The Kill

The Killing

BOOK 2
PARTS 7–11

David Hewson

Based on the BAFTA
Award-Winning TV Series
Written by Søren Sveistrup

W F HOWES LTD

This large print edition published in 2013 by
W F Howes Ltd
Unit 4, Rearsby Business Park, Gaddesby Lane,
Rearsby, Leicester LE7 4YH

1 3 5 7 9 10 8 6 4 2

First published in the United Kingdom in 2013
by Macmillan

Based on Søren Sveistrup's *Forbrydelsen* (*The Killing*)
– an original Danish Broadcasting Corporation TV series
co-written by Torleif Hoppe, Michael W. Horsten and Per Daumiller

A CIP catalogue record for this book is available
from the British Library

ISBN 978 1 47124 422 3

Typeset by Palimpsest Book Production Limited,
Falkirk, Stirlingshire
Printed and bound by
CPI ⸻⸻⸻ ⸻ ⸻ ⸻ ⸻ ⸻0 4YY

**Life can only be understood backwards;
but it must be lived forwards.**

Søren Kierkegaard

PRINCIPAL CHARACTERS

Copenhagen Police

Sarah Lund – *Former Vicekriminalkommissær (a post now known as Vicepolitikommisær), Homicide*

Lennart Brix – *Chief, Homicide*

Ulrik Strange – *Vicepolitikommissær, Homicide*

Ruth Hedeby – *Deputy Commissioner*

Madsen – *Detective, Homicide*

Svendsen – *Detective, Homicide*

Erik König – *head of Politiets Efterretningstjeneste (PET), the internal national security intelligence agency, a separate arm of the police service*

Folketinget, the Danish Parliament

Thomas Buch – *newly appointed Minister of Justice*

Karina Jørgensen – *Buch's personal secretary*

Carsten Plough – *Buch's Permanent Secretary, a senior civil servant*

Erling Krabbe – *leader of the People's Party*

Birgitte Agger – *leader of the Progressive Party*

Flemming Rossing – *Minister of Defence*

Gert Grue Eriksen – *Prime Minister*

Frode Monberg – *former Minister of Justice*

vii

Danish Army

Jens Peter Raben – *former sergeant*
Louise Raben – *Raben's wife, an army nurse*
Colonel Torsten Jarnvig – *Louise Raben's father*
Major Christian Søgaard
Allan Myg Poulsen – *former comrade of Raben's*
Lisbeth Thomsen – *former comrade of Raben's*
David Grüner – *former comrade of Raben's*
General Jan Arild – *assistant chief of staff, army headquarters*
Gunnar 'Priest' Torpe – *former army clergyman, now a civilian pastor*
Torben Skåning – *former captain*
Frederik Holst – *army doctor*
Peter Lænkholm – *former lieutenant*

Others

Anne Dragsholm – *a lawyer and activist*
Stig Dragsholm – *Anne Dragsholm's husband*
Abdel Hussein Kodmani – *an Islamist activist*
Connie Vemmer – *a journalist, formerly a press officer with the Ministry of Defence*

CHAPTER 7

Saturday 19th November, 09.03 a.m.

Erik König looked more and more like a man under unbearable pressure. A man, Brix thought, with secrets too.

'Raben abandoned the chaplain's car two kilometres from Hareskoven. He stole an old Volvo nearby. We picked him up around two in the morning. Kept watch.'

'Kept watch?' Brix asked.

'We were lucky to get sight of him. He's tired. Desperate. Got his guard down. A good Jægerkorpset soldier would never—'

'He wasn't Jægerkorpset though, was he?' Brix asked gently and enjoyed the PET man's discomfort. König had kept them in the dark from the start. Brix wanted to let him know this was over.

'Close enough. He slept for three hours in a lay-by. Now he's near Ryvangen Barracks, in a side street on a housing estate.'

'Bring him here when you pick him up.'

Ruth Hedeby stared at the plain grey desk and said nothing.

1

'Raben's the last one in the squad,' König replied. 'We know where he is. We know we can stop him doing any further harm.'

'Bring him in!' Brix demanded.

'No.' König took off his wire-rimmed glasses. 'If the Islamists have been tracking the squad he's the next potential victim. Raben stays free, under surveillance.'

'As bait?' Brix asked.

The PET man leaned back in his chair and frowned.

'There's a limit to how many religious lunatics we can arrest. Sooner or later one of them is going to put his head above the parapet.'

'We can help with surveillance,' Hedeby suggested.

König had the coldest and most insincere of smiles.

'We're better equipped for this kind of work. Besides, after that farce with Lund—'

'That's dealt with,' Hedeby said briskly.

'I'm sure the Ministry will be pleased to hear that. They're looking for scapegoats. I'd like you to look at these . . .'

He pulled a sheaf of photos and identity documents from his briefcase and threw them on the table.

'They're refugees from Helmand, living in Denmark for the last couple of years. They might be after revenge.'

Hedeby passed the pile to Brix.

2

'I want them watched,' König added. 'A few questioned.' A dry laugh. 'No one need be exhumed.'

Brix didn't look at the photos.

'How did a refugee from Helmand break into Ryvangen Barracks and steal explosives with a current security code?' he asked. 'How's it possible they've access to military records—?'

'Lennart.'

There was a hard, scolding note to her voice, one that silenced him.

'I'll leave that to you to find out,' König said. He glanced at his watch. 'I've got a meeting at the Ministry.'

Then he was gone. Hedeby looked at Brix across the table.

'I can't save you from yourself,' she said quietly. 'Someone's going to pay. One way or another.'

'König's thrashing around in the dark trying to save his own skin.'

'You dug up a dead soldier for no good reason. I'm struggling to make sure no one but Lund picks up the blame. Try and help me, will you?'

In the adjoining office Strange was interviewing Gunnar Torpe. Brix leaned on a filing cabinet and listened. Lund had never said Strange was a poor cop. It wasn't necessary. Brix could read the occasional impatience in her eyes.

'Why did Raben take you to the woods at gunpoint?' Strange asked.

Torpe sat pale and tired in a chair.

'How am I supposed to answer that? Maybe because he's sick. Here . . .' He tapped his forehead. 'Crazy. Delusional.'

'He must have had a reason.'

'Crazy people don't need them. I tried to reason with him. To get him to think about his wife and son.'

'What did he say?'

'It was just . . .' Torpe shrugged. 'Crazy stuff. War does strange things to people. They don't know the difference between right and wrong sometimes. Between what's real and what's not.'

Strange placed something on the table.

'We found this in the office in your church. Anne Dragsholm's business card. What was it doing there?'

'Raben must have dropped it.'

'Did you know her?'

The priest twisted on the chair then said, 'Raben asked me that too. I never met her. I never saw that card before. Can I go now? I've got a committee meeting.'

Brix took a deep breath, stared at the lean officer seated in front of Torpe. Waited.

'OK,' Strange said. 'We'll probably need to get back to you later.'

'PET have located Raben,' Brix said when Torpe had left. 'They've got him under surveillance.'

Strange scratched his cropped hair.

4

'Surveillance? We need him brought in.'

'We do as we're told.' Brix passed him the names and photos König had given Ruth Hedeby. 'I want every last one of them checked out. Bring in any that are marked. Some are outside the city. You've got some driving ahead of you.'

'Lund thought we need to check out the chaplain. So do you—'

'Lund's not here any more.' Brix tapped the papers.

Strange frowned.

'So what are we supposed to say if someone calls up and wants to speak to her?'

'Tell them the truth. She's gone to a wedding,' Brix said.

Men and vehicles. Loading orders and schedules. Torsten Jarnvig felt he'd been watching these rituals all his adult life. Dispatching men to uncertain fates in Bosnia, the Middle East and now the bleak and distant provinces of Afghanistan.

Most came back.

Most unharmed.

Not all.

Christian Søgaard had been round to see Møller's mother. An initiative of his own. Jarnvig hadn't asked for it.

'She's livid,' he said. 'Who wouldn't be? She says she's going to sue the police for trespass. For pain and suffering.'

5

The two men were walking from the main head-quarters building towards the car park. A security barrier rose as they approached. Men in combat fatigues saluted.

'I spoke to Gunnar Torpe,' Søgaard added. 'He's very upset.'

'You've been busy.'

'The police were on your back. I didn't think you needed to be bothered. It was welfare. I usually look after that on my own.'

Jarnvig raised an eyebrow.

'Welfare? This is welfare?'

'What's Raben going to do next?' Søgaard asked, avoiding the question. 'He seems desperate. I've told everyone to keep their eyes and ears open when they leave the barracks.'

He hesitated.

'That means everyone,' Søgaard repeated. 'How much does Louise know?'

'Enough,' Jarnvig answered, watching a line of trucks roll past. 'Until this happened I thought he was one of the best soldiers I ever had. Brave. Intelligent. Resourceful.'

Torsten Jarnvig thrust his fists deep into the pockets of his fatigues.

'Didn't like him much. But when everybody else gave up Raben just kept going.'

'A pity he couldn't take the pressure,' Søgaard said. 'I always thought there was something brittle about him. Ready to snap.'

Jarnvig stopped and looked at him.

6

'How very observant, after the fact. Did we get to the bottom of that story of his?'

'Damned right we did,' Søgaard replied straight away.

'You were certain?'

'One hundred per cent. It was bullshit. He was covering up for his own mistakes. Why?'

Jarnvig didn't answer.

'It's not easy when these things turn personal,' the younger officer added. 'The past few days have been tough. I could relieve you. Maybe you and Louise and Jonas could—'

'Could what? Go on holiday? That won't be necessary.' Jarnvig cast his eyes around the red-brick buildings of the barracks. 'This place is good enough for me. Louise grew up with the army. It's good enough for her too.'

'What I meant was—'

'No,' Jarnvig said and left it at that.

The artificial beach of Amager Strandpark in November. Stained concrete shiny with winter rain. A few children wrapped in thick anoraks, struggling against the wind, their faces hidden inside tightly drawn hoods.

Louise Raben watched her son zigzagging on his little scooter across the dun slabs by the grey sea, beneath the grey sky, no smile on his face, no expression there at all.

Slowly he scooted back to her. They stared at the empty beach.

'Are you hungry?' she asked.

He didn't eat enough. He didn't do anything much except play with his toy soldiers, slaughtering fantasy enemies in his head.

Jonas took a sandwich then she watched as he pushed the little scooter towards a group of kids who had ignored him before and doubtless would now.

Children had their own rules, their own sensibilities. They suspected anyone who stood out. And Jonas, in his loneliness and misery, always did.

While he was wheeling down the sea wall she walked slowly in his wake. A figure emerged from a metal shelter, gestured.

Green jacket, pale grey hood. Beard and watchful eyes.

Her heart fell. She wanted to flee and would have if she didn't know he could always outrun her.

'We've only got a couple of minutes,' Raben said, dragging her back into the dark of the shelter.

'Jens—'

'Listen to me!'

His voice sounded fragile and broken. His eyes were as wild as she'd ever seen. She wondered whether to feel afraid. For herself, for Jonas.

'You've got to leave the barracks,' he said, clutching at her cold fingers.

'You followed me here?'

'It doesn't matter.'

'What's wrong with you? Why did you treat Gunnar Torpe like that?'

'I didn't do anything to him!' High, fractured, his voice echoed round the darkness of the shelter. 'They're lying to you.'

'You hit him. My father said—'

'He's lying too.'

She took one step back. The hood came all the way down. He looked so hurt and vulnerable.

'No,' Louise said. 'He told me about what happened in Helmand. How you feel guilty.'

He shook his head.

'It's not that.'

'What is it then?'

'They're covering up for something an officer did.'

'Who?'

'I don't know. I don't remember it all. Maybe Søgaard . . . Maybe others.' His eyes wouldn't leave her, and they had the expression she'd learned to hate. That of a soldier hunting his prey. 'Maybe your father.'

'My father's a good man. He tried to help you.'

A sound outside. A kid going past kicking a can. Raben recoiled from her, fell against the wall, hand going to his belt. She saw the gun there, the fear and tension in his eyes. Found she had no feeling for him at that moment but contempt.

'I don't believe this,' she said, glaring at him. 'Two years I've waited. Two years I've looked after our son. And look at you. Cowering like a thief . . .'

The kid with the can was still outside, making a din kicking it against the wall.

'Get hold of that woman from the police,' he ordered. 'Sarah Lund. I called the Politigården. She's at her mother's wedding. You've got to go there. Tell her to check—'

'Is it true you volunteered for active service? Abroad? When Jonas was born?'

His face could change so rapidly. From the hard, unfeeling coldness of a warrior, to the boyish gentleness she'd once loved, all in an instant.

'Who told you that?'

She took a step towards him, looked up into his pained, pale face. Knew she wouldn't leave this place without an answer.

'Is it true?'

A moment of hesitation. His eyes pleaded with her.

'Can't you see what they're trying to do? They want to separate us. They want to lock you inside the barracks for ever.'

She turned her back on him, watched the kid with the can wander away.

'It's not what you think,' Raben said, placing his arms around her shoulders.

There was no colour in this world, she thought. Not for her. Not for Jonas. They deserved better. There was a limit to the sacrifices you could make.

'I've been a soldier since I was eighteen,' he

went on, still clinging to her shoulders. 'It's all I've ever known. The things I've seen. The things I've done . . .'

'My father's a soldier. A good man. Ordinary like the rest of them . . .'

'I wasn't like him. There are things you shouldn't know.' He tapped his lank, greasy hair. 'Things here. I didn't deserve Jonas. I didn't deserve you. He was so pure. I wasn't. I thought if I stayed I'd poison you both . . .'

'Let go of me,' she said as his grip tightened on her jacket.

'I've changed.' His fingers still held her. 'All I want is to come home and be with you. To learn to be a good father. A good husband.'

Her blood began to boil. He no longer held her in an embrace. It was as if she belonged to him. As if he'd captured her.

'I've heard that shit too often, Jens. And where are we now? How many years in jail? How many visits am I supposed to make a week and I still can't even drag you into bed in that stinking little room? Fuck it—'

'Louise . . .'

Half an order, half a plea. His arms wound round her more tightly.

Through the door a tiny figure flew, screeching curses too old for a child to know. Jonas was on them, little arms beating at Raben's legs, little feet kicking at him.

'Let Mummy go! Let Mummy go!'

Raben retreated, fell back against the grille and the leaden light outside.

Crouched down, looked at the child, young face full of fury, tears in his eyes.

'You've grown, Jonas,' Raben said. 'It's me. Daddy.'

He smiled. Jonas didn't.

Raben's hand went out to the toy soldier sticking out of the boy's jacket pocket. Retrieved the figure. A warrior with a shield and a raised sword.

'What's he called?'

'Mummy,' Jonas said, wheeling his scooter to her side, 'I want to go.'

She took the boy's hand and led him to the door. Stopped there. Looked around. In summer this place was full of happy voices, kids playing with their parents, running, laughing, feeling alive. Jonas had never known that. Nor had she. Raben had fled from them through some inner fear he'd never been able to share. And now she hated him for that too.

'Don't ever try to see us again,' she said, aware of the spiteful fury in her voice. 'I mean it . . .'

'Louise?'

He could turn on the charm when he wanted, like a naughty child caught stealing. But she'd been tested, so many times.

'Never again,' she said and walked out into the first few drops of winter sleet starting to fall from the heavy sky.

Jonas tugged on her hand. He was pointing at

the man hiding in the doorway. In Raben's hand was the toy soldier, shield raised, sword at the ready.

'I'll buy you a new one,' she told her son and dragged him to the car.

It took a lot of arguing to get permission to visit Monberg in a private room in the Rigshospitalet. But Karina won through in the end and accompanied Buch in the car from the Ministry.

They stopped in the corridor outside.

'You don't have to come in if you don't want to,' he said. 'If it's embarrassing.'

The remark seemed to puzzle her.

'Why would I be embarrassed?'

'Well . . .' Buch struggled for an answer.

'Let's go in, shall we?' she said and led the way.

Frode Monberg was in a bed by the window. Unshaven. Looking tired and pale. As a backbench MP Buch had never mixed much with ministers. Now he could see Monberg was a handsome man, with a narrow, smiling, genial face, a mop of unruly brown hair and lively, roaming eyes.

Buch stepped forward and placed a box of expensive chocolates on the bed.

'Karina,' Monberg said warily. 'My successor. Congratulations, Thomas. I hope you're having fun.'

'It's good to see you. How are you doing?'

No tubes, no wires. The monitors by the bed

13

were switched off. This was a man in recovery. Barely sick at all. And yet behind the bright facade there seemed something gloomy and desperate about Frode Monberg. The politician's smile vanished much too quickly.

'I'm OK.' His melancholy brown eyes roved over Buch's huge frame. 'It seems quite a storm's been brewing while I've been in here.'

He looked at Karina.

'And how are you?'

She nodded, said nothing.

'It was good of you to take the job,' Monberg added, turning back to Buch. 'You must have wondered what the Prime Minister was thinking. But now . . .' He patted his chest. 'I can take better care of this old heart.'

He moved to put the chocolates on the bedside table.

'I doubt I'll be allowed things like this for a while. The doctors . . .'

Karina folded her arms. Buch said nothing. Monberg's face turned sour again.

'So. It gets around.'

'I took over your job,' Buch said. 'I had to be told. It's not general knowledge. It won't be. Don't worry.'

'Don't worry?' His voice became fragile and old. 'That's easy for you to say. I was sick for ages. No one noticed. No one cared. You're stuck in that damned office, day in, day out. Nights too. It all . . .'

14

His eyes turned briefly to the smartly dressed blonde woman by his bed.

'It all becomes unreal after a while. You find yourself doing things you'd never dream of. I don't want my family to suffer any more. You hear that?'

'Of course,' Buch said. 'I guarantee it. We just want to talk about that old military case. The one you were looking into. Before . . .' He nodded at the bed. 'You know. The Dragsholm woman.'

'There's nothing to tell,' Monberg said too quickly. 'Anne came to me with this odd story. She wanted me to look into it. A favour for an old friend.'

'And?' Buch asked.

'We had a meeting. Talked about the past. She was going through a divorce. I think she was getting a bit . . . obsessive. She gave me a folder when I was leaving. The case seemed to mean a lot to her. God knows why. I never got to look at it, of course.'

Buch took a deep breath, folded his arms, said nothing.

'Why do you ask these questions, Thomas?'

'You already knew about the case before she came to you. You sent that envelope to a dead address for a reason. Please. Try to be clear on these things. The Defence Minister called a meeting about a soldier.'

Karina extracted the papers from her bag. Buch showed them to the man in the bed.

'A certain Jens Peter Raben.'

15

Monberg took the documents, did no more than glance at them.

'I'm still a bit hazy about some things.'

'Let's dispense with this nonsense,' Buch said, aware his voice was rising. 'Just tell me what you and Rossing spoke about at that meeting. It's important.'

Monberg shrugged, got a pair of reading glasses from the table, scanned the papers.

'This was ages ago.'

'You withheld information about a serious military investigation! You kept it hidden from the police, from PET, from your own civil servants.' He pulled up a chair, got close to the bed. 'Why? What are you and Rossing hiding?'

Monberg turned to Karina, pleaded for her help. She kept quiet.

'Why did you have a meeting about Raben?' Buch persisted. 'What did Rossing say to you? Why were no minutes kept?'

'What is this, Buch? What are you going on about?'

'You met with Rossing. Later Dragsholm raises the case with you. But you never let on. Never told the police or PET, even when she was murdered. I need to know—'

'If you've come to blame me for your screw-ups you can get out of here now,' Monberg barked.

'What did Rossing say at that meeting?'

A noise at the door. A woman in a dark-blue

16

suit. A doctor by her side. Monberg's wife. Buch recognized her.

'Visitors again, Frode?' she said, rushing to his side, kissing his head as Monberg scowled like a child. 'That won't do.' She stared at Buch. 'I appreciate your concern. But the doctor needs to examine my husband.'

Monberg held up the papers. Karina took them then went to the window and began to sift through the get-well cards.

'This kind of pressure isn't good for him,' the wife added.

'I'm supposed to rest,' Monberg agreed.

Karina nudged Buch. One of the cards was from Flemming Rossing. A bunch of roses on the front. A standard handwritten greeting inside, then a scribbled addition – *It was so good to see you better, Frode. We are brothers always.*

Buch read it and nodded.

'I believe the minister's about to leave,' Monberg noted.

'Yes,' he said. 'Get well soon, Frode.' He threw Rossing's card on the sheets by Monberg's knees. 'All of your friends want to see that.'

Outside in the corridor, breathing in the hospital smells, listening to the beeps and whirrs of the machines in the wards around them, Buch waited for Karina to catch up with his furious pace.

'Rossing got there before us, didn't he?' he snapped when she reached his side.

17

'He knew what you were going to ask. And what he was going to say.'

'Shit,' he muttered. He couldn't take his eyes off her. 'What's Monberg like? Really?'

'Witty. Funny. Charming.' She thought about it. 'Weak.'

'We need more options,' Buch said, and tried to imagine what they might be.

'Here's an idea,' Karina said as they sat in the back of the ministerial car, trapped in traffic on the way back to the Ministry. 'Why not issue an apology for the exhumation of the soldier?'

Buch grunted something wordless and looked at the crowds of shoppers beyond the window. Ordinary people with ordinary lives. He envied them.

'Thomas,' Karina went on. She always used his first name now, when they were on their own. He liked that. 'It'll take off some of the pressure. Krabbe's getting impatient. He's pestering Plough for an urgent meeting.'

'Plough can tell Krabbe to go and sit outside the Prime Minister's office, begging for an audience with him if he wants.'

'An apology would go down well.'

Buch kept several packs of chocolate biscuits in the back of the car, in the small cabinet where others stored booze. He opened the nearest, offered it to Karina, took two when she shook her head.

'How can I say sorry for something I never knew about?'

'You're the minister. It happens all the time.'

'That doesn't mean I like it. Whose idea was it to dig up this poor bastard anyway?'

'A policewoman. She was fired.'

'That was quick.'

'She had history. Remember the Birk Larsen case a couple of years ago?'

Buch shuddered.

'That was horrible.'

'She solved it. Got fired after that too.'

Buch looked at her, interested.

'There was a possibility a few local politicians were involved,' Karina went on. 'She wouldn't let go of that either. If you put out a statement you could mention this wasn't the first time she ran into disciplinary issues. Say something like . . . we expect all officers to uphold the fine traditions of the force.'

Buch stared at her.

'OK,' Karina agreed. 'That's not your style. I'll leave the wording to you.'

'What's her name?'

'Sarah Lund.'

'I want to talk to her.'

She burst out laughing. The thought that he could amuse this sharp, intelligent woman cheered him somehow.

'You can't possibly talk to her! She's just been booted out of the force.'

'I'm the Minister of Justice. I can talk to anyone I like. If this Lund woman solved the Birk Larsen case she can't be stupid. Maybe she knows something.'

He offered her the biscuits again. This time she took one.

'If you do that you'll compromise your relations with the police.'

'And haven't they been forthcoming! No. If Monberg won't speak to us we'll have to try another avenue. Get me Sarah Lund, please.'

'Thomas,' she said, and her voice was that of a mother scolding a child. 'If they find out you could be in big trouble.'

'Oh for pity's sake. If I don't get to the bottom of this I'm out on my ear anyway. Let's not pretend otherwise, shall we?' He tapped her bag. 'You're very good on the phone. Find me this Sarah Lund please. We'll go there straight away.'

A Danish working-class wedding. A hotel banqueting room full of friends and relatives. A happy couple. Soft music. A civilian registrar pronouncing the familiar refrain, 'I now pronounce you man and wife. You may kiss the bride.'

Bjørn, a playful little man, full of good humour and mischief, grinned like a wicked pixie and did as he was told.

Lund was glad her cake hadn't poisoned him much. He was nice and her mother was finally happy after so many years of solitary bitterness.

So she stood in the best dress she had, purple silk, applauded them both, smiled at Mark, tall and handsome beside her.

All the world moved on. Everything shifted with the times. But not her. She was in the same place she occupied two years before, after that black night when Meyer was shot and everything unravelled in her life. That was why she took so much awkward guilty comfort in the sight of her mother like this, consumed by the smothering bliss, the contentment that came from giving one's life selflessly to another, burying an individual identity in a shared love that would whisper the perpetual lie 'Now you're safe for ever.'

This was a sacrifice she could never make and those who knew her understood. Mark was no longer the surly teenager who once snarled, 'You're only interested in dead people.'

He still thought that, she guessed. He was just too kind to say it.

It was a fine banqueting hall in Østerbro. Marble walls and the scent of too many bouquets. When the applause faded Bjørn clapped his hands and declared, 'Now let's have something to eat and drink, please. Then another drink! Then another!'

Her mother was in a green silk dress she'd made herself. She looked so perfect, so complete, Lund felt the tears start to well in her eyes.

'You can tell Bjørn used to be in the Home Guard,' Mark chuckled by her side.

'Oh yes,' she said, watching a couple of men in

regimental blazers embrace the old man and slap him on the back.

Vibeke came over, hugged them both, kisses on the cheek, arms round each.

'This idea about me making the toast . . .' Lund began.

'Nothing to it,' Vibeke said quickly. 'A short speech for your mother's wedding. Small price to get rid of me.'

'I've never been much good at speaking.'

'All the more reason to keep it short. There has to be time for dancing. Next you'll tell me you're no good at dancing too. And I know that isn't true.' Vibeke's joyful face became serious for a moment. 'I remember you when you were Mark's age. I know you can dance, Sarah.'

'Wife! Wife!' Bjørn's squeaky voice rose above the hubbub. 'We've got to have our pictures taken.'

Still she didn't move. The two of them stayed where they were, mother and daughter. Mark retreated as if seeing something.

'But I won't make you,' Vibeke said quietly. 'I've tried so hard over the years to force you to be someone you're not. I'm sorry. I just wanted . . .'

Lund threw her arms round her mother, brushed her lips against Vibeke's warm and powdered cheeks.

'You are who you are and I love you for that,' her mother whispered into her ear, then fled back

22

into the crowd as if terrified by this sudden outburst of intimate honesty.

A hotel worker in a white shirt appeared with a small bell in his hand.

'You ring this for attention,' he said, as if she'd never been to a wedding before. 'The presents are on the table. Along with the flowers. Oh, and the bouquet that came for you.'

'Who sent me a bouquet?'

'Search me,' he said, pointing at one particular bunch of flowers.

Three red roses in cellophane amidst the stacks of gaudy boxes.

'Everybody . . .' the photographer announced. 'Take your places, please.'

Bjørn in the middle, Vibeke and Lund on either side. She remembered her own wedding, recalled how a nagging question had dogged her even as she posed for the pictures: could it last?

This one would. A peace had been declared. Vibeke's long and sorrowful years of loneliness, a war of a kind, was over.

Mark knelt in front. Lund found her hand straying to his soft hair, stroking it, was pleased when he smiled, didn't recoil as once he would.

Ten minutes later, everyone seated round the table, watching the first course come out from the kitchen, the singing began. Wedding tunes with ridiculous words, half chanted, half bellowed from the lyric sheets that sat next to the menu. The wine was white and lukewarm. She'd been deliberately seated next to a bachelor cousin of Bjørn's, an accountant from Roskilde whose principal topic of conversation, between the choruses, concerned the future of double-entry bookkeeping.

Lund didn't touch the drink. She felt heady enough as it was.

The man appeared sufficiently cognisant to notice the subject bored her.

'You're a police officer?' he asked.

'Sort of.'

'I heard they dug up a dead soldier. It was in the papers.'

Lund changed her mind, gulped at the too-sweet white wine and said, 'Really?'

Then, before he could utter another word, rang the bell.

Vibeke was on her feet. The hotel man was back by Lund's side.

'I'm sorry,' he said. 'Someone's here to see you. She says it's important.'

A blonde woman in smart office clothes was standing just outside the door. She nodded when Lund looked.

'I've been looking forward to this speech,' Vibeke declared, rising to her feet. 'So . . .'

Lund slid back her chair and started to leave the table.

The woman at the door introduced herself as Karina Jørgensen from the Ministry of Justice.

'A toast!' Vibeke ad-libbed behind her. 'Cheers!'

Lund followed into the serving area.

'This conversation happened by accident,' the woman said. 'There'll be no record of it. You won't inform anyone in the Politigården.'

They went downstairs. White tiled corridors. The smell and noise of a kitchen nearby.

There was a large man at the end, next to a woman folding tablecloths. He had a phone in one hand and a chicken leg in the other. The half-gnawed leg got thrown into a bin as she approached. Then the phone went into his pocket.

He wiped his hands on the nearest napkin then shook hers.

'I'm Thomas Buch. Minister of Justice. For now anyway.'

Lund said nothing.

'Karina says we met here by coincidence.' He had a genial face with an untidy brown beard. 'Some coincidence, huh?'

'My mother just got married upstairs.'

'I know. The truth is I'm in dire need of some answers. And I think—'

'Look. If it's about the exhumation, I'm really sorry. It was my mistake. Don't blame Brix or Strange . . .'

He waited until the waitress disappeared.

'Do you know about the accusations against Danish troops in Helmand?'

'A bit.'

'Did you see any indication that civilians might have been murdered by our own soldiers? Any—'

'Like I said. You should call Lennart Brix or Ruth Hedeby. They're in charge now—'

'I'm not sure about that. And I'm the Minister of Justice. There's a suggestion an individual officer was involved in an atrocity. Do you know about this? Did you see evidence that someone was trying to cover it up?'

Lund shook her head.

'That story came from a soldier who was mentally disturbed. There probably wasn't any officer.'

The big man stuffed his fists into the pockets of his trousers and didn't move.

'So why did you go to all the trouble of digging up a soldier?'

'Because I screwed up. I don't know anything. I've got to get back to the wedding. I'm sorry.'

'What about the squad leader, Jens Peter Raben?'

'I thought he knew something but . . . he's mentally ill. He had good reason to escape. He'd just been turned down for parole.'

'By whom?'

'By the Prison Service. The medical director said he was fit to go but . . .'

Buch glanced at the blonde woman.

'Herstedvester gave him a clean bill of health?' he asked. 'And the Prison Service blocked his release?'

'That's right. He was desperate to get out. His marriage is falling apart. Probably has by now.'

Buch put a finger to his mouth, thinking.

'Bear with me a moment.'

26

He turned to the woman.

'Monberg was working on a bill about the Prison Service, wasn't he? When was that abandoned?'

She thought for a moment.

'Just after he met the Minister of Defence.'

'Quite. Get Plough for me.'

A broad smile, the big hand again. Lund took it.

'Thank you,' Thomas Buch said. 'And congratulations on your mother's wedding.'

'What's this about exactly?'

His finger went to his bearded face again. Another wry smile. Then a wink.

'Enjoy your day, Sarah Lund,' Buch said as he waved goodbye.

Bjørn was in full flow by the time she got back to the wedding.

'Vibeke,' he said, standing next to her, reading from his notes. 'You make me so happy. I just want to sing and dance and make speeches, all the time.'

Lund walked to her seat saying a silent prayer this wouldn't happen.

Then thought about the man she'd just talked to. Thomas Buch was the Minister of Justice. And he was in the dark too, just like her.

'Sometimes,' Bjørn went on, 'I wish we'd met earlier in life. But then we wouldn't have been ready for one another. So I'm glad I walked into the second-hand shop that Tuesday in May. And walked out with the woman who would one day be my wife.'

Lund ignored the dubious jokes of the man next to her, stared at the presents and the three red roses.

No one sent flowers to a solitary daughter at her mother's wedding. Even the cheapest bouquet a delivery company would handle.

The guests were getting up. Glasses in hand. Bjørn was making a toast.

'Long live the bride!'

As Bjørn bent down to kiss Vibeke, Lund crossed the room, found the bouquet, picked out the white envelope tucked into the top.

She was aware of the silence, of the fact they were all watching.

The hotel man was going past with a fresh bottle of wine.

'Who brought these flowers?' she asked.

'A courier,' he said with the same dull tone he'd used before.

A scribbled message inside.

Tjek hundetegnet – Raben.

Check the dog tag.

Vibeke was watching her, smiling but tense. She rang her knife against her wine glass and stood up.

'Now that we're all gathered together I'd like to say my piece too. Before Sarah . . .'

Lund picked up her little toastmaster's bell.

'Dear Bjørn . . .' Vibeke began, then stopped, watching as her daughter approached.

Lund came and stood by her. So many years of difficulties between them. So many arguments and

28

tantrums. And now she would fail her mother one more time, on her wedding day.

Something changed in Vibeke's face. She smiled. Lund placed the bell by her plate, embraced her, kissed her on both cheeks and got the same in return.

'What is this?' Bjørn asked, a faint note of outrage in his voice. 'You can't walk out on your mother's speech! What kind of guest leaves before the wedding party has begun.'

Lund wiped something from her eye.

'That's exactly what my daughter's doing, Bjørn,' Vibeke said in a voice that was close to rebuke. 'And it's OK.'

'OK?' he asked, wide-eyed.

Lund said nothing, just started to slip from the room.

'Yes!' Vibeke said very brightly. 'It's very OK. The women in this family are busy and have minds of their own.' She slapped him on the back. 'Get used to it, boy. And try to keep up.'

Lund marched out of the room. There was laughter behind. Nervous, perhaps. Laughter all the same.

They'd talk about her but they always had.

Then her mother's voice, strong and forceful boomed at her back.

'Now, dear Bjørn. Where were we?'

She didn't listen any more. She walked down the stairs, and knew exactly where she had to go.

★　　★　　★

29

Hanne Møller was clearing out her garage. She had a photograph in her hands, a wistful look in her eyes.

Lund walked in, a worn blue donkey jacket over her purple wedding dress.

'I came to apologize. I know the police said sorry too. It's not enough. I wanted you to hear it from me.'

She could see the photo. A handsome young man in an army beret, smiling for a standard portrait. Hanne Møller put it back in the box.

'I realize I can't put it right,' Lund continued.

'No,' the woman said in a low and bitter voice. 'You can't.'

'I need you to understand.' One step closer. She wasn't leaving until this was said. 'I had to be certain.'

'And are you?'

She picked up some of her son's clothes and placed them in a black rubbish bag.

'I'm certain he's dead. I'm sorry. But there's something we still don't know—'

'Just go, will you?'

Lund looked around the garage. Wondered.

'I need you to listen.'

Hanne Møller's voice rose and it was full of pain and anger.

'Why do you never leave when I ask? Why do you keep coming back here? Haunting me?'

'Because something's wrong. I think you know it too.'

'Do I?'

She was holding a sweater. Blue military wool. Or part of a school uniform. They looked so similar.

'It's about your son's dog tag. The chain the army gave him with the metal name tag on it.'

Lund found herself gesturing awkwardly with her hands to describe the thing. From the look on Hanne Møller's face this wasn't necessary.

'Do you know where it is?'

'Why's a piece of metal important?'

'They give the dog tag to the nearest of kin. Did you get it?'

'I asked,' the woman said, shaking her head. 'They never found it.'

'But you got his other possessions?'

The woman gestured at the box.

'No. These were what he'd left at home. We got nothing. Just a body they wouldn't let us see. Why do you keep asking these questions?'

Lund wondered whether to say it. But Hanne Møller was owed something after the debacle in the cemetery.

'I think someone found your son's dog tag. I think he used it to take on Per's identity. And then cover up an atrocity.'

'Per was a good boy,' his mother said in a soft, hurt voice. 'I never wanted him to go into the army. When he was little there were no wars. I thought he'd be a teacher. Or a doctor. But then he grew up and the world was different.'

31

She stared at Lund.

'It was as if it was just another choice. Go to work in a school. Go to some country he'd barely heard of and fight a war none of us understood. I never imagined for one minute he'd wind up in a uniform. We need soldiers, I suppose. But not Per. He was too gentle for that.'

Lund stayed silent, thinking of Mark.

'You think you can guide them towards something good,' Hanne Møller added in that same soft, pained whisper. 'But you never know what's waiting out there. Not really.'

'I'm sorry for the hurt I caused. It was stupid of me. I won't bother you again.'

Lund walked towards the garage door.

'Wait a moment,' the woman said. 'There's something you need to see.'

She went to the corner and dragged out another box.

'I thought it was a mistake. Maybe it is. But it still bothers me.'

'What does?'

'Now and then things turn up. As if Per were still alive. Here . . .'

She pulled out a sheaf of opened envelopes.

'Letters. The last one was a few weeks ago. Look.'

Lund took it.

'When they started I thought . . . I dreamed maybe he was still alive,' Hanne Møller whispered.

32

'But he's not, is he? And then that woman came along. And you . . .'

Receipts mostly. Posted long after Per K. Møller died in an explosion, suicide maybe, in Helmand more than two years before.

'It is a mistake, isn't it?' the woman asked.

'Probably,' Lund said. 'Can I keep these?'

Just before six Buch was back at the Rigshospitalet determined to take a second tilt at Frode Monberg.

The reception desk was empty so he walked straight in. Found Monberg in white pyjamas, seated on the edge of the bed reading a newspaper.

'If you must come,' Monberg said, 'you should ask in advance and do it during visiting hours.'

Then he got up from the bed, walked to the window, put on a dressing gown. He still hadn't shaved. He looked gaunt and worried.

'I've nothing more to say to you, Buch.'

'There's not much I need to hear. I know it already.'

Monberg turned and grinned. It wasn't a pretty sight.

'Oh, do you?'

'Pretty much. You were preparing a bill. You'd promised to cut the cost of the Prison Service. It was in the manifesto.'

'There was too much overcrowding. Why does this matter?'

'And you wanted fewer mentally ill criminals locked up, didn't you?'

33

The thin man glared at Thomas Buch and kept quiet.

'You'd asked for every case to be reassessed, and parole for all those who weren't perceived to be a threat to society.'

'Digging through old files is a job for civil servants. Not ministers.'

'One of those who was going to be set free was Jens Peter Raben. A soldier. A man who claimed to have witnessed an atrocity committed by our own forces in Afghanistan.'

'I don't remember . . .'

Buch took a step towards him.

'Don't lie to me. Rossing came to discuss Raben's case with you. And then, for whatever reason, you abandoned your proposal entirely. Nothing came of it.'

Monberg nodded.

'True. There were other reasons for that.'

'I won't disturb you any longer,' Buch announced, and headed for the door. 'This is a matter for Plough and the legal team now . . .'

'Buch!'

He stopped.

'For God's sake will you listen to me?' Monberg pleaded.

Buch came back and looked at the skinny, stricken man by the side of the bed. He wanted to feel a sense of guilt for punishing him like this. But it was hard.

'What do you plan to do?' Monberg asked.

'That depends on you. I don't want to punish anyone. I just want the truth.'

'Rossing was adamant Raben shouldn't be released. All the reports from the hospital said he was fine. But Rossing regarded him as a security issue. He said it was against the national interest to release him. He had to stay in Herstedvester.'

Buch almost laughed.

'The national interest? What does that mean? We don't lock up our enemies unless they give us reason. Why should we do it to our own soldiers when they've fought for us, for their country?'

'Rossing didn't elaborate and I didn't ask.'

Buch raised a finger, pointed it at the frail man in front of him.

'Jens Peter Raben was aware something had gone terribly wrong in Afghanistan. Rossing wanted him locked up because he feared the political fallout if that were made public. That's not the national interest.'

'I don't know about any of this! Rossing asked for my help. He told me what to do.'

'And then Anne Dragsholm wanted to reopen the case.'

Monberg scowled, went to the bed, started to tidy the sheets, turned his back on the big man throwing questions at him.

'What did Dragsholm say? What had she discovered?'

'I can't go into these details . . .' Monberg muttered and began to reshape his pillows.

Buch lost it.

'Dammit!' he roared. 'Do you think you can hide in this place for ever?'

His arm shot to the door.

'People are dying out there! And you . . .' His finger stabbed at Monberg's haggard features. 'You're the one they'll set up to take the blame. Not Rossing. They'll condemn you as a sick lunatic the way they condemned Jens Peter Raben. Can't you see that?'

Frode Monberg gripped the end of the bed, fighting for breath. Fighting for some courage too.

'I only came into politics to do something. To serve.'

'So tell me,' Buch begged.

The thin man hesitated, took a deep breath.

'She said she'd found proof the soldiers were telling the truth. There was a massacre. A Danish officer was responsible. It was an injustice Raben had been locked away like that.'

'How did she know?' Buch asked.

Monberg closed his eyes, looked like a man on the edge.

'Because she'd found him.'

'Found who?' Buch demanded.

'The one who did it. She knew who he was. She wouldn't say. She was too frightened. I was in the government, wasn't I? I don't think she really trusted me.'

Buch didn't say the obvious: Dragsholm was right.

'That's all I know,' Monberg added.

He turned from Buch, looked out of the window.

'What the hell am I going to do? It just gets worse and worse.'

'You tell the truth, Frode. That's all.' He put a hand on Monberg's shoulder, was shocked that he felt little there but wasted muscle and bone. 'Tell the truth and everything will be all right. I promise. The Prime Minister's behind me all the way. He asked me to get to the bottom of this. We'll back you, I promise.'

Frode Monberg turned and glared at Buch, said nothing.

A rap at the door. Karina.

'I'm sorry,' she said. 'Excuse me. But I have to talk to you. It's important.'

'Two minutes,' he told Monberg. 'Then we'll work out what to do.'

The lean man glared at him.

'You're an infant, Buch. Rossing won't say a word.'

Karina was still bleating.

'Two minutes,' Buch repeated.

'You can't make him,' Monberg said and there was fear in his eyes. 'You don't know. He's not like me. Not like any of us.'

Out in the corridor, Karina dragging him away from Monberg's room, Buch was finally beginning to feel he'd made a breakthrough.

'Thomas . . .'

37

'I got him to talk. He confirmed what we guessed. We need to get PET over here right away.'

'Will you listen to me?' She dragged him into an alcove. 'Monberg's not your problem now. It's Krabbe.'

Buch took a deep breath.

'What's the Boy Scout up to now?'

'He's demanding your resignation.'

'Oh come on.'

She looked miserable and that wasn't like her.

'Krabbe's given the Prime Minister an ultimatum. Either you go or he withdraws his support for the administration. He wants your head or he could bring down the government.'

'No, no, no.' He couldn't get the conversation he'd just had out of his head. 'Listen to me. Monberg has confirmed he spoke to Rossing. That he kept a Danish soldier in Herstedvester at Rossing's request. This is what matters now.'

She folded her arms and gazed at him.

'Let's get to the truth and then everything will work out,' Buch insisted. 'It usually does. Come . . .'

He led her back down the corridor.

'You can hear it for yourself.'

'This is serious,' she replied, following him.

'Everything's serious. It's just a matter of degree.'

He marched back into Monberg's room. A nurse was changing the sheets. The bed was empty.

Buch looked at the nurse.

'He said he wanted a bit of exercise,' she said with a shrug.

'And you let him go?'

She bridled.

'This is a hospital. Not a prison.'

Buch swore, went back into the corridor. Monberg had to have turned left. If he'd gone the other way they'd have seen him.

'Thomas . . .' Karina bleated.

'Not now.'

He wasn't a nervous man. Anxiety wasn't in his nature.

'Thomas! You need to call the Prime Minister.'

'No!' He was shouting at her and he regretted that. 'We've got to find Monberg. Don't you get it?'

'Tell me,' she said and folded her arms.

'I pushed him, Karina,' Buch said quietly, almost to himself. 'I pushed him very hard.'

She watched, listened, then walked in front of him, scanning the rooms left and right.

'Frode?' she cried, and got no answer.

Jarnvig's house in Ryvangen Barracks. The basement was almost finished. Painted by Christian Søgaard, bright wallpaper in Jonas's new room. A cot bed, a small yellow chair, a standard lamp, a little desk. It was the first time he'd ever had any space of his own. Louise watched her son standing by her father as Jarnvig placed a poster of fantasy warriors on the space above the bed.

'Is it level, Jonas?' he asked when the picture was in place.

'Yes, Granpa. Like that.'

Jarnvig turned and grinned at him, took some drawing pins out of his pocket and stuck the poster to the wall.

'Right then,' he said, patting the boy on the head. 'It looks smashing, doesn't it? All yours now.'

'You have to knock before you come in,' Jonas told him.

'Sir!' Jarnvig said with a salute and a click of his heels.

Jonas did the same. The two of them laughed. Louise Raben saw this and felt both happy and sad.

Then she walked back to the kitchen and started to clear up.

Her father followed.

'I'll leave you to it now,' he said. 'It looks nice down there. This was always a bachelor place before. Now . . .' A foolish grin. 'It feels like I've got a family again.'

'Thanks for helping, Dad.'

'What else can I do? I said some stupid things yesterday. I'm sorry. It gets to me too. I hate . . . I hate seeing you like this.'

She took off her rubber gloves, came and touched his cheek.

'It's all right. I've been an idiot, haven't I? I always thought for ever meant for ever. That's stuff for kids, isn't it?'

40

'Sometimes,' he agreed. 'Come to the cadets' ball. I'd like that. You could be my guest.'

She remembered them from when she was a teenager. All the young soldiers aching to dance with an officer's daughter.

'I'm too old and fat for that.'

'Nonsense. You're neither. It would do you good.'

'I should be with Jonas.'

'Jonas is OK. I can get someone in to babysit. It's you I'm worried about. Come on . . .'

She ran a cloth across the sink. The gold band of her wedding ring was by her watch next to the tap. She always took it off to wash up.

For ever.

Pipe dreams for children. She'd stuck by Jens through more than most women would bear. And got what in return? A coward who ran away to fight in the Middle East the moment she had a child. A criminal fleeing from everyone.

'Just a couple of hours,' he pleaded. 'We can leave when you like.'

She couldn't take her eyes off the wedding ring. Once it had seemed so important. A symbol of something they shared. Now it was a relic, a bitter reminder of everything she'd lost.

'Of course,' Jarnvig said. 'I understand. It's up to you.'

He laughed.

'But I always loved to watch you dance. You thought you were no good at it. You'd no idea . . .'

41

Louise folded her arms.

'So what time are you going?'

Jarnvig clapped his hands, his face wreathed in the kind of delight she hadn't seen much in recent years.

'As soon as you've picked the right dress. So God knows . . .'

One hour later, outside the wire fence of the barracks. Raben was in the second car he'd ripped off that day, slumped in the driver's seat, hood round his face. Door open, ready to flee at the first sign of trouble.

A good place. A clear view of Jarnvig's house. Lights on. Toys just visible in a downstairs window. The sight made his heart ache. For what he'd lost. For what he had to recover.

The door opened. Torsten Jarnvig walked out in full dress uniform. Black jacket and gold epaulettes. White shirt with bow tie. A long Mercedes limousine was waiting.

Raben knew this routine. It was the ball for the new intake of cadet officers, in a hired hall near Kastellet. Men like him were never allowed near. They just had to imagine the music, the cackle of laughter, the odd drunken jape. To grit their teeth and hope these raw, green youngsters didn't get in the way of fighting, of staying alive, once the unit hit the hard terrain of Helmand.

Officers had their place. But it was men, ordinary

soldiers, enlisted squaddies, little in the way of education and social background, who decided whether the battle was won or lost. Their blood, more than any other, that was spilled on dry, foreign soil.

He watched Jarnvig get to the car, throw a cigarette in the gutter, look around, wondering what he thought of this man. The commanding officer. Louise's father too. Raben never really understood if he was family or just one more soldier waiting for his orders. Perhaps Jarnvig struggled with the same conflict too.

The door to the house opened again and Raben's thoughts froze, the breath caught in his mouth. Louise was walking out. Fur stole, scarlet silk dress. Hair perfect. Face pale with make-up. Ready for the cadets' ball, the officer's daughter all the junior men would dream of.

And yet she'd ignored every one of them and picked him instead.

She walked slowly down the steps. Reluctantly, Raben thought. As if a decision had been made.

Jarnvig held open the limousine door. A uniformed soldier sat erect at the wheel. Louise got in, looking ahead all the time. She'd slipped back into their world now, was a part of it again. And he wasn't, never would be.

Raben watched the car move slowly to the guardhouse, the men salute as Jarnvig and his daughter were driven out of Ryvangen.

Then slowly, carefully, he took his stolen Peugeot

into the road behind them, following from a safe distance, wondering what to do when they were there.

In the back of a cab, on the way into the city from Mrs Møller's house, Lund called Strange.

'You don't sound like you're at a wedding,' he said.

'I need you to check something.'

'You're off the case.'

'I need you to check something,' she said again, impatiently.

'I'm in Helsingør.'

Forty minutes north of Copenhagen by car.

'What are you doing there?'

'PET want us to drag in every last Afghan in Denmark. I'm with an interpreter at a refugee centre. Waste of time. Let me step outside . . .'

She waited. The car was getting stuck in night traffic. Her mother's flat might be half an hour away like this.

'So what's up?' Strange asked after a while.

'Someone used Per K. Møller's identity. His dog tag is missing.'

'They're fighting a war, Lund. Things get lost.'

'It's not just that. Someone's been buying things using his name. In the last few months. The letters have been coming back to his mother.'

'Oh.'

'You need to talk to the priest again. And Søgaard. Run Møller's name through the credit agency system and see if anything else turns up.'

'I'm in Helsingør, remember? Talking to people who hate me.'

'Fine. Get in the car and come back. You can do it in thirty minutes if you put your foot down.'

'I've got work to do! It's going to be a couple of hours.'

He went quiet for a moment.

'Have you told Brix about this?'

'Not yet,' she admitted. 'I will. Honest.'

That long pause again.

'Please tell me you're not going to do something stupid.'

'Like what?'

'Like . . . I don't know. Going off on your own again. That never works out well, does it?'

What do you care? she thought. You're just another cop they gave me. One who's not so good at the job. Too nice for it in many ways.

'I'm not going to do anything stupid,' Lund said, and realized she didn't want to hurt his feelings. 'But thanks anyway.'

That was it. Rain now. Cars in slow-moving lines ahead of them.

'I want to go somewhere different,' she said to the driver. 'Vesterbro. How long?'

He laughed. Shrugged.

'You tell me,' the man said with a chuckle. 'You're sure?'

'Yes. I'm sure.'

Cutting through Indre By in the city centre the cab turned down a narrow lane and knocked a cyclist off his bike. The inevitable argument ensued. The cyclist, a big man, plenty of beer inside him, reached inside the taxi and stole the keys.

She waited a couple of minutes watching the two men dance around each other in the street. Then she left her card on the dashboard and told the driver she'd stand witness if he really wanted someone to testify how bad he was behind the wheel.

It was a short walk back to Nørreport Station. From there the trains ran in all directions. She could be in Vibeke's apartment in a few minutes, calling her mother, trying to make amends for walking out of the wedding. Or she could head out to Vesterbro and try to find the priest, Gunnar Torpe.

Normally it would have been an easy choice. But Strange's closing words bothered her. It wasn't stupid to chase things she didn't understand. This was what she did. Who she was. And besides . . . what was it to him? A decent, half-competent cop who seemed to have stumbled into the police because he was sick of being a soldier. Ulrik Strange didn't look much like a man with a career. He'd fallen into what he did and that was never the case with her.

Lund walked into a cafe opposite the station, bought herself a cappuccino and a sandwich.

Strange was so unlike Jan Meyer, a man she'd found amusing and infuriating at the same time. There was a seriousness to him. A sense of solitary devotion and duty, one that seemed strengthened by his self-awareness. He knew he was struggling with this case. That was why he clung to her, listened to her, did as she asked, even though they were both, nominally, equals in rank until Brix kicked her out once more.

She sipped her coffee slowly, took time over the sandwich. Looked at her watch. Quarter to eight. If Strange had done what she asked he'd have been back in the Politigården by now chasing the leads she'd suggested. She could call. But that would be checking. It might annoy him and she didn't want to do that.

So she finished her drink, walked to the metro, went down the stairs, looked at the two platforms, one leading to home, the other to Vesterbro and Gunnar Torpe.

It wasn't much of a choice at all.

Thirty minutes later she was in the church. The place seemed deserted. The only lights were on the altar. Three gold candelabra on a white cloth in front of a painting of Mary weeping over the dead Jesus.

47

Lund walked down the aisle, looked around. There was a noise from an open door to the right. A dim light beyond there.

'Hello?' she shouted, and found herself hearing Jan Meyer's voice out of nowhere. That rough, familiar cigarette-stained croak. It said, *You're not going to go in alone again, Lund? And without a gun?*

These were the tricks your head played sometimes. She went to the door and cried, 'Anybody there?'

No answer. She pushed it open.

'Hello?'

Her voice sounded musical in the echoing interior. It was dark in the room. She found a switch, turned on the single bulb. Jumped back with shock when the first thing it threw at her was a tiled sink stained with splashed blood.

Hand to the pocket. Nothing there but a phone.

'Shit,' Lund whispered and did what came naturally. Walked on.

A second room. In semi-darkness this time, since there was a window to the outside, and a street lamp leaking its wan light through the glass.

A familiar shape, both obscene and holy, in the centre. A figure, arms outstretched like a crucified man, tethered to an iron bar strapped between two tall wooden candle holders.

Gunnar Torpe, face bloodied, in a combat jacket, black tape over his mouth.

Lund walked to him, snatched the tape away.

48

Blood poured from the priest's mouth. His head went down. His eyes were closed.

She got to his arms, removed the fastening there with one hand, supporting him with the other. Right arm first, then the left. A heavy man. She struggled as she let his body fall slowly to the hard concrete floor.

He was breathing. Just.

Phone.

Lund called control.

'Sarah Lund. Send an ambulance to St Simon's Church, Vesterbro. Tell Brix. I just found the priest. He's still breathing but . . .'

Something glittered near Torpe's body. She looked. A dog tag cut in half, blood on the sharp severed side.

'You need to be quick. Tell . . .'

A sound nearby. Footsteps at the back of the room.

Lund looked at Torpe. At the blood. Fresh. At the wounds. So many, so livid.

A shape. A hooded man, head down, crossed briefly in the light from the window, ran out towards the rear.

'Tell Brix I'm in pursuit,' she said then left the bleeding priest and raced for the door.

An hour they'd been looking. An hour wasted. The hospital administrator, a bad-tempered woman, was with them.

'How can you lose a patient?' Buch demanded.

49

'How can you walk in here and berate him without his permission or ours?' the administrator demanded. 'This is outrageous. I don't care who you are. It doesn't matter—'

Her phone rang.

They were on the third floor. Intensive Care. No sign of Monberg. No one had seen him anywhere.

Buch watched the way her face changed. He knew what bad news looked like now. There'd been so much of it of late.

'What is it?' he asked when she put the mobile in her jacket pocket.

'I think we need to call the police.'

'I'm the Minister of Justice!' Buch bellowed. 'The police answer to me.'

'Fine,' she grumbled, and led them to the end of the corridor, through what looked like a storage area. No rooms. No wards. Just equipment and boxes.

'Patients aren't allowed here,' she said. 'Under no circumstances . . .'

There was a service lift. With his bulk and the two women it was just about full. The administrator pressed the button for the ground floor. Said nothing more.

After a while the door opened. Three men in green overalls, bent round something.

Buch pushed through.

Monberg lay on the floor face down. A pool of scarlet blood ran out from his haggard features.

His smashed spectacles lay by his side. The red stained his white pyjamas. His eyes were open and looked puzzled. In some cruel way more alert than they ever had been in life.

'Jumped from the third floor just now,' one of the men said.

'Patients are not allowed . . .' the administrator began.

Karina had turned to the wall and was sobbing.

'There'll be an inquiry,' the woman added.

'You're sure he jumped?' Buch asked.

No one answered.

He got up, took hold of one of the men by the shoulders. Got a filthy look in return.

'You're sure he jumped?' Buch repeated.

'I was down here sweeping up,' the man snapped back at him. 'I saw him standing there. Smoking a cigarette. Then he saw me. Got on the railing.' His hand pointed up the winding staircase. 'I heard him screaming all the way down.'

'You're sure?' Buch asked again but quietly.

'I don't think I'll forget that in a while. Would you?'

Ten past seven. The meat-packing district was coming to life. Trapped between the railway lines and Vesterbro, it was the place that fed much of Copenhagen: butchery wholesalers, fish companies, bakers, grocery firms crammed into low metal buildings ranged across a sprawling industrial estate. Then, in the evening, another side emerged.

The spare space, on the first floor, sometimes the ground, opened up to the night crowd, with bars and tiny restaurants where the glittering party types flocked to dine and drink near the rows of cattle carcasses and trays of freshly gutted salmon.

Lund chased the distant hooded figure out from Gunnar Torpe's church, saw him dash left at the Bosch sign above a fashionable organic hangout.

Still she ran and ran, arms pumping, breath coming in short, rhythmic gasps. Brix could deal with the priest. Lund had the man in her sights and nothing else mattered.

She rounded the Bosch sign, scanned the square ahead. Warehouses and commercial outlets. Vans loading. Taxis turning up with women in garish dresses out for the night.

A hooded figure disappeared into the building in the far right corner. Lund set off, ran through the half-open doors behind him.

An empty loading area. Forklift trucks parked for the morning. Steam rising from grates in the grey concrete floor. An iron staircase winding up to the timber ceiling.

A sudden noise. Lund jumped. It was the thump of a sound system from the floor above. Loud, rhythmic disco music. The sound of laughter, squeals of delight.

One door open ahead. She walked on. Found herself back in the chill night. A yard full of black rubbish bags, pigeons pecking at the waste.

The place was empty.

She called Brix, heard the sigh in his voice as he answered.

'Lund. I'm busy. I'll call you back.'

'The priest—'

'What about him?'

'You didn't get the message?'

'I told you. I'm busy.'

'I found him half-dead in his church. I called control. Told them to get an ambulance there. To tell you—'

'What in God's name are you doing?' he yelled. 'You're supposed to be at a wedding.'

'Someone ran from the church when I got there. I'm trying to track him. He's in the meat-packing district.'

She glanced around. So many buildings. But there was broad open space between them. If she got lucky . . .

'He can't be far away. Send me all the backup you can spare. We can isolate this place—'

'Stay where you are,' Brix ordered.

She could hear him snapping his fingers at the officers around his desk. *See* him doing that.

'We're coming. You're unarmed. I don't want you going near—'

'Talk to the priest. Get us an ID. He saw him.'

'Lund?' His voice was back to a bellow. 'How many times do I have to say this? You're off the case. I don't want you anywhere near.'

'I'm here. You're not.'

A hazy shape moved across her line of vision. A

hooded figure racing out of the empty loading bay towards the building opposite.

'Just get here, will you?' she said and put the phone in her pocket.

She saw him push through a plastic ribbon curtain, the kind they used in the loading areas. Lund walked towards it, got the raw, sharp smell of freshly slaughtered meat in her face and the chill of refrigeration.

Went through. The place ahead was in darkness. Her fingers fumbled on the brick wall, found switches, flipped them. Harsh fluorescent tubes burst into life, crackling, flashing, sending their blue-white light everywhere.

Through the next ribbon door. Sides of bloody red beef hanging from hooks on the right. Naked dead pigs, as bare and pink as gigantic babies, ranged on the left, snouts up to the ceiling, eyes closed.

Line upon line of dead flesh set against white-tile walls. Lund caught sight of herself in a shiny metal door. Black donkey jacket, purple wedding dress. Gunnar Torpe's blood on her chest.

Walked on.

A cutting room now. Tables like the morgue, clean and shiny. Saws and electric knives. The stench of blood and severed tissue.

She walked through slowly, moving the wheeled cutting slabs out of the way.

Looking. Listening.

Another room ahead. A handle turning. Lund

got to another set of plastic ribbons then saw it coming. A trolley laden with rubbish bags and cartons, flying through the grey sheeting, straight at her.

She caught the metal frame with her hands before it could strike, took the blow, rolled with it, fell backwards, half into a bloody gutter stinking of disinfectant, turned on the ground, trying to see, to judge if he was coming for her.

Just the trolley.

She got up, started running. A corridor. Long enough so she could see him. A man. Not big, not small. Not broad, not skinny.

Unremarkable.

They usually were.

He could run too, scooted right at the end, scattering bins and pallets as he fled, throwing shut an iron rollaway grating behind him.

She ran too quickly, slipped on the greasy floor, took a hard fall into a waste bin, smashed her head against the metal side. Stumbled upright, ran on.

A staircase leading towards the light and the noise and the people.

Night in the meat-packing district. No one came to buy dead cow or fresh fish. They were here to party, and Lund was fighting her way through them, pushing, scrabbling, staring everywhere.

Kids and their stupid music. A relentless, idiot beat. They screamed as she spilled their hundred kroner cocktails, fell silent when they saw her, bloodied and furious, clawing her way through their party dresses and designer denim.

Looking.

A shape far ahead. The one hooded figure in the place.

Lund raced past a psychedelic purple light, got blinded for a moment, refocused, saw him escaping by a distant door.

A bare narrow corridor. Empty and dimly lit. Offices maybe. Closed for the night.

He had to be exhausted. She was.

One door at the end. She opened it and found the cold wet night blowing in her face.

The roof. One floor up. Somewhere not far away the sound of sirens.

And nothing.

Nothing.

Lund started to turn. Saw the briefest shadow sweeping through the air. Felt something hard and cruel connect with her neck, send her stumbling towards the roof edge, then over, feet turning as she fell into empty space, drop like a stone onto what felt like corrugated plastic.

Her head felt loose, her mind ranged. She hadn't fallen a full floor. That was impossible. She was alive, conscious, could think. There was another part to this structure. He'd sent her flying onto that, not the ground which would surely have killed her.

Face side on against the sheeting, blood trickling into her eyes. She couldn't move. Could barely breathe.

A sound. Footsteps on metal stairs. Slow and deliberate. Getting closer.

'Not yet,' she whispered, willing her dead limbs to move.

A crazy memory. Her mother at the wedding. The stupid songs. Mark laughing, behaving like the responsible, careful adult she'd never been herself.

Then, so quiet only she could hear, 'Not now.'

He was there and she knew it. Knew too that if she had the strength she'd turn and stare him in the face.

Another sound, one too familiar. The slide of a semi-automatic pistol racking the first shell into the chamber.

One last sentence in her head.

Let me see you.

But she lacked the strength and the means to say it.

Only her eyes could move at that moment. So she kept them open and looked ahead. At the black Copenhagen night, and the bright-red neon Bosch sign of the restaurant on the corner.

Waiting.

The office in Slotsholmen, the evening news on TV, the little rubber ball bouncing against the wall, back and forth.

The only story was Monberg's death. Plough was pacing the floor, tie undone looking distraught. Karina moped around as if she took some responsibility for what had happened.

Buch threw the ball again, misjudged the way it would come back, watched it fly off behind the sofa.

He'd disabuse her of that notion soon enough. He'd badgered Monberg. No one else. And now the TV news knew too. They were reporting that shortly before he killed himself Monberg had been visited by his successor, and a confrontation had taken place.

Karina, shirtsleeves rolled up, perspiration on her brow, came over and turned the TV to mute.

'The Prime Minister's called a meeting with Krabbe and Rossing. You're not invited.'

Buch went to his desk, pulled out another rubber ball, bounced it against the wall. Monberg's photo was on the TV. Back when he was minister. A good-looking, confident politician. Nothing like the man who succeeded him. Frode Monberg liked to tell everyone how he dined in all the finest places, Noma across the harbour, and Søren K in the Black Diamond Library that sat by the water in Slotsholmen. Thomas Buch wanted nothing more than to sit a short distance away from Søren K, in the garden near the Jewish Museum, close to the statue of Kierkegaard, the Danish philosopher who gave the Black Diamond restaurant its name. No fancy food. A sandwich. A hot dog. He was happy like that, would have been content to stay a foot soldier in politics until his early retirement.

But then Grue Eriksen called, just the previous Monday. And everything changed.

'Thomas!' Karina said in that matronly, scolding voice. 'Will you please stop behaving like this? If you hadn't pressured Monberg he'd never have admitted anything.'

'If I hadn't pressured him he'd still be alive.'

'You don't know that. He'd already tried to kill himself once. Flemming Rossing was in there before you. How do you know he didn't say something?'

Buch didn't answer.

'How hard did you lean on him?' Plough asked.

'He did what was necessary,' Karina retorted.

'You don't know that,' Plough said. 'What happened? Exactly?'

The ball went to the wall, came back. The fat man with the walrus beard said nothing.

'This mess is Monberg's fault,' Karina insisted.

Plough dragged his tie away from his neck and threw it on the desk. In a man like him it seemed an act of rebellion.

'You don't understand the politics of this. The way things connect.'

'I understand we've got to focus on the meeting with Grue Eriksen!'

Buch kept throwing the ball. He hated this stupid habit as much as they did now. But it was hard to stop.

Plough's phone rang. He answered it.

Karina came over and stood next to Buch.

'From what I gather Krabbe and the Defence Minister will take over responsibility for the

59

anti-terror package. They're going to side-line us completely. So we'll never get to the bottom of this. You'll be paralysed. Or fired. Dammit, Thomas! Will you at least say something?'

Marie, his wife, had been phoning his mobile. He hadn't the heart to answer.

'The meeting's started,' Plough said, coming off the phone. 'We should wait and hear what they have to say.'

Karina glared at him.

'We've got to stop this! The Prime Minister hasn't a clue about the games Rossing's been playing.'

The TV was murmuring in the corner. A familiar voice. Buch abandoned the ball and turned up the volume. Rossing was there, smart suit, black tie, being interviewed outside the Defence Ministry before going to meet Grue Eriksen.

'I'm shocked by the loss of a good colleague,' he said to the camera with a stony face. 'Frode was a great political personality. A man who made an enormous personal contribution to Denmark. Above all, a very dear friend.'

Buch turned up the volume to make sure the row between Karina and Plough didn't catch fire again.

'It's a great loss,' Rossing went on. 'Especially at a time like this, when our country faces serious problems.'

The ruse didn't work. Plough was taking aim at Karina again.

'Don't defend Monberg!' she yelled at him. 'He doesn't deserve it.'

'I want to know what happened,' Plough barked back. 'You should know. All things taken into consideration—'

'What happened?' She slammed her fist on the table. 'What happened is the damned coward killed himself because he couldn't face the consequences of his own actions? Impeachment. Shame. Don't blame me. Don't dare blame Buch. Blame the man himself.'

She pointed at the TV.

'Blame Rossing. His fingerprints are all over this. For Christ's sake, Plough. I'm sorry I offended your puritanical sensibilities by sleeping with the man. Doubly so now. But don't make that more than it was. Nothing to me. Nothing to him either. It just happened. The way they do between normal human beings, not robots like you.'

The pale civil servant looked dumbstruck. No words. No answer at all.

Buch threw the ball away, turned off the TV and said to both of them, 'I want you to call in the press. Straight away.'

'The press?' Plough gasped. 'Please tell me this is a joke.'

'Just do it,' Buch ordered.

The curtains were closed to keep out the black night. The Prime Minister, Flemming Rossing and

61

Erling Krabbe alone. No civil servant to keep minutes. No pens, no notepads on the table.

'Here's the truth,' Krabbe began. 'You've got much better candidates than Buch. You should never have appointed him in the first place.'

'He's an honest man,' Grue Eriksen noted. 'Intelligent and hard-working. Lacking in experience. But . . .' He smiled at the thin, dour man across the table. 'We all are until it happens to us.'

'He's unfit for the job,' Krabbe insisted. 'Now there's all this publicity about Monberg, too. What the hell is going on?'

'Leave Monberg out of it,' Grue Eriksen replied. 'Buch's my minister. Get off his back.'

Krabbe bridled.

'If you want my support you're going to have to listen to me.'

'We are,' Rossing broke in. 'I told you already. We can alter the anti-terror package to accommodate the People's Party. We'll proscribe the organizations you want—'

'Buch must go,' Krabbe insisted.

'Will you listen for once?' Grue Eriksen barked. 'I decide the ministers in this government. Not you. Buch got the sharp end of the stick. There were irregularities on Monberg's part he never knew about and neither did the rest of us.'

'What irregularities?' Krabbe demanded.

'You don't need to know. Now he's dead . . .'

Flemming Rossing coughed, glanced at Grue

Eriksen, and said, 'Frode wasn't quite master of the situation. Let's leave it at that.'

Krabbe threw up his skinny arms in despair.

'Every day there's a new surprise. When's it going to stop? Rumours about this. One of your ministers killing himself. Buch flapping around like the fat idiot he is . . .'

A man in a grey suit walked in, whispered in Grue Eriksen's ear.

'And now!' Krabbe's whiny voice was approaching falsetto. 'There's talk about some old army case. What the hell's that about? Did the Islamists do this or not?'

Grue Eriksen got up and turned on the TV.

'Let's do the deal on the anti-terror package,' Rossing went on. 'Get that out of the way. It'll bring you closer to government. You can learn from us. Things will settle down. I guarantee it.'

The news came on, a caption: *Live from the Folketinget*. Buch on the screen, blue shirt open at the neck, looking tired but determined. A line of microphones pushed into his face.

'These are very critical questions which must be faced,' he was saying. 'I will demand a report from the Defence Minister concerning a military case which may be connected to the recent murders.'

'Fuck,' Flemming Rossing murmured.

'It seems,' Buch went on, 'the Defence Minister has withheld important information from the police in order to cover up his own negligence. My predecessor Frode Monberg confirmed my

63

suspicions before he died. That's all I can say at present.'

A fusillade of questions shot from the unseen faces in front of him.

Grue Eriksen watched the impromptu press conference end in chaos.

'Is that what you mean by settling down?' Erling Krabbe piped up.

Madsen was in the first car to get to the meat-packing district. He briefed Brix as they walked through the nightclub full of sullen, puzzled people, then out to the roof.

'Lund chased him through the warehouses, then the club, then out here,' he explained. 'She didn't even have a gun. Crazy cow.'

They stopped by a line of metal steps leading to a level below the roof.

'As far as we can work out he hid behind the door and slugged her when she came out.'

Brix stared at the drop.

'Did Gunnar Torpe say anything?' he asked.

'He was unconscious by the time we got there. Really badly cut, like the others. With a dog tag by the looks of it.'

Madsen looked at the crowds of clubbers getting ushered from the building.

'He died in the ambulance. Never recovered consciousness.'

Forensic officers were working the steps, brushing for evidence, taking photographs.

'What did Lund say?'

'She didn't see his face. She wants us to look for the dog tag belonging to the soldier she exhumed. It's missing.' Madsen shrugged. 'Seems crazy to me.'

'Usually does. How is she?'

'Stubborn.'

The older man glared at him.

'Tough as old boots. She wanted to walk to the ambulance. I think a stretcher was . . . beneath her.' Madsen scratched his head. 'She had some crazy idea that the guy was about to shoot her then changed his mind.'

Brix looked interested.

'I don't think so,' Madsen went on. 'There were people coming out of the club by then. They knew something was happening. He just legged it.'

'And Møller's missing dog tag?'

Madsen stared at him.

'What about it? We've got another murder. We've got an officer almost killed.'

'Just look into it, will you?' Brix ordered.

A black car flew into the loading space below, blue light flashing. Strange was out of the driver's door straight away.

'Where's Lund?' he shouted.

'On her way back to the Politigården from hospital,' Brix called down to him.

'Is she OK?'

'Yes,' Brix answered. 'Shaken but . . .'

Strange didn't stop to listen. He got behind the

wheel, slewed the car across the wet concrete, disappeared the way he came.

Brix watched him go, nodded to Madsen to get on with it.

Then called Ruth Hedeby.

'We need to talk,' he said.

Half an hour in Casualty then back to an interview room in headquarters. A wound above her right eyebrow. Bruises. A thick head. And questions. Lots of questions, none of them the ones the young detective who was with her thought of asking.

'Are you sure you didn't see his face?'

She sighed.

'If I saw his face I'd tell you, wouldn't I?'

'There must have been something special about him. The way he dressed—'

'Black anorak. Hood up. Is this the best line of questioning you've got?'

'I learned from you, Lund!' he cried, a little hurt.

She looked at him. A cadet she'd mentored a few years before.

'You always said to keep asking.'

'I did,' she answered. 'And you should. But sometimes there's nothing to say.'

'You told me,' he said, pointing an accusing finger, 'I was supposed to be part of a team.'

She nodded.

'You are.'

'But not you?'

Before she could answer the door opened and Strange strode in. He looked pale and worried.

'Are you all right?'

Lund got up. Her hand went to the wound above her eye.

'Fine.'

Strange nodded at the officer. He left straight away. She went back to the seat, quietly cursing the bruises and the pain.

'OK,' Ulrik Strange declared. 'You should not be here. I'm driving you home. Is there anyone I should call?'

She sipped some of the lukewarm coffee they'd brought her.

'No. I'm not going home.'

'For God's sake. Will you stop being the hero?'

'I'm not! My mother's getting married. Some wedding guests are staying over. I don't want to see them like this.'

She put her head on the table, closed her eyes.

'I can sleep in one of the night rooms here. Get me a bed. Find me a cell if you like. Won't be the first time.'

'You're a complete pain in the arse.' He got up. Put a gentle hand on her shoulder. 'Come on. We're going now.'

Head on the table, eyes barely open, she glowered at him.

'I used to pick up my kids and sling them over my shoulder when they did this shit to me,' Strange said. 'Don't try it. You won't win.'

'Sleepy,' she whispered.

'You're leaving this damned place. Even if I have to carry you.'

Lund didn't budge.

He bent down, whispered in her ear. His breath was warm and smelled of liquorice.

'Even if I have to carry you,' Strange repeated.

Madsen had contacted Møller's mother by the time Brix got back to the Politigården. There was a message for him with one of the uniform men on the desk: someone had misused her son's identity.

'Also . . .' Madsen went on.

Ruth Hedeby was wandering down the corridor ahead, looking to avoid him.

'Later,' Brix ordered and followed her.

'Ruth,' he said when they got to her office.

She turned on him, finger jabbing in his face.

'What the hell was Lund doing in that church? If I find you've gone behind my back—'

'I didn't know she was there. She told Strange. Wanted him to look. He was in Helsingør—'

'The woman's a liability.'

She walked off to her desk. Brix took her shoulder.

'Lund's the only one who's seen this right from the start. It's nothing to do with terrorism. We've got to get König in here and find out what he really knows.'

She sat down. Brix took the seat opposite.

68

'We need to start afresh—'

'König's got problems of his own,' she broke in. 'The Minister of Justice called a press conference this evening. He's making accusations against the Defence Ministry and demanding PET look into them. Meanwhile Raben's parked outside a hall in Østerbro where the Ryvangen cadets are having their ball. Do you feel a spectator in all this?'

'Ruth—'

'PET will decide what to do. We just sit back, listen and take orders.' Her acute, dark eyes fixed on him. 'That means you. That means me. That means Lund too.'

He got up, closed the door.

'We can't go on like this.'

That irked her.

'There's a dividing line, Lennart. Work and pleasure. We agreed that from the start. Don't pretend otherwise.'

'That's not what I mean.'

'What is it then?'

'If you don't trust me any more.' He hesitated, made sure she understood. 'After all we've done together.'

Ruth Hedeby's mouth dropped. She looked younger. Looked vulnerable, and a part of Brix said he shouldn't pull a trick like this.

'Then really,' he added, 'what's the point?'

'How can you use that against me?'

'I'm not.' He put his feet on her desk, leaned back, stifled a yawn. 'I can work round König.

69

We don't have to sit here like junior partners waiting on their lead.'

'Listen—'

'König's had us running all over Denmark chasing immigrants who don't know the first thing about these murders. Was that out of incompetence? Or did he have a reason? I'm not asking you to step out of line. I'm demanding you do your duty. *We* do it.'

She was wavering. Torn.

'I want Lund back and I want a free hand,' he said.

'You're a bastard.'

He smiled.

'Sometimes. But not now. They're jerking us around. I know you hate that as much as I do. So . . .'

'Let me think about it,' she said.

'Ruth . . .'

'Enough. You've got work to do, haven't you?'

The cadets' ball was in a whitewashed army hall close to the Kastellet fortification near the waterfront. Lights in every window, a string quartet, young men in fine uniforms, girlfriends on their arms.

Torsten Jarnvig had an unexpected guest: Jan Arild. Once a fellow lieutenant in the Jægerkorpset in Aalborg, now a general at army headquarters. A short, stocky, sly-looking man a couple of years older than Jarnvig. With his fine ginger hair, ruddy complexion and sharp features he'd earned the nickname 'Fox' back then. Appropriately, Jarnvig thought. They'd served together, in hard times on occasion. Arild was a survivor. An important man now, in dress uniform covered with ribbons of service. He held divisional responsibilities over Ryvangen. It was important to cultivate him. And never call him Fox again.

So Torsten Jarnvig smiled and laughed at his bad jokes. Didn't complain when he smoked at the table even though it was frowned upon. Didn't mention his poor manners, or the coarse way he'd whistle at anything, his own crass remarks or a woman walking past.

Instead Jarnvig looked at his daughter and raised an eyebrow. He wanted her to know this offended him too. Wanted her to understand it was one of the burdens of being Colonel of Ryvangen.

'I could tell you stories about me and your old man,' Arild said and nudged Louise's elbow. He didn't notice when she shrank from him. 'Places we were never supposed to be. Doing things they'd never want to hear about in Geneva . . .'

'Jan,' Jarnvig began.

'See! I'm still Jan.' He leaned forward. 'Not so good here, you know.'

'General . . .' Jarnvig said with a sigh.

'Things we never talk about,' Arild repeated. 'That's the way of the army.'

Arild admired the couples on the floor. Let loose a low wolf whistle at a woman in a low-cut red gown.

'I gather the only surviving member of this rene-gade squad of yours is your own son-in-law,' he said, still eyeing the dancer. Arild stubbed his cigarette into the smoked salmon on his plate, glanced at Louise. 'Never works when men and officers meet outside duty. They know their place. We know ours. What do the police say he's up to?'

'I really don't know much about it,' Jarnvig replied. 'We've more important things to focus on. How was . . . how was the hunting season?'

Arild scowled.

'I don't have time for that. If Raben attacked the army chaplain he must be quite mad, don't you think? A lunatic.'

Louise stared at him.

'What?' Arild asked. 'Did I say something out of place?'

She was about to speak when Søgaard turned up at the table. A bright smile broke on Arild's face. He got to his feet, shook the newcomer's hand briskly.

'Major Christian Søgaard,' Arild cried. 'Behold the future.'

'I believe,' Louise broke in, 'Major Søgaard was about to ask me to dance.'

She got up, took Søgaard's arm and pushed, half-dragged Søgaard to the floor.

Arild scowled at Jarnvig.

'Spirited young woman. Do you think she'd feel the same if she knew about our little games together all those years ago?'

'I did what I was told and so did you.'

'A man should know his duty,' Arild agreed and lit another cigarette. 'Even better if he doesn't need to be told. PET's about to pick up that renegade of yours. They've been following him for a while.' He tapped his sharp nose. 'That's confidential. Keep it to yourself.'

'Why are they waiting?'

'Because they hope to pick up the killers, of course. If he's stupid enough for PET to track him down I can't see a bunch of Muslim fanatics having much problem, can you?'

Jarnvig's phone rang. The music was too loud. He walked out, went down the hall, found an empty room. White walls, a glittering Murano chandelier.

The call was from Bilal, on security duty outside the ball. Gunnar Torpe was dead. A policewoman had been attacked.

Jarnvig leaned against a wall and closed his eyes.

'What are the police telling you?'

'Not much,' the young officer said.

'Leave it with me.'

He pocketed the phone, wondered what to do. Looked up and saw Jens Peter Raben by the long curtains. He was as filthy as a tramp and had a pistol in his left hand, the barrel pointed at the floor.

'Do as I say, tell the truth,' Raben ordered. 'That's all I ask. Then you can go back to the ball and push Søgaard at my wife again.'

73

'How the hell did you get in here?'

'The way I was taught. Your security stinks.'

'I just got a call to say Gunnar Torpe's dead. They found him murdered in his church this evening. And someone attacked that policewoman, Lund.'

Jarnvig watched him. He was used to judging soldiers. He knew when they were scared and lying. He knew when they were just scared.

'Wasn't me,' Raben said.

'Maybe not. I know you didn't start this but by God you're not helping yourself or Louise any more.'

'I'm staying alive,' Raben barked back. 'I'm the only one who managed that. I need to see the personnel files.'

'It's the cadets' ball,' Jarnvig said, spreading his arms wide. 'They keep old records at Holmen now, in the personnel office.'

'I need—'

'PET know where you are. They've been following you all along.'

'Bullshit.'

'It's true,' Jarnvig insisted. 'They let you stay loose because they hoped you'd bring these terrorists out into the open.'

'What terrorists? You don't believe—'

'Do everyone a favour and give yourself up.'

'I need those files.'

'Are you listening to me? PET are here tonight. They know you're inside. If you got this far it's only because they let you. Be smart for once.'

Raben checked the gun, the magazine.

'Oh for God's sake,' Jarnvig cried. 'Don't make it worse. I'll come with you. I can speak up for you—'

'Speak up for me?' Raben yelled and the gun came up a fraction.

'If you give me a chance.'

'The same chance I had before?'

The scruffy man with the unkempt beard, grubby clothes and scruffy hair seemed so far from the immaculate soldier who'd taken Louise down the aisle. Torsten Jarnvig had been proud that day, even if he had his misgivings.

'I was coming home,' Raben said in a low, bitter tone. 'I had two weeks to go. Then I was back with Louise and little Jonas. Out of the army. A new life. A new home. And now . . .'

The gun shook in his fingers.

'It's been two years of hell and it's never going to end, is it? You could have given me a chance back then. You could have investigated Perk—'

'There was no Perk, Jens. You ruined everything. For yourself. For Louise and Jonas.'

'I told the truth! Priest knew it too. Why would he lie? Or the others? I tried to stop him.'

'Who?'

'Perk! He had the officers' academy badge tattooed on his shoulder.' Raben tapped his temple with his free hand. 'I can see him now.'

'You said the man you attacked first of all was Perk—'

75

'I know what happened! I know what I saw.' He glared at Jarnvig. 'You were my commanding officer. You should believe me first. Not PET. Or whoever's spinning these tales. To hell with it . . .'

He went for the door.

'Stop.'

Raben had his fingers on the handle.

'They're looking for you, Jens. I told you. Go that way.' He pointed to a side exit. 'There's a corridor. It leads out into the garden. Keep your head down.'

The man in the grimy clothes stared at him.

'Just do it, will you?' Jarnvig pleaded.

Raben shambled off. With trembling fingers Torsten Jarnvig lit a cigarette, looked at himself in the mirror as he smoked it.

Halfway through a man marched in. Dark suit. Earpiece. PET. Had to be. Said Bilal was behind him.

'The toilets are at the end of the hallway,' Jarnvig told him. 'Show him, Bilal.'

The man looked the colonel up and down, checked the room, the curtains, everywhere, then left.

Torsten Jarnvig finished his cigarette and went back to the ball.

Jan Arild sat on his own, furious, his vulpine face flushed with booze and anger.

'That was a long call,' he said. 'Any news?'

'No,' Jarnvig said. 'Just personal.'

76

Arild folded his arms, watched Louise still on the dance floor in the arms of Christian Søgaard.

'Now that,' he said, 'is a couple.'

Thomas Buch was starting to know too well the labyrinth of corridors from his office opposite the twisting dragons to Grue Eriksen's quarters. So when he was summoned he broke recent habit, got a coat, walked outside, behind his own ministry past the little square where he used to eat sandwiches by the statue of Søren Kirkegaard, ambled all the way to the Christianborg Palace through the cold damp night.

Along the way he called home. He and Marie had married when they were nineteen and Buch was still working on the farm, learning the business. They seemed to have been together for ever but that night, in the chilly Copenhagen drizzle, she felt distant from him. She hated the city, the noise, the commotion. He no longer noticed. There were other, more pressing matters. The conversation was difficult and trite, which was less than she deserved. He'd abandoned her in a way, and the pressing questions Monberg had left hidden in his papers meant Thomas Buch barely had time to feel regret.

The call ended outside the imposing facade of the palace. Buch walked in, went upstairs. The Prime Minister didn't look too mad. But he was.

'I had no choice,' Buch said, taking a seat opposite the silver-haired man behind the vast shiny desk from which he ran the nation. 'I wanted to prevent—'

'Be silent, Thomas, and listen to me for a moment.' Grue Eriksen leaned back in his chair, put his hands together. 'I didn't hesitate when I appointed you. Nothing in your past suggested you'd be rash enough to stab your own government in the back.'

'You didn't hear me out . . .' Buch began.

'You called a press conference without my knowledge. Accused one of your own colleagues of criminal behaviour. These accusations cannot be retracted . . .'

Buch shook his head.

'I've no wish to retract them. The facts—'

'I've worked with Rossing since he first entered politics. I know him. I trust him.'

'Then let me ask him some questions, in front of the Security Committee. That's all I want.'

'You've backed me into a corner, haven't you?'

'It's important we get to the bottom of this!'

The Prime Minister leaned back in his chair and muttered a quiet curse.

'And there I was thinking I was raising a simple farm boy to Minister of State. You learn more quickly than I thought. And a few tricks I'd rather you'd missed. Do you realize what you've started?'

'Tell me,' Buch answered miserably.

'A witch-hunt, one I'm now forced to play out in public. If there's something amiss it's got to

78

come out. In the open. For all to see, whatever the damage.'

'Transparency is all I ask.'

'But if this is nothing but gossip and speculation,' Grue Eriksen added in a cold and vicious tone, his finger raised, his eyes blazing, 'I will send you back to Jutland to sweep up cow shit for the rest of your life.'

The Prime Minister glanced at his watch.

'You can go now,' he said.

Back in the office Plough and Karina were dissecting the latest news from the Politigården.

'They found the priest badly injured in his own church in Vesterbro,' Plough said. The tie was gone, the jacket too. He was changing, Buch thought. Maybe they all were.

Plough went on: 'Gunnar Torpe. He died in the ambulance. A former field chaplain attached to troops from Ryvangen. He was in Helmand at the same time as Raben. That's five dead. Six if we count Monberg.'

'Monberg killed himself,' Buch snapped. 'The hospital porter saw him jump. Did the priest have a dog tag?'

'Yes.' Karina sat on the edge of Buch's desk. Jeans and a shirt. She looked tired. A little dishevelled for once. 'It seems Lund interrupted the murder.'

Buch blinked.

'The woman we met at the wedding?'

79

'Her. The priest was with Ægir. He knew the first victim, Dragsholm. She'd visited him. Maybe all the victims knew what really went on in Afghanistan.'

Plough shook his head.

'We know what happened. Nothing. The army investigated. An official inquiry. It said Raben's claims were nonsense. Just a way of shifting the blame.'

He threw a report in front of Buch.

'Read it for yourself. Nothing points towards the killing of civilians.'

'Things get covered up sometimes, don't they?' Buch asked. 'If there was an atrocity they'd have good reason.'

Plough tugged at his open shirt, as if struggling to come to a decision.

'There must be someone inside the Defence Ministry who bears a grudge against Rossing.' He looked at Karina. 'Can you think of anyone he's fired recently?'

Buch grinned with surprise.

'That's the spirit,' he said.

'But it isn't.' Plough looked offended. 'It's petty and dishonourable.'

'We need to get close to the police and find out what they uncovered about this officer,' Buch added.

Karina frowned.

'Not easy. They've taken Lund off the case. It's being run by PET.'

80

'And what do they say?'

'They're still chasing what we told them about Monberg. König doesn't think it's relevant to the investigation. They feel . . .'

She was reluctant to say it.

'They still think we can solve this by locking up every last Muslim we can find?' Buch asked.

'Pretty much.'

'And these clowns are running the show? While Lund's fired?'

'König's a very experienced officer,' Plough said carefully. 'He's very . . .'

'Very what?'

'Very well connected.'

'I think we need to make some calls,' Thomas Buch said, waving at the phones. 'Let's get busy.'

Thirty minutes later Erik König was back in an interview room in the Politigården. It felt, Brix thought, a little formal, and he was happy with that.

'Don't you think it's odd no one ever found Møller's dog tag?' he asked.

König laughed.

'Not really. The man was blown to bits. How many pieces do you expect them to pick up?'

'You've had us chasing Islamists for days, Erik. Up and down the country. But there's nothing, not a thing, that indicates fundamentalists are behind these killings.'

'Only the video and the material we found at Kodmani's.'

81

'Faith Fellow planted that on him. And we don't have a clue who he is.'

'Speculation—'

'Why aren't we investigating the army and Ægir?' Brix asked. 'Do they have some kind of immunity?'

'Stop this. I won't answer to you, Lennart. We're PET. We never have.'

'I want Raben brought in here for questioning. If you know where he is fetch him now.'

The PET man took off his rimless glasses, polished them carefully with his handkerchief, placed them back on his face.

'That's not possible. He's got away from us.'

'You've lost him?' Brix roared. 'If you were one of my men—'

'I'm not. We're looking. We'll find him. When we do . . .' König sat back in the hard interview room chair. '. . . I'll let you know.'

Brix threw up his hands in despair.

'Lennart.' König leaned on the table, looked him in the face. 'Do you honestly think that if I knew there was something to hide in that barracks I'd be sitting here, lying to you?'

Brix didn't answer. Hedeby came in.

'I just had a call from the Ministry of Justice,' she said. 'Monberg told Buch he knew the first victim, Anne Dragsholm. She'd found the officer Raben talked about. The one responsible for the massacre. They want a full investigation. By us.'

82

She sat down next to König, very close, looked into his grey, emotionless eyes.

'Us,' she repeated. 'And if anyone stands in our way they want to know.'

'Do they indeed?' the PET man said and got up, put on his coat and left.

Ruth Hedeby watched him and didn't say a thing. That took guts, Brix thought.

'Thanks,' he said.

'Don't thank me. Thank the Ministry. They're even more pissed off with PET than they are with us.'

'There's the question of staffing—'

'I don't want Lund back. We're on thin ice as it is. The answer's no.'

Her phone rang again. She looked at the number.

'Dammit. Don't these Ministry people ever sleep?'

Brix watched her take the call, followed the expression on her face.

'Minister Buch . . .' she said quietly. 'It's not normal for a politician to become involved in personnel issues here.'

The response was so loud and furious Ruth Hedeby held the phone away from her ear.

When it was over she said, 'I'll see what I can do.'

Brix sat and waited. When she stayed quiet he said, 'So you told them Lund wasn't coming back?'

'No,' she said haughtily. 'But they found out anyway.' She glared at him. 'I wonder how.'

He glanced at his watch and said, 'Search me. I'm going home. We can put everything together in the morning.'

'Lennart!'

He stopped at the door.

'For God's sake keep an eye on her this time. If you can. She scares the living daylights out of me.'

'I'll tell her.'

'No.' Hedeby got up and pulled her coat around her. 'No need.'

Lund didn't object when Strange drove her to his flat. The last thing she wanted was to bump into a bunch of happy, drunk guests from her mother's wedding.

The place was barely furnished, the way Danish bachelors liked. Two bedrooms, the second with a couple of single beds for his kids when they visited.

They sat next to each other on the low sofa, opposite one of the giant TVs she hated so much. He had a menu for pizza from a place round the corner.

'Number thirty-eight,' she said.

He was on the phone to them already.

'Number thirty-eight,' Strange said in his calm, genial voice.

'With extra cheese,' she added.

He sighed.

'With extra cheese. Same for me. No cheese.'

The hospital had given her something for the wound. She was pouring some fluid onto a piece of cotton.

'How's your head?' he asked.

'I took some pills.'

She dabbed the cotton onto her forehead and missed.

'Let me,' Strange said and tried to take it from her.

'I'm not an invalid.'

'You can't see what you're doing. Is it so hard to be helped?'

She let him take it. Sat there like a child as he brushed back her hair, looked carefully at her face.

'It's not so bad. You won't even get a scar.'

'Wonderful.'

'You're a tough old bird.'

'You're too kind.'

He dabbed at the wound with the cotton. She gasped.

'I know. It stings.'

'Why am I here? I could have stayed in the Politigården?'

'You could have put yourself up in a hostel too.' He looked round the room. 'It's not so bad is it? No dirty underwear on the floor. No porno mags lying around. And I wasn't expecting you. Give me a break.'

There was a photo on the low table by the sofa. Black and white and old. A tall, upright man in uniform.

'Your father was a soldier?'

His face turned grim and she couldn't guess why.

'Uniforms run in the family. Army usually, not always. That's my grandfather. He was a policeman. That's the old uniform. Didn't I tell you?'

'No.'

'Well he was. In the Politigården during the war.' Strange stopped and looked at her. 'He was working with the Resistance. The Germans found out. Someone, some *stikke*, informed on him. My father said he died with all the other heroes at Mindelunden. Tied to one of those stakes, I guess. I don't know why I keep that picture really. To remind me of something but I have forgotten what it was. Such a long time ago. There's enough shit happening now without worrying about yesterday.'

She pulled back from him, picked up another photo of a man in uniform, army this time, more recent but still old.

'Is this your father? He looks just like you.'

'Soldiers, you see. There's something in our blood. We're born to serve.'

He laughed, looked vulnerable at that moment.

'I'm not like you. I'm best when I'm part of the pack and someone's telling me what to do. I guess I inherited that—'

'What happened to him? Your father?'

Strange stared at her.

'Who said anything happened to him?'

'It's an old photo. If he was still around you'd have a recent one.'

'Good God. You're a piece of work. Do you ever stop?'

'Not really. If you don't want to tell me—'

'He quit the army. My mum nagged him to leave. He bought a franchise for some stupid insurance agency with his pay-off. Was never going to happen. Remember what I said? We're born to serve. Not lead.'

Something on his face made her wish she'd kept quiet.

'We didn't know he was going bust. I'm not even sure it would have made a difference. I was only nineteen. That summer I was in the Politigården. When I thought the police uniform was for me.'

'How long will the pizzas be?'

He frowned at her.

'You asked. You've got to listen now. Only polite.'

'Strange—'

'I came home one day. He was hanging in the garage. I remember seeing the shoes first.'

'I'm sorry. I shouldn't have said anything.'

Strange scratched his stubbly cheek.

'You can't stop yourself. Besides, why not? You weren't to know. I hated him for that. For years. Then, when I was looking to come out of the army, my wife started giving me the same line. You're bright enough. Start your own company. Get a job in management. Be your own man.'

He brought the cotton wool to her face and dabbed again.

'That was enough to get me to re-enlist. I know who I am. I like being told what to do. By you. By Brix. Suits me. You're brighter and you know it.'

'I never said that.'

He laughed.

'You think you need to? You've got a face like an open book.'

'I've got a face like a football.'

'Still nice to look at.'

It had been so long since she'd had a conversation like this.

'I don't understand,' Lund said.

'What?'

He went back to working on her bruises and cuts.

'Why he didn't pull the trigger?'

He took away the cotton wool.

'Sarah. You don't know what happened. Don't worry about it.'

'I know. I heard. The gun . . .'

'There were people around.'

'He had time. He made a decision. I could feel it.'

'OK.' He put down the bottle and the swab. 'Listen to me. This won't happen again. You will not run away from me—'

'You were in Helsingør!'

'You could have waited.'

'Well I didn't.'

'Next time I'll make you. That's a promise.'

It was her turn to laugh.

'A promise? What am I to you? Just a crazy woman you fetched back from Gedser because Brix told you to . . .'

He put his hand on her arm. Then his fingers ran to her cheek, brushed back her hair, gently stroked for one brief moment her lips.

She didn't know what to do. Her head still hurt. She ached all over.

He moved towards her. She recoiled but just a little. So he persisted, tried again, got the meekest of pecks on her cheek, as much as she'd allow.

'This is a hell of a time to hit on me,' Lund whispered.

'When's a good one?'

He was so close, so full of a quiet and caring interest in her. Lund leaned towards him, tried to remember the last time she kissed a man.

The doorbell rang.

'Dammit,' Strange muttered. 'That was quick.'

He got up and a part of her was relieved. When he returned he looked grumpy.

'It's for you.'

Ruth Hedeby was outside in a heavy wool coat looking as if she'd rather be somewhere else.

'I'm sorry for the intrusion, Lund. I won't take much of your time.' She had an envelope in her hands. Opened it. There was Lund's police ID inside. 'Lennart . . . Brix can fill you in on the details. We were a bit rash, it seems.'

Hedeby handed her the ID, a sheaf of new

reports from PET and the Politigården's own team.

'There are developments in the case and a change of attitude in the Ministry of Justice.'

She glanced at Strange.

'We'll see you both tomorrow,' Hedeby said then walked to the lift.

'Wait,' Lund said.

Hedeby stopped.

'I want your guarantee I can stay on the case until it's closed.'

'My guarantee?'

'Yes. It's my case. I work with Strange. We handle it together. OK?'

'If the two of you can get along—'

'I want no restrictions. I don't want PET or anyone else telling me what to do. All the officers involved in Ægir are to be questioned. And maybe . . .'

'Maybe what?'

'Maybe something else I haven't thought of yet.'

Hedeby walked back, faced Lund.

'Let me make the position clear. This is not my decision. The Ministry want you back on the case. I don't know why. I don't want to know. But if you say that's how it is then so be it. The shit won't land outside my door.'

'Good. And stop the tail on Raben. I want him in for questioning.'

'PET have lost track of him. We've no idea where he is.'

Lund shook her head.

'No idea . . .'

'I'm sorry. König screwed up. On lots of other things too. The Ministry notice these things. Let's make sure they don't turn the heat on us, shall we?'

The lift came. Hedeby stepped in and left.

'Where am I supposed to sleep?' Lund asked.

'In one of the kids' beds. Don't you want your pizza first?'

'Save it till tomorrow.'

She waved the sheaf of documents at him, then wandered into the little bedroom, closed the door behind her and started to read.

CHAPTER 8

Sunday 20th November, 8.10 a.m.

B rix let Strange brief the team the next morning, Lund listening near the door. After more pills her head didn't hurt so much. The wound over her eye was swollen but behaving. She stood at the back of the room, casting her eyes across the latest intelligence reports on the board, listening but not much.

They'd barely talked. Strange went out and got coffee and warm pastries from the bakery across the road then, in silence, drove her to the Politigården.

'Lund never saw the man's face,' he told the group of detectives assembled before him. 'We're working on the idea he was one of Team Ægir's officers. There were twenty-eight in all. I want every one considered a suspect. Get them in for questioning. I don't care where they are or what they're doing. If the army kick up a stink let me know.'

Lund marched into the middle of them, stirring her cup of coffee back to life.

'They never found Møller's dog tag either,' she said. 'We've reason to believe someone used his identity. There's a list of bills . . .'

She went to the table, picked up the papers she'd got from Møller's mother.

'These are all items ordered in his name. After he was dead. I want them checked. Anne Dragsholm found out who the officer was. The one who called himself Perk. That's why she was killed.'

Lund looked at the line of detectives in front of her.

'If a woman lawyer can find him so can we.'

They went off. Brix waved to her. He had something in his hand.

'This is PET's report on what happened outside the cadets' ball last night. They saw Raben go in. Never saw him come out. He abandoned the car he stole.'

She scanned the document.

'You look better than I expected,' he said.

'It says Raben's wife and Torsten Jarnvig were there. He must have talked to one of them.'

'You don't know that.'

'Then why did he go? How did he give PET the slip?'

Brix didn't like being contradicted. It showed on his craggy face.

'What about this row between the ministers?' she asked. 'Which one do I talk to first?'

'Who said anything about getting involved in Slotsholmen?'

'It's all the same thing,' Lund said, baffled that he couldn't see this. 'We have to . . .'

The door opened. Christian Søgaard was marched in by two uniformed men. He stared at Lund, gave her a furious, bitter nod as he was walked off to an interview room.

'Do we know anything about this man?' Brix asked.

'Born soldier,' Strange said. 'Tough guy or so he thinks. If there's a fight somewhere he's up for it.'

'That narrows it down,' Lund said, still going through the papers.

Søgaard was moaning even before they started.

'This is outrageous.' He sat slumped in his combat fatigues. 'We're sending a new team to war. And here you are screwing around—'

'You do want to know who killed your men, don't you?' Strange interrupted.

No answer.

'You turned up late for the cadets' ball,' Lund said. 'Why was that? Where were you between five and nine?'

Søgaard blinked.

'You're watching us now? Do you really have nothing better to do? While these terrorists—'

'Forget about that,' Strange told him. 'We were being led up a blind alley. Where were you?'

'One of my officers asked for a talk. He was uncertain whether he wanted to go.' A sour smile. 'Worried about leaving his family behind.'

'You talked him round, I bet?' Strange asked him.

'That's my job.'

Lund passed over her notepad.

'I want his name and address.'

Søgaard scribbled something on the page.

'You'd better get a move on. He's off to Helmand for six months.'

'We will,' Strange said. 'Don't worry. According to the phone records you called Torpe, the priest, not long before he died. Why was that?'

'I had nothing to do with what happened to Torpe.'

'Frightened he was going to tell tales?' Strange went on. 'He knew everything, didn't he?'

'There's nothing to know. Raben had attacked him. Torpe was scared he'd come back. I told him not to worry. That you people had the case in hand.'

He stretched out his feet, banged his big boots on the floor.

'More fool me.'

Lund took back her notepad.

'Anne Dragsholm had been in touch with Torpe, about what happened in Helmand. Raben's accusations. The ones the military tribunal rejected.'

'Really?' Søgaard shrugged.

'That case bothered you,' Strange said. 'You called Raben unpatriotic and cowardly for saying those things. It's on the record.'

'What if I did? His fairy tales damaged us. He

95

should have taken responsibility for his own failings. Not tried to blame some imaginary officer called Perk.'

Lund checked her notes again.

'You like his wife,' she said. 'What's your relationship with her exactly?'

'What's that got to do—?'

'You took her home last night. You danced with her at the ball. She looked as if she was with you. So—'

'So?'

'How long have you known her?' she asked. 'What's the deal? Did Jonas just get a new daddy? Has Colonel Jarnvig finally got an officer for a son-in-law, not a scruffy lowlife from the ranks?'

Søgaard waved away the question and stared at the wall.

Strange had more papers.

'According to army records five years ago you had three cadets tied to a tree on a training ground in Jutland. You left them there overnight. Middle of winter. Freezing cold.'

'You have been busy, haven't you?' Søgaard sneered.

'You said they'd been disloyal. Is that an approved punishment, Søgaard? Did you make a habit of it?'

'I train them for battle,' the army man yelled at him. 'When we're out there anyone can take a shot at us, put an IED by the side of the road. We have to trust one another or we're dead. If I have to strap a mouthy cadet to a tree to teach him that lesson I'll do it. He'll thank me one day.'

'Not all of them,' Lund said. 'Raben's got as much field experience as you have. Was that the problem with him and his squad? They didn't toe the line. They let you down by accusing an officer of killing civilians when really they should have kept their mouths shut?'

Strange pulled his chair closer to the man in the combat fatigues.

'Which if you think about it gives you and your fellow officers quite a motive to shut them all up. Especially when a civil rights lawyer comes knocking and says she knows who impersonated Perk. Who killed those people.'

'Bullshit,' Søgaard replied. 'You're dancing in the dark. I'm not talking to you clowns any more. Not without an army lawyer here.'

Strange laughed.

'We could have got you Anne Dragsholm if she wasn't dead. I'll put you on the request list, Søgaard. We've got twenty or thirty of your mates coming in here soon. Maybe we'll stick you in the same hole and let you swap war stories.'

Christian Søgaard closed his eyes, leaned back in the chair and yawned.

'For an innocent man you don't have much to say,' Lund noted. 'Do you?'

He smiled at her, a sour, confident face, and kept quiet.

★   ★   ★

97

Ryvangen Barracks was in the semi-organized chaos that came with any new troop deployment. Trucks moving everywhere, teams of men handling pallets, weaponry and vehicles. Raben's wife was in a white nurse's uniform with a pink sweater against the bright, cold day, helping with the medical supplies, sick of the young cop called Madsen who kept badgering her.

'Let me get this straight,' he said, following her as she walked from the infirmary to a green army truck, her arms full of medication boxes. 'You left the ball with Søgaard? You were with him afterwards?'

'He gave me a lift home. That was all.'

'Did he seem different?'

She gazed at him, puzzled.

'No.' She handed the boxes to a woman soldier. 'This is for the armoured vehicles. Bandages, pain-killers, morphine. The usual . . .'

'And the day Grüner was killed?'

'Why do you keep asking me the same questions? I already told you. Søgaard gave us a lift back here.'

'And after that?'

She ordered the woman soldier to get more supplies.

'After that I've no idea. Maybe he drove to Sweden to deliver some explosives. Or went down the mosque to say his prayers.'

Madsen didn't appreciate the joke.

'Look,' she said. 'I told you all this. He helped us with some decorating and after that he talked

98

to my father. I don't know what you think he did but really . . .' She put her hands on her hips. 'This is pretty ridiculous if I'm honest.'

'And you didn't see your husband last night? At the ball?'

'Oh God.' She wanted to scream. 'Of course I didn't. How could Jens possibly be there?'

'He was,' Madsen said, and left it at that. Then he shook her hand the way the police always did. 'If anything comes up I'll let you know.'

She didn't like being left in the air. A car drew up. She saw who was getting out and bristled at his presence. Her father was wandering across to the warehouse with a clipboard. Louise walked over and said, 'I need the keys to the storeroom. I want to get some of Jonas's things out for him.'

'I'm busy right now.'

'It's a key, Dad.'

He frowned.

'I said—'

'Never mind. You've got a visitor. That idiot from last night.'

Jarnvig peered at the long black army limo and the wiry figure climbing out of the back. General's uniform, flat cap, long raincoat with gold epaulettes.

'I can't believe you used to be friends with a moron like that,' she added.

'Dammit,' Jarnvig snapped, reached into his pocket and gave her the key. 'Best leave us.'

★   ★   ★

99

Arild wanted a meeting in Jarnvig's office. When they were alone he looked around, scowled at the meagre, bare room.

'If you'd listened to me years ago you'd be doing better than this, Torsten. You're too wedded to your men. You could have made general if you'd wanted.'

'I'm happy here. I like it.'

'Do you like having the police poking round the place day and night? I got a call from PET. The Politigården say they're now focusing on Team Ægir. It's nothing to do with terrorism apparently. This is all down to us.'

'So I gathered,' Jarnvig replied.

'They've put this damned woman back on the case. What's she called?'

'Lund.'

'What's so special about her?'

'I don't know,' Jarnvig admitted. 'She seems . . . determined. She asks good questions too. A few I'd like answers to if I'm honest.'

'Don't be ridiculous! She's pointing the finger at some of our best officers. They're not murderers or terrorists.'

Jarnvig wondered why Arild had come. It wasn't just for this casual conversation.

'I've told everyone here,' he said. 'We'll do all we can to cooperate with the police. It's in our interests this is cleared up as quickly as possible. Just as much as theirs.'

Arild laughed.

'Is it just the police you're helping, Torsten?'

'I'm sorry . . .'

'PET tracked Raben to the ball last night. He was in the building.' Arild's vulpine features narrowed and his acute eyes focused on the man opposite him. 'But you knew that already, didn't you?'

'No. Why should I? What was he looking for?'

'Raben seems interested in the officers too. I find this all rather . . . disconcerting. An escaped prisoner gets into the ball. Then somehow manages to evade PET on the way out. It's as if he was warned.'

'Really?'

'And then, early this morning, there's a break-in at the personnel office in Holmen. We've got CCTV. It's Raben. He didn't steal anything of value. Just all the files on the officers attached to Ægir. Every last one's missing.'

Jarnvig sat in silence.

'The thing is,' Arild went on, 'we only moved personnel records from Ryvangen to Holmen three months ago.'

He looked into Jarnvig's face and smiled.

'I have to ask myself. Since he's spent the last two years locked up in Herstedvester . . . how the hell did he know where to look?'

'Jens Peter Raben's a resourceful man,' Jarnvig said. 'He always was.'

'But he's only human. Isn't he?'

★　★　★

101

Another ripped-off car, this time an old yellow VW Polo that felt ready to give up the ghost at any moment. Raben had briefly fled the city, parked in wasteland by the water in Amager Øst. He reached beneath the dashboard, pulled the wires to kill the engine. There was half a tank of fuel. He didn't want to risk buying any more with the scant cash he had.

The documents from Holmen were on the floor of the passenger seat. He scanned the bleak flat land around him, felt confident he'd thrown off PET. Reached down and pulled out the files: identical brown envelopes, each with a mugshot attached.

Familiar faces, part of the jumble of confused memories from that last fateful tour.

One photo was missing. It was from a file on a captain, Torben Skåning. Raben rifled the envelope. There was a typed report inside.

But for the rank it could have been talking about him.

Skåning was sent home from Helmand around the same time. Withdrawn from active service for uncontrollable fits of violent rage and mental instability. Someone reading the report had underlined the most damning parts. There were scribbles, rings and exclamation marks, in different coloured pens.

Raben closed his eyes, listened to the traffic wheeling into the nearby oil depot.

Skåning.

He'd never heard the name. There was no face

to put to it. Yet somewhere in his own head lay the key, buried deep beneath the pain of that last day in Helmand when the bomber hit and the explosion almost killed him.

If he saw the man he'd know him. Raben had told Torsten Jarnvig that and it was true.

He reached down, found the wires, brought the ancient Polo back to life.

Torben Skåning.

A man much like himself. Consumed with rage and fury and violence.

Raben turned the rusty VW back to the main road and trundled on towards the city.

Plough had assembled what information he could glean from the Ministry of Defence. Karina was at her desk making calls. The Security Committee was less than an hour away. Buch had nothing new to tell it.

'Three soldiers died on the mission. Afterwards the Ministry received accusations from a local Afghan warlord. He said a family in the village was executed by Danish soldiers.'

'Was he the kind of man we'd believe?' Buch asked.

'It's Afghanistan,' Plough answered with a shrug. 'Raben's team said they answered a distress call from an officer. They came to relieve him, found themselves trapped. The officer killed the family. According to the judge advocate this was a propaganda effort by the Taliban. After they were questioned the soldiers withdrew their story. All except Raben . . .'

'Why did they change their story?' Buch asked.

Plough frowned.

'It seems no one pressed them on that point. And now they're all dead. Save for Raben. PET seem to have lost him completely by the way. Idiots. König's put up a bad show—'

'Forget König for a moment,' Buch cut in. 'Rossing knew something was amiss. We've got to work on that.'

'He's hardly likely to admit it.'

Karina came in.

'There's a journalist to see you.'

Buch rolled his eyes.

'I don't have time for that.'

She smiled.

'Oh yes you do. I worked all night tracking this one down. She's got an axe to grind with Flemming Rossing. I think you should hear what she has to say.'

Plough took a deep breath and began to knead his brow.

'She's next door,' Karina added. 'Shall I ask her in?'

Connie Vemmer was a tall, striking woman close to fifty, pearl necklace, long tidy blonde hair, elegant top, smart blue jeans, all a little too young for her. She smelled of cigarettes and the faintest whiff of booze.

Buch got up when she entered the room, found her a chair and said, 'Well?'

The woman stretched her long legs.

'I worked in Flemming Rossing's press centre,' she said. 'I was legit before that, though. A real journalist. You can check.'

'We will.' Plough promised.

'Your aide . . .' She glanced at Karina. 'She told me you were interested in the Helmand case two years ago. I was there. On the watch when the accusations came in. I killed them. That's why they never made the papers.'

'Should they have done?'

'Depends on your point of view. On the day the soldiers were buried, when Rossing gave his speech, a fax came in.'

She fumbled in her bag and came out with a packet of cigarettes, lit one.

'It was from Afghanistan. Anonymous. That wasn't so unusual. Do you mind if I smoke?'

'Not in here!' Plough cried. 'It's forbidden.'

'Just the one,' Buch said with a smile.

She lit the cigarette, looked grateful. Karina fetched a saucer for an ashtray.

'It was a medical report from the field hospital at Camp Viking,' Vemmer said. 'That's the part of Camp Bastion we use under the wing of the British. The body parts didn't match.'

Buch's eyes narrowed.

'What do you mean?'

'A hand,' she said with a shrug. 'There was a hand too many. It wasn't from any of the soldiers.'

'You mean it was a civilian's?' Plough asked.

'Seems a reasonable guess. So I passed on the fax to the Permanent Secretary thinking he'd want to look into it. After all it seemed to confirm the soldiers' allegations. But . . .'

A long drag of the cigarette, then she waved the smoke away from her own face, unaware that it was drifting straight towards the horrified Plough.

'Nothing happened.'

Connie Vemmer looked at each of them in turn.

'I checked. No one acted on it. The fax didn't even enter the file. The judge advocate never saw it.'

'I need you to tell this to the Security Committee,' Buch said. 'We meet in half an hour.'

She laughed.

'Are you serious? I signed the Official Secrets Act. I could go to jail just for talking to you.'

'I'm the Minister of Justice.'

'And I'm a freelance hack trying to stay alive. Sorry. If I could go public with this do you think I'd be trying to get you interested? I'd have written the damned story myself.'

Plough retrieved the dying cigarette from her shaky fingers and took it away with the saucer.

'If it's a deal you're after . . .' he said.

'I don't want a deal! What do you think I am? I want someone to look into this case. It stinks to high—'

'If you won't step forward there's nothing I can do,' Buch interrupted. 'We can talk to our lawyers. I'm sure the Official Secrets Act doesn't cover every eventuality. If there's good reason—'

'I doubt Flemming Rossing thinks there's good reason, does he? And from what I read in the papers he's likely to be around a lot longer than you, Buch.'

He smiled at her, said nothing.

She dug around in her bag.

'You can have this,' she said, retrieving some crumpled sheets of paper. 'It's a copy of the fax. I made one before passing it on. Seemed a good idea at the time.'

Three pages. Highly detailed. Buch started to read.

'That's as far as I can go,' Connie Vemmer said.

She let herself out after that. The smell of tobacco hung in the air.

'I don't like this,' Plough moaned. 'We don't know that woman from Adam. She's a journalist, for God's sake. It gives me a bad feeling . . .'

Buch kept reading.

'You can't possibly put that in front of the Security Committee,' Plough insisted.

'Do you have something else?'

No answer.

The Security Committee consisted of the Prime Minister, Flemming Rossing, Gitta Spalding, the

Foreign Minister, and Kahn, the ambitious Interior Minister.

Buch had Plough to back him up. That would have to do.

'I'm sorry I'm late,' he said with a smile when he entered Grue Eriksen's office. 'I was delayed.'

No one spoke. Buch dragged two chairs from the side of Grue Eriksen's desk, sat down with his papers on his knee, smiled again as Plough joined him.

'This meeting,' the Prime Minister dictated into a voice recorder, 'has been called to discuss the accusations the Minister of Justice has made against the Minister of Defence concerning some recent past cases. Present are . . .'

Rossing was drinking a cup of tea.

When Grue Eriksen was finished Buch leapt straight in.

'Let me begin two years ago,' he said briskly. 'When an incident in Afghanistan was reported to the Ministry of Defence. I will refer to it as the Helmand case.'

Rossing raised his teacup.

'Very melodramatic, Thomas.'

But he listened all the same.

The office looked like an outpost of Ryvangen itself now. It was full of army officers dragged in by Strange on her instruction. Men in combat fatigues mainly, unhappy to be painted as anything but heroes.

Madsen came in.

'We've found someone interesting.' He gave Lund a personnel file. 'Peter Lænkholm. They had to pick him up. He didn't come in for questioning like we asked. He was a lieutenant. Got kicked out once Ægir came back to Denmark. Bad apple.'

Peter Lænkholm was in an interview room. He looked a mess. Unshaven, ragged clothes. Dead, unfocused eyes. No money. No life. No hope. One step from the gutter, she thought.

'Why are you bothering me?' Lænkholm said when she started throwing questions at him. He had a droning, lazy voice. Scared too. 'I'm not in the army any more.'

Strange sat at the back of the room. Madsen left them to it.

'You were part of Team Ægir,' Lund said. 'Tell us about Søgaard. Did you like him?'

'Oh!' Lænkholm put on the most artificial of smiles. 'Very much so. Søgaard was great. He trained me at the officers' academy. I learned a lot from him.'

'Is that so?' Strange asked.

'Yeah. He was terrific. I asked to serve under his command. That's how much I respected him.'

Strange flipped through some records.

'You didn't serve very long.'

'I got as far as Afghanistan. How much do you want?'

Lund pushed a report across the table, tapped her finger on one of the passages.

'It says here you were uncooperative. There were disciplinary problems. You and Søgaard don't come across as buddies.'

'I'm not here to slag him off.'

'Listen, mate!' Strange got to his feet, came to the table, planted his fists next to Lænkholm. 'Let me tell you how it is. You've got enough weed in that squalid little pit of yours to put you in jail.'

'It's p-personal. I'm not a dealer.'

'Pull the other one. Tell us about Søgaard.'

'It's personal.'

'Oh for God's sake . . .' Strange looked at his watch. 'I can have you in court by two o'clock.'

'Just tell us what went wrong, Peter,' Lund broke in. 'Do that and we'll send you for counselling. Get you some help.'

'Help?' he laughed. 'You believe that?'

'I believe it's better than jail . . . Søgaard?'

He wiped his mouth with the sleeve of his threadbare, grubby jacket.

'It doesn't come from me, right?'

'It doesn't come from you,' Lund agreed.

'He's fine.' Lænkholm stared at her, alert now, as if the memories brought back a trace of the officer he once was. 'So long as you follow the rules. *His* rules. Do what he says and it's cool. But . . .'

'But you didn't, did you?' Strange asked.

Peter Lænkholm stared at the table.

110

'You can get weed out there. And worse if you want it. All I did was smoke one fucking joint, for God's sake! I was no more high than the Taliban.'

'And for that he kicked you out?' Lund asked.

He glared at her.

'Søgaard doesn't kick you out. If you fail him it's like you've insulted him. You pay the price. I got the full treatment.'

'What treatment?'

Nothing.

'What treatment?' Strange bellowed in his ear.

'They fetch you at night, when you're asleep. You've no idea it's going to happen. They've got hoods on. You don't know who they really are.'

His shaking hand went for the cold coffee cup on the table. But Lænkholm's trembling fingers couldn't hold it so he gave up.

'They strip you naked and tie you up with cable binders and duct tape. Then they take you outside, shove a flare up your arse and string you up from a post.'

'A flare?' Lund asked.

'A flare. That's what I said. It's not so great, I can tell you.'

Strange was shaking his head, laughing. She scowled at him. He walked to the window.

'Didn't anyone help you?'

'What? And get the same?'

'Couldn't you complain?'

'Jesus. You don't understand what it's like, do you? Out there Søgaard's God. Nobody moves, nobody breathes, nobody takes a shit without his say-so.'

Strange came back, pulled up a chair.

'What about Raben and his squad?' Lund asked. 'How did Søgaard like him?'

No answer.

'Come on,' Strange cried.

'Not a lot. Raben's team used to get into some stuff the rest of us were never told about. There were people around sometimes . . . I don't know what they did. I didn't want to know.'

His head went down again. Lund bent over and tried to look into his glassy, lost eyes.

'Raben was one of them?'

'We all heard the rumours after he was hit. Then this officer got discharged. Me they just let go. But discharged . . .'

Lund shook her head.

'You're losing me.'

'It didn't happen often. You didn't get a formal discharge for smoking a joint.'

Strange pushed a pad onto the table, followed by a pen.

'Name,' he said.

Nothing.

'Peter? Hello? Is there anyone still awake in there?'

'A name,' Lund repeated. 'Then you're out of here. To counselling, not court.'

'His name was Skåning.'

She began to flick through the papers.

'Anything else?' Strange asked.

'No.'

Lund found the file. A photo of a bearded man in a beret. Torben Skåning.

'Him?' she asked.

Lænkholm nodded.

'Great,' Strange said, slapping his shoulder. 'Then we're done, aren't we?'

He grabbed the personnel records off the table, ran his finger down his clipboard.

'Skåning's on the list of men to bring in. Shall we pay him an early visit?'

Lund got up, followed Strange to the door, watched him walk to the circular stairs, never looking back.

She hesitated. After so many days in the dark they seemed to be getting closer to something that might resemble the truth.

That had happened towards the end of the Birk Larsen case too. She was still living with the consequences, and she wasn't alone in that.

You learn from your mistakes, she thought, hearing Jan Meyer's voice in her head, and all the warnings he kept throwing at her, mostly unheeded.

Lund walked to her private locker, undid the padlock, sorted through her things. Got out the 9-millimetre Glock in its leather and canvas holster. Looked it at. Knew she'd always hate the thing.

Caught her reflection in the metal door. Cut

over the eye. Bruises. Swelling. But she was still alive, not that she knew how or why.

The gun went into her bag with the gum and the tissues.

'Are you coming or not?' Strange called up from the floor below.

'On my way,' she said and walked to the stairs.

Thomas Buch had prepared what he wanted to say in his head. It didn't change when he delivered his concise and simple speech to the Defence Committee. It couldn't. That was all he had.

'Why was the Folketinget not informed of the accusations? Why . . .?'

'Oh come on, Buch,' Rossing intervened. 'I can hardly go running to Parliament every time the Taliban try to pull a publicity stunt on us.'

'You saw no reason to investigate the alleged killing of civilians? By our own officers?'

Kahn, who'd looked bored throughout, broke in.

'The minister's already answered the question. Whose side are you on?'

'That,' Buch said, 'offends me.'

'It offends me to sit here listening to you question the integrity of one of our most senior ministers. Five seconds in government and look at the mess you've created.' Kahn swore under his breath, stared across the room. 'Do you have anything to support these wild accusations?'

Buch nodded at Plough. The civil servant got

up, walked round the room, handed out copies of the fax Connie Vemmer had brought.

Rossing laughed.

'What the hell is this?'

'It's a report from the field hospital in Camp Viking. This fax was sent to you on the day of the soldiers' funeral. Among the body parts was a hand too many. The hand of an Afghan.'

'This is a Ministry of Defence document,' Rossing complained. 'I'd like to know where you got it.'

'The doctors' report concludes the alleged killing of civilians must be investigated. You buried this—'

'No, no, no. I called a judge advocate's inquiry. It's all on the record. The case was investigated and to tell you the truth—'

'The truth is you did bugger all!' Buch cried, getting to his feet, a little unsteadily. 'You knew something was wrong and you were determined it wasn't going to get out. You made Monberg keep silent when he found out. And when Anne Dragsholm got wind of it and was murdered for her pains you didn't do shit!'

'You're overwrought, Thomas,' Rossing said idly.

'Damned right I am! Five people are dead.' Buch put up his hand, fingers spread. 'Five lives that could have been spared if you'd done your duty. It makes me—'

'You've made your point,' Grue Eriksen broke

in. 'Take a seat. Calm down if you can.' The Prime Minister turned to Rossing. 'Do you have an explanation?'

'Yes. Of course.'

He went through the copied fax again.

'I asked for this to be kept out of the case files because it was inaccurate.'

'Oh no, Rossing!' Buch bellowed. 'You can't get away with this nonsense. The time and place is on the fax. It all fits.'

'I'm sorry you force me to go into such macabre details, Buch. It seems I have no alternative. When the medics in Afghanistan looked into the case further they realized the hand was that of the suicide bomber himself.'

'Not good enough.'

'It may not be good enough for you! But it's in the corrected medical report which was placed on file later.' Rossing glanced at Grue Eriksen. 'I really don't want to waste any more of your time with this. You're all welcome to read the documents if you wish. Had Buch asked for it beforehand I would happily have supplied it. Instead he goes off half cock once more. Really . . .'

Rossing wiped his forehead.

'What with poor Frode's death this has been quite an ordeal.'

'That was all very quick,' Buch snapped. 'How did you know I was going to talk about that fax?'

Rossing shook his head.

'How did you know?' Buch repeated.

'You're prone to conspiracy theories,' Rossing said. 'You ignore expert opinion. You force the police and PET to hound our soldiers.'

Voice rising, he leapt to his feet, jabbed his hand in Buch's face.

'You put pressure on Frode Monberg when you knew he was unwell. You, Buch! And now you dare to make me responsible for your own stupidity and incompetence! Enough.'

He strode to the door, walked out of the room. Kahn followed. Then Gitta Spalding and finally Carsten Plough.

Grue Eriksen stayed in his seat, staring at the wall.

'There's more to this,' Buch said tentatively. 'I promise . . .'

The silver-haired man by the window closed his eyes, rolled back his head, said nothing.

Buch left.

Just after six, icy rain on the windscreen, streets covered with a greasy winter sheen. Lund and Strange driving through Copenhagen still trying to find the missing Torben Skåning.

He lived in one of the old military houses off Store Kongensgade. His wife hadn't seen him all day. They'd checked the local pubs he liked and got nowhere. His one interest outside drink seemed to be the nearby Frihedsmuseet in Churchillparken close to the Kastellet garrison and the Amalienborg Palace. It was a museum dedicated to recording

117

Danish resistance to the Nazis, a small building with a home-built tank from the conflict near the entrance.

Lund stared at the ramshackle vehicle as they drove up outside. It looked like a kid's toy, a large Christiana trike covered in armour, with the message 'Frit Danmark', Free Denmark, scrawled on the front. There were lights on in the building, figures behind the glass drinking wine. A reception of some kind.

She followed Strange into the entrance, told him to talk to the people there, wandered round the nearest exhibits. Lund hadn't stepped inside this place since she was a school kid and barely remembered the stories from those days. War, she recalled once again, was a distant nightmare when she was young. Something that affected other, older people, never her.

Briskly she walked through the exhibition areas, followed the murky, awkward story of how Denmark reluctantly allowed an all-powerful German regime to invade in 1940 then steadily found the courage to resist in the ensuing years.

It was all here. The amateur acts of sabotage by schoolchildren bearing names like the Churchill gang. The more daring and serious attacks by the Communists, aided by secret agents from British special forces. Then, from 1943 on, the terror. The round-up of Jews. Routine arrests, torture, banishment to concentration camps, the execution of those suspected of working with the partisans.

And the response. This part she looked at most closely. Not all Danes resisted. Not everyone stayed neutral. Some joined the Nazis, worked with them, benefited from their patronage. By doing so they risked their lives. When the terror took hold the Resistance formed ruthless assassination groups, published clandestine newsletters with the names and photographs of the collaborators they intended to murder.

Then shot them dead on the street, in their homes, at work.

War was everywhere, in the basement cells of the Politigården where suspects were tortured before being shipped to concentration camps in Germany or, worse, driven to Mindelunden and a quick, brutal death.

Stikke.

That word stared at her from almost every exhibition case, on the underground pamphlets the Resistance printed on their home-made presses, in the newspaper reports, the history books.

Informers. Traitors. Danes who'd lost the right to live.

Everything from that time seemed to be recorded here, in old guns, children's paintings, scraps of newspaper, and score upon score of photos. Dead soldiers in the snow. Home-made pistols and pipe bombs. Mugshots of informers to be shot. Photos of squads like the Lorentzen gang, Danes trained by the Germans to infiltrate the partisans. Bullet diagrams from the shooting of Resistance fighters

119

cornered during raids. Lines of men being rounded up by Nazi guards at the Horserød internment camp near Helsingør, a place Lund knew well since it was now an open prison used for offenders deemed to be of little threat to society.

She'd been an idiot to think that war belonged to history, an accident of the past, something the world had outgrown. Its dark ghost still lurked in the corridors of the Politigården, in the prisons the state now used, in the minds of those who came after her and grew up in a world less secure, less peaceful than the one she'd enjoyed.

Lund stood in front of a shocking display about an attack on a group of Resistance fighters caught unawares, slaughtered without a second thought. Men who'd delivered a similar fate to a Danish *stikke* a few days earlier.

Strange came and stood next to her. He didn't look at the case at all.

'They haven't seen Skåning today. But . . .'

'Is there a picture of your grandfather here?'

Strange shook his head.

'What?'

'I always thought it was so distant. For me it was. But it's not really.' She looked at him. 'Is he here? Haven't you looked?'

'I never knew him,' he said, and seemed offended. 'How could I? My dad didn't talk of him much either. I've only got now. Here. This moment. I don't have time for . . .' He gestured at the display. 'For this kind of stuff.'

120

'That's what I thought too.'

'You're starting to scare me.'

'Why?'

'I don't like it when you do reflective.'

'Doesn't happen often.'

'Good. Back to the real world. Skåning's wife just called. She said someone else has been trying to get in touch with him.'

Lund turned away from the old photos and home-made guns.

'Who?'

'He didn't leave his name. Just said he was an old army colleague.' He pointed to the door. 'Skåning's still not answering his mobile. His wife says that's unusual.'

'What did the wife say to him?'

Strange frowned.

'Something she never told us. Sunday nights Skåning has a key to use a local library in Nørrebro. He's studying languages there and locks up.'

Two minutes later they were back in the car. Strange took out the blue light as they pulled away from the museum, placed it on the roof, set it going, hit the siren.

The Yellow Polo was the only car outside the little library. Raben had been there the best part of an hour, lights off, slumped in the driver's seat, gun in his pocket. Waiting.

The name troubled him. Skåning. He'd heard it before somewhere. There was a face he thought he could attach to it. Troubled, like his own. Tough and relentless.

Someone who might answer to the name Perk.

In the badlands of Helmand identity meant nothing. All armies had men, sometimes women, who roamed the dangerous terrain behind the front, spoke many languages, wore clothes that disguised who they truly were and where they came from.

The soldiers of Jægerkorpset weren't the only shadows around. There were spooks like the phantom Perk, seemingly beyond the usual command structure, allowed to move freely, unhindered by convention, by rules of battle and engagement, the inflexible norms of the military.

If his head would only work right he'd see this man and know. If . . .

Lights behind. A car drew up. Parked next to his own. Raben stayed low, let his eyes stray to the window.

A bearded man with a hard, unforgiving face. A black beret. Army fatigues.

Raben's mind reeled. He was back in Helmand in that instant, listening to the bombs and the screams, men and women, children too.

Gunfire and flames. Agony and blood.

All these memories raged through his head and he'd no idea what was real, what was imaginary.

The man got out. He was big and muscular. Walked to the library door. Pressed the bell. Shouted, 'Hello. Anyone at home?'

A loud, firm voice. That of an officer.

'Hi, Skåning,' said the man who came out to answer. 'I didn't know if you were coming or not.'

A brief exchange. Raben watched Skåning walk in then climbed out of the yellow Polo.

Felt the gun. Felt something else in his other pocket. Took it out. Jonas's toy, the one he'd left when he got angry at the beach. A toy soldier. Raised sword. Furious face.

Such a small thing. All that was left.

Raben looked at the library, walked to the door. Found it open.

Footsteps ahead inside. Heavy military boots on wooden tiles. He walked through into the main room. Lines of bookshelves, the smell of damp and old wood. A figure just visible in the low security lights, heading for the desks at the end.

He looked even bigger now. Broad and strong. A full head of hair that needed combing. Some heavy hardbacks under one arm. A paper cup in the other.

Torben Skåning placed the books on the last desk, turned on the light above it. Shuffled the titles, took a sip of his drink. Screwed up his lined, haggard features. Yawned.

Arms behind his head. A face like a church gargoyle. Ugly, exaggerated, unkind, with a full ginger beard and wolf-like white teeth.

When he opened his eyes Raben was there.

Buch made the mistake of going back to the Ministry by the public roads. Couldn't face the maze of corridors any more. The briefers had been at work. A mob of reporters and TV cameras hung around the door of the Ministry, under the gaze of the Børsen's dragons.

He strode through them without speaking, eyes ahead, trying to think about everything in his life that was not in Copenhagen. About Marie and the kids. The farms and the cooperative's finances.

It wasn't easy. Wasn't possible.

'Buch,' barked one of the TV hacks. 'The Defence Minister denies all your accusations. Will you apologize?'

On, past the security guards who brought the rabble to a halt at the front door, and let him walk upstairs to his office.

There he sat on the sofa and turned on the TV news. No surprise to see the lead item.

'After only one week in office, the Minister of Justice Thomas Buch faces an uncertain future after what observers describe as an unprecedented political blunder.' Buch sat down and listened. 'The People's Party is likely to move a vote of no confidence in him tomorrow which, if passed, would seal his departure from government.'

Karina was on her phone again, whispering to someone. He didn't much care who.

'The party expects to press for a more draconian anti-terror package as a result . . .'

Plough marched in, turned on her.

'Have you managed to contact this journalist of yours?'

'She's not answering. I left a message.'

'Brilliant! You realize this was all a set-up. Rossing fed her to us and by God we took the bait.'

She didn't answer. Flemming Rossing came on the screen. All three of them watched.

The Minister of Defence was in ebullient mood, smiling, neatly dressed, grey suit, white shirt, scarlet tie.

'No one likes to be smeared,' he said to the interviewer. 'So I'm relieved to hear the Minister of Justice has been asked to withdraw these unfounded and appalling accusations.'

Buch turned off the set.

'This is all my fault. I don't want either of you to think you're to blame. Rossing was right. I pushed Monberg too far. I kept on at him without thinking for a moment about his health. Not for a second.'

'You had good reason to ask him those questions!'

It was Plough who spoke, which surprised Buch.

'I did, but . . .'

'As far as you knew Monberg was recovering,' Plough went on. 'There were serious issues he needed to address. They haven't gone away.'

'But it seems they have.'

'May I call you "Thomas"?' Plough shot a look at Karina. 'She does.'

'If you wish.'

The civil servant took a deep breath.

'You do not have the bearing of a minister. The panache. The guile. The sophistication.' Plough looked visibly upset. 'But by God you're the most honest and decent and open man I've seen hold office in Slotsholmen in all my years here and I will not let those . . .'

His arm shot out towards the Folketinget and the Christianborg Palace.

'Those . . . those *fuckers* do you down if I can help it. I swear to God I won't.'

Buch stared at him. Karina too. Plough was shaking with visible fury.

All three of them were grateful when there was a knock on the door and a pale and puzzled Erling Krabbe blundered in.

'I'm sorry,' Krabbe stuttered. 'Was I interrupting something?'

'Yes,' Buch said.

'Do you have a minute?'

Buch eyed Plough and Karina. They both retreated, still shocked.

He went to his desk, put his big weary feet on the polished walnut, leaned back and relaxed. Krabbe fell into the chair by his side, looked round at the portraits on the wall. A century and a half of Buch's predecessors.

'If you've come to gloat, Krabbe, you chose the wrong moment.'

'Do you mind if I smoke?'

'So long as you don't bore the arse off me with some stupid demands about the anti-terror package.

126

You'll get what you want. And my head on a plate too. Don't expect me to butter you up . . .'

Krabbe pulled out a packet of cigarettes and lit one.

'I will get what I want,' he agreed. 'And I do want rid of you. I don't think you're fit for this job, Buch. You've proved it, haven't you?'

Buch smiled for one brief moment and said nothing.

'How sure are you about your accusations against Rossing?' Krabbe asked.

'Why? I don't see you losing any sleep over it.'

'Do you still believe what you said?'

'What is this?'

Krabbe scowled.

'I'm not an idiot. I don't like being fooled with any more than you do.' He took a drag on the cigarette, blew a cloud of smoke out into Buch's office. 'Rossing seemed remarkably well prepared for all this. Too much so. It makes me . . . uneasy.'

'Of course he was well prepared. He had a reason. I was tipped off about a fax that incriminated him. It looks like he set it up. I walked straight into his trap and he cut off my head in front of Grue Eriksen and the Security Committee. Satisfied? I was outsmarted, Krabbe. I was not proved wrong.'

'You told no one about this fax?'

'Of course not! What do you think? I phoned Rossing to warn him in advance?'

'So . . .' Krabbe was thinking, working

something out for himself. 'The only people who knew were your own staff?'

'Krabbe! For heaven's sake, what is this?'

'Did you outline to the Prime Minister what evidence you were bringing to the meeting?'

'We had a short conversation. You don't think I'd park my tank on Rossing's lawn without giving Grue Eriksen a clue of what I was going to say, do you? He wants . . .' Buch stopped. 'He wants the truth as much as anyone.'

Krabbe drew on his cigarette, stayed silent.

'You're not suggesting . . .' Buch began.

The door opened. Plough came in.

'We've just had a call from the Prime Minister's office. He'd like to see you later. He suggests nine o'clock.'

'I should go,' Krabbe declared, getting to his feet. 'I won't disturb you any longer.'

He came and shook Buch's hand.

'Thank you for listening. I know you must hate me. I imagine that's inevitable. I'm sorry. If . . .' He looked around for somewhere to dump his cigarette. Plough found him a saucer. 'If you want to talk again do call.'

The two men watched him go.

Plough emptied the saucer into a waste bin.

'What was that about?'

'I honestly don't know,' Buch admitted.

Marriages didn't end with an argument or a dismissive wave of the hand. They were like

128

bereavements. Traces lingered. Physical objects that carried with them memories. Barriers that needed to be removed so a life could move on.

Louise Raben was in her father's storeroom, sorting through the detritus of the life she would now abandon.

Practical material: box files of medical reports, guarantees for cars and washing machines, insurance certificates, receipts and invoices.

Personal things: letters in airmail envelopes from parts of the world she'd never see. Photographs that tugged at the heart. An ancient video camera, unused in years.

There was a cassette next to it. The date on it was a few months before Jonas was born.

The past would not be buried. What happened had happened. It would live with her and carry with it some love, if only in the shape of their son.

And she would not hide from it.

She put the cassette into the video and walked into her empty bedroom, hooked up the cables to the little TV opposite the bed.

Sat down, listened, watched and wondered.

It was Amager Strandpark on a hot summer's day. So unlike the cold, bleak place where she'd finished with him.

Jens, younger, clean shaven, happy and fit. Grinning into the lens saying, 'It's fantastic. Come on! Come on! Get wet, Louise. I dare you . . .'

She blinked. There was a tripod. Still in the

storeroom. He liked to set the camera on it and let the film run.

A wavering shot of the beach then it was still. She could see the black shadow the stand made, like that of a stiff mechanical crane.

She was pregnant, wearing the gaudy flowered swimsuit he'd picked for her.

Squealing, 'No! Don't film me! I'm too fat. Too ugly.'

She looked so much younger. It seemed as if nothing could possibly go wrong with the world.

He came into the frame, wagging his finger as if cross.

'Nonsense, young woman,' he said in that firm sergeant's voice. 'You are beautiful, Louise Raben.' She laughed at him. 'You are so beautiful.'

He kissed her. She kissed him. Hands round his rough cheeks, fingers in his hair.

The older Louise watched and felt a tear emerge, roll slowly down her cheek.

She looked at the pile of letters. So many. When she thought about it she felt she could remember every last loving word he wrote, week in week out, however hard the fighting, however remote the place.

A noise behind. She quickly wiped her face with her sleeve. Christian Søgaard was marching in with a box in his arms. More paint. She'd asked for it. He wore combat fatigues. Had that confident officer's face. Nothing like Jens. Never would be.

'I'm sorry I'm late. They kept me at the Politigården all day. Idiots.'

When she wiped away the tears more came. Too many to hide.

'OK,' Søgaard said softly. 'Bad time. I'll come back later.'

'No. Stay.'

She froze the video. It captured the two of them in each other's arms, crackly lines running across the screen as if this love between them was already broken, gone for good.

Søgaard glanced at the picture, looked away.

She removed the cables and the cassette. Placed it in the box with the letters. Turned off the TV. Put the box on the floor then kicked it away with her foot.

'Is Jonas at home?' Søgaard asked.

'No. He's staying over with someone from kindergarten.'

A friend she wanted to say. Except it wasn't that. Jonas had none really.

She couldn't take her eyes off the dead TV.

Søgaard put down the paint, sat next to her, took her hand.

'Louise. You didn't let him down. You put up with more than most women would. You held out. You fought. I know. I watched.'

'Did you?'

'Every minute.'

He looked ready to leave. She didn't want that. There was a break to be made. A decision to be faced.

'What are you going to do now?' she asked.

Hands in his pockets. He looked embarrassed. Hopeful.

'Not much.'

She laughed.

'All alone?'

'As usual.'

'Me too,' she said. 'You want some wine?'

'Wine's good.'

'And a bonfire?'

He looked at her, baffled.

Louise Raben picked up the box with the letters, the video, all the memories.

'I want to burn some things. I want a witness.'

She paused, felt a decision closing in on her.

'I want it to be you.'

The library was at the end of a dark cul-de-sac. Barely a light inside. Lund made Strange turn off the blue light and the siren then stop the car some way from the entrance. There were two vehicles out the front, both old and battered.

She walked up, shone her torch through the windows of the first. An old Ford. Nothing. Then the second. In the footwell of the yellow Polo was a pile of manila folders. Army logo. Personnel records with the stamp of the Holmen office.

Lund felt her gun tight against her waist in the holster on her belt.

She called control, got them to run a check on the registration of the Ford. It took a minute.

'Skåning's car,' she said when the operator got

back to her. She looked at Strange. 'Do we go in? Or do we wait?'

He laughed.

'You're asking me now?'

'Yes. I am.'

'You did bring your weapon?'

Lund slapped her jacket and nodded.

'Well then you stay back, let me handle the front. We'll take it from there.'

She still wasn't sure. The night Meyer got shot was rattling round in the back of her head.

'We could wait for backup—'

There was a sound from inside the library. A yell. A shout. A scream.

'No,' Strange said, and got out his Glock, checked it, went for the door.

Raben had Skåning strapped to a chair, shirt dragged down to show the officer's tattoo on his left shoulder. He'd punched the bearded man in the gut a couple of times, was getting madder with each failed blow.

This ugly face was familiar. The bent, exaggerated features, the low brow, the broken nose.

'Jesus . . .' Skåning muttered through bleeding lips. 'What do I have to do . . .?'

'Shut up and listen!' Raben shouted, his voice echoing through the dark empty belly of the library. 'You said your name was Perk. You stole his identity. You were with us in that house . . .'

He whacked his fist into Skåning's face again.

'You had that dog tag. I saw it. I was there, remember? It was you.'

'No, Raben! You didn't—'

Another punch. Blood spattered the blue tattoo on Skåning's arm.

'Admit it, dammit!'

The man in the chair fell forward, retched blood and broken teeth onto his army trousers.

'I know it was you,' Raben snarled. 'We came to your rescue.' He brought up his knee, fetched it hard beneath Skåning's chin.

Another screech. Another howl.

'Leave me alone, for fuck's sake. I never fought in Helmand. I went crazy there. They discharged me.'

A hand whipped round his cheeks.

'I had a breakdown.'

'I saw you—'

'Yeah!' Skåning cried in a high, pained voice close to falsetto. 'And I saw you. On the plane home, with all the other wounded soldiers.'

Raben stood back, felt a sudden, agonizing pang of doubt. A flash of unwanted memory.

'What soldiers?'

'*Your* soldiers! The men who were with you. Grüner and those other guys. They told me what happened. They said you were under siege in a village for two days.'

'You were on that plane?'

'With all of you! I remember seeing you strapped to a stretcher. You were awake, just. But you couldn't talk. They didn't think you'd live. I tried to speak to you. The others told the same story. About some guy called Perk . . .'

One stride closer.

'No!' The bearded man looked terrified. 'No more!'

Raben sat on a chair. Looked at what he'd done. Put his head in his hands. Wanted to weep.

A sound at the back of the library. He turned, reached automatically for the gun in his pocket.

'Raben?' Lund said, walking through the cold, dark hall of the library, seeing two figures silhouetted in the dim light ahead. Two men on chairs, both head down. One strapped, breathing heavily. The other . . .

She wasn't sure.

'Raben!'

She had the gun on him. Held it the way they taught on the range.

'Just come with us. It's all going to be fine.'

Strange had disappeared the moment they came into the library, fallen into the shadows. She'd no idea where he was now.

'You think?' Raben asked, head cocked, beard rough and straggly, next to Skåning, wounded and bleeding.

'Just get your hands up and walk towards . . .'

He dashed for the stairs that rose at the end of the hall. Something in his right hand. A gun. No doubt about that.

135

'Raben!' Lund shouted again and followed him up the wooden staircase.

It was an old library. Had the smell, the feel of a church. At the far end, beyond the tall bookcases, was a circular stained-glass window. Blue with pale figures, scriveners at their desks.

Another shape there. A bedraggled man beneath its soft light, erect by the wall, holding a gun firmly beneath his chin, both hands to the grip.

She put her own weapon back in the holster. Walked on. He was rocking backwards and forwards, eyes closed.

'Don't be stupid,' Lund shouted. 'You've got a wife and a kid. You've got a future.'

A noise came from him and she wondered if it was wry laughter.

'I need your help. We know Perk's real. He's behind this. We know you got framed.'

Still the same motion, to and fro, the gun hard to his throat.

'You're so close to winning,' she said, taking another step closer. 'Do you give up now? You didn't in the army.'

No words.

'Put the gun down,' she ordered. 'Drop it to the floor. Kick it towards me.'

Eyes tight, face wracked with pain.

'You're the only one left! Think about it. If you're dead he's won. If you're dead Louise and Jonas . . .'

136

The weapon came away. Raben fell to his knees, stumbled forward gasping for breath.

'Come on, Raben. It's easy.'

He looked at her. Blank, exhausted eyes. A man at the end of the road.

'Put the gun down,' she repeated and he did, very slowly, then raised his hands.

A noise from the library below, big shoes on tiles. Raben stayed crouched, close to the weapon.

Lund glanced. Strange was there, staying close to the walls. Gun raised, ready.

'It's just my partner. You're safe with us. Walk away from the gun.'

Strange's footsteps got closer. His silhouette was emerging from the gloom.

Raben could see the shape of him now. His fingers crept back to the weapon, clutched it, raised it.

'Leave the gun alone!' Lund barked at him. 'Come over here.'

Three more strides and Strange emerged from the darkness, stood on the floor beneath them, Weaver stance, Glock ready, pointing.

'Put it on the floor,' he ordered.

She watched so closely. Couldn't work out why this was going wrong. Raben was getting to his feet, the weapon in his right hand again, a look of astonishment and horror on his haggard, bearded face.

'Perk . . .' he murmured.

'Put the gun down!' Strange roared. 'Do as I say or I fire. Now!'

Lund wondered if she'd heard right.

'Do as he says,' she said. 'Please—'

'Perk, you bastard!' Jens Peter Raben roared, racing to the balustrade, weapon up, at the ready.

She screamed something and wasn't sure what. Saw the bright light burst out from beneath her, heard the single gunshot burst through the darkness, echoing off the old brick walls.

Jens Peter Raben flew back, thrown hard against the wooden shelving, tumbled to the ground in a sea of falling books.

She was there first, had a hand to his chest, feeling for breath.

Torsten Jarnvig couldn't get the conversation with Arild out of his head. Ryvangen was his dominion. What happened to the men there mattered. And now he felt he was in ignorance. Had been kept that way.

Søgaard's phone was off, the man was nowhere to be seen. Jarnvig pulled in Said Bilal and talked to him instead. Bilal was something of a mystery. A loner who didn't mix much, didn't drink, didn't do anything except his job.

Jarnvig had the papers from two years ago in front of him.

'Raben said the officer they were relieving was called Perk. Yet Søgaard had attended Perk's funeral three months earlier. Didn't he think this was strange? There's nothing in the report . . .'

'It couldn't be the same Perk,' Bilal replied. 'Why would Søgaard think anything of it?'

'Because he was in charge.' Jarnvig knew how he'd have approached such an investigation. There would have been questions. Plenty of them. 'What about the radio call Raben said he received? He said it was from a Danish unit in trouble.'

'We didn't pick up any radio call.'

'Would it have been in range from that village?'

'We're on a really tight schedule, sir. Could I suggest we postpone these questions—'

'Do you? Till when? For ever?'

'But there was no officer!' It was the loudest he'd ever heard Bilal speak. 'We had no troops in that area.'

'True,' said Jarnvig. '*We* had no troops. It doesn't mean there wasn't someone there. Perk—'

'Perk was a myth. An excuse.'

'I want a transcript of all radio communications. Ours. Other Danish units. Any allied logs you can get hold of.'

'And our schedule, sir?' Bilal said wearily.

'Ask Army Operational Command to send it. I want everything on my desk tomorrow.'

The young officer said nothing, went for the door.

'Oh, and Bilal?'

He stopped.

'Mum's the word,' Jarnvig ordered. 'This is between the two of us. No one else.'

★   ★   ★

139

A corridor in the surgical wing of the Rigshospitalet. Raben on a gurney. Oxygen mask, lines in his arm. Blood. A surgeon dictating to a nurse as they raced him towards the theatre.

'Bullet wound, shoulder. If we're lucky it hasn't punctured the lung.'

Lund followed, saw the wounded man open his eyes.

'Has he eaten recently?' the surgeon asked.

'We don't know. He's been sleeping rough.'

The surgeon wore a green mob cap, mask pulled down over his chin.

'He's lost a lot of blood. Do you know if he's allergic to any drugs?'

'We've sent through his medical records,' Lund said. 'The army had them on file.' She hesitated. 'He was badly wounded in Afghanistan two years ago.'

'Well he's badly wounded now,' the man said in a curt, low voice. Then louder, 'Get me a suction drain! Let's get on with this!'

The theatre doors opened. One of the nurses put a hand to Lund's chest.

'What do you think you're doing? You can't come in here.'

She stood outside, watched the door close, wished she could still the furious thoughts in her head.

Strange was a few steps behind, coming off the phone.

'We've brought Skåning in for questioning,' he

140

said. 'They want to know whether to start or wait for us.'

Her wrist was still bandaged from the night before. Her head was starting to hurt. She couldn't think straight and answer his question.

'Is he going to be all right?' Strange asked.

'They didn't say. He seemed pretty bad.'

'I had to shoot. You saw that, didn't you? He was waving that gun about. Looking crazy.'

She flexed her fingers. They still hurt from the fall.

'Why the hell didn't he drop it?' Strange went on. 'If he'd done that we wouldn't be here.'

'He seemed scared, didn't he?'

Strange blinked.

'Of what?'

'I don't know. He did put the gun down. Then he saw you approaching. And . . .' She watched him closely. 'He seemed to think you were Perk.'

Ulrik Strange didn't seem the same man at that moment. He looked angry, unpredictable.

'Oh for God's sake . . .' he muttered.

A voice from behind.

'Where is he?'

Brix in a damp raincoat. Unhappy.

'In theatre,' Lund said.

'What the hell happened?'

The three of them began to walk down the corridor, towards the waiting room. Strange first, silent and angry.

'He took Skåning hostage,' Lund said. 'Beat him

up. He had a gun. He took off and wouldn't put down his weapon.'

'Who shot him?'

'I did.' Strange shrugged. 'I aimed for his arm as best I could. It was dark. He was upstairs.' A glance at her. 'So was Lund. I was worried.'

'I want armed guards on the room. No one has access to him unless they come through us.' He stared at Strange. 'Well?'

'OK.'

He walked off to make the calls.

'Is he going to pull through?' Brix asked.

'Maybe.'

'Why the hell didn't he put the gun down?'

A couple of nurses raced down the corridor pushing some equipment into the theatre. Strange was gone through the double doors. She was glad of that.

'I don't know,' she said.

It had been so long she'd almost forgotten what it was like to have a man, to take him to bed, to get so close she could taste his sweat and feel his strength inside. Christian Søgaard lay back grunting, eyes closed, face for once suffused with pleasure. Louise was above him, back arched, thrusting, not too quickly, trying to make it last.

To make him happy the way she once did for Jens. He liked it this way too. Liked to give over some of his power, if only for a short time and then life could go back to normal.

But Søgaard wasn't Jens and it was more curiosity that drove her. Curiosity about herself.

Another man, the first in thirteen years.

How did she feel? Elated? Ashamed? Or just plain dead?

He was getting there. She could sense it, hear it. And she felt nothing at all, but mirrored his growing rhythmic grunts and cries anyway because that was what you did.

Too long? Too short?

She didn't know. Didn't care. With Jens there was something else. Beyond the physical. A bond between them, a mutual shared mystery that bore the name of love. With Søgaard . . . nothing except his desperate need to have her. Which, like the good army woman she was supposed to be, she'd acknowledged, acceded to. Taken him to her lonely bed and given him what he wanted.

He moaned. He thrust at her. A damp warm feeling.

Louise Raben rolled off him, sweating, head spinning, wondering where the pleasure was and if it turned up whether it would outweigh the pain.

She didn't feel guilty. Jens had seen to that. But she did feel bad, and that somehow was worse.

Sweating, gasping, his arm around her, clinging to his new possession, Christian Søgaard lay on her crumpled, damp bed sheets, eyes closed, content.

This was one more of his battles, she thought.

Another victory. Another piece of the world claimed.

Neither of them spoke. It seemed unnecessary. As she rolled from him there was a rap on the door. Loud and urgent.

She dragged on her nightgown, the one she used to go to Jonas when he had the terrors, went to answer it.

Her father was there. He could see inside, she was sure. At that moment though he didn't seem to care.

'Something's happened,' he said in a nervous, worried voice. 'The police called. I . . .'

'What?'

'You need to go to the hospital now.'

A sound behind her. Søgaard coming towards them. She moved the door to block the sight of him. A big man, with the officers' tattoo on his arm.

'What is it?' she asked.

'Jens has been shot, Louise.' Her father cast a glance at the tall figure in her room. She couldn't read it. 'They need you there now.'

Thomas Buch felt hungry. He needed a drink. There was a late-night reception at the South Korean Embassy that evening. Music, art and food. He loved kimchi even if it did smell foul.

There was just the meeting with the Prime Minister to get out of the way first.

Grue Eriksen was at his desk going through some

papers. He didn't look up as Buch marched in and apologized for being late.

'There are developments. The soldier we were searching for has been shot.'

'I know.' Grue Eriksen smiled at him. 'Would you like a drink?'

'No, thank you. I'm anxious to find Rossing so we can talk things over.'

'Talk about what?'

'I realize I was a bit rash in what I said. I'm new to government . . . I'm sorry about the misunderstanding. I'll offer him my apologies.'

Grue Eriksen smiled and shook his head.

'I hope we can continue our working relationship,' Buch added. 'And Krabbe too. The anti-terror package has put us under pressure. But I'm determined . . .' He rapped the desk with his knuckles. 'Absolutely determined to put this right.'

'Very noble.'

'If I can just have a talk with Rossing. I'm sure—'

'Thomas. You've been a minister for six days. God created the world in just one more. And you've destroyed everything.'

Buch nodded, listened.

'I was never made for the spotlight, Prime Minister. Never sought it.'

'All these accusations have left you damaged,' Grue Eriksen continued. 'I listened to you. I tried to believe a little of the fantasies you were spinning. But honestly. They're incredible. You've

145

picked up a tiny thread of rumour and woven it into the most ridiculous of fairy tales.'

Grue Eriksen pushed a piece of paper across the desk.

'You have to resign. There's no alternative.'

'But I'm not ready to resign,' Buch said as if the idea were ridiculous. 'There are far too many loose ends for one thing. I defy anyone else to pick them up. How did Rossing know I'd mention that fax?'

'The fax?'

Buch laughed. Started to get mad.

'The fax I briefed you on! About the medical report and the surplus hand.'

'Don't shout.'

'Don't shout?' Buch roared. 'How else do you get someone to listen to you in this damned place? It was so convenient Rossing knew, wasn't it? And I didn't tell him. So who did?'

The Prime Minister seemed more amused by his anger than offended by it.

'You want me to call Rossing over here? Would that make you happy? If I indulge you one last time?'

Buch hesitated.

'No,' he murmured.

He looked at the sheet of paper in front of him. Times for meetings. Everything set out.

'This is your final agenda,' Grue Eriksen said. 'Tomorrow we pass the anti-terror package. With Krabbe's amendments. Then you call a press conference to announce your resignation. Tell

146

them . . .' He waved a dismissive hand. 'Say you want to spend more time with your family. No need to be original.'

Buch glared at him.

'Don't worry, Thomas. We've short memories around here. In a few years you can come back. Not to justice, of course. I'm not sure you have the temperament—'

'Did you pick me because you thought I'd be useless?' Buch asked straight out. 'Amenable. Pliable. Someone like Monberg who'd do as he's told?'

The Prime Minister laughed.

'I picked you because I liked you. I still do. Give it time. You'll see.' He pointed to the door. 'But right now your career's over. Go home and think of what you'll say.'

Grue Eriksen saw him out.

Home.

That was in Jutland, which seemed a million miles away. The invitation to the embassy was in Buch's pocket. Music. Art. Beer and rice wine.

And kimchi.

Plough and Karina were waiting on a bench seat downstairs. Something on their long faces told him they knew his fate already.

'Thomas . . .' Karina began.

'I need some time to myself,' Buch said quickly.

Then left the Christianborg Palace, walked out into the chill, open space of Slotsholmen, thinking of the places he used to linger back before he became a minister. When he was free.

Lund waited as close to the operating theatre as the hospital staff would allow. Strange went back to the Politigården to interview the badly beaten Torben Skåning. Brix stayed to talk to the medical staff.

After an hour Strange called.

'This doesn't work. Skåning's got an alibi. He had a nervous breakdown in Afghanistan. He flew home with Raben and the wounded soldiers. He says Raben recognized him from the flight but didn't remember it.'

'Check that out. I'm coming in.'

She was about to leave when the double doors opened and Louise Raben walked through, pale-faced and anxious.

'What happened?' she demanded.

'He just came out of surgery. You need to talk to the doctors.'

'I asked what happened!'

'He took a soldier hostage. Your husband had a gun. He tried to escape. Then . . .'

Lund didn't want this conversation. She tried to get past the woman. It wasn't possible.

'Why the hell did you have to shoot him?'

She tried to recall what had happened, to get it clear in her own head. It wasn't easy.

'He had a gun. It was dark. He looked crazy. I'm sorry—'

148

'Jens isn't like that.'

'You weren't there. He put the gun to his chin. We thought he was going to take his own life. Then he changed his mind . . .' She shrugged. 'For some reason. He wouldn't put down the weapon. We didn't know . . .'

Louise Raben's hair was a mess. She looked as if she'd come straight from bed.

'That isn't Jens . . .'

'But it was,' Lund insisted. She pulled out a plastic evidence bag. 'He had these with him. We don't need them.'

A pair of gloves. A toy soldier, sword raised. The woman took them, stared at the little figure.

Brix was at the end of the corridor.

'Excuse me,' Lund said and went to see him.

'Any news from Strange?' he asked.

'They questioned Skåning.'

'I know. He called me. Skåning's alibi checks out.'

'It's got to be him. We've been through all the other officers on Ægir. The rest of them are clean.'

'If he was from Ægir . . .'

'If he wasn't God knows where we start. What did the doctor say?'

'Raben's stable. We can interview him tomorrow.'

Brix took a deep breath, looked around, made sure they were on their own.

'We've got a problem. Raben was talking before he went under. He claimed the policeman who shot him was Perk. Strange.'

149

Lund kept quiet.

'The surgeon said he was delirious,' Brix went on. 'But we can't ignore that. It's got to go on file. There'll be an inquiry into the shooting. You know what they're like, don't you?'

Oh yes, she thought.

'I need to hear this from you, Lund. Is your report accurate?'

'Of course.'

He watched her, interested. Brix didn't like swift and easy answers.

'What exactly did the surgeon say?' she asked.

Brix waited. He knew.

'OK. Something wasn't right,' she admitted. 'When Raben saw Strange he called him out as Perk. I heard that. I thought—'

'You're sure of that?'

'He's crazy, isn't he? A couple of minutes before he'd been beating the life out of Skåning thinking he was Perk. Then he had a gun to his own throat. You can't believe—'

'It has to go on the record. It has to be in the report.'

'Yes! Yes! I know. Raben was in a state. He didn't know what he was doing. I need to get back to the Politigården.'

His hand caught her arm as she tried to leave.

'Listen for once, will you? When we took on Strange a year ago I read his CV. He was in the army for a long time.'

'Yes! I know. He told me. At Vordingborg. He

150

had back trouble. He was a squaddie. Hardly a suspect.'

Brix scowled.

'He wasn't a squaddie at Vordingborg. He was Jægerkorpset. An officer. He came over to us on a transfer programme. He's got weapons training. Lots of . . . skills we probably don't know about.'

'No . . .'

A figure striding down the corridor towards them.

Strange came and stood next to Brix, looked at both of them.

'I thought I'd come and fetch you,' he said. Hands in pockets, mild face miserable and tense. 'I never shot anyone before. How is he?'

'He'll live,' Brix said. 'We need to talk.'

Back in the Politigården. Strange in a chair on his own. Lund, arms folded, next to Brix in his office.

'How long did you serve with the special forces people?' Brix asked.

Strange took a deep breath, looked at both of them.

'Is this serious? Come on . . .'

Brix stared at him.

'Serious? What do you think? You shot a man. He identified as you Perk. Every firearms incident gets an inquiry. In circumstances like these . . . We have to know where we stand.'

'This is crazy,' Strange complained. 'I was in

the army. They asked me if I wanted to serve with Jægerkorpset for a while.'

'Why did you lie to me?' Lund asked.

'Because we're not supposed to say! Look. I served. I got sick of it. I wasn't tough enough for that shit frankly. So I quit and applied for the Police Academy.'

'But you went back?' Brix said.

'Yeah. After 9/11 they came and said they needed people. I had a boring job in the drugs squad. They seemed desperate. So I gave it another go.'

He frowned.

'Great idea. Cost me my marriage. I finally quit eighteen months ago and came here. Didn't make any difference.'

He looked around the place.

'I think this suits me better. Maybe you two don't agree . . .'

Lund asked, 'Were you in Afghanistan?'

It took a while for him to answer.

'These things are supposed to be classified,' Strange said. 'But yes. Three times. Not with Jægerkorpset. And I wasn't with Ægir either. I was demobilized six months before they left.'

He leaned forward, stared at both of them.

'You're clear on that? I wasn't there when any of this happened. I never met Jens Peter Raben till tonight. I mean . . .' He tried to laugh. 'Don't you think I'd have told you?'

'You could have said something,' she threw at him.

'What? I hated those last few years. It destroyed things . . . things that mattered to me. I just want to forget about the whole damn business.'

'You could have said.'

It was Brix this time.

Strange threw back his head and looked ready to howl.

'My life came apart while I was pissing around playing boy soldiers out there. My marriage. My kids. I lost them all. It's taken me a long time to get back on my feet. I like it here.'

'Very good,' Brix said and picked up his notebook. 'According to Skåning, Raben seemed interested in a tattoo. A logo with a message. *Ingenio et Armis*. With wisdom and weapons.'

'We're wasting time,' Strange sighed. 'Let's talk to Skåning some more. He's got a tale to tell—'

'He's not the only one,' Brix cut in. 'We sent him home. He's got an alibi, remember?'

'Then there's something we're missing. Something we've overlooked.'

Brix pointed.

'Take off your shirt. Let's get it over with.'

Strange shook his head. Removed his black sweater. Pulled up the arm of the T-shirt beneath.

The tattoo was there. A red-handled sword stabbing through a crest. The motto *Ingenio et Armis* in blue lettering.

Lund stared at him. Brix made a note.

'Before you cuff me,' Strange said, 'you ought to check how many officers have got that tattoo.

153

Skåning has it. I'd place a good bet you'll find it on Søgaard too. We all did. It was part of the induction, part of—'

'I need your gun,' Brix ordered, holding out his hand. 'And your ID. We're going to hand you over to the inquiry team. After that you'll go home and stay there until this is cleared up.'

Ten minutes later the inquiry team had Strange in a room. Brix was looking through the glass, Lund and Madsen by his side.

'This is where we are,' he told the young detective. 'I'm suspending Strange until we get to the bottom of this. You're taking over his assignment. You report to Lund and me.'

'We need to talk to the army,' Lund said. 'Get a list of officers who worked for special forces in Afghanistan two years ago.'

'Good luck,' Madsen said. 'My cousin was with the spooky people for a while. They won't tell us a thing. Those guys barely talk to each other.'

Madsen nodded at the glass.

'If Strange was one of them he won't give you the time of day. Not that you can trust anyway. It's part of the code.'

'Ask for it,' Brix ordered. 'If they object let me know.'

'If it was Strange I'd have known,' Lund said, watching him, arms folded, waiting patiently.

Brix shook his head.

'The case is connected to the army. He should have told us. You know that.'

That was too easy, she thought.

'We didn't know that to begin with, did we? It was all about terrorists.'

'When he shot Raben . . . was there really no alternative?'

'It was dark. Raben was behaving unpredictably. He had a weapon.'

Brix stared at her.

'Were you with him when those people died?'

'Yes. I mean . . .'

She'd been trying to think this through.

Myg Poulsen and Grüner were dead when they turned up. She didn't know what Strange was doing in the hours before they were murdered. And Helsingør . . . He could have got to Torpe's church in Vesterbro before she did, with the traffic and her indecision along the way.

Brix turned to Madsen and said, 'Look into it. Until I see something that says otherwise he's a suspect. Lund?'

She was lost somewhere, trying to fit together the pieces of an impossible jigsaw.

'Lund!'

He took her arm.

'Either Raben's crazy or Strange's lying. I'd rather believe the former. But until we know, we do this by the book.'

★   ★   ★

155

Louise Raben sat in the hospital corridor watching the doctors and nurses come and go. There were two uniformed cops outside her husband's room. They didn't want to talk which was fine by her.

An awkward, hurtful memory stuck in her head like grit beneath an eyelid. Christian Søgaard grunting and panting beneath her. She didn't feel ashamed. Didn't even feel guilty. Just stupid. Boredom and an infantile curiosity had tempted her to take him to her bed. Not even a mindless desire.

It was Jens she wanted really. Had all along. The idiotic adventure with Søgaard was her way of punishing him. Ridiculous. Pointless.

No one had spoken to her for the best part of an hour. She was beginning to doze off when a young woman doctor came up, stethoscope round her neck, green surgical gown beneath a white coat, and tapped her shoulder.

'How is he?' Louise asked, getting up.

'Drowsy. He'll probably sleep until tomorrow.' She hesitated. 'But we're pretty sure he's going to be all right. He's healthy. He's young.' She smiled. 'He's lucky.'

'No he isn't. Not at all.'

'He was lucky tonight. You can go and see him if you want.'

It felt wrong. After Søgaard . . .

'I can come back tomorrow. Will someone look after his things?'

'He might wake up,' the woman said in a hard,

156

cold voice. 'It's important he feels there's someone there. Someone who cares for him.'

She had very large, keen eyes. Like the police-woman, Lund.

'I can show you the way,' the doctor said and it wasn't an offer to be refused.

Five minutes later she was alone with him in the private room. Machines on stands. Monitors. Louise Raben was a nurse. She could read these things, understand the clipboard at the foot of the bed. He was fortunate really. It was much worse two years before when he came back from Helmand.

He lay half beneath the sheets in white hospital pyjamas, chest open, shaved in places for the sensors. Lines and drains and monitors. Cannulas in his arms and hands and neck.

Unconscious on the single hospital bed, crooked at a slight angle, he looked at peace for once. They'd cleaned him up. Maybe even trimmed his beard. Like this he was the man she remembered. The one she'd fallen for so deeply.

She looked at him and said, in a low, certain voice, 'The doctor told me I should talk to you.' Her hands fidgeted. She felt nervous and, finally, guilty. 'And I don't know what to say.'

The image of Søgaard refused to leave her head. It shouldn't, she thought. That vile picture was there to remind her. To guide her towards a place she needed to find.

'I saw an old video this evening,' she said,

157

watching the lines on the monitor, listening to the machines click and whirr. 'You and me at the beach, just before Jonas was born. Remember?'

Why ask a sleeping man? She'd no idea. The video was molten plastic and burned tape in an old dustbin in the garden, alongside the ashes of their letters. Gone for ever. Except in her head . . .

'I was fat and ugly and we couldn't think of a name for him. You remember that?' She laughed, couldn't help it. 'We wrote such a long list and they all seemed wrong.' Her voice fell to a whisper. 'In the end you wanted to go for a swim.'

This memory wasn't on the video. It went deeper than that. Was still real.

'But I didn't because I thought I looked like a whale.' She closed her eyes, felt the tears start. 'And you took me in your arms. You carried me, big fat me, all the way to the sea. You kissed me.' Another quiet moment of laughter. 'Then you said you knew what his name should be. Jonas. Because Jonas was inside the whale. And then set free . . .'

Alone but not alone, she found the tears running down her cheeks.

'What a piece of shit I am,' Louise Raben whispered.

Then stood up. Touched his still fingers. They were warm. Life there. Hope there. Love still. He'd never lost that. Never would and now she knew.

Took them away. Wondered. Looked at the man in the bed, eyes closed, shallow breathing. Hurt

158

and damaged by so many things. And now she was among them.

Then she touched his fingers again and knew she wasn't mistaken. There was the faintest of responses there. A flicker of movement as she took his hand in hers.

'I'm so sorry, Jens,' she murmured, her voice breaking, then leaned over him, kissed his rough cheek, placed her head next to his on the soft hospital pillow.

There was only one place to be and it wasn't with Christian Søgaard. This difficult, damaged man was all she wanted, with his faults, his troubles, his pain.

Her cheek brushed his rough beard. Her fingers tightened on his. Somewhere outside a siren sounded. Through the glass door she could see the tall cops in their blue uniforms.

Here, at least, he was safe.

Carsten Plough and Karina Jørgensen were back in the Ministry of Justice, desperately trying to track down Buch. His mobile was turned off. He'd gone walkabout after leaving the Christianborg Palace. Even the hot-dog stand hadn't seen him.

The phones kept ringing constantly, media mainly, screeching for a statement.

'We've no comment,' Karina told the latest, the political editor of one of the dailies. 'There's nothing to say. Nothing at all . . .'

She put down the phone, looked at Plough.

'The driver's not seen him. He's been gone for an hour now. How can he do this to us?'

She tried his mobile again.

'It's still on voicemail. I called his wife. She's not heard from him either.'

'The rumours are flying!' Plough said anxiously.

'Forget the rumours. Let's hear it from Buch directly, shall we? Maybe he tracked down Connie Vemmer and had a word with her.'

'Maybe, maybe, maybe,' Plough grumbled. He phoned security. 'Hello? Plough here. Our minister's missing. I want you to find him.'

Nothing.

'Is there a committee meeting or something?' Karina asked. 'Does he have any invitations?'

Plough raised a finger. They walked to Buch's desk, found the diary.

It was scribbled in there for the evening. The address of the South Korean Embassy. And a single word, seemingly written with enthusiasm.

Kimchi!

She called, talked to someone there.

'Oh crap,' Karina muttered as she came off the phone.

Kimchi.

There was lots of it. And skewers of beef. And things he didn't recognize. Beer too. Rice wine. Whisky. Thomas Buch had his jacket off, his tie halfway down his neck. Sat on the floor like a fat Buddha, sweating heavily, only half-listening to a

160

woman in traditional costume play some kind of oriental harp.

He'd no idea whether the semicircle of people in front of him understood a word of what he was saying. A Chinese woman. A kindly but puzzled-looking young black man who wore some kind of African dress. A Korean in a grey suit and some others who didn't seem happy at all.

'I was so . . . so very angry,' he went on in a slow, slurred tone. 'Because I thought there was an extra hand in the coffin. And it was proof. But . . .' Buch's voice rose, as if volume might bring sense to what he was saying. 'But it wasn't an extra hand, you see. Oh, no. There was another medical report.' His fingers gestured through the air, then the right one found his strong beer. A swig of it. 'And it was the hand of the suicide bomber.'

He raised his glass.

'What happened was . . .' He puffed up his cheeks. Said very loudly, 'Boosh!'

Buch nodded.

'Boosh. And there it was.'

He stopped. There was movement at the back of the room. Someone there, a very serious-looking individual who had the appearance of security, had been eyeing him for a while. A blonde woman marched in. Karina. Then the tall figure of Carsten Plough.

'Hello! Hello!' Buch called. 'Come, come! Have beer. Try kimchi!'

161

The two approached.

'I was telling my new friends about the hand.' His fat, bearded cheeks puffed up again. 'Boosh!'

He waved at the semicircle of silent people on chairs in front of him.

'These are my colleagues. Plough and Karina. Kimchi!'

Plough smiled and gestured with his hand, fingers waving towards himself.

'What?' Buch asked.

'Come, Thomas,' Karina said. 'Time to go home.'

Buch struggled to his feet, smiled, brushed himself down.

'One more beer and a bit of kimchi,' he said and struggled to the buffet.

The two of them came over.

'We need to go back to Connie Vemmer,' she said.

'Kimchi,' Buch replied, forcing a small plate of fermented cabbage on her.

'I don't want kimchi!' she said very loudly. 'Rossing set you up, remember?'

'Oh Karina,' he moaned. 'I'm not cut out for all this intrigue. Haven't you noticed?'

'This isn't finished,' Plough said.

'But it is. And so am I,' Buch whined.

'Thomas!' Karina's voice was hectoring and insistent. 'They've got Raben in custody. He's been shot but he'll live. We can look into this—'

162

'No!' Buch cried. 'I'm resigning tomorrow. For God's sake let me go quietly, will you?'

Carsten Plough made him sit, then took the chair next to him. Tidied Buch's tie. Stared into his sweating face.

'Give up? Give up?' he said in a low and caustic voice. 'How can you possibly say that after all we've done?'

'Something's amiss,' Karina added. 'You know it.'

Plough picked Buch's jacket off the floor and returned with it.

'We're in this together, Thomas. We have to keep calm. Behave responsibly . . .'

Buch shook his big head, got to his feet, angry all of a sudden.

'Stop it, Plough? The truth is we weren't up to it. We were out of our depth—'

'No,' Plough interrupted. 'That's not justified at all. Let's go back to the office and discuss this.'

'Fuck the office!' Buch roared. 'Fuck Slotsholmen. Twice over.'

The room fell into silence.

'The truth is you'd no idea what Monberg was up to! He was a loose cannon. And you . . .'

His finger jabbed at her.

'You even slept with the man. Bloody hell!'

The two of them stared at him.

Buch blinked, wondered why he'd said such a stupid thing.

The two of them turned and walked out.

'Oh don't leave,' Buch cried. 'I apologize. Come here, won't you? Please . . .'

He fell back into the chair, grabbed for the glass. Wondered if he could manage more kimchi.

The one who looked like a security guard came up. He had a coat in his hand. Buch realized it was his.

It was cold outside and Buch wasn't exactly sure where he was.

Then remembered something. Erling Krabbe. He lived nearby.

In a nearby cafe he drank two large cups of espresso. Close to midnight he went to Krabbe's house and let his finger rest on the doorbell.

It took a while but eventually he heard a familiar voice cry, 'All right! I'm coming, dammit!'

'Hello?' Buch yelled, peering through the spyglass.

Eventually he saw an eye on the other side.

'What in God's name are you doing here?'

'We've got to talk, Krabbe. Honestly. It's important.'

Buch paused.

'Also . . . I need to use the toilet.'

Krabbe let him in, showed him the bathroom, then took him into a smart modern kitchen, gave him a glass of milk, put out some food. Cheese and biscuits.

'Dig in!' he said. 'You look as if you need it.'

Buch was too drunk to be sure but a part of him

thought Erling Krabbe was mildly amused by his condition, and not in a cruel way either.

There were photos on the fridge. An attractive Asian woman with a couple of kids. Thai maybe.

Glass of milk in hand, Buch stared at them.

'We talked about that too. Me and my wife.'

'Talked about what?' Krabbe asked, neatly dividing up some coffee cake.

'Getting an au pair.'

'That's my wife,' Krabbe told him.

Buch gulped at the milk. Wondered when he'd be able to open his mouth without saying something deeply stupid.

He sat down.

'May I ask,' Krabbe said, 'what exactly you're doing here?'

Buch gulped at the milk, looked at him, and ate some cheese.

'I'm sorry if I left you confused,' Krabbe said.

He was in a T-shirt and pyjama bottoms and wore a heavy pair of glasses. Must use contacts during the day, Buch guessed. He was different like this. Less robotic, more human. Krabbe munched on a piece of cucumber and got himself some carrot juice.

Buch stared at the glass of orange liquid as if it were poison.

'I wondered why you came to see me,' he said. 'That's all.'

'It was nothing.'

'Didn't look like nothing.'

'Buch. I'm sorry. I didn't mean any of this personally—'

'Oh no! Listen, Krabbe. I had the Prime Minister's confidence. Then you march in there.' He raised a fat forefinger. 'I demand to know what you talked about. I demand it. I'm still a government minister, you know. Maybe not for much longer . . .'

Krabbe sipped at his carrot juice.

'You're an infuriating man. After that stunt of yours at the press conference I was furious. All the work with Monberg on the anti-terror package was in ruins.'

Buch kept picking at the food, listening.

'Because of you . . .' Krabbe shook his head as if this were somehow hard to believe. 'I had to call a meeting of the executive committee.'

'Big deal.'

'It might have been. But on the way there I got a call from Grue Eriksen's office. They said the whole thing had been investigated and Rossing was in the clear. That was it. You were going to be hung out to dry and the package was up for the vote tomorrow.'

'Wait, wait.' Buch was struggling to work this out. 'You're saying they told you that before I'd even gone in front of the Security Committee?'

'Exactly. I couldn't understand that either. But I think I get the picture now.'

'Going to share this revelation with me?'

Krabbe rolled his eyes.

'What does it matter if Grue Eriksen had prior knowledge? They knew your accusations were false. They were just calling me in advance to make sure I didn't stir things up. They'd lost confidence in you.'

Buch raised his glass of milk in a silent toast.

'So Rossing made a fool of you. It doesn't mean Grue Eriksen was a party to the whole thing, does it? Surely he's above this kind of back-stabbing.'

'Krabbe,' Buch said, aware his mind was starting to clear. 'This isn't about a political row in Slotsholmen. It's to do with murder. Conspiracy. Maybe an army atrocity—'

'I spoke to the Prime Minister this evening. I'm fine on this. We vote tomorrow and put it all behind us. I'm sorry, Buch, but I'm glad he gave you the push. You're not up to the job.'

He pointed to the clock on the wall. Half past midnight.

'Shall I call you a taxi?'

'Are you happy now?' Buch asked.

'I've got what I wanted.'

Buch got up, looked at the photos on the fridge. The pretty Asian woman. The kids.

'Funny, isn't it?' he said. 'We're different people when we step outside that place. When you throw all those fixed positions to one side and talk about things without all that . . . crap around.'

'A taxi,' Krabbe repeated.

'Are you happy?' Thomas Buch asked again. 'Truly? Honestly?'

Lund got home at close to one in the morning, a pizza going cold in her hands. Her head was hurting again. The wound above her eyebrow itched. Walking up the stairs on the way into Vibeke's apartment her phone rang. Madsen with the latest on Strange.

'We need to know exactly when he came out of the army,' she said, listening to his excuses. 'He claims it was six months before Raben's squad got hit.'

'They won't give us that information, Lund. Once it's about someone who's been in special forces—'

'Tell them we've got to have it! This is a murder inquiry.'

'They're sending some top brass guy to see us tomorrow morning. General Arild.'

'They can send who they like. We still want that information. And Strange's CV. All the personnel information we got when he transferred to the police. Send me that too, will you?'

She put the pizza on the step and hunted for the door keys in her bag.

'Lund,' a low, miserable voice said out of the darkness near the lift.

She jumped as Strange walked out of the gloom.

'How the hell did you get in here?'

'I waited till someone turned up and said I wanted to see your mother. I'm not breaking in, for God's sake. This is for you . . .'

He had a plastic wallet in his hands. She didn't take it.

'You shouldn't be here. What's that?'

'Reports on the soldiers who died on Raben's mission. I left them in the car. You should have them now you're taking over.'

'Thanks,' she said and took them.

He'd been home and changed. Nice brown coat, clean shirt, scarf. He didn't look worried at all. Just pissed off.

'You know you shouldn't be here . . .'

'I don't care what Brix thinks.'

'Jesus, Strange. We can't talk about any of this. You're suspended. There's an inquiry—'

'What do you think? That's all I want to know. What do you believe?'

She looked at him, wished she didn't have to face this.

'You should have told me. I had the right to know.'

He nodded, as if he took the point.

'Why? Did you tell me about every last thing in your life? About the Swede you were going to live with? About the cop who got shot?'

'It's not the same . . .'

She tried to push past. He took hold of her. Wouldn't let go.

'The guys in the Politigården said you went

169

nuts and that's why Jan Meyer wound up in a wheelchair.'

'Did they?'

'I told them to shut up. I stood by you, all the time, and you didn't say a damned word. Offer me a thing either.'

The communal light was on a timer. It flicked off at that moment. Just as Ulrik Strange's face came close to hers.

Lund punched the switch and got the light back on.

He waited for an answer. When he didn't get one he swore in a whisper and set off down the stairs. Turned after a couple of steps.

'I told my kids about you,' Strange said. 'They were asking why I looked so happy. I said . . .'

She wanted to yell and scream at him but didn't.

'I told them I'd met someone at work. And maybe they'd meet her too one day.'

'Stop it,' Lund whispered.

So quietly he didn't hear.

'Maybe,' Strange said and then was gone.

CHAPTER 9

Monday 21st November, 9.15 a.m.

General Arild was a cocky, ginger-haired man who looked Brix and Lund and Madsen in the eye the moment they called him into an interview room. Early fifties, Lund thought. Short but muscular, confident as he stood by the window, laughing at the conversation. She could imagine him as a soldier in the field, looking for the nearest fight.

'Cooperation?' Arild asked when Lund questioned the responses she'd been getting from the military. 'You think we haven't helped you already? You've been all over Ryvangen. Interrogating our officers while they prepare for the next tour. Goodness . . .'

He wore an immaculate blue uniform covered with ribbons and medals.

'Did you have special forces operatives in the area in question, two years ago?' Lund asked.

Brix stood by the filing cabinets, listening.

'I wouldn't normally answer a question like this,'

Arild said. 'But since you seem to think it so important, yes, we had officers there.'

'While Team Ægir was in place?'

'Didn't I just answer that?'

'And Ulrik Strange was demobilized six months before this incident in Helmand?'

'Too far,' Arild replied. 'You know I can't discuss names.'

'I want a list of who was there!' Lund insisted.

He laughed at her.

'You don't want much, do you? Do you understand the kind of people we're talking about? The work they do?'

'Not really,' Lund replied.

Arild's confident, smiling face fell.

'We're fighting animals who'll decapitate their own daughters for wearing the wrong clothes. Hang a man in the street for listening to the radio. Geneva's a long way from Helmand. They know it. We do too.'

He didn't like women, Lund thought. Except in their place.

'I want that information, General.'

'I'm not at liberty to disclose anything about individual officers. What I will say is this. No one from Jægerkorpset or any other special forces unit was involved in that particular incident. It happened without our involvement and our knowledge.'

A knock on the door. Someone asking for Brix. He left the room.

Arild came a step closer.

'I'm trying to help you,' he said. 'We don't go around murdering innocent civilians. Here or in Afghanistan. Now . . .' He picked up his cap. 'You must excuse me.'

'These officers were deployed too,' she said, passing him the latest list of soldiers attached to Ægir from other regiments. 'I want what you have on them. They're not special forces. You've no reason to object—'

'The ramblings of a traumatized soldier do not merit this nonsense,' Arild barked, close to losing his temper. 'And how is it Jens Peter Raben could elude PET so easily? Tell me that. I thought you people had him under surveillance . . . You've no idea what you're getting into, woman. Any more questions before I leave?'

She wanted to ask if he dyed his hair but didn't. Instead she folded her arms, gave him a jaded look and said, 'If you stand in my way I'll go public. You'll have every hack and TV crew in Denmark banging on your door demanding answers. Your choice.'

He didn't like that.

Brix came back. Arild marched with him to the black marble corridor outside.

'What information we can provide,' Arild said very deliberately to Brix alone, 'I will send you. You'll hear from my office this afternoon.'

Then he left.

'What changed his mind?' Brix asked.

'Female charm.'

'How are you feeling?'

The wound didn't hurt any more. The bruise was just a red weal.

'Fine,' Lund said.

'Raben's conscious. He wants to talk. Doesn't mind whether a lawyer's present or not.'

Lund got her keys.

'Take Madsen with you,' he called as she left.

But Madsen was on the phone. Lund walked on without him.

Buch had brushed his teeth four times already that morning. But he could still taste stale kimchi in his mouth. He'd called together the most senior staff in the Ministry, stood in front of them in the reception area outside his office.

No energy for a tie. Just a clean suit, a blue sweater and a white shirt that was in need of an iron.

Plough and Karina stood behind him looking mutinous.

'I'm sorry my ineptitude embarrassed you all,' Buch said. 'The newspapers are telling everyone I'm just a simple farmer from Jutland.'

Karina muttered something.

'It seems,' Buch went on, 'they were right. Which is a shame because I enjoyed working with you greatly. You deserved better. I trust my successor, whoever he or she turns out to be, will bring you that.'

Plough led the applause. Karina took it up. Soon

174

they were all clapping him, which made Buch feel rather odd. As if he'd touched these people, not that he understood how.

He went back into his office. Plough and Karina marched in behind, closing the door.

'Today's schedule,' she began, placing a sheet of paper on his desk. 'The Prime Minister's office will vet your leaving statement and arrange a suitable exchange of letters.'

Buch put a couple of headache pills in a glass, topped them up with water, swilled them around.

'About Raben,' she began.

'Oh, forget it, Karina,' Buch cut in. He looked at her, at Plough. 'Please. I'm really sorry for last night. It was inexcusable. Can you draft a letter of apology to the poor Koreans?'

They said nothing.

'You've both been so kind. So supportive, from the beginning. And all I did was foul things up.'

'Thomas . . .' she began.

'No. Let me finish. This is the best solution for the government and the Ministry.' He thought of the difficult, strained conversation he'd had with Marie that morning. All she knew was what she'd read. It was hard to explain over the phone. 'For me too. I want to go home. I need to. Here . . .'

He reached beneath the desk and pulled out the bottle of expensive Armagnac he'd picked up for Plough.

'I wish you all the best, Carsten. And for you . . .'

He handed Karina a box of chocolates.

Plough's phone rang. He excused himself and walked away to take it.

'Was it the wrong Armagnac?' Buch asked, watching him go.

'It's fine.' She looked at Carsten Plough, talking in low tones in the corner of the room. 'He's got worries of his own.'

'What worries?'

She took a deep breath.

'He's been called to a meeting in the Prime Minister's office. There seems to be some kind of reorganization on the cards.'

Buch gulped at the headache pills and the water. He'd offered his own head. It was never part of the deal that Grue Eriksen would take others too.

'They want to appoint Plough to an EU consultant's post in Skopje.' She shrugged. 'If they're going to pick on Plough then I'm gone too. But that's fine by me.'

'This is wrong . . .'

'It's the way things happen. Connie Vemmer called. She wants to explain . . .'

'Oh no . . .'

'She says she needs to speak to you personally. Only you. I really think . . .'

Buch tried to smile, took another sip of the water.

'We lost, Karina. It's done with. I'll talk to Grue Eriksen about your careers. It's quite unacceptable that you should pay for my incompetence and stupidity.'

'Don't say that!' she shouted. 'It's not true.'

'I'll put this right. If I can.'

Lund sat next to Raben's bed in the private ward, amidst the racket of the medical machinery, listening to his firm and insistent voice.

She left the recorder running, took no notes. Raben claimed he was starting to remember more of what happened in Helmand. There was a decision to be made here: who to believe?

'We were in the Green Zone. We got a message at nine thirty in the morning,' Raben said. 'It was on an emergency frequency. It said a Danish unit was under fire.'

His shoulder had a fresh dressing. The doctor said some of the lines from the night before had been removed. Raben was a hard man. He recovered quickly.

'We crossed the river to help. Did Thomsen tell you what happened?'

'I want to hear it from you.'

'The bridge was mined. I left her to sort it out. We made it into the village.'

He looked at her from the pillow.

'There was no Danish unit. Just one officer who'd got himself trapped in there with the family and didn't dare come out.'

'What made you think he was called Perk?'

'He told me. I saw his dog tag.'

'Did you know him?'

'No. He hadn't been through Camp Viking. I'm sure of that. But the special forces guys came from all over. Kabul. Direct sometimes. He said he got cut off from his squad.'

'You didn't believe him?'

Raben clutched his injured arm.

'I didn't know what to think. He said he'd been on a mission and the Taliban had caught wind of it. They were hounding him. He was waiting for backup.'

She folded her arms and waited.

'We weren't supposed to ask men like that what they were doing,' Raben said eventually. 'It wasn't our business.'

'Do you have any idea?'

'No. But he was scared. We all were. Just five of us left. Myg, HC, David, Sebastian and me. And Perk. Dolmer got hit by sniper fire on the way in. Dead. Grüner's leg was shot to bits. He needed help. There were Taliban in the village. Too scared to come for us but that wasn't going to last. We'd left the radio with Thomsen.'

'What about Perk's radio?'

'He said it got hit by fire after he called for us. I didn't see it. I didn't . . .' His head went from side to side on the pillow. 'I don't remember too clearly. Perk was an officer. It was like he was in command straight off. He said we had to wait. Not try to fight our way out. There were too many of them.'

178

Raben swore, closed his eyes for a moment.

'We should have just gone for it. The family were getting really jumpy. We couldn't let them leave.'

He stared at her.

'Grüner was screaming. The place stank of shit and blood and . . .' A moment of pain and bewilderment. 'I kept thinking they'd come for us but they didn't. Perk was getting madder and madder. Then he decided we had to get out, whatever.'

Raben went quiet.

'And?' Lund asked.

'It's in here!' Raben shrieked, tapping his forehead.

'Tell me what you can.'

'He said . . .' Raben spoke very slowly, as if unsure of himself. 'He told me he wanted the father to help him get hold of a radio. If we got that we could call in a helicopter and backup. But the father was just a villager. He didn't have one. He didn't have anything.'

He wiped his face with the sleeve of his hospital gown.

'Perk didn't believe him. So he grabbed one of the kids. A little girl.' He shuffled on the bed, dead eyes, face full of pain. 'Put his gun to her head. He said the father had to decide. Was he with the Taliban? Or with us?'

Head thrust back into the pillow.

'Then he shot her right in front of us. Seven years old. Eight maybe. Just gone like that.'

'You remember this? You're sure?'

'I remember!' Raben shrieked, eyes open, full of shame and fear. 'I watched him grab hold of the mother and he shot her too. He was crazy. The man held his son. He was crying, screaming. Begging Perk to spare them. But he just blew them away, there in the room. In front of us.'

She waited till he took hold of himself.

'There was one kid left. A little girl. Four maybe. I held her. I didn't think he'd shoot. Perk just snatched her from my arms and blew her head off.'

'And the others?'

'They were shouting. Sebastian was crying.'

She checked her notes.

'That's Sebastian Holst?'

'Yeah. The youngest. He was more interested in his camera than his gun. Wanted to be a press photographer when he came out. I put my arms round him. Made him calm down. It got dark. Suddenly we heard the sound of a motorbike outside. Some guy drove into the courtyard and blew himself up. They said Søgaard had almost found us by then. He came into the village, got us out of there. I don't recall.'

'And Perk?' she asked. 'Where was he?'

He shrugged.

'I don't really know what happened after that. Perk was a clever guy. I think he maybe found a way out before Søgaard came in. Either that or . . .'

'Or what?'

'Or someone helped him. We were just ordinary soldiers. He was higher up the food chain.'

Another look at her notes.

'Søgaard filed a report. He said there was no sign of any civilians. No bodies.'

'Yeah. Well . . .' A sour expression on Raben's bearded face. 'Maybe Perk got rid of them. Or someone didn't look too hard.'

He stretched up, gazed into her eyes.

'They were there. I'm telling the truth. Ask Perk yourself. He's one of yours.'

'Raben . . .'

'He's the one who shot me.'

She put the notebook to one side.

'What makes you think that?'

'I remember!'

'You said you don't remember well. You said Skåning was Perk. That man you kidnapped two years ago. He was a librarian—'

'I remember now!'

Lund frowned.

'Clearly?' she asked. 'Everything?'

Raben closed his eyes, looked desperate.

'Not everything. No. But I know he's Perk. He killed those people. I saw that. He's got a tattoo on his shoulder. He's—'

'Skåning's got the tattoo. So have lots of officers.'

She pulled out a set of photographs. Black and white mugshots from the files. Men she didn't know.

The moment Ulrik Strange's face appeared Raben picked the photo and thrust it in her face.

'Him,' he said. 'That's Perk.'

Brix and Hedeby were talking about Strange when Lund got back from the hospital. They listened to what she had to say. But Hedeby wasn't interested in Raben at that moment. She wanted to know about Strange.

'So now you're telling me one of our own officers killed these people?' Hedeby asked. 'Seriously?'

'I don't know,' Lund admitted. 'Raben's got good reason to tell a tale like that. He's facing criminal charges. I guess he might get off more lightly if he can throw the blame on us.'

Hedeby muttered a quiet curse.

'We need Strange cleared by name,' she said emphatically.

'We won't get it,' Lund said taking a seat.

'Raben's mentally unstable,' Brix added. 'We've got proof of that. He could easily have confused Strange with someone else. He's done it before. Besides . . . Strange has been an active member of the team here. He didn't have time to invent nonsense like the Muslim League.'

Lund sighed.

'There are gaps in his movements,' she said. 'He was at home on his own before we found Myg Poulsen. Grüner was killed by a bomb detonated

182

by a mobile phone placed in advance. Same thing. No alibi.'

'Lund—' Brix began.

'He left me in Sweden while I was talking to Lisbeth Thomsen. He was gone for two hours looking for Raben. We were in his car, not mine. He was at the barracks the night the explosives were stolen.'

'And when you found the priest Strange was in Helsingør,' Brix added.

'He was there,' Lund said. 'No one knows what time he left.'

She got her coat.

'I'm going to see Sebastian Holst's father. Raben said he used his camera all the time. It was never found.'

'And Strange?' Hedeby said. 'What do you propose we do with him?'

'Same as we'd do for anyone else,' Lund told her. 'Put him in an interview room and throw some questions his way.'

When she was gone Hedeby turned on him as he knew she would.

'The people upstairs are asking why you took him on in the first place.'

Brix tried to control his temper.

'I didn't appoint him, Ruth. He came with the police reforms. When the Ministry of Defence dumped all those people on us they didn't want on the payroll any more.'

'Someone let him in here.'

He pointed at the ceiling.

'They did,' Brix said. 'And they can wash their hands of him if they like.'

The anti-terror bill was in front of the Folketinget. Three readings and then it was through. TV teams stood outside the Parliament building, reporters delivering live to camera. Someone, from Grue Eriksen's office Buch, assumed, had briefed the media already. They were expecting his resignation once the measure was through.

He walked out for some fresh air during a break in the debate, looked round the lobby.

Grue Eriksen and Flemming Rossing were in a huddle by one of the pillars. Buch hadn't bothered with a tie. His career as a minister was over. No need for protocol any more.

He walked over, interrupted the two of them, asked Grue Eriksen for a moment of his time.

A public place. The Prime Minister was all charm.

Rossing stayed there, listening in his smart grey suit, checking his phone for messages from time to time.

'It's about Plough,' Buch said. 'I gather he's being moved sideways. It must be a mistake—'

'It's no mistake. That department was unfit for purpose when Monberg was there. We all know it now. It's time to signal a new beginning.'

'He's a good man!' Buch said, voice rising. 'A

decent, hard-working civil servant. You shouldn't punish him for a politician's errors. Mine and Monberg's . . .'

Rossing pushed his way into the conversation. That big beak nose looked triumphant.

'The Prime Minister tells me you've apologized, Buch. I'm glad to hear it. No hard feelings.'

'Yes, yes. About Plough . . .'

The two of them stared at him. A team, Buch thought. Maybe they had been all along.

'Did you see our draft for your speech at the press conference?' Grue Eriksen added. 'Put in a little personal touch if you want. But don't change anything substantive. I mean that. Now . . .'

Buch was flapping, losing him.

'I've got to talk to someone,' Grue Eriksen said, dashing off. And Rossing was gone just as quickly too.

Buch's phone rang. Plough.

'Everything's ready for the press conference,' he said. 'We can do it whenever the package is done with.'

'Fine . . .'

'Also your wife's turned up at the Ministry. Karina's looking after her.'

'What?' Buch exploded. 'Marie? Who's looking after the kids? Her mother goes to yoga on Mondays. I mean really . . .'

A long silence on the phone.

'I said you'd meet her outside,' Plough responded

185

in an arch, distanced voice. 'Perhaps you'd better ask her.'

Buch marched out of the Parliament building, through the quiet centre of Slotsholmen, past the statue of Kierkegaard, out into the narrow street in front of the Ministry. It was a fine bright day for the moment. The weak winter sun made the twisting dragons opposite look sad and comical.

Karina stood by a black official car near the steps. She wore a black coat and looked dressed for a funeral.

Buch stumbled across the steps.

'Where is she?' he asked, panting as he turned up. 'I don't understand . . .'

He walked up to the big estate. Connie Vemmer was hanging out of the passenger door, long blonde hair blowing in the stiff winter wind, cigarette in hand, coughing smoke out of the window.

'Oh no,' Buch groaned, turning on Karina. But she smiled at him, shrugged, walked off.

'Don't be an arse,' Vemmer barked at him from the car. 'Just listen to me, will you? Get in and let's go for a drive. We need to talk about those medical reports.'

'You cost me my job. What in God's name . . .?'

He turned and started to walk back towards the door.

'Buch! Buch!' She moved more quickly than he expected, was by his side, tugging at his sleeve.

'Do you think I was running errands for that bastard Rossing? He's the man who fired me.'

Still he kept walking. She hung on his arm like an importunate beggar.

'If Rossing knew about that fax in advance someone must have tipped him off.'

Buch marched on.

'OK. Let's leave that for now,' Vemmer suggested. 'Here's the truth. The evidence you wanted was sitting right under your nose all along.'

They were at the door. Buch was opening it.

She let go, swore at him.

'Hey, genius! Why didn't you check the dates on those two medical reports? Why—'

Buch slammed the heavy wooden door behind him.

Connie Vemmer stood out in the bright cold street, finished her cigarette, threw the butt into the gutter along with a few coarse epithets.

The door opened. Buch came out, eyed her.

'What dates?' he asked.

Sebastian Holst's father lived in a half-finished apartment not far from the Amalienborg Palace. Modern paintings everywhere, on the walls, on the floor. Suitcases and building materials. An old building on the way up. Still some distance to go. Walls to be plastered, ceilings to be painted.

He made Lund a coffee and sat next to her at a table by the window.

'I believe Sebastian always had his camera with him,' she began.

He was a hefty man not much older than she was. Bright-blue shirt, hair long and unkempt.

An artist, she guessed. Or an architect. He never said.

'He was always taking pictures. That kind of thing runs in the family. We see the world through our eyes. Why not try to record it?'

'Everything?'

'Everything he could. He took lots of pictures in Afghanistan. The army kept them. They said they were theirs.' Holst frowned. 'You mean you haven't seen them?'

'I saw them. Did the army tell you why his camera was missing?'

'Who told you that? He sent it home a couple of weeks before he was killed. He'd broken it. Sebastian was always a bit clumsy. I was going to get it repaired. Or buy him a new one.' Holst sighed. 'Probably the latter.'

He got up, went to some boxes beneath a line of gaudy paintings. Took out an old-looking camera.

'Film only,' Holst said. 'He was very fastidious about some things.'

'Were there more pictures?'

'No. Only the ones the army have as far as I know. They wouldn't let him post stuff like that back here, would they?'

It was a slender hope and now he'd dashed it.

188

'I guess not. I'm sorry I bothered you,' Lund said, picking up her bag.

'I heard you'd found his squad leader, Raben. I suppose that whole business is going to get dragged up again.'

'What business?'

Holst stared at her. He was no fool.

'Please,' he said. 'I never believed all that bullshit. About there being an officer. Raben made that up as an excuse. He wanted to go into that village anyway. It was his fault Sebastian and the others got killed.'

He was turning the old camera in his hands. A Leica, she saw. Expensive. Marked and worn. His mild, plain face was suddenly wreathed in anger.

'Sebastian said something was going to happen.'

He walked back to the table unsteadily and Lund saw now that everything was a mask, an act of subterfuge. Inside Holst was breaking, weeping.

'I've lost both my sons to a war I don't understand,' he whispered, falling heavily onto a chair near the door. 'One came home in a coffin. The other's not the same.'

He rubbed his eyes with the backs of his hands. 'What did we do wrong? Why did they deserve this?'

The room was quiet except for the low murmur of traffic beyond the window. These walls would stay unplastered, unfinished for a long time. This man was lost in a limbo created by a distant conflict that was beyond him.

His hands played fondly with the old, battered Leica. His mind seemed somewhere else.

'I'm looking for answers,' Lund said.

Holst snapped awake. His sad, dark eyes fixed on her.

'Answers,' she repeated. 'And it's hard.'

'No one asked me any questions before. They just came here to tell me things. What to do. What to say. How to feel.'

'I'm struggling, Holst. People don't talk to me. They want to bury things . . .'

He was frightened. She could see that.

'If there's something you haven't told us—'

'This stops with me,' he said quickly. 'Don't blame anyone else. Not Sebastian. Frederik.'

'Frederik?'

His eyes went to one of two photos on a nearby rollup desk. Two young men in uniform.

'If he doesn't come back God knows . . .'

'It won't go any further,' Lund told him.

Holst got up, shambled back to the boxes, picked up a tiny pocket video camera.

'He had this too. He used to sneak off and keep a diary. It came back hidden inside the Leica.'

He pressed some buttons. Nothing happened. Her heart was in her mouth. Holst rifled through the boxes, found some batteries, put them in the thing.

Flicked a switch. A face came on the tiny screen.

It didn't take long. When she'd finished Lund called Madsen.

'Is Raben fit for questioning?' she asked.

'He's in hospital. How hard can it be?'

'I mean,' she said patiently, 'is he fit to be brought into the Politigården?'

'Wait a minute.'

She did.

He came back.

'The hospital says we can bring him in here for an hour or two. He'll need to go back afterwards. His wife was coming to see him. I guess we can tell her to come here now.'

'She can see him first. Then it's a full interview. I want Brix there as well.'

'That's generous of you.'

She watched the tiny picture on the screen.

'Not really,' Lund said.

They put Raben in a secure waiting room with a uniformed guard. When Louise arrived, mad with the police and fearful about the meeting, she found him waiting for her, standing, arm in a sling. No blood, no visible sign of hurt.

She stayed at the door, didn't know what to say.

'Can we get a bit of privacy?' Raben asked the officer in the room.

'Sorry,' the man said. 'I have to stay.'

'For God's sake . . .' he pleaded.

The officer stared at him, leaned against the wall, watched.

'Let's sit down, Jens,' she said, and they took two chairs at the far end of the room.

He didn't look bad at all. There was something dogged, relentless about this man. The more they threw at him, the harder he came back.

His fingers reached over, took hers. She was cold from waiting outside and didn't respond.

'It was just . . .' He was staring at her in that importunate way he had. The one that said: *forgive everything*. 'I was beside myself.'

He held her more tightly. The familiar smell of hospital soap and medication.

'It won't happen again,' he promised.

She didn't speak.

'I know I said that before. This time—'

'Let's not talk about it now.'

His eyes were on her, pleading, insistent.

'I let you down. You and Jonas. I know that. I was a rotten husband. A rotten father. If I could turn back the clock I would.'

She saw the previous night in her head. Søgaard beneath her. A physical act, nothing more. But one that haunted her.

His voice rose, a note of hope in it.

'Things are looking up. They're listening to me now. They know I was telling the truth. You and Jonas . . .'

'Two years,' she whispered. 'All that time on my own. Even when I came to see you. Even when they left us together in Herstedvester. You scarcely touched me. You just talked about yourself. About the army. About what happened . . .'

'We can put this back together.'

It had to be said. She couldn't bear it any more.

Eyes on his, words forming already in her head.

'No we can't. I slept with Søgaard.'

The shock on his face hurt her. He looked like a child who'd seen something real, something terrible for the first time.

He didn't speak. She slipped her fingers out of his.

'I'm sorry. It didn't mean anything. I was just . . . lonely. I missed you, every single day. I knew you weren't coming back. Not after all this. I just couldn't stand it any longer. Being alone.' She wouldn't cry. That wasn't right. 'Can't you see? It's no use. It's never going to happen for us now. They won't let it.'

His eyes fell to the floor.

'You won't let it, Jens.'

The door opened. The detective she knew as Madsen strode in.

'Sorry,' he said, 'but this meeting's at an end.'

'We're talking,' Raben shot at him.

The uniform cop came and stood next to them. Ready for trouble.

'This is important,' Madsen insisted. 'We need you now.'

Lund had Holst's video on her laptop. Raben opposite her, Brix next to him.

'Do you want to see a lawyer?' she asked as she worked the keyboard, finding the file.

'No.' A surly, juvenile tone in his voice. 'I want to see my wife.'

'Sebastian Holst sent his father a video diary not long before he was killed. Did you know about that?'

Raben shook his head.

'He shouldn't have done. Against regulations.'

'Lots of things are against regulations,' Lund said, turning the laptop round so he could see the screen. 'But he sent it all the same.'

A face there. A young man with a beard and curly hair. He wore a white T-shirt and looked tired and scared. A bare wall in the background, crude plastering and a tourist poster of Copenhagen.

'. . . Don't get worried, Dad,' Sebastian Holst said in a quiet voice, 'but something's not right in our squad.'

Raben watched, caught by the dead man on the screen.

'Why do I have to see this? He was one of my comrades . . .'

'. . . Raben's the worst.' Holst's voice was clear and unmistakable in spite of the tinny speaker. He shook his head, blinked, looked terrified for a moment. 'He's going crazy. He sees Taliban every-where. All he thinks of is killing. Like there's one round every corner and we've got to shoot them first. Christ . . .'

The man in the blue prison suit went quiet, eyes locked on the screen.

'. . . He runs so many risks. We do things we

194

shouldn't. Sometimes . . .' Holst's voice was close to breaking. 'Sometimes he makes up radio messages just so we can get out there and kick ass. This morning . . .' There was shame on Holst's face, alongside the fear. 'We crossed the river to raid a village for the third time. Raben thinks one of the men there's Taliban.'

Holst's hand went to his head.

'They're farmers or bakers or something. Maybe they're running dope. Maybe they're bribing someone. Who isn't here? We still took the place apart. Raben yelled at the guy, called him an informer. Poked a gun in his face. I thought he was going to shoot him.'

'Turn it off,' Raben said, reaching for the laptop.

'No,' Brix said, and pushed back his hand. 'You need to hear this.'

'. . . The kids were screaming,' Holst went on. 'The mother and the old women were crying. They thought we were going to kill them all. Raben's running wild, Dad. He wants to do it all over again tomorrow. It's like he's in the Wild West or something. I talked to the others. They say it's going to be OK. We're back home in a couple of weeks.'

Holst didn't look at the camera.

'They don't want to cross him. They're scared. Me too. But I guess . . .' A nod of his head. 'I guess he knows what he's doing. He's the boss. Good guy when the shit hits the fan. Someone gave him that job. We're just . . .'

195

A smile. He was trying to pull himself together for home.

'Anyway,' Holst said. 'That's me done moaning. Raben says I do it all the time. In a couple of weeks we'll be back in Copenhagen. I can't wait to see you.' He shook his head. 'I'm not coming back here. That's a promise.'

A broader smile.

'I miss you all. I'll see you soon. I'll give your love to big brother when I see him. Bye.'

The dead man in the white T-shirt reached out and turned off the camera. Lund closed the laptop lid.

'Is it true?'

A knock on the door. A call for Brix. He went out to take it.

'Is it true?' Lund asked again.

'Sebastian was only there because his older brother enlisted. It was like a competition between them. He wasn't up to it.'

'He said you broke orders. Threatened civilians.'

'It's war! Not a game! This isn't about Sebastian. It's about Perk.'

'The family he mentioned. Are they the ones you say Perk killed?'

'He murdered them all right.'

'So you and the rest of the squad had been in the house before?'

'The bastard was a crook. Selling dope. Feeding our movements to the Taliban. Scum . . .'

'And you were determined to go back until you proved that?'

Raben shook his head wearily.

'You're not listening to me. What I think's irrelevant. We got that radio call. Perk must have been sent there because whoever was running him knew too.'

'It's not irrelevant, Raben. There's no record of any radio traffic calling you to that house. There was no officer called Perk.'

He swore and there was a look on his face she couldn't quite read. Unless it was defeat.

'What I've told you is the truth. I can't . . .'

Lund was getting mad. She took out some scene of crime and autopsy photos.

'Look at these,' she insisted, spreading the pictures across the table. 'Five people have been killed.'

Anne Dragsholm. Myg Poulsen. Grüner. Lisbeth Thomsen. The priest. Savagely murdered. Still torn corpses caught for ever.

'I've done everything I can to track down that officer,' she told him. 'If you're lying to me and he doesn't exist . . .' Her voice was cracking. 'For pity's sake tell me now and let's bring this nonsense to an end. I'll do my best to help you. That's a promise, and it's more than you deserve.'

He seemed calm. Calmer than her.

'It was my decision to enter the village. The others didn't want to go.' He stared at her. 'They were right. I should have listened to them.'

'You should—'

'But there was an officer. We got that radio message. His name was Perk.' He paused, made sure she was looking at him. 'He's the man I saw. The one who tried to kill me.'

The door opened. Brix came back, sat down.

'We just received documentation from the army,' he said. 'It shows beyond any doubt that the police officer you accused yesterday . . .'

Brix shuffled the photos on the table, glanced at them.

'He wasn't in Afghanistan at the time. He wasn't Perk. Couldn't be.'

The man in the prison suit swore and shook his head.

'What about Sebastian's older brother?' Lund asked. 'Do you know him?'

'Not really.' His voice was low and miserable. 'He was a doctor working out of Camp Viking.'

'An army surgeon? Frederik?'

'Why ask me?' Raben shot back at her, punching his head with his fist. 'I'm just crazy, aren't I?'

Then he stamped hard on the pictures of the mangled corpses in front of him.

'Someone killed these people, didn't they? And that wasn't me.'

'We need to talk to Frederik Holst,' Brix said. 'Fix it.'

The debate on the anti-terror package had dragged on into the early evening. Birgitte Agger's MPs were doing everything they could to stall it. Buch had spent an hour driving round Copenhagen with Connie Vemmer, watching her smoke, listening all the time.

When he marched back into his office Karina and Plough were waiting for him. In the room outside a desk was set up for the resignation press conference. Microphones in place already.

'I'm sorry I tricked you,' Karina told him as he marched to his desk. 'You needed to see her.'

Buch took his chair. It felt familiar. Comfortable. Right.

'We know you can't tell us everything,' Plough added. 'But if you felt able . . .'

He had a set of papers inside a yellow document folder. Buch read the top page again, absorbed in what Vemmer had said.

'Even if you don't act upon it, Thomas,' Karina added, 'I thought you deserved to hear what she had to say.'

Still Buch kept quiet.

'I'm resigned to going to Skopje,' Plough added. 'It's in Macedonia apparently.'

Buch stared at the microphones.

'Thomas,' Karina added quietly. 'If you're going to do something you need to do it—'

'When does the vote start?'

'Soon.'

'And Krabbe's there?'

'Of course.'

He grabbed the yellow folder from the desk and got up.

'But Krabbe's got nothing to do with it!' she cried as he bustled for the door.

'He's a decent man,' Buch cried as he left. 'Not my type but . . .' He waved the papers. 'Krabbe is all I've got.'

The Folketinget before a vote was like a theatre between acts. An interval was in place, men and women in serious business suits conferring in whispers in the anterooms outside the chamber.

Buch saw Krabbe chatting to one of Grue Eriksen's aides at the far end of the room. Then he disappeared into the toilets.

No one at the urinals. Buch walked up and down the stall doors, saying, 'Krabbe? Are you here? You are. I know it. I saw you come in. Krabbe?'

He paced the length of them, looking for the red locked sign and feet underneath the door.

Only one appeared occupied. Yellow folder in hand, Buch hitched up his trousers, got down and placed his bearded face against the cold tiles to peer through.

'Krabbe? Is that you?'

All Buch could see were two black trouser legs down around skinny ankles, some shiny shoes and a very colourful pair of underpants.

'Bloody hell,' said a disgruntled voice inside. 'This really takes the biscuit. If you want to talk to me, Buch, call my secretary. I'm enjoying a private moment if you please.'

'The medical report about the extra hand was faxed in August,' Buch said, squinting beneath the door. 'But the revised report didn't arrive until October!'

'Is that so?' Krabbe sighed.

Buch pushed the yellow folder beneath the door.

'So you see the implication?' he said, thrusting the documents towards the hidden Krabbe. 'First there's one report suggesting civilians have been murdered.'

A hand came down from above and took the folder.

'What a pathetic attempt to cling to office!'

Buch got up, wondered how hard it would be to force the door open.

'This is nothing of the kind. All I want is the truth and so do you. You see what I mean? In spite of the initial report nobody did anything for two months. Two whole months!'

His hand was banging on the door. Buch regretted that but he was getting mad again.

'There was no need for any urgency, was there?' Krabbe called. 'It was the hand of the bomber.'

Before Buch could reply the door opened and the man inside walked out, marching for the sink.

'Why did no one say anything in all that time?' Buch asked. 'What were they up to?'

He followed, watched Krabbe wash his hands

in a very precise and punctilious fashion, plenty of soap and hot water.

'When the first report arrived Grue Eriksen was proposing additional funding to get more troops in Afghanistan.' Buch jabbed at the papers in Krabbe's hands. 'Here and here. See for yourself. The money was promptly approved when the Folketinget came back from recess in October.'

Krabbe was reading the sheets in front of him.

'You and your party voted for that,' Buch went on. 'So did I. Would we have been so keen if we'd known our troops had been accused of a civilian massacre?'

'This proves nothing. It's just speculation.' Krabbe passed the folder back to Buch. 'I can't believe Grue Eriksen would manipulate things—'

'That's what happened, dammit! See for yourself.'

Krabbe looked at his hands and thrust them under the dryer.

'Go ahead and push for a stricter anti-terror package if you like. But you'll be picking on an innocent party. Those pathetic immigrants didn't kill our people. It was someone—'

'Who?' Krabbe asked.

'I don't know. Someone closer to home. I'm asking for your help. I think—'

'We've worked so hard for this . . .'

'Krabbe!' Buch's voice was high and hard. 'Let's be candid. What you believe in mostly I abhor. You feel the same about me I'm sure. But this I know . . .' His fat forefinger waved in Krabbe's narrow pale face. 'You don't like being lied to. And you don't like being used.'

Buch took the yellow folder and waved it in front of him.

'There,' he said. 'We've something in common. Now the question is . . .'

Krabbe was listening intently.

'What are we going to do about it?'

The farewell ceremony for the new detachment was over. Torsten Jarnvig stood outside the Ryvangen Barracks hall watching the men and their families saying goodbye. Søgaard was there too.

'I think they're going off in a good mood,' he said as Jarnvig approached.

'You never told me we'd got radio traffic five days before Raben started shrieking.' Jarnvig threw the documents on the bonnet of Søgaard's G-Wagen. 'I've been through every last one of the traffic logs. I saw this . . .'

He was still mad. The bitter look on Søgaard's face didn't help.

'What?' he asked.

Jarnvig slammed his hand on the papers.

'We got a message. August, two years ago. When I was in Kabul.'

Søgaard picked up the logs.

'Five days before the incident.'

'So you said,' Søgaard muttered. He flicked through the pages.

'It was from a special forces unit. No ID in the records. No names.'

Søgaard shook his head.

'I don't understand. What are you implying?'

'Implying?' Jarnvig bellowed. 'It's here in black and white. We had a unit operating just thirty kilometres from the village where Raben's squad ended up.'

'I never saw any of this.'

He put the papers back on the bonnet.

'You were officer in command in my absence. Every message comes through the office—'

'I'm telling you. I never saw it.'

Jarnvig's fist pummelled the vehicle.

'It's in the file, Søgaard. Even if you were half asleep on duty, which I doubt, you investigated Raben's claims. He said someone from special forces was in the vicinity. We didn't believe him because you . . .' Jarnvig's hand went out. 'You told us no one was there.'

Nothing. Not a word.

'You said they were seeing ghosts.'

'They were. This doesn't prove he wasn't lying.'

'It proves he could be right! And you never mentioned it.' Jarnvig took a step closer to the tall precise man in the neat dress uniform. 'Why was that? Come on. Out with it.'

'I've no knowledge of this. I never saw the message. I never knew special forces were in the area.'

'It's here!' Jarnvig roared, waving the papers in his face.

'If there's an official complaint being filed I'd like to see the details. I want Operational Command informed. General Arild's team was involved in the investigation too.'

Jarnvig stared at him, waited.

'Look,' Søgaard pleaded. 'I don't have time for this now. I've got to go to the airport. We're due to fly in five hours.'

'You're going nowhere. I'm suspending you from duty as of now. I've got someone to take your place on that plane. You're confined to barracks until I know what the hell went on there.'

'I'm due in Helmand!' Søgaard shouted.

'Not this time,' Jarnvig told him. 'You're staying here.'

Forty minutes later, after eating supper with a silent Louise and a tired Jonas, Jarnvig retreated to his office. Jan Arild was waiting for him.

Jarnvig tried to smile at him. It was obvious what had happened. Søgaard had been on the phone.

'I'm glad you came,' he said, taking a seat opposite the general. 'I was about to call you.'

'You've been unreachable all day, Torsten,' Arild said, leaning back in his chair, hands behind his head.

'I was checking out the hunting,' Jarnvig lied. 'We ought to pick up on that again. Get out of these uniforms once in a while.'

'I told you,' Arild said with a scowl. 'I don't have time for that any more. Not your kind anyway.'

'That's a shame.'

'Not really. Those days are long gone. I went somewhere, Torsten. You just . . .' He looked round the little office. 'You just served, didn't you?'

'Raben could have been right,' Jarnvig said, ignoring the taunt. 'There was radio contact with a Danish special forces unit five days before his squad was attacked.'

Arild, in his green uniform, cap on the desk, ginger hair perfectly combed, looked bored.

'We must tell the police,' Jarnvig said.

'Aren't we putting up with enough shit from them already? Why invite their attention any more?'

'Because Raben could be telling the truth!'

'The man's mad,' Arild declared. 'A shame. He was a good soldier once, or so I gather. We're the army. We don't need civilians to come and tell us what to do. I don't understand why this concerns you so much.'

'It's possible Søgaard withheld information. Covered up what went on. I was in Kabul at the time. He was in sole command. He says he never saw the radio traffic. That can't be true. It came across my desk every single day.'

'That's a very serious accusation.'

'I know.'

'And you're right,' Arild agreed. 'Something is amiss.' He stared at Jarnvig. 'But it isn't Søgaard, is it?'

Torsten Jarnvig looked at Arild's smiling face and knew this was going wrong.

'You're a rotten liar,' the general said with a laugh. 'Always were. Let me prove it. Look me in the face and tell me. Did you help Raben escape PET the night of the ball?'

'What do you mean?'

'It's a simple question. So simple I already know the answer. I told you in confidence he was under surveillance. Yet he still got out of the building. Someone saw you go into a side room. Raben was in there, wasn't he?'

'What happened in Helmand is important, Jan. We need to investigate.'

'Don't use my name, Colonel. Twenty years ago that might have worked. Not now.'

Arild picked up his cap.

'You're a small man. With limited ideas and meagre ambitions. Dammit!' Arild's voice rose in sudden fury. 'You can't even lie to save your own skin.'

'Can't we leave the personal issues to one side . . .?'

'Come on!' Arild urged. 'Just answer, will you? Look me in the face and say it. Did you see Raben or not?'

Torsten Jarnvig took off his glasses, stayed silent.

Arild threw back his head and laughed.

Then was serious in an instant.

'I've called the military police. You'll go with them. Don't make a fuss.'

'This . . .' Jarnvig brandished the documents from Operational Command. '. . . will not go away.'

Arild smiled.

'But it has. And so will you.'

He looked at the down-at-heel office Jarnvig had occupied for the best part of a decade.

'This place can be Søgaard's now. It needs a lick of paint if you ask me.'

Lund spent the best part of an hour trying to track down Frederik Holst. It seemed hopeless. Then Brix walked in, something in his hand.

She finished the call, thanked Holst's father who was playing scared and ignorant again.

'No one wants to talk about Frederik Holst,' Lund told Brix. 'Even his relatives.'

'Maybe they've got good reason. I got through to someone in Operational Command. We just missed him. Holst's back in Afghanistan. He's been on home leave in Copenhagen for a month. It seems he was renting a short-term apartment in Islands Brygge, not far from where Grüner died. Maybe he didn't tell anyone.'

'Why would he do that?'

Brix showed her a plastic evidence sleeve. A photograph inside.

'We found this in the rubbish he left when he cleared out.'

An army picture. Soldiers in a brief moment of relaxation. Raben's team set against the Danish flag, cans of beer in their hands. Happy. Drunk. Sebastian Holst was at the front shouting, arm raised in the air. Behind the rest of them. Myg Poulsen. Lisbeth Thomsen. Grüner. The others.

Combat fatigues. A table full of food and drink. A moment off-duty.

There were cross marks in black felt pen through all of the faces except one: Jens Peter Raben.

Lund walked to the desk, checked her calls, her papers. The idea had been nagging her for a while.

'You can get us on the soldiers' flight tonight.' She thought for a moment. 'If I need my passport I'll have to go home first.' Lund looked at him. 'Will I need my passport? It's Danish territory, isn't it? We've got jurisdiction.'

Brix was so surprised he couldn't help but laugh.

'What the hell are you saying?'

'We've been running round in circles.' Lund pulled out some files she thought she might need. 'Frederik Holst saw his brother's video diary. He sent the camera back. The father confirmed it.'

'Lund—'

'Frederik was at the field hospital when they brought in his brother's body. If he was here we'd be bringing him in for questioning right now. We can't let it go just because he's in Helmand . . .'

'I need to talk to Hedeby. There are avenues to go through. The permission . . .'

It was her turn to laugh.

209

'Come on. That'll take days. We can't wait on paperwork.'

'There are procedures.'

'Don't give me that.' She kept her eyes on him, wouldn't let go. 'You pulled that information about Holst out of Operational Command when I couldn't. You know the people to talk to.'

She picked up the files, asked one of the desk officers to check some medical reports.

'I can't get you on the army flight,' Brix told her. 'It's too late.'

'There's nowhere else left to look.'

'It's a war zone!'

She gazed at him and knew it had to be said.

'If this was Ruth Hedeby's show I'd be back in Gedser already. I don't know what you've got over her and I don't care. Just do it, will you?'

He was wavering.

'You can't go into Afghanistan on your own.'

'I know that.'

'So what . . .?' Brix went quiet for a moment. Knew what she was thinking. 'Is that a good idea?'

'Fix the flights and the paperwork. Leave the rest to me.'

Brix was on the phone straight away. This would happen, she thought. There'd be a brief chance to see the distant, enclosed world of Helmand. Then home, with answers.

The last stamp in her passport was for a holiday in Mallorca with Mark two years before. Her

210

son had moped most of the time. Lund had hated it.

She walked down the black marble corridor, found the interview room, kicked out the uniform man deputed to watch Strange.

When he was gone she sat next to him on the bench seat. Jeans and a T-shirt. Tattoo just visible on his shoulder. Strange looked like the kind of man who could go anywhere at the drop of a hat.

He puffed out his cheeks, sighed, said nothing.

'My old partner . . . Jan Meyer,' Lund said. 'We got to this warehouse.'

Strange stopped staring at the floor, looked at her instead.

'It was dark. I went inside. I didn't think there was anyone in the building.' Lund's hands wouldn't keep still. This was so hard to say. 'Then Meyer came in too. He knew someone was in there with me.'

Strange's eyes wouldn't leave her.

'I shouldn't have gone in on my own. It was all my fault. We found the man who shot Meyer.' She wiped her mouth with the sleeve of her black and white Faroese jumper for no reason. 'What good does that do? He's still stuck in a wheelchair.'

A pause. She didn't know whether to say it or not.

'Sometimes I wonder if he wishes he was dead. He looked that way when I saw him in hospital. But—'

'People can change. Get better,' Strange said.

'Sometimes,' she agreed. 'Sometimes they're who they are for ever.' Another moment of hesitation. 'Like me.'

He watched her, hands on knees, that odd, calm, angular face interested as usual.

'I shut myself down. I got that job in Gedser and I told myself . . .' Her voice was firm and unwavering. 'If you can't feel anything then it can't hurt you. Gedser suited me fine.'

Strange raised an eyebrow.

'I wanted to stay buried there for ever. If you hadn't turned up I would have done too.' She fidgeted a little closer to him, looked into his eyes. 'Not happy. Not sad. Not anything.'

The eyebrow went down. A ghost of a smile on Strange's stubbly face.

'I'm sorry,' she said, staring directly into his grey-blue eyes. 'It's hard to trust people if you can't trust yourself sometimes. Do you understand?'

A moment of indecision. It could go any way.

Then he laughed, that low, self-deprecating chuckle she'd come to like.

'Yeah,' Strange said. 'I always pick the difficult ones. Now what?'

Closeness.

It frightened her. Always would.

'We have to leave.'

'Where to?' Strange looked at his T-shirt and jeans. 'They didn't even let me get my jacket when they dragged me in here.'

She slapped his leg, got up.

'We'll pick it up along the way. And your passport too.'

Ulrik Strange sat on the bench seat, mouth wide open.

'Are you coming or not?' she asked. 'We've a plane to catch.'

One hour later. Kastrup airport. Brix had organized for the scheduled flight to be held for fifteen minutes so they could make it. He walked with them down the gangway. Passed over a folder.

'There's Frederik Holst's personnel details and a warrant for his arrest. Some contact phone numbers in Afghanistan. Here . . .'

A satellite phone in a case with some instructions.

'This should work anywhere you're going. If the army give you trouble call me. Strange?'

He had his jacket back, and his swagger.

'Yeah?'

'According to your file you speak Pashto.'

Strange laughed.

'Don't shoot. Where's the toilet? Can you get a beer round here? That good enough?'

Brix wasn't in the mood.

'You've got military experience. Lund hasn't. I want you to take the lead on the ground.' The chief looked at her. 'You hear that? You do what he says.'

Strange laughed again and shook his head.

213

'It's three hours to Istanbul,' Brix said. 'The visas and authorities have been sent ahead by fax. When you get to Turkey the army will meet you and put you on board one of their flights to Camp Bastion. Five hours. You'll be there in the morning our time. Midday theirs. Try to get some sleep.'

'You haven't been on an army plane,' Strange told him.

The door was open. The flight attendant was beckoning them on board.

'You're under military control for the duration,' Brix added. 'Don't go wandering off. You've got one day there only. You come back the same way. The flights are fixed. You'll be in Kastrup thirty-six hours from now. Any questions?'

Neither of them spoke.

Brix sighed.

'For God's sake take care,' he said.

Then watched as they got on the plane.

When Brix got back to his office there was a string of messages from the army. Operational Command, Ryvangen and more distant branches too.

He ignored them, called together the team, told them to dig up everything they could on Frederik Holst. Phone records, credit card activity while he was on leave. A full profile.

'I want his movements day by day, from the moment he got off the plane to when he got back on it. Where was he at the time of the murders? What does his father know?'

Hedeby was standing in the shadows at the end of the room, close to the corridor that led to her office. She didn't need to beckon him. The summons was in her face.

Brix read through some notes Madsen had made after talking to Holst's neighbours in the rented flat in Islands Brygge. They didn't amount to much but he took his time over them. Then, when he was ready, he followed Hedeby into her room, took a chair, watched as she closed the door behind her.

She was furious. She often was since Lund had returned to the Politigården. Hedeby was once a reliable detective. Promotion had turned her into a civil servant, a manager of budgets and resources and she never even noticed.

'I've had a call from the Ministry asking for an explanation,' she said.

'Understandable,' Brix agreed.

'Along with half the army.' She stood by the window, looked down at him.

Brix shrugged.

'It happened very quickly. Strange was cleared and Lund picked up this lead . . .'

She walked to the filing cabinet, slammed her fist on it. Brix tried not to laugh.

'I don't give a shit about Lund and Strange! What the hell——?'

'We found a suspect. He's just returned to Helmand. His brother was in Raben's squad. One of the men who died.'

'And no one told me?'

'The brother, the one we're looking at, is called Frederik Holst. He'd been tracking the members of Raben's squad.' Brix offered her some of the papers Madsen had given him. 'He's a doctor at one of the field hospitals in Lashkar Gah.'

She seized the sheet, looked at it.

'Holst has a motive. He was here in Copenhagen when the murders occurred, so he had the opportunity too. We couldn't ignore—'

'Dammit, Lennart,' she bawled at him. 'You know this has to go through me.'

Brix leaned back in the chair, put his long arms behind his head, thought about his answer.

'But you'd have said no, Ruth. So what was the point?'

For once she seemed speechless.

'You'd have pushed some papers around the desk,' he went on. 'Called someone in the Ministry who wasn't there. Waited until morning.'

No answer. Just those wide, wide eyes.

'I hate waiting,' Brix went on. 'I don't much appreciate being lied to either. Holst looks like our man. There was a flight going. I managed to rush through the visas and the authorizations—'

'I can't believe you'd do this to me. After all that—'

'The plane's gone. They're in the air. It's done,' he said with a shrug. 'That's it.'

Brix got up, made for the door. Madsen was there, holding a phone.

'It's the Ministry of Justice,' he said, looking at Hedeby. 'They want an update.'

Brix went to see Raben in the interview room. Tired, arm still in a sling, moaning for painkillers, not that he looked as if he needed them.

One of the younger detectives was trying to get him to talk. Raben glanced at Brix as he came in. A look that said: is this the best you've got?

'Tell me about Frederik Holst,' the young cop said.

Raben yawned.

'What was your relationship like?'

'We didn't have one. He was a doctor. Didn't mix with the troops unless he had to.'

Brix sat down, said, 'How's it going?'

'It's not. He just sticks to the same stupid story.'

'Maybe that's because the same stupid story's the truth,' Raben said wearily.

'Smart arse,' the cop replied. 'You just start coming up with something or you're here all night.'

'All the time in the world,' Raben said with a smile.

'Leave us,' Brix ordered and waited for the two of them to be alone.

Raben didn't look quite so confident then.

Brix sorted through his papers, glanced at him across the desk.

'I talked to Herstedvester. Frederik Holst wanted

217

to visit you there. Phoned five times. You said no to each one.'

'I want to see my wife.'

'We found several letters in Holst's flat. They were addressed to you.' He pushed a folder across the table. 'He posted them to the prison. You sent them back.'

'Why are you telling me things I already know?'

'Holst was angry with you. He saw that video. He blamed you for his brother's death.'

'Ask Holst about that. Not me.'

'We plan to. Lund's on her way to Helmand now.'

Raben's tired eyes opened.

'This isn't going to stop until we get to the bottom of it, Raben. Until we know what happened. It's in your interests to help us—'

Raben's free hand thumped on the table.

'I did help you! I told you the truth!' His face was stern and fixed. His eyes on Brix. 'An officer executed that family. He brought the Taliban down on us. Not me.'

'You said it was one of our men. But we checked. He wasn't even in Helmand at the time. How can we believe—?'

'I want to talk to my wife.'

Raben's eyes were on the table.

'You need to reconsider the statement you gave us. The one that incriminated Ulrik Strange. Do that and we can try to move things forward. I'm telling you. It can't have been him.'

218

Raben was starting to get mad.

'Talk to Colonel Jarnvig. He believes me. It's all there in the files. You just have to look in the right places. You've got to ignore their lies.'

'Whose lies?' Brix wondered.

'The special people,' Raben yelled. 'The spooks. The ghosts. The guys . . .' His hand jerked towards the door. 'The guys who come and go and you never even know their name. That's who. Ask Jarnvig.'

'Jarnvig's under arrest. The military police are questioning him. They say he helped you get out from under the noses of PET.'

Nothing.

'You've got a preliminary court hearing tomorrow. Do yourself a favour.'

'You mean do you a favour?'

'Just come up with a story we can believe, will you?' Brix looked at the man across from him. 'Is there anything I can get you? Some medication? A doctor?'

'I told you already. I want my wife.'

Brix got up from the table.

'I called her before I came in here. Trouble is . . .' He sighed. 'She's got more than you to worry about now.'

Christian Søgaard was in Jarnvig's house, going through his papers in the study with Said Bilal.

'Let me get this straight,' he said, looking at the young officer squirming in the seat opposite.

'Jarnvig came to you and wanted details of all the radio traffic from two years ago?'

'That's right,' Bilal said.

'Why didn't you tell me?'

Bilal blinked.

'He said no one else was to know.'

'Why?' Søgaard asked. 'What did he think was going on?'

'I don't know! The colonel didn't seem to be himself. He was . . . asking all kinds of things.'

A noise behind. Søgaard glanced and saw Louise Raben, jeans and leather jacket, as if she was ready to go out somewhere.

'Quiet,' he said to Bilal and got up from the desk.

A big smile for her. Søgaard felt more than a little awkward.

'Hi,' he said. 'How's things? Going somewhere?'

'Where's my father? I've been looking all around the camp. Isn't he back yet?'

Søgaard perched on one of the chairs. Jarnvig's house. Soon it could be his. And all it contained.

'Your father's been taken in for questioning. The military police are holding him.'

She blinked, looked at him, said nothing.

'He talked to Jens at the cadets' ball. Helped him shake off PET.'

'That's a lie,' she said straight off. 'I was with him. You were there too.'

'He went off on his own when we were dancing. Someone saw him.'

'Who?'

'I don't know,' Søgaard said. 'But they told General Arild. Your father confessed immediately. You know what he's like. He wouldn't . . .'

His voice trailed off.

'Wouldn't what? Lie? Try to hide things?'

'He wouldn't do that,' Søgaard agreed. 'I'm sorry but . . . it's serious. He's been acting strangely ever since this began.'

A shake of his blond head.

'Tonight he was accusing me of things . . .'

'What kind of things?'

'He seems obsessed by the murders.'

'What kind of things?' she repeated.

A noise behind. Søgaard could see Bilal in his green uniform trying to stay out of sight.

'He said I'd been concealing radio traffic from the investigation. It's ridiculous. As if he believes all that crap Jens made up.'

She hugged herself in the black jacket, stared at the living room with its plaques and photos and memorabilia. The debris of Torsten Jarnvig's army life.

'I'll do what I can to help him,' Søgaard said, coming to stand behind her. 'It's a serious charge. He's been under a lot of pressure. With a record like his it won't come to anything—'

'So you're saying he believed Jens? After all this time?'

Søgaard shrugged.

'Sounds like it. The whole idea's crazy . . .' He

wasn't used to this kind of conversation. It felt uncomfortable. 'What about you? Jonas? Can I get you some food or something?'

'We can look after ourselves, thank you. I want to see my father.'

'They won't allow that. Not until they're ready.'

'He gave everything he had to the army, Søgaard! How can they treat him like this?'

'Your father talked to Jens. He helped him get away. What do you expect?'

'If you hear anything I want to know. Do I at least get that?'

'Of course.' He touched her arm. She pulled back, glared at him. 'If you and Jonas—'

'I told you. We're fine.'

She was going. He got up, put out a hand to stop her.

'Louise. You don't think I'm involved in this, do you?'

'No,' she said too easily. 'Why would I think that?'

Søgaard watched her go then went back to the desk.

'You should have told me,' Søgaard said. 'I don't give a shit about Jarnvig's orders. I shouldn't have to hear it from Arild.'

He put his fist in Bilal's dark face.

'You answer to me. You did then. You do now.'

Then he looked at the documents on the desk, radio logs, maps, details of troop movements, and brushed them to the floor with a single violent sweep of his arm.

Bilal sat there in silence.

'Now pick it all up,' Søgaard ordered and got to his feet.

Around the time Lund and Strange's delayed flight lifted off from Kastrup, Thomas Buch found himself watching the Folketinget's decision on the anti-terror package hang in the balance.

Krabbe's sudden demands for more information had led Grue Eriksen to postpone the vote. The Prime Minister had summoned Buch to a brief and ill-tempered meeting in his office. There Buch revealed that a police team had been despatched to Helmand to investigate the alleged atrocity. Flemming Rossing had shrieked about being kept in the dark once more and threatened Buch with expulsion from the parliamentary group. Grue Eriksen listened and said little. Slotsholmen was in the midst of a feverish crisis, one Thomas Buch had never witnessed before.

One, he knew only too well, of his own making.

Back in the Ministry afterwards Plough gave him a judgemental stare and said, 'You're not a man for cards, are you?'

'Of course not. Why?'

'It's called overplaying your hand. All we know is the police sent a team to Helmand. We've no idea what if anything—'

'Do they have any idea what the doctor might say about the hand?'

'No!' Plough replied. 'If you'd only allow me to brief you before shooting off your mouth. The doctor's now their prime murder suspect—'

'I need more ammunition by tomorrow. Grue Eriksen won't let this run for ever.' He turned to Karina. 'See if you can get any communication between the military and the Ministry of Defence on this.'

'By tomorrow?' she asked, wide-eyed.

'Don't we have the right of access?'

'Up to a point. It would normally take a week—'

'We don't have a week! Oh for pity's sake . . .'

He marched into his room, sat at his desk, stared at the growing mountain of papers.

Karina pulled up a chair.

'What is it?' he asked.

'Here's a thought. We stop shouting at people. Instead let's try persuading them it's in their own interest they talk.'

Buch pulled out a drawer, found a chocolate bar, bit on it.

'I've no idea what you're talking about,' he said, mouth half full.

'The only one who can deliver you Grue Eriksen's head is Flemming Rossing.'

Plough groaned.

'Even if that's true, Karina, why on earth would he talk to us?'

'To save himself?' Buch suggested. 'If we make

224

Rossing feel he's more to lose by sticking with Grue Eriksen than coming clean . . .'

He scratched his straggly beard.

'If Rossing knows it's all going to come out anyway he's going to want to limit the damage. When will we hear from Lund?'

'They land in the morning,' Plough said. 'They've only got one day. It seems a lot to ask—'

His phone rang. Without thinking he answered it.

Home. Jutland. His wife, Marie, going on about the kids, about how he hadn't called.

She was mad. So was he. The dam burst. All the suppressed rage and misery came out at that moment, engulfing the wrong person, the last one he would have blamed for anything. Thomas Buch shouted at her, called his wife bad names, used words he never liked.

When he finished he put down his mobile and stared at it on his desk as if the phone was responsible somehow. Karina and Plough stared at him, embarrassed, silent.

'No more family calls for now,' Buch ordered in a meek and miserable voice. 'Not until I say.'

It was close to midnight. He wondered what the time was in Afghanistan. How the curious and persistent woman he'd met just once, in a banqueting hall kitchen beneath a wedding, would fare in such a distant, hostile land.

CHAPTER 10

Tuesday 22nd November

Lund slept on the passenger jet to Istanbul. Slept after they got on the basic, uncomfortable military transport plane from Atatürk airport to Camp Bastion. Halfway through she woke up, opened her eyes, found her head on Strange's shoulder. He didn't know she was watching him. His placid, ordinary face was staring ahead, at nothing at all.

Memories, she thought. He was recalling the army. Perhaps they never lost it. There was nothing to say. So she shuffled her head from him, slumped in the seat, tried to sleep again, was unsure whether she managed it on the long, boring flight into a place she couldn't imagine, let alone picture.

At Bastion airfield they were driven to Viking, the Danish quarter. It looked like a shanty town of mobile accommodation blocks and tents, with constant traffic, the to and fro of men and equipment.

After their documents had been checked a bored,

taciturn officer gave them a soldier as a driver then pointed them to some equipment in the corner of the office. Strange helped her. A hard helmet, covered in khaki material. A jacket so heavy and uncomfortable she hated it the moment he started putting it on her.

'Why do I need a bulletproof vest?' Lund asked. 'We're just going to interview a doctor, aren't we?'

The soldier and the officer stared at her.

'Are we going behind the front line?' she asked, shrugging off the thick, heavy vest.

'This is Helmand,' the officer said. 'There is no front line. Put it on or you can go back to Copenhagen right now.'

Strange was gently pulling it over her arms.

'It's called body armour,' he said. 'It isn't magic. But it can stop an AK47 round from distance. Keep you alive if we hit an IED. Block a knife—'

'Not much use if they shoot you in the head. Or blow your legs off.'

'Dammit, Lund. We've got these back in head-quarters. You're supposed to wear them whenever you go out on an armed incident. Don't you even bother then?'

She didn't want to tell him: usually a gun was too much trouble.

'Not much need in Gedser,' she said, then let him drag the khaki vest over her slender frame, tried to shuffle to a position that chafed the least.

'Very fetching,' the officer said. 'Your flight out

of here is at seven this evening. You will be on it. Even if I have to strap you in myself.'

Twenty minutes later the Land Rover was bouncing along a rough stony track that seemed to lead to nowhere. The terrain was dry and bare and mountainous, the air cold and dusty. Snow covered the peaks of the surrounding hills. No villages. No other traffic. The driver, twenty-five at the most, with sunglasses and a skimpy moustache, seemed to know the way by heart. Travel had never interested Lund much. Helmand wasn't going to change that.

'This is a bad time for us,' the soldier said. 'We had two suicide bombers this morning. Been quiet for weeks. Then the bastards come back.'

They sat next to one another in the back, Strange at home in the body armour and helmet, Lund fidgeting with it.

'The hospital's frantic,' the driver added. 'Buckle your helmet, please. And your vest. Otherwise they're useless.'

Strange sighed, reached for the straps and did them up before she could say anything. The soldier didn't look happy having a woman in the vehicle.

'Do you want to . . . freshen up when we get to the base?' he asked.

'Just take us to the hospital, will you?' she said. 'We want to see Frederik Holst.'

Thirty minutes later they met the first traffic. A truck with locals in the open back. Farm workers maybe. They squatted in the rear, stared at the Land Rover as it went past. Lund saw the driver tense as they got near. Soon there were more vans, a few battered cars, some army vehicles. Troop carriers, jeeps, armoured cars.

After an hour they pulled into a small town. Women and girls walking round a few vegetable stalls, faces hidden inside gaudy burkas. Men by the roadside sipping tea from glasses, watching the army Land Rover with keen dark eyes.

A checkpoint. Soldiers in uniform with the Danish flag, rifles in their arms. They looked at the driver's papers and waved them through.

It was more like a run-down market hall than a hospital. A single-storey grubby brick building; on the side a large red cross crudely painted against the crumbling plasterwork. She thought of the spotless, shiny corridors of the Rigshospitalet. Copenhagen was a world away. She was a stranger here, a foreigner, unwelcome to locals and soldiers alike.

Lund climbed out of the door. A man in a turban was hacking a side of raw lamb on a wooden table just outside the perimeter fence, flies all round. He watched as she gathered up her clipboard and folders.

'They all look like that,' Strange said. 'Ordinary. Innocent probably.' His calm, intelligent eyes scanned the area, the way they must have done so many times when he was serving here. 'You never know until it's too late.'

There was a sign by the hospital entrance: No weapons. The driver checked his with security. They had none anyway.

It was dark inside, the smell a fetid mix of medicine and decay. A couple of locals, an elderly man and a young woman, sat in a corner, crouched on the floor, back against the wall, the woman wailing, the man glassy-eyed.

'You couldn't wait, could you?' the soldier at the desk asked. 'We've got casualties. Ours and theirs.'

'No,' Lund said. 'We can't.'

She walked on. Peered in and out of the side rooms where men struggled on crutches, lay moaning on ancient gurneys. Further along three Afghans sat patiently on chairs, their clothes covered in blood, bandages round their hands.

Someone pushed at her from behind, barked an order to get out of the way.

A stretcher, a figure on it, legs just visible. Or the remains of them, flesh and bone.

A look of pain and disbelief in the soldier's face. A nurse was fixing a drip into his arm, feeding what Lund guessed was painkiller into a vein.

A memory: Jan Meyer unconscious, leaping with the electric shocks they gave him in the ambulance when he was shot.

She hated hospitals. This place more than any she'd seen.

'I'm going home in a week,' the man on the

stretcher said in croaky Danish. 'Home. You hear that?'

He struggled to get his head up, peered down his body.

Lund looked again. Two stumps where his feet should have been.

The soldier didn't cry. Just puffed out his cheeks in a big, deep breath then lay back on the grubby stretcher pillow and gazed at the ceiling.

Strange was by her side, silent, watching too.

'Let's get this over with,' she said.

The operating theatre was nothing more than a small area closed off with curtains. One circular light, two nurses in white uniforms, a surgeon in green. A body on the table, mask on, eyes closed, unconscious. A gaping wound in his torso. Peeling walls, barely white as if someone had been fighting a losing battle to keep them clean. A ragged piece of fabric at the window, the white winter sun pouring through the holes.

'Holst?' Lund said, when the man in green came away from the table and issued some orders to the nurses. 'We're—'

'I know who you are. Wait outside, fifteen minutes. Then we'll talk.'

They sat in a small room with an arched ceiling and a single light. Strange let her take off the helmet. The body armour stayed. It took thirty minutes then Holst marched in, tore off his paper mask, threw it into the bin, began to wash his hands in the simple basin.

'We want to know what you did in Copenhagen,' Lund said, watching him.

'I was on leave. Three weeks. A month. Something like that.'

He sat down. A big, unsmiling man with the face of a surly teenager. The faintest resemblance to his dead brother. Frederik looked tougher, more worn by the war. Lund was struck by a thought: he should have been the soldier, Sebastian the doctor.

'So what?' he said and reached for a drawer, took out a packet of cigarettes, lit one, blew smoke towards the window.

'Where were you?' Strange asked.

'What business is it of yours?'

'We've got a warrant for your arrest. Come up with some answers or you'll be on a plane with us tonight.'

He looked surprised.

'I wanted some time to myself. That's all.'

'You didn't talk to your father?' Lund wanted to know.

'Not much. I told you.' He pushed back some boxes of dressing and drugs on the desk, a stethoscope. 'Do you mind telling me who I'm supposed to have murdered? Just out of politeness, you know.'

She took out the photos from her bag: Anne Dragsholm, Myg Poulsen, David Grüner, Lisbeth Thomsen, Gunnar Torpe.

Holst picked up the picture of Dragsholm.

'The rest look familiar. Who's she?'

'Where were you?' Lund repeated. 'What did you do?'

'I'm a surgeon. I spend my life saving people. Not killing them. You could have phoned. I would have saved you the trip.'

Lund placed the photo of Dragsholm back among the others.

'She was the woman who was going to prove they were innocent. Two years ago you tried to save your brother. We saw his video diary. What he said about Raben.' She reached into the case, took out the squad photo with the crosses on it. 'We found this in the rubbish you threw out from the flat you rented in Islands Brygge.'

He looked at the faces, the marks through them.

'You think Raben was responsible for Sebastian's death, don't you? Anne Dragsholm was going to get him vindicated.'

'I don't even know who that woman is . . .'

Holst stubbed out his cigarette. Someone came to the door and tried to talk to him. He waved them away.

'We know you tried to contact Raben,' Strange went on. 'He sent your letters back.'

'Really?'

'Start talking,' Lund told him. 'We've come a long way. We're not going back empty-handed. You'd better believe that.'

'You're wasting your time. I didn't kill anybody. Why—'

Strange bellowed a curse, slammed his fist on the table. The noise was so sudden and so loud it made Lund jump.

'Don't give me this shit! You had their photo. You crossed them out, one by one.'

'Just a game,' Holst said calmly, with a shrug. 'Something to pass the time.'

'You were here when they brought in your brother.' Lund looked round the miserable little field hospital.

He blinked, didn't look at her.

'It must hurt whoever it is,' she went on. 'But your own brother, wounded alongside the rest—'

'Yeah, yeah! You made your point!'

'And then you find out Raben and the others were to blame. They're alive and he was on the slab.'

Holst pointed a long pale finger at her.

'Stay away from heroes,' he said in a quiet, damaged voice. 'That's my advice. They get you killed.'

'So Raben's got your brother's blood on his hands?'

'Oh yes!' he cried. 'And I hope the bastard burns in hell. But . . .'

They waited. It took a long time.

'That's the way it goes,' Holst said in the end. 'Raben was in command. There's no law that said

234

he couldn't force a kid like Sebastian into that hornet's nest. What could I do?'

He laughed.

'Except put a little surprise in there myself. There was another body part in all the pieces they brought in. A hand.'

His eyes were somewhere else. Holst was remembering.

'I thought if I threw that in then maybe someone back in Copenhagen would start asking a few questions. There were lots of rumours going round. How a family had been murdered.'

'You think they did it?' Strange asked.

'Who else? No one believed that fairy story about an officer. I thought . . .'

He reached for the cigarettes, lit another one.

'I thought the army would get to the bottom of it. Check it out. Find the truth. We don't cover things up. Not like that. But . . .' A grim, brief smile. 'I was wrong there too. The judge advocate dismissed the idea that any civilians had been killed. They walked away scot-free, until Raben got himself locked up anyway.'

Lund checked through the documents.

'The hand belonged to the suicide bomber,' she said.

'It was a hand. I don't know whose.'

'You were pissed off. You worked up a false medical report—'

'The hand came from the village! Someone should have looked into what went on there!'

'You're in trouble, Holst,' she said.

That short laugh again.

'Oh dear. How very worrying.' He leaned forward. 'Sebastian died here, just round the corner. From a punctured lung. That was all. If it had happened back in Copenhagen he'd be walking round now. It's nothing. But here . . .'

His eyes ranged the room, beyond.

'I couldn't save him. I had to watch him die. And that psychopath Raben, the idiot who made him go into that village, had a fancy lawyer who got them off scot-free. It's a wonder he didn't get a medal. Pissed off?'

The anger broke in him. Both hands, straight from the operating theatre, hammered the desk.

'Yes!' Frederik Holst roared. 'You bet!'

Lund waited.

After a while Holst recovered, said in the same low, flat tone he'd used before, 'But it doesn't matter how pissed off I am. It won't bring Sebastian back. So what else can I do? Except try to save him again. Every single day on that wreck of an operating table.'

Holst sniffed, stubbed out the half-smoked cigarette.

'That's all it amounts to,' he said, pushing the photo with the crossed-out faces back across the table. 'Sorry to disappoint.'

They got nothing more out of Frederik Holst. He had work to do. Another patient, a Taliban

236

fighter, badly wounded and screaming at the nurses.

Lund used the satellite phone to call Copenhagen.

'Holst can't account for his movements during any of the murders. Or won't,' she told Brix.

'Never mind that. Did he do it?'

Even over thousands of miles and a satellite connection his anxiety came through clearly.

'I don't think so.'

'Jesus, Lund. Are you telling me this was all a waste of time?'

'I don't know yet.' They were back in the main reception area. Nurses and another doctor were gathered round the soldier she'd seen earlier. The one who'd lost his feet. 'Has Raben said anything new?'

'He's sticking to the same story.'

'Søgaard's name keeps coming up here,' she lied. 'He was commander when it happened. Everything must have gone through him.'

'Just pack your sunglasses and come home, will you? Søgaard's a surly, unhelpful bastard. We've got nothing on him.'

Silence.

Then, 'Lund? *Lund?*'

She couldn't stop herself looking. The nurses round the trolley had moved back. Except one, a young woman with glassy, sad eyes. She was pulling up the green sheet. Covering the face of the Danish soldier who'd only wanted to go home.

237

To escape the maelstrom for another week. To survive.

Strange stood next to her. He walked in front, blocked her view.

'What does Brix say?' he asked.

'He says we should come home.'

Strange picked up her helmet, placed it carefully on her head, did up the strap, looked into her eyes.

'Brix is right.'

Ruth Hedeby was watching from the end of the corridor as he came off the phone. They knew one another well enough by now. She was a smart, sensitive woman. Could read his face.

'For God's sake, Lennart, tell me this whole adventure was worth it. That we're not just taking a shot in the dark.'

Brix walked to join her. He didn't want anyone else listening in.

'Everything's dark to begin with.'

'Don't get cryptic on me. I've got the Ministry, Parliament, PET on my back every minute of the day.'

Brix nodded.

'They think we've made a breakthrough in the case,' Hedeby added.

He smiled.

'Have we, Lennart?'

'I'm sure the Minister of Justice will understand—'

'He's hanging on to his job by a thread. Probably not for much longer.' She had a newspaper under her arm, took it out. A photo of Thomas Buch looking furious, making accusations he seemed unable to substantiate. 'Don't count on him.'

'I'm still working on this.'

'That's not good enough. We're under a microscope here. Everything we do's under scrutiny.'

'What's new?'

'This,' she said, prodding his jacket. 'Do nothing without my knowledge from now on. I want no more surprises. Or I will suspend you in an instant.'

He watched her go, went back into the office. Asked Madsen what had been happening.

Precious little. The trawl of officers had led to nothing.

'If it's not Frederik Holst,' Madsen said, 'we're left with Raben.'

'How could Raben have done all of this?' Brix asked wearily. 'He was in a cell in Herstedvester.'

One of the detectives came over with a new file.

'We've been chasing the things he was buying in Per K. Møller's name. He didn't use a credit card. Just cash, bought second hand from individuals mainly. If a couple of them hadn't sent receipts to Møller's mother we'd never have known.'

'What did he buy?' Brix asked.

'So far,' the man said, reading from a list, 'we've

239

got a video camera, a laptop, and a copy of the Anarchist's Cookbook. A bomb-making manual. They all got sent to a PO box at the same place Faith Fellow used when he set up that box for Kodmani.'

Brix took the sheet.

'Did he use Møller's name to rent accommodation? Storage space somewhere?'

'Not that we can find. But there may be something.' More notes on his pad. 'The mobile we think was used to set the bomb that killed Grüner was stolen. The SIM's active again.'

Madsen came and stood next to him.

'Where?'

'Somewhere near Ryvangen.'

'Inside the barracks?' Brix demanded.

'Don't know, boss,' the detective replied. 'The signal was weak.'

Brix found himself wishing Lund was back already.

'This doesn't add up. Why would he use the phone again? He knows we're looking for it.'

'Everyone makes mistakes, don't they?' Madsen suggested.

Brix thought for a moment then ordered up a team for immediate dispatch. Decided in an instant he wouldn't tell Ruth Hedeby.

'They're having the funeral service there today,' Madsen pointed out. 'For those dead soldiers. The army won't like it.'

Brix snatched a look at his watch. Wondered

240

what time it was in Helmand. Lund had hours to spare. That worried him.

'I can live with that,' he said.

The Land Rover was back in the rough mountainous hills between the field hospital and Camp Viking. The driver had orders to take them straight to the Camp Bastion airfield for the plane to Istanbul.

'Maybe we could stop by Viking and ask some questions about Søgaard,' Strange suggested as they got bounced around in the back of the vehicle. 'We've got time.'

She wasn't much interested in that idea. The army said what it wanted to say. It seemed unlikely their guard would drop in a war zone.

'Tell me what happens when you're on a mission,' Lund said. 'Special forces.' She looked at him. 'The kind of thing you ended up doing.'

'Such as what?' Strange replied. She'd half expected him to turn cagey.

'How do you operate? How do you communicate?'

He looked at her.

'I didn't do a lot. Honest.'

'Just tell me!'

'It was always a group of five men. We'd go places sane people didn't. Mostly intelligence. Not fighting. That was too risky.'

'Did you stay in contact with other forces? Ours? The British? The Americans?'

He laughed.

'There aren't any Americans around here. And the answer's no. We were undercover. If it turned hot we shot at anything that moved and hoped we'd get out in one piece.' He pointed at the bleak terrain. 'This is no man's land. You don't stop for a conversation. But we always moved five at a time. A team. Besides . . . didn't Arild say there were no special forces in the area?'

The helmet wasn't too uncomfortable. The vest still annoyed her. Lund tapped on the driver's shoulder.

'Can you stop the car, please?'

'Can't you hang on till we get to the airfield?' he said and kept driving.

'No.'

He swore, pulled in by the side of the rough track.

Lund got out and looked around. After a while Strange joined her.

'What's up?' he asked.

The driver got out too, scanning the rocky hills anxiously.

'How far's the village where Raben's team got attacked?'

Strange slapped his forehead.

'You must be joking.'

'I want to see it.'

'We're not tourists on a day trip!'

'I know that,' she said and looked at the driver. 'Can you take us there? How long?'

The soldier shook his head.

'You don't have authorization.'

'What do you mean we don't have authorization?' Lund yelled at him. 'Do you think they sent us all the way from Copenhagen to get ordered around by a driver? We've got arrest warrants and visas. We can go—'

'You can't leave the military zone,' the man said. 'That's that.'

A step closer, hands on hips.

'We've got full authority from the Ministry of Justice. Here . . .' She pulled out the satellite phone. Brix was right. It did seem to work everywhere. 'I'm going to call Copenhagen. I'm going to get through to the minister himself right now and tell him some adolescent squaddie won't let us go where we need to—'

'Lund!' Strange cried.

She stared him down. Started hitting the buttons.

'What's your name again?' She read the tag on his combat jacket. 'Siegler. OK.'

The soldier went back to the Land Rover, started looking through his documents. Lund didn't place the call.

'Does it say we can't go to the village?' she asked.

No answer.

'Well, does it?'

The man was scanning the hills again, looking for movement.

'I've still got to get you back to Bastion on time.'

'Agreed,' Lund told him. 'And call in the local

chief of police. He was in the judge advocate's report. I want to talk to him too.'

The police had found Raben a lawyer. A young, doleful woman who looked as if she'd drawn the short straw from that day's prisoners.

'You're going to be charged with burglary, vehicle theft, possession of a firearm, unlawful imprisonment, violent and threatening behaviour.'

She sat at the interview room desk, flicking through the papers.

'That's for starters. How will you plead?'

His arm was still in a sling though the pain was so muted he could move it with some ease.

'Guilty on all counts?' the lawyer asked.

'Has my wife been in touch?'

She shook her head.

'What about the police officers who went to Helmand?'

'Don't expect any miracles there. That story about the officer is doing you no favours.'

'But it's true.'

She gestured at the papers in front of her.

'Things look bad enough as it is. There's no need to make them worse by provoking people.'

He laughed.

'I'm provoking them?'

'You are. This looks like a long sentence. If they decide you're too unbalanced to be allowed out in public it could be indefinite.' She waited

244

for that to sink in. 'You understand what I'm saying? The judge may say you should never be released.'

'Do you know if Louise has tried to visit me?'

'She hasn't.' The lawyer brushed the papers into her briefcase. 'Someone else has. The police allowed it. He's waiting. I don't think they had any choice . . .'

She got up, went to the door, rapped on it to be let out.

'Help me, Raben. Give me something to work with.'

Then she was gone, and a short, active figure was there instead. Blue uniform. Badges and ribbons. Ginger hair, bright, alert eyes, a smile so insincere it ought to hurt.

'No need to salute,' Arild said as he took a seat. 'It's not as if you're in the army any more, is it?'

Raben was at the window, leaning on the sill, looking enviously at the grey world outside.

'Funny, you know. I've heard so much about you. I looked at your records. Quite a story. You don't mind this little visit, do you?'

Arild held out his hand.

'General Arild from Operational Command. This is official business.'

Raben didn't move.

'Ah well,' Arild murmured, giving up. He took the lawyer's chair, made himself comfortable. 'Make things awkward if you want. I understand

245

you feel we've let you down. I can assure you I'm very sorry you feel that way.'

'Really?'

Arild took out some papers.

'You were a good soldier. Loyal, talented.' A glance. 'Ingenious. If you stick to this nonsense you'll be hurting yourself and the military. I can't believe you want that.'

A pen, a sheet with what looked like a space for a signature.

'The solution to this problem lies with you. Sit, for God's sake!'

Raben did as he was told, couldn't stop himself. There was something in the man's tone.

'Let's help one another,' Arild suggested. 'Instead of this pointless fighting—'

'If you want me to withdraw my statement, forget it.'

Arild had a distant, penetrating stare. He tapped the papers on the table to straighten them.

'On behalf of the military I'd like to offer you compensation. We have the option to adjust the insurance policy you took out with your service contract. At our own discretion—'

'Just fuck off out of here.'

Arild stared at the ceiling for a moment, then at the man.

'This isn't for you. It's for your wife and son. If you'd been killed in action she'd have been entitled to a pension. With a little good will on both sides we can change the conditions of the policy.' He lifted the papers, waved them. 'So it also applies to long-term illness.' The bleak, cold smile again. 'That would make life a lot easier for Louise and Jonas. I'm sure you appreciate that.'

Arild brandished his fountain pen.

'All I ask in return is . . .' The man in the uniform shrugged. 'You know perfectly well. It's up to you.'

He picked up the papers, held them out.

'Your decision entirely. Louise is a fetching young woman. I'm sure she could find herself a new husband. An officer, perhaps. Without any form of income . . .'

Arild peered around the room.

'Who could blame her?'

Louise Raben had placed one call to the Politigården to check on her husband's condition. And five to the army custodial facility at headquarters, trying to talk to her father.

At nine thirty she made another effort to get through to the military police, walking out of the infirmary, standing in the road, coat on, scarf round her neck, dealing with the switchboard, pleading with an officer to talk to.

Finally she got through to the same man she'd spoken to twice that morning.

'You again?' he said cheerily.

'Look. My father's been with you since yesterday. I'd like to talk to him.'

'He's being questioned.'

247

'Jesus Christ! If he was a common criminal I'd be able to talk to him.'

'From what I gather you're in a good position to know that,' the man said, laughing. 'I'll take your word—'

'He's my father. A good officer. Won't you—?'

'Can't talk individual cases. Not over the phone. When he's allowed visitors we'll let you know.' A pause. 'Didn't I tell you that earlier? Oh, right. I did. And here you are wasting my time again.'

She wanted to scream. Thought of her husband, furious and making things worse.

'I'm sorry I yelled at you. It's difficult here. We've got the memorial service today.'

He didn't say anything. She could see him mouthing at the phone: really?

'Just do me one small favour,' Louise begged. 'Pass him a message. Tell him—'

'No messages. I told you that already.'

'Well, fine! Thanks for nothing. You . . .'

The line went dead. She was mouthing one long, loud curse when a police car screamed through the red-brick barracks entrance arch, blue light flashing on the roof. Three more followed, lights too. And a white van that came to a halt and started to disgorge men.

Søgaard was in dress uniform. Immaculate, ready for the service. He marched over to the tall, taciturn cop she recognized from the Politigården as he climbed out of the first car and started barking orders to the men assembling around them.

'What the hell is this?' Søgaard shouted. 'I didn't get advance notice—'

'We don't give advance notice of raids.' He pulled out an ID, flashed it at Søgaard. 'Lennart Brix. Head of homicide. Remember me?'

'There's a memorial service today.'

'We'll try not to get in your way,' Brix said, pulling a sheet of paper from his heavy blue winter coat. He brandished it at Søgaard. 'This is a search warrant. We've reason to believe there's crucial evidence hidden here.'

'If you told me what you were looking for . . .'

The cop was smiling at him.

'I gather you're in charge now, Søgaard. That was a rapid promotion, wasn't it?'

No answer.

'Unless you want an equally rapid demotion don't get in our way,' Brix added. 'I want someone with all the keys. No one's to leave. Not until I say so.'

He tucked the warrant down the front of Søgaard's jacket, walked off and started to direct his men towards the stores complex.

Louise Raben edged closer, interested by the sudden flash of fear on Søgaard's face. She hadn't seen that before.

Said Bilal had joined him. Just as smart, black beret, ribbons. Never a smile.

'What's up?' he asked.

'Get hold of General Arild,' Søgaard ordered.

Bilal was watching the police.

'What do they want now?'

'Just do as I say!' Søgaard bellowed. 'For fuck's sake . . .'

She walked closer, watched him, noted his anger, didn't smile.

'Deal with it, Bilal, will you?' he said more quietly and didn't meet her eye.

Stalemate on Slotsholmen. Karina was working the phones. Buch was desperately waiting for news from Afghanistan.

'Krabbe's getting kickback from his own party,' she said coming off a call. 'They don't like kicking up a stink.'

Buch was walking round the office cleaning his teeth with a brush she'd found for him. The moving people were in, ready for his departure. Boxes stacked everywhere.

'I'll talk to him. Krabbe wants to get to the bottom of this just as much as I do.'

She winced.

'What is it?' Buch asked.

'One way or another he's going to want some political gain, Thomas. Where is it?'

'Never mind that.' He finished brushing, got a glass of water, gargled with it then spat everything back into the glass. 'Are the police really coming home without any evidence?'

'Plough knows more about that than I do.'

'Then where the hell is he? Why does he always disappear just when I want him?'

She was barely listening. One of the transport people wanted instructions. He went off with two boxes of folders.

'The press have given up on you. Three members of Parliament have accused you of treason.'

'What?' Buch's face lit up with rage. He ran his fingers through his hair. 'Treason? What century are these morons living in?'

Plough came through the door. Grey suit, tie. Always the civil servant.

'We need evidence the Prime Minister shelved that first medical report,' Buch said. 'And where in God's name have you been?'

Plough came and stood in front of him, hands in pockets. The surest sign of rebellion he had. He gestured at Buch's face. Toothpaste on the beard. Karina passed him a napkin and told him to wipe it away.

'All the evidence we've seen,' Plough went on, 'suggests the doctor was happy with the revised report. No one's suggesting Grue Eriksen's murdered civilians. These accusations of yours . . .'

Buch's mind was wandering.

'Thomas!' Plough pleaded. 'At least fight battles you've a hope of winning! We should focus on Rossing. We know he was involved. We know he hid things.'

'Rossing would never do all this on his own. He doesn't have the balls. Where is he now?'

Karina checked the government diary on the nearest computer.

'At the memorial service in Ryvangen. For the dead soldiers.'

Buch went for his jacket, a tie. And, almost as an afterthought, stripped off his shirt from the night before and found a clean one.

'Get me a car.'

Flowers and four coffins draped in the Danish flag set in a line next to the black stone font. A lone trumpet echoing through Ryvangen's tiny chapel. The place was cold. Flemming Rossing shivered next to the biers, staring at the bouquets and the regimental caps by their side.

The service was postponed. The police were searching the barracks. Army personnel had been confined to quarters during the investigation. Only a lone undertaker, black jacket, black tie, white shirt, joined Rossing and the trumpeter in the chapel. The relatives were in the mess hall. If the search continued no soldiers or officers would be able to take part.

The door opened. A large, heavy figure marched through. Rossing turned, saw, took a deep, pained breath.

Buch sat down in the pew behind him.

'More fairy stories to throw at me? What are you doing here? Were you invited?'

Buch's voice was low and croaky.

'I know you don't trust me. But we've more in common than you think.'

Rossing kept his eyes on the coffins and the red and white flags.

'I seriously hope that isn't so. I hear your little adventure in Afghanistan proved fruitless. There's a surprise. No wonder you're stressed.'

A low, muttered curse close to Rossing's ear.

'Don't play the pompous ass with me,' Buch hissed. 'You think you served a higher purpose.'

'I have.'

Buch's heavy arm came up by Rossing's face and pointed ahead.

'Do you think they'd agree?'

'They're the reason. Every coffin reminds me we've got to continue until no death's in vain.'

'That's politician's claptrap and you know it. This wasn't about war, about victory. Not for Grue Eriksen. It was about power and money and votes.'

Rossing turned and stared at him, said nothing.

Buch got up, came and stood in front of him.

'I know you didn't do this on your own, Rossing. You got your orders and you obeyed them. These men . . .' His voice was louder than ever, his bearded face contorted with anger. 'They died because of what happened.'

'You don't know that—'

'Deny it then!' Buch roared. 'You've got a responsibility, for fuck's sake. At least Monberg had a conscience.'

'And it killed him . . .'

Buch threw up his hands in fury.

'And who killed them?'

The undertaker strode towards him.

'You have to leave now. I demand it. This behaviour's quite inappropriate.'

'Inappropriate?' Buch stared at Rossing, shook his head. 'That's a good word, isn't it?'

'You must leave or I will order the guards!' the undertaker said more firmly.

'He'll load the blame on you,' Buch yelled, going for the door. 'Just like he did with Monberg. And me.'

Rossing sat, eyes closed, face stony and grey.

'We need each other,' Buch added. 'If you can find yourself a spine you know where I am.'

Forty minutes into the search, Brix and Madsen were walking through the main officers' quarters, watching the teams go through desks and lockers and filing cabinets.

They hadn't found a single thing.

'Try calling the phone again,' Brix ordered.

'Done that,' Madsen replied. 'Maybe the battery's dead.'

'Have you looked in the basements? The cellars? The . . .'

They went into the entrance hall.

'Big place,' Madsen said, admiring the elegant ceiling and the curved staircase. 'With the men we've got this is going to take a couple of days.'

'I want every inch searched. I don't care how long it takes. There's something here. There has to be . . .'

He stopped. A man was walking down the stairs, blue uniform, ginger hair, sharp, intelligent face hard with anger. General Arild had a phone to his ear and was speaking in a whisper.

'Stop!' Arild said in a voice so full of authority he barely needed to raise it.

He'd put the call on hold, not finished it.

'I know what you're going to say,' Brix told him. 'Don't waste your breath. This is an official police investigation. We're here for the duration. Live with it.'

Arild's bleak eyes fixed on him. He held out the phone.

'For you.'

Brix snatched the mobile from his hand. He knew who'd be on the other end.

'What the hell are you doing?' Hedeby shrieked down the line.

'This isn't a good time.'

'Pack your things and get out of there. That's an order. How dare you . . .?'

Søgaard had come to join Arild. The two soldiers stood next to one another, arms folded, faces calm and confident.

'I'm in charge here,' Brix said. 'I take full responsibility for the situation. Once the search is finished I'll get back to you.'

'Not this time. I've talked to the commissioner. You've no authority any more. Get out of there.'

He took the phone away from his ear. Heard her ask quietly, 'Lennart . . .?'

Arild reached out and removed it from his fingers.

'If you're not gone in five minutes,' he said, 'God help you.'

The coldest of smiles then Arild turned on his heels and left, with Søgaard walking obediently behind.

Brix stood in the chilly hall, unable to think for a moment. He'd suspended officers himself in the past. It was never easy.

His own phone rang.

'Yes?'

'We've got something in the basement. You need to come now.'

Two floors down beneath the officers' hall. Central heating pipes, low lights, dusty and cold. Brix and Madsen put on latex gloves, walked to the team of men huddled by the door at the end of the corridor.

A locker room. Rows and rows of wooden doors, all of them open now. A woman forensic officer was shining a torch into the space of one in the middle. The man with her reached inside.

A phone with a flashing green light.

'It's the number,' the officer said. 'The same SIM used to trigger the call that killed Grüner.'

There was a long red metal box on the shelf below the phone. A small brass padlock keeping it secure.

Brix pointed at it.

'Let's have a look.'

The woman got a pair of bolt cutters and removed the padlock. Brix walked in front of them, bent down, opened the lid with his gloved hands. Someone shone a torch.

He picked up the first thing he found. A glittering piece of metal. Dog tags on a single chain, severed in half, one of them covered in dried blood.

Brix stood up, closed the door. Looked at the name on the locker.

Søgaard.

Called Ruth Hedeby.

'Just listen for once, will you?' he said as she began to squawk.

It was barely a village at all. Just a collection of wrecked buildings inside a low perimeter wall breached by force and weather. A few houses made of mud and brick, every one reduced to broken shells. A boy of ten or so was feeding a small flock of goats outside what was once a gate. He fled the moment the Land Rover appeared.

Lund got out with Strange. The driver picked up his assault rifle and joined them. The place lay in a long valley surrounded by barren fields. A burnt-out pickup stood by the nearest house. The marks on it, black and ugly, could have been a bomb blast.

Beyond stood a white truck with a blue lamp on the roof. A stocky man in a blue police uniform leaned on the side smoking a cigarette. Two others in long robes, turbans round their heads, sat in the back, rifles slung round their shoulders.

'Salam Alaikum,' the soldier said as he approached them.

The policeman threw his cigarette to the ground, stamped it out, looked into their eyes and shook their hands, Lund last.

He didn't say a word, just grabbed his rifle out of the back then led them inside the compound, with the two men making up the rear.

Strange had the file. It was hard to connect what it contained with the wrecked house the cop showed them. Black smoke stained the front from the suicide attack. The windows were broken and open to the bitter winter blasts. Most of the furniture was gone. Just a few broken chairs and a tiny table in the living room.

Strange led the way upstairs.

'According to the investigation Raben's people got the family up here.'

Three rooms, only one of any size. More trashed furniture. A grubby cooking pot. On the floor broken glass and bullet casings. She picked one up. Strange came and looked at it.

'That's a 5.56,' he said. 'Danish army M-95. This is the place.'

She went into the small room next door. Kicked open an old chest. Tried to rifle through the broken doors and cabinets. The place looked as if a deadly hurricane had hit it.

Back downstairs. A big fireplace, sooty and damp. A rickety kitchen table.

'The soldiers slept in shifts in here,' Strange said, going through the notes.

A single mattress. She picked it up, looked. No sign of blood.

Next to it the entrance hall, behind a door off its hinges.

'This is where the family were killed?' Lund asked.

'According to Raben,' Strange agreed. 'He said the corpses were moved one room along.'

He took out a torch, opened another rickety door. One more empty space.

'So they didn't dare go outside?'

Raben shook his head.

'Not if there were Taliban out there. How could they?'

'But there's nothing here! Just some casings. No blood. No sign of rations. You wouldn't . . .' It felt so wrong. 'You wouldn't think anyone lived here.' She opened the ragged, grubby curtain and looked at the bleak parched countryside. 'Died here either.'

The driver was getting worried.

'Are we done yet?' he asked.

'We've plenty of time,' Lund said. 'I want to talk to the policeman. Can you translate?'

They went back into the big room. The cop was seated on a chair, the two men he came with stood over him like guards. They were all smoking. The man in the blue uniform looked bored and surly.

'Who lived here?' Lund asked.

Waited for the translation.

'A family of five. Some people thought the father was a drug lord who gave money to the Taliban,' the soldier said eventually.

'Does he think they were killed by Danish soldiers?'

The cop yawned, got up, brushed the dirt from his cap, picked up his rifle. Said something slowly.

'No,' the soldier translated. 'He said there was no sign of the family.'

Lund kept her eyes on the man.

'So they just disappeared?'

'People do,' the soldier said. 'Don't push it.'

There was something on the floor. It looked like a big wooden paddle with a handle. Lund picked it up.

'What's this?'

The cop made an eating gesture, said something.

'It's for bread,' the soldier said. 'The family ran a bakery.'

'As well as selling dope for the Taliban?' Lund asked.

'It happens.'

'Where's the oven?'

A long stream of Pashto.

'He says everything was destroyed.'

'In that case show me where the oven was.'

'Lund,' Strange whispered.

'What?'

'We're not welcome here. We need to get back.'

There was a back yard. Some low buildings in it.

'I'm not done yet,' she said.

Buch sat at his desk, watching the boxes move out of the office, listening to Plough whining about the confrontation in the Ryvangen chapel.

'Thomas . . .' Plough began. It was always first name terms now. 'What could you possibly hope to gain?'

'Rossing's no fool,' Buch said. 'He knows Grue Eriksen may come gunning for him next. I gave him a chance. He didn't take it. I've called in some private lawyers to discuss our options. I want you to sit in with them—'

'We've got bigger things to worry about!' Plough cried.

'Such as?'

'Lund's investigation in Afghanistan.'

'So what?' Buch replied, shaking his head. 'If she's going to go all that way—'

'She's left the military zone without authorization.'

'Then send her some.'

'You've no idea how these things work. Afghanistan's a NATO operation. There are international rules. We've broken them. Operational

Command are furious. The British are pissed off—'

'When aren't they?'

Karina rapped on the door. She was dressing down these days, as if her time was numbered too. Red shirt, tight jeans.

'I've got the Minister of Defence outside,' she said, looking more than a little surprised. 'He wants to see you in private. Shall I . . .?'

Buch clapped his hands, was out of his seat in a moment. Rossing walked in, waited for Karina and Plough to leave.

'If you've come about some trivial clearance issue for the police in Helmand, forget it,' Buch said.

'No,' Rossing said with a wry smile. 'I've given up trying to guess what you'll do next there.'

'Then what can I do for you?'

Rossing took a seat by the window. He looked different. Defeated maybe.

'I've always been loyal to Grue Eriksen. Why wouldn't I be?'

'Congratulations.'

Rossing's hooded eyes looked him up and down.

'Sometimes that meant I had to compromise. On policy. On principles. That's politics.'

'I would have said that was compromise.'

'One week in office and you're lecturing me?' It was said more with sorrow than anger, Buch thought, and that surprised him. 'It's never easy.

262

Never simple. When we heard these stories about civilians being killed . . .'

Rossing looked out of the window.

'There was a lot going on. We needed more money. More soldiers.' He looked weary, jaded. 'One decision always impacts on another. You tip over a domino here. Another falls somewhere else, and then a line with it. The Prime Minister and I agreed to put off the investigation of the hand. I'd no idea where it could lead.'

Rossing leaned forward, looked into Buch's eyes.

'If I'd known for one moment . . . Poor Monberg. All these murders . . .'

Buch sat down next to him and waited.

'Maybe some alarm bells should have been ringing,' Rossing murmured. 'I'm not proud—'

'What bells?'

'The doctors who looked at the hand saw some inconsistencies. We felt it was inconclusive. Military intelligence told us none of the victims were civilians.'

'Rossing. You're the Minister of Defence. You of all people can find out the truth . . .'

The aquiline head went back and Flemming Rossing let loose a long, hearty laugh.

'Oh God. You're such a child sometimes. Do you think I know everything? Do you imagine for one moment they tell me every last detail? Or that I want to hear it? This is war. This is government—'

'What inconsistencies?'

263

Rossing's face was back at the window, distant, as if he didn't want anyone or anything to witness this. He reached into his jacket and took out some papers, read from them.

'There was a henna tattoo,' he said then passed over the sheet.

Buch looked. A photo of a severed hand. The palm marked by a brown circular tattoo.

'We consulted some experts,' Rossing went on. 'They said it was typical of the Hazara people. They hate the Taliban. Fear them too, with good reason. There's this . . .' He pointed to the second finger. A band of pale metal there. 'It's a gold ring. The Taliban don't wear gold. This is a woman's hand. It can't possibly be that of a suicide bomber.'

There were no words in Thomas Buch's head for a while. Then he dared to ask the question.

'Did the Prime Minister know about this?'

Flemming Rossing closed his eyes.

'It's not on the record.'

'But did he know?'

A brief laugh.

'Haven't you worked that out yet? Gert knows things he's never been told. Gets favours he's never asked for. That's why he's Prime Minister. The man in charge. The one to whom we're all beholden.' Rossing eyed him carefully. 'Even you if you knew it.'

Then he got to his feet.

'Why are you telling me this?' Buch asked.

'It's what you wanted, isn't it?'

'But why? Why now?'

'Poor Buch,' Rossing said with a shake of his head. 'You can't feel the earthquake coming, can you?' He tapped the papers. 'I'm going now. Those are for you. Do with them as you see fit.'

Buch thought about it for the best part of five minutes after Rossing was gone. Then he called in Plough and Karina, asked them to sit in front of his desk, keep out the moving people for a while.

'What is it?' Plough asked warily.

'A change of strategy,' Buch said, passing them the papers about the hand.

'I didn't like the look on Flemming Rossing's face,' the civil servant grumbled. 'Are you telling me it's you two against Grue Eriksen now?'

'Read what he gave me,' Buch demanded and waited till they'd both looked at the photo with the tattoo and the report attached to it.

'How can you trust him?' Karina asked. 'After all the lies. All the tricks he's pulled? Why would he get an attack of conscience now?'

'This has nothing to do with conscience,' Buch replied. 'He's scared. He's using me to warn off Grue Eriksen. I'm going to talk to Krabbe. Get me something from Lund. Let's find out what we can from PET. The police . . .'

Plough wriggled on his seat.

'Well?' Buch asked.

'Erik König's been summarily dismissed. On the order of the Prime Minister's office.'

'I'm still the Minister of Justice! He's mine to fire!'

'And Grue Eriksen's the Prime Minister. It's done. König's gone.' Plough wrinkled his nose in puzzlement. 'I asked him why and he wouldn't tell me. A replacement will be announced tomorrow. I find this somewhat disturbing . . .'

Brix put Søgaard in an interview room with Madsen. No major's jacket any more. Just a plain military shirt, beret on the table. He didn't look cowed in the slightest.

'This is ridiculous,' Søgaard complained. 'I told you a million times. I haven't used that locker in months. It's just coincidence it's still got my name on it.'

'Coincidence?'

'Exactly.'

'Here's another one.' Madsen was standing by the window, looking down at the man at the table. 'The phone we found there was used to murder Grüner.'

Søgaard shrugged.

'If you say so. It's not mine.'

Brix was getting bored with this game. He opened the folder that had just turned up from forensic. Photos of the severed dog tags found in Søgaard's locker.

'Take a look at these and tell me they're a

266

coincidence. The lab's gone through and examined all the halves.'

Søgaard glanced at the pictures and said nothing.

'Every one matches a half found with the victims,' Brix said, spreading out the five photos: bloody metal and chains. 'This places you in the crime, Søgaard. Start coming out with some answers.'

'Like what?' He barely looked at the pictures. 'I haven't seen these things before. I've no idea how they got there.'

Brix threw a plastic evidence bag onto the table and asked, 'What's that?'

Søgaard loosened his black tie. Picked up the envelope, threw it on the table.

'A key. New to me. I've never seen it before.'

'I'm charging you with all five murders,' Brix told him.

'Then you're making a big mistake.'

'You said you'd never met Anne Dragsholm. That's a lie. You knew she was reopening the old case.'

'God this is tedious . . .'

'You're going to be charged,' Brix repeated. 'You'll be put in solitary pending the investigation. We'll let the army see you when we feel like it.' He scooped up the photos, turned to Madsen. 'Get him out of here.'

'Wait.'

Søgaard didn't look so cocky any more.

'So I did meet the Dragsholm woman. She phoned me at Ryvangen pushing for a meeting.

267

Mouthy cow who wouldn't take no for an answer. I told her Raben's story was a pack of lies. She didn't believe me so I said she could go to hell.' He picked up his beret. 'End of story.'

'You lied,' Madsen repeated.

'I didn't want to get involved. Why would I kill my own men?'

Brix shuffled the photos, listened.

'And if I did,' Søgaard went on, 'do you really think I'd be dumb enough to leave an incriminating phone, switched on, in a locker with my name on the door?'

'Let's see what the judge thinks, shall we?' Brix said.

'No!' Søgaard was getting scared. 'This is all wrong. We didn't care about Dragsholm. Raben's story was just bullshit.'

'We?' Brix asked. 'You mean you and Jarnvig?'

'No. The colonel's too damned nosy for his own good sometimes. I wasn't going to push this in front of him.'

'Then who?'

'Said Bilal. He was my number two when Jarnvig was in Kabul. He handled all the radio traffic reports when the investigation happened.' Søgaard tapped the table. 'He can confirm everything I say.'

Brix took out a pen and a pad, scribbled a few things.

'How did Bilal react when Dragsholm starting flinging the mud around?'

'Mad as hell. You'd think it was personal. Bilal's a Muslim but he's a Dane first. He hates those fanatics more than anyone. A good man. Operational Command like him. Arild especially. He was the one who saw Raben with Jarnvig and told Arild about it. I guess . . .' Søgaard broke into a sarcastic smile. 'A dark face looks good on the recruiting posters these days.'

'Does Said Bilal have access to those lockers in the basement?'

'Knock it off. He can barely think for himself.'

'Does he have access?'

A memory from somewhere. Søgaard scratched his head.

'He said something a week or so ago about how we weren't supposed to use the place. The ceiling was unsafe or something. Maybe it could collapse.'

'No one mentioned that when we went down there,' Madsen said.

Søgaard was gripping his major's beret, pummelling it nervously.

'I didn't kill anyone,' he said. 'You're wasting your time if you try to pin this on me.'

The lawyer was back. She'd spoken to Arild. That much was clear.

'So,' she said as they walked through police headquarters, towards the car back to the hospital, 'this is all agreed? You'll withdraw your statement about the officer and civilian casualties?'

Three cops with them. Burly men. One jabbed

Raben in the chest when he wouldn't walk quickly enough.

He made a low, pained noise. Arm still in a sling. He was limping too.

The lawyer was getting irate.

'You shot this man yesterday,' she yelled at the cop. 'Don't push him around too.'

'We're with him all the way to hospital,' the detective said. 'Once they tell us he's fine to be released he goes to jail.'

They were passing through the main investigation room. Photos on the wall. Bloodied corpses. Weapons. Dog tags.

Raben stared at them, glanced at the three cops.

Sleepy men who thought being tough was all you needed.

There was a huddle of detectives by the photos. The lawyer, a smart, quick woman, he thought, one who never missed an opportunity, told him to wait a moment and went to talk to them.

Raben looked at the cops and smiled. Then held his arm, the one in a sling, and winced.

'Getting shot's no fun. Twice in two years. I must be unlucky.'

'Must be something,' the one who pushed him muttered.

Raben just smiled again. The lawyer came back. She seemed happy too.

'We won't be having a hearing tomorrow.' She glanced at the men around him. 'I'm going to ask for him to be kept in a secure room in the hospital. Until we can get to court—'

'What's the delay?' he asked.

'They think they've got their man. Major Søgaard's in custody, about to be charged. They found incriminating evidence in his locker.'

'Oh for God's sake,' Raben yelled. 'Søgaard? Are you serious?'

She didn't like his response.

'You're a hard man to please. You've been telling all the world someone in the army was involved.'

'It wasn't Søgaard. He wasn't Perk. He couldn't be . . .'

The big cop said. 'Can we go now?'

Then pushed Raben towards the exit.

They took the long way out. Down the black marble corridors, to the tall staircase leading to the front entrance.

'I can't come with you to the hospital,' the lawyer said, looking at the cops. 'You're not allowed to question him without me present. Is that clear?'

No answer.

He was limping again, taking the steps one by one.

'Søgaard might cover something up but he's not a murderer,' Raben went on.

'Why don't you just shut up and walk?' the first detective barked. 'You're boring me.'

'He's an injured man,' the lawyer shrieked at him.

'He's a piece of shit who's been giving us the runaround—'

'Søgaard's not your man!'

'Really?' The cop folded his arms, stopped on the stairs. 'We found the other half of the dog tags in his locker. How do you explain that, smartass? Now move, will you?'

The gentlest of pushes and Raben almost stumbled, would have done if the cop's arm wasn't through his.

Bottom of one flight of steps. Another ahead.

'My wife and son are at the barracks,' Raben yelled at him. 'This matters—'

'You're really getting to me now . . .'

Raben was screaming. The second cop came in, told him to relax, jabbed him in the back.

The lawyer was shouting again. They watched Raben in his blue prison suit stumble forward on weak legs, one arm flapping, the other trapped in a sling. Over the second flight of steps then down them, tumbling all the way to the bottom.

'Shit,' the big cop said when he got there. He held Raben's head, felt his pulse. 'He needs the hospital now.'

Night in the barracks. Quiet and deserted with the latest troop dispatch headed for Helmand. Louise Raben had spent most of the evening trying to track down her father. Now Søgaard was missing. The place seemed rudderless.

She walked round the empty offices looking for

someone to talk to, to nag. Finally found Said Bilal in the weapons store cleaning a service rifle.

He didn't look up as she walked in. Never smiled. Never responded.

'Bilal,' she said. 'What the hell's going on here? The military police still won't tell me when they're going to release my father.'

He cradled the weapon in his arms, stroked the oiled barrel. Glowered at her, said nothing.

'What the hell were the police doing here anyway?' she demanded.

'I don't know,' he said with a shrug. 'The last one's gone. They took Søgaard.'

She crouched down next to him, tried to see into his blank and surly face.

'My father found out someone had concealed the radio messages during Jen's mission. Kept them from the judge advocate.'

He went back to the rifle, took out the magazine, checked it in the dim light of the store.

'Who would have done that?' she asked. 'It's got to be a soldier here. Someone who was serving with the unit.'

He stood up, ran his eye down the sight.

'Don't you care, Bilal? Don't you see how important this is? It shows Jens was right. Someone fitted him up—'

'It's war!' Bilal roared and his dark eyes were full of such fury she felt frightened for a moment. 'You've never been there. You don't know what it's like.'

'Don't say that,' Louise Raben said quietly. 'I've seen what it does. Someone set up my husband—'

'There were no messages. No one concealed anything. Raben was a rogue soldier. Just a shame he took others with him.' A fierce glance into her face. 'Not himself.'

She stood her ground.

'That's not what my father thinks, is it? He's got evidence. Maybe the same man put those things in Søgaard's locker—'

Bilal swore. It was the first time she'd ever heard that. Put the rifle back on the table, got up, walked to the boxes of weapons.

'If they found those things Søgaard must have put them there,' he said. 'Who else? He's an idiot. I told everyone to keep out of the place. The ceiling's not safe—'

'Who was running the radio two years ago, Bilal?'

Another rifle was in his hands. He held it the way they all did. As if the weapon was a part of him.

'You're a nurse. Stick to what you're paid for.'

'I'm Raben's wife! Your colonel's daughter. The two men who matter to me most are in shit because of this—'

'There's a computer log!' he yelled at her. 'It's just a list of traffic. That's all.'

She wasn't going to leave this.

'Let's say someone worked out how they could delete messages. I guess Søgaard could have done that. He was in command. Who else?'

He took out the rifle magazine, looked inside, ran a finger across the breach, slammed it back into the body.

'I can't talk about this any more,' Bilal said. 'It's army business. Not yours.'

'Call that bastard Arild! Find out who ratted on my father about the cadets' ball.'

He stared at her.

'What?'

'God you're slow. As soon as my father started digging someone got him arrested. Why? Because he *was* digging. If we find out who . . .'

He came and stood in front of her, young, foreign face devoid of expression.

'Make the call,' she insisted. 'Tell the police too. They need to know.' She shook her head. 'If you won't do it, I will . . .'

Slowly Bilal pulled his phone out of his pocket. She watched as his fingers ran across the keys.

He wasn't dialling.

'I'm waiting . . .' she began.

He looked round the empty store, put the phone back into his pocket.

Stretched out his hand, gripped her round the throat, squeezed hard.

The driver watched Lund breaking up the shattered tables in the outside bakery. He was getting jumpier all the time.

'I've talked to the base,' he said. 'They want us out of here right now.'

275

She'd got splinters in her fingers. Cut herself a couple of times. Found nothing at all.

Strange leaned against the doorway, arms folded, silent.

'I want to see this oven,' she said. 'Where is it?'

The Afghan cop called through from the adjoining room. He'd found another fireplace, full of soot and burned logs.

Lund looked.

'That's not an oven,' she said. Stared at the man, said, 'Oven!'

'That's helping,' Strange muttered. A trilling sound. The satphone in his pocket.

The Afghan threw up his hands in despair. Said something she didn't understand but couldn't miss the tone.

Lund marched back into the first room. A pile of timber had been set up at the end. She began to tear at it as one of the Afghans behind her turned his torch beam on the wood.

Finally she saw a stack of broken bricks and boulders. They looked as if they'd been pushed in place to hide something.

The Afghan and the soldier were behind her.

'Right,' she said. 'We have to remove all the debris and see what's behind here.'

The two of them started talking in Pashto. The Afghan put a hand to his head, made a gesture.

'He thinks you're crazy,' the soldier said. 'I'm with him on that.'

'What happened here led to murder!' she yelled at them. 'An entire family.'

'We don't know that, Lund,' Strange said, coming off the phone.

'But we do!' she cried. Finger pointed in the face of the Afghan. He didn't like that. 'If you know something about this tell me now. A family, for God's sake! Mother and father. Three children.'

The soldier was translating again. The cop looked bored.

'I need to know what happened to them!' Lund yelled.

To her amazement the burly bearded cop looked at her and started laughing. He said something to the soldier.

'Families round here die every day in case you didn't notice,' he translated. 'Since when did you people care?'

The Afghan glared at her, lit a cigarette.

Lund shook her head, astonished, furious.

'What the fuck is that supposed to mean? Hey. Hey!'

Strode over, grabbed his arm. Bad idea. He didn't like a woman doing that, had his hand on his rifle. Not that she cared.

'Hey! Mister!' she bawled. 'When people get killed it matters, even here. What in God's name's wrong with you? Don't you give a fuck or what?'

Lund glared at the soldier.

'Translate that, damn it.'

He was saying something. She wasn't sure it was right.

'Tell me what happened,' Lund said, patting his blue chest. 'Or is that uniform just a big fat joke like you? What happened to the bodies? You're the law around here. You must have seen something, heard something.'

He was very still, peering straight into her eyes. Not a pleasant look.

'Did someone bury them? Cremate them? Take them somewhere else?'

Something the soldier didn't translate.

'You don't care, do you?' Lund yelled. 'Don't give a shit. No wonder they're dead . . .'

He was in her face then. Pushing her back with his fat belly. That made her even madder.

Strange was the first to get between them. Hand out, keeping back the man in blue. He said something in Pashto to the cop, then to her in Danish, 'Easy now, Lund. It's their country. Not ours.'

'We came here, Strange! If we killed this family we're responsible—'

'We've been through everything. There's no oven. No bodies. No sign of any anything.'

'It happened—'

Strange held out the phone.

'It's Brix. He wants to talk to you. He thinks he's got his man.'

Lund took the mobile, went outside, heard them making consoling noises to the fat Afghan cop.

'I want you on a plane now,' Brix said. 'I've

got the Ministry of Defence and the army all over us.'

'What's up?'

'It looks like it's Said Bilal.'

She stared at the wrecked courtyard, the house reduced to rubble in front of her. A family died here. She knew that somehow. She could still hear their cries.

'Bilal knew Dragsholm was opening the case,' Brix continued. 'We found the other halves of the dog tags at the barracks. He tried to fit up Søgaard.'

'At the barracks? Why would Bilal hide things there? He's not Perk—'

'Bilal's gone missing. Louise Raben could be with him. Just get on the damned plane, will you?'

The line went dead. Lund tried to picture the young soldier. He seemed so subservient. A follower. Not a leader.

The driver seized her arm.

'Now we really are going,' he said.

Buch had called the Prime Minister's office demanding another meeting. To his surprise he got it. Gert Grue Eriksen sat in the centre of the table, Kahn on his left. Buch took the seat opposite. Rossing came and sat next to him.

The Prime Minister watched as his Minister of Defence took that seat. A long, hard stare.

'Plenty to talk about,' Buch began without being asked. He'd found his best suit, a clean blue shirt, a dark tie. His hair was tidy, his beard trimmed. Karina had insisted on all these. 'As you may know, little new has so far come to light in the investigation in Afghanistan. That changes nothing. We have a scandal on our hands. A stain on the history of this party, and our government.'

'Same old, same old,' Kahn cut in. 'That's it? The police have come up with nothing?'

'Not yet. But if I may continue—'

'You've launched a personal attack on the Prime Minister's integrity,' Kahn interrupted. 'I'm not listening to more of your rants.'

'Then why are we here?' Buch laughed. 'If it's not to consider the facts?'

Grue Eriksen shook his head and said, 'For better reasons, Thomas. Please listen carefully. This isn't easy for me. I've received information . . .'

He handed a brown leather folder to Kahn who knew straight away what to do. A set of papers was distributed round the table.

'It's clear the Minister of Defence has deceived us,' Grue Eriksen went on.

Rossing stared at the shiny table as if expecting every word.

'He withheld a certain expert's testimony.'

The papers arrived in front of them. The severed hand with the Hazara tattoo. Rossing stared at it, looked at Buch.

'This testimony suggests the hand found in Afghanistan and shipped here did not belong to a Taliban suicide bomber. This information was suppressed to avoid the suspicion of civilian casualties.'

'That's not true . . .' Rossing began.

'If only I could believe that,' Grue Eriksen replied. He paused, stared at Rossing across the table. 'But I don't. You're dismissed as Minister of Defence with immediate effect. Your actions will be investigated by PET to see if criminal charges are appropriate—'

'Say it, Rossing!' Buch cried. 'Tell Kahn. He ordered you to hide those papers.' A finger pointing across the table. 'This bloody, scandalous trail leads directly to him—'

'With regard to the Minister of Justice,' Grue Eriksen went on, 'the situation is equally grave.'

'Oh for pity's sake,' Buch grumbled.

A shake of the silver head. A politician's look, more sorrow than anger.

'You could have used your talents to benefit your country, Thomas. Instead you abused your office to pursue a misguided and unwarranted personal campaign against me.'

Buch tried to catch Kahn's eye.

'Listen, will you? The Prime Minister instructed Rossing to do these things. For his own reasons—'

'In this prolonged smear campaign,' Grue Eriksen continued, 'the Minister of Justice has been scandalously careless in his handling of confidential and privileged information. He has distributed classified documents to people who should never have seen them. There's an apparent

281

breach of the Official Secrets Act which the new director of PET will be investigating alongside Rossing's actions—'

'Ha! So you squeezed him out to get in your own man! Now I understand. Wouldn't even König do your bidding? Is this the Middle Ages again, Gert? Are you a medieval king who'll march me out into the parade ground for a beheading?'

At a signal from the Prime Minister the clerk got up and opened the door. Police in uniform. Plain clothes men too. Rossing stood up and buttoned his jacket, as if ready for this. Buch kept yelling abuse at the short, composed figure opposite.

'You won't get away this,' he barked as someone brusquely took his arm.

'Both of you will leave the building immediately and be taken into custody. You can't take anything with you. I think it's evident you've stepped down now.'

Two of the uniformed cops had hold of Buch's big frame. He was screaming, fighting them.

'Go with dignity, Thomas!' Grue Eriksen cried, raising his voice for the first time.

Buch was a big man. With his two fat arms he threw them off, sent the cops scuttling to the back of the room.

Then he went to the door.

'I can walk on my own,' he yelled and did until they caught up with him, shoved him out into the public area and the media scrum.

He should have guessed they'd be tipped off. Everyone was there. TV, radio, newspapers.

Rossing walked on, head high, silent. Buch followed, sweating, panting, dishevelled again, struggling through the mob.

A microphone in the face. A single stupid question.

'Are you guilty? Buch? Rossing? Are you guilty?'

Marie would see this on the news in Jutland. Their last conversation had not been good.

So Thomas Buch managed to wriggle free from the police officers who'd seized his arms one last time.

Then he got to the nearest camera and said a single word.

'No.'

It was dark by the time the Land Rover got back on the road. Lund was dog-tired, her head full of questions. The body armour felt heavy and unnecessary. But Strange was onto her the moment she tried surreptitiously to loosen it.

There was a bright moon. With the snow on the hills the place almost looked enchanting.

'Why did this happen?' she asked.

He didn't answer.

'Why? If there were no civilian casualties there was nothing for Dragsholm to investigate. Why kill all those people?'

'Jesus, Sarah. You can't know everything. We'll

be back in Copenhagen tomorrow. Let's ask Brix then.'

He sighed.

'You shouldn't have talked to the Afghan like that. They don't appreciate it.'

'He didn't give a shit.'

'Maybe he's got more on his plate than you know. This is Helmand. Not Vesterbro.'

'Why would Bilal take Louise Raben with him? You don't think . . .? The two of them?'

Strange laughed.

'Søgaard had his beady eyes on that one. Didn't you see?'

'Maybe,' she murmured. 'I'm not sure I've seen anything much since you dragged me out of Gedser.'

'Well then,' he said grandly. 'We must get you home. And there . . .' His arm swept the moonlit horizon ahead of them. 'Vicepolitikommissær Lund will ensure all is revealed. The bad guys get their comeuppance. The world will be one again . . .'

'Sarcastic bastard,' she said but she was laughing.

He smiled.

'No I'm not. I mean it. You pick up things that aren't there. You know where people come from when they don't know themselves. What makes them. What hurts them. On top of which you're the most stubborn, awkward, infuriating—'

It was automatic. She reached out, squeezed his hand. Looked into his eyes. Then let go.

'There's something wrong at that house,' Lund said. 'I'm telling you—'

'Shit!' the driver cried as he stomped on the brakes so hard they were thrown against one another in the back. 'Now we're screwed.'

Lund leaned round his shoulder and stared.

A white pickup blocking the narrow dusty road between two rocks. Five men, long, heavy Afghan robes, rifles in their arms, walking towards them.

One yanked open the Land Rover door, the other two kept their rifles on them. A torchlight flashing over the interior. Words she couldn't understand.

Orders. They had that sound.

'They want you two.' The driver had his hands up. He looked terrified. 'Best do as they say.'

Fifteen minutes down a track so rough she wondered how the truck stayed upright. Then somewhere ahead there were lights. Another pickup. Lund's night vision was adjusting.

They were back in the wrecked enclosure, in front of the house.

'Go,' one of the Afghans ordered, picking up an ancient oil lantern, putting a match to it.

The fat police chief sat on the one good chair, beaming.

'So?' he said in broken English. 'Did you get a surprise, angry woman?'

Lund stayed quiet.

'Lots of surprises here.' He grinned then said

285

something in Pashto to the others, made them laugh. 'Some not so nice.'

He got up, stood so close to her she could smell something sweet on the man's breath.

'I didn't want you to leave empty-handed. So I got a little present for you. Come! Come!'

Someone pushed her in the back. Lund walked out to the courtyard behind the house. Strange followed.

Two more men there. They'd been removing the bricks and rubble from a filled-in hole at the back. To reveal a large, blackened space.

Two lanterns on the floor cast their waxy beams into the hole. The cop walked forward. The men got out of his way without a word. He bent down, looked inside, came out with something in his hands.

Lund felt cold and scared and a very long way from home as he gave it to her with all the slow ceremony that might come with a treasured gift. It was a child's skull. Blackened with smoke and flame. A ragged tear in the temple from a bullet wound.

'This make you happy?' the cop asked in his lilting, half-tuneful English.

Lund took the lantern from him, walked to the oven. Peered inside.

More bones. Ribs. A hand. And something metal in the dust.

She picked it up with a pencil. Old habits died hard.

It was a dog tag, stained with smoke. A name: *Per K. Møller* and a number, 369045–9611.

The cop had a bag in his hands. Made of raffia. A little battered, but with a pretty pattern on the side.

'Take home what you want,' he said. 'It's yours now.'

Ten minutes to the Rigshospitalet from the Politigården. Raben stayed in the back, eyes flickering, moaning, breath ragged.

Just the cops with him now. Worried men.

They got out when the police car pulled into the ambulance area, blue light flashing, ran into the emergency area shrieking for help. Doctors. A stretcher. Something to save them.

He waited till they were out of sight then let himself out of the passenger side away from the hospital. Half walked, half hobbled out into the damp night, keeping in the shadows all the way.

From the trees he heard them screaming, looked back briefly. Saw nurses with a gurney, doctors in green coats, the puzzled cops yelling curses.

But didn't wait.

He had things to do.

CHAPTER 11

Wednesday 23rd November, 11.04 a.m.

The flight from Istanbul took them straight back to a busy Kastrup and a world Lund knew. Strange picked up a newspaper the moment they stepped onto Danish soil. The headline said the government was in crisis. Rossing, the Defence Minister, had been fired for covering up an atrocity in Afghanistan. Buch was in custody accused of a breach of the Official Secrets Act.

Lund glanced at the stories, said nothing. The battered raffia holdall hung from her right hand, a collection of blackened bones, a child's skull and a dead soldier's charred dog tag inside.

Strange was busy on the phone all the way into Arrivals. She was glad of that.

'Bilal's taken an army Land Rover,' he said when he'd talked to headquarters. 'We've got an alert out for him. With the border guards too.'

'He thinks he's more Danish than we are. Bilal's not going abroad. What about Louise?'

A frown. He didn't look tired. Didn't look upset or surprised by what they'd found either.

'Seems he snatched her from the barracks. Raben's gone missing again too.'

'Oh for pity's sake . . .'

She wasn't feeling well after the long, difficult journey. Too many thoughts running round her head.

That shrug again.

'He gave our guys the slip when they took him to hospital,' Strange said. 'It's no big deal. In his condition . . .'

'He trained with Jægerkorpset. Special forces and God knows what else. He thinks he's immortal.'

She couldn't stop herself looking at him when she said that.

'I never did,' Strange replied with that same, self-deprecating innocence. 'But I guess I wasn't in Raben's class. I put a bullet in his shoulder. We'll have him before long.'

Out into the Arrivals lounge. The bag felt heavier than it was.

'They found a key in Søgaard's locker,' Strange went on. 'Bilal had rented an industrial unit where he planned all five murders. There's a machine for making fake dog tags there. Other stuff—'

'Where's Brix?'

'I'm not his keeper.'

He was starting to sound angry and that was unusual.

'I need the bathroom,' Lund announced.

She didn't. Just some space. But she walked off towards the toilets anyway, and Strange followed her.

'Sarah?' he said, catching up. 'What's up? You've hardly said a word to me all the way back.'

She stopped, looked at him, tried to think of something to say.

'I'm tired. It's a long journey . . .'

'That's it?'

A familiar, unexpected voice close by shrieked, 'Yoo hoo! Hello there!'

Lund felt the earth was falling beneath her feet. Her mother and Bjørn were beaming joyously as they walked arm in arm from another gate.

'How sweet of you to come and meet us,' Vibeke said and kissed her.

Her mother smelled of perfume. Lund guessed she didn't.

'Where did you go exactly?' she asked, shaking her head.

'Prague! I told you.'

'Living it up!' Bjørn added, making a drinking gesture with his right hand.

Vibeke put her arms round Lund, held her closely, whispered in her ear, 'What have you been up to, Sarah? I had a terrible nightmare in the hotel. I dreamt you were all alone somewhere, lying lifeless. Nothing I could do would bring you back to life.'

'Mum—'

'I was crying! Mark was crying! It felt so real.'

Strange said he'd get the car. Her mother pinched her arm.

'I'm so glad you're not mixed up in that horrible job any more. You should leave that to the men.

Bjørn and I have decided we're going to visit you in Gedser. There must be lots to see there.'

She told Strange she'd take a cab with her mother and Bjørn.

He didn't move.

'You're sure?'

She shrugged.

'Why not? You take the car.'

'Oh!' Vibeke cried. 'What a lovely bag! So pretty. Where did you get it?'

Her fingers were on the top, reaching inside already.

'It's nothing,' Lund said and snatched it away. 'Honest. Shall we go?'

Lund let them sit in the back of the taxi, tried to talk as quietly as possible from the front. Brix was busy. Satisfied for once by the sound of it.

'Why did your friend leave?' Vibeke asked from the back.

Lund turned and pointed at the phone.

'I like him,' her mother declared. 'He seems a nice man.'

Lund went back to Brix.

'We found the remains of two adults and three children.'

'This is definite? No mistake?'

The raffia bag was between her legs on the floor of the taxi.

'It's definite. They'd been burned in an oven. Someone covered it up with debris afterwards.'

'Well done.' He sounded impressed. 'I passed on your initial report.'

'There's a bullet hole in the child's skull. It looks like an execution, not a firefight.'

'Did you pick up anything on Bilal?'

'No. We found Møller's dog tag. Raben was telling the truth. Did we get a list of active special forces officers from the army?'

'That doesn't matter any more.' The old impatience was back. 'I told you. We're looking for Bilal. Any killings in Helmand are for the army to investigate.'

Her mother was listening intently from behind. There was no way of hiding this.

'We can't leave it at that. Bilal wasn't there pretending to be Perk. He was in the base, handling the radio traffic. Maybe he was part of the cover-up but he didn't kill this family.'

'The army—'

'It was like a ritual killing, for God's sake. Like the ones here.'

'Bilal—'

'Bilal's not your man. It's someone else.' A pause. It had to be said. 'We need to look at Strange again. He was so . . .' This was what had kept her awake all the way back from Helmand and she had to face it. 'So at home. Like he belonged there.'

She could hear the instant anger in his voice.

'Arild told us categorically that Strange was never in Afghanistan when this happened.'

'You think you can believe him?'

A long pause on the line.

'I'm going to forget you said that.'

He gave her an address in Vesterbro, told her to come when she could.

'Brix. Brix!'

Then he was gone. Vibeke's street was coming up.

'We need to tell the driver where to stop,' Bjørn said from the back.

Her mother was pale. No longer smiling.

'Mum,' Lund said and put a hand to her cheek. 'It was just a dream. Everything's all right. This is just work. What I do.'

'I don't know what you do, Sarah. I don't want to.'

The quickest of showers, a change of clothes. Then a cab to the place they'd found. It was near the Det Ny Teater close to Vesterbrogade. Brix met her at the door.

'Bilal left the key in Søgaard's locker with the mobile phone,' he said, leading her through the grubby entrance into a small workshop. 'Along with the broken-off halves of the five dog tags.'

A large room, white tiles, yellow markers everywhere, bright winter light filtering through the high windows.

'This is a starter building for small businesses,' Madsen said, padding along in blue forensic shoe covers. 'No one else has moved in yet. He had it to himself.'

A laptop on the table. Anne Dragsholm's terrified bloodied face frozen there.

'Shouldn't we wait for Strange?' Brix asked.

'Let's get on with it.'

She lugged the raffia bag with her as they talked.

'We've got the camera he used,' Madsen said, pointing at the long work table by the window. 'The computer. Traces of explosives. Ryvangen personnel records on the hard drive.'

Six mobile phones in a neat line. Instructions for making explosives.

'They all match the evidence from the killings,' Brix said.

Books on the Taliban and Islamist extremism. Terrorism and secret forces.

'Knives.' Madsen held up a plastic bag. Two blades inside.

So much evidence, so neatly laid out.

'Bilal's a Muslim,' Brix went on. 'But everyone says he hates Islamists.'

Lund looked at the sharp curving blades, the bloodstains.

'Why—?' she began.

'Because he saw Raben's squad as traitors,' Brix cut in. 'Bilal thinks he's a loyal Dane. Raben's accusations would damage the reputation of the army by incriminating officers in the killing of civilians.'

She turned on her heels, looked round. Five forensic officers in white suits going over everything.

'And he did all this? On his own?'

Brix pointed to the wall. Printouts from Kodmani's website.

'He invented the Muslim League. He was Faith Fellow. We've got the emails on the laptop. He was trying to frame Kodmani.' Brix stared at her. 'Might have done if it wasn't for you.'

It didn't feel like consolation.

There were photos near the printouts. Old pictures, some she recognized. Executions of traitors during the war. Hunted down by the partisans, shot in the street. The same pictures she'd seen in the Frihedsmuseet in Churchillparken when they were chasing Skåning. Bodies curled up and bloodied on grubby cobblestones. Notices giving warning of the next *stikke* on the list.

'I guess he knew his history,' Brix said watching the way she stared at them. 'That's why he took Dragsholm to Mindelunden.'

Lund hated false logic.

'They didn't kill traitors at Mindelunden. They murdered heroes. That doesn't add up.'

He glared at her.

'Dragsholm was his first victim. She wanted to reopen the case. They met a few months ago.'

More photos. The three original stakes in Mindelunden. A victim in South Africa, incinerated by a tyre around the neck. A young man, a woman about the same age, both staring at nothing, looking bored, unconcerned, as a Nazi officer placed a noose round their necks beneath a makeshift gallows.

Then army mugshots of the soldiers in Raben's squad and a snatched photo of Dragsholm walking down the street.

'Bilal rented these premises not long after.'

'You know that?' Lund demanded. 'You can place him here? Fingerprints? DNA? Documentation?'

'Give us time, for God's sake,' he replied wearily. 'The man's fled Ryvangen. He's taken Jarnvig's daughter hostage. We've enough evidence . . .'

She was sick of looking at the walls. There was a determined, obsessive mind at work here. She just wasn't sure whose.

'Did anybody see him here?'

'The building's empty. Who's going to see him?'

She walked up and stood in front of the tall homicide chief.

'So the only proof you have this belongs to Bilal is the key at the barracks?'

'Lund!' He was getting mad again. 'First he gets the colonel fired because he was investigating the old radio messages. Then he snatches Louise Raben and takes off God knows where. Do they sound like the actions of an innocent man?'

'He's scared. Did Jarnvig trace those radio messages?'

He folded his arms.

'So you're telling me Bilal's of no significance? And no one else can see this except you?'

'He's significant,' she agreed. 'He can help us find that officer. But it doesn't make him the killer.

Why would Bilal hide a key and a mobile phone at the barracks? Who got you to search there in the first place?'

'You were in Afghanistan—'

'Dragsholm said she'd found the officer. The one pretending to be Perk. That's what kicked this off. Bilal was at base when Raben went into that place, fixing the radio logs. It couldn't have been him.'

Lund's hand swept towards the table, the photos on the wall.

'This proves nothing. Raben's been right all along. We should have listened to him. He accused Strange—'

'We double-checked Strange!' the chief bellowed at her. 'He was demobilized long before the incident. He wasn't in Afghanistan. It can't be him. What the hell is wrong with you?'

She picked up the raffia bag, emptied it onto the table. A tiny blackened skull with a bullet hole. A skeletal hand. Dry, sooty bones.

'That's what's wrong with me.'

The forensics officers were torn, staring at her, staring avariciously at the bones. Then at the door.

Lund sighed. Knew what she'd see there.

Ulrik Strange. Hair freshly washed. Stubble newly shaved. Face perky and innocent. Clean clothes. Ready to start again.

She still felt grubby, even after the shower. And a little guilty. But not so much.

Brix said nothing.

Strange said nothing, just turned his back and walked outside.

A bright day, chilly. Not much different from Afghanistan. It was the same sun after all. He was leaning on his black Ford. She took off her blue shoe covers and plastic gloves, walked straight up to him.

Leaned on the car too, hands in pockets.

Strange was watching her. Hard to read his expression. Sorrow? Disgust? Anger? His face seemed so calm, so impassive that extreme emotions simply passed it by.

'What's the matter with you?' he asked in a quiet, calm voice. 'Why do you do these things?'

She coughed, shrugged.

'I didn't sleep all the way back. Jet lag. I don't know.'

He watched a uniformed officer take in some equipment, dodging beneath the Don't Cross tape.

'It's like the whole world's guilty until you prove it innocent.' He caught her eye. 'You. No one else.'

That wasn't such a bad observation, Lund thought. Or a bad idea.

'Sometimes,' Strange went on, 'I get the feeling you like a few things about me.'

'I do!'

'You've a damned funny way of showing it.'

'True.'

298

She waited for him to say more. There was nothing.

'So,' Lund said and clapped her cold hands. 'Now we've cleared the air—'

'Jesus!' Strange cried, so furiously one of the cops guarding the building turned and stared.

'I'm sorry. OK?'

'You're sorry?' He nodded. 'That's all there is to say?'

Lund frowned.

'What more do you want? I'm sorry. I was wrong. My head's somewhere else. I'm trying to get it straight.'

Nothing.

'OK?' she asked.

Still nothing.

'OK? Or do I go and see Brix and ask for a bus fare back to Gedser?'

'As if,' he said with a low laugh she couldn't interpret. 'So what now?'

'Isn't that obvious? We need to find Bilal.'

As she spoke Lund was looking round the neighbourhood, trying to picture a soldier coming here. Even out of uniform.

'We need to talk to Søgaard about the radio messages too.'

She crossed the street, looked at the posters in the immigrant bookshop opposite.

'Bilal must hate the extremists,' Strange said, following her. 'He sent the video just at the end of Ramadan.'

'Is that significant?' she asked.

'I don't know. Maybe he's kind of an extremist in reverse.'

Lund pointed at the walls. Posters for a rabble-rousing preacher, in Danish and Arabic.

'If it was Bilal he didn't have far to look for inspiration.'

There was an old book in the window. *Muslimsk Liga*. Muslim League.

'Hello!' Brix cried. He was coming out of the building with Madsen and some of the others. 'Bilal took a military G-Wagen from Ryvangen. He's been seen heading west. Let's go, shall we?'

She couldn't stop staring at the shop window.

'Lund!' the chief yelled. 'That means you too. Doesn't it?'

'It does,' she said and followed Strange to the car.

The army let Torsten Jarnvig out of custody at midday. He went straight back to Ryvangen. The place was crawling with police. No one was complaining any more.

'Any idea where your daughter is?' a young detective asked when Jarnvig got to his office. Søgaard had begun rearranging things already. Filing cabinets. The computer.

'No. She was looking round for things. She believed Raben from the start. Maybe I should have . . .'

Her picture was on the desk. Søgaard must have made the decision to leave it there.

Jarnvig was in plain army fatigues. No sign of rank any more. Maybe they were gone for ever. It didn't feel such a loss at that moment.

'We need to go through all the places Bilal kept things.'

'To hell with that!' Jarnvig shouted. 'My daughter's missing. What are you doing to find her?'

The cop didn't seem interested in answering.

'Do you think Bilal was hiding more than we know?'

'Ask Operational Command,' Jarnvig barked. 'Ask Arild. Bilal was the general's pet.'

The detective frowned.

'Yelling at me won't help. Do you have any idea where he might go?'

Jarnvig glared at him, furious.

'Do you specialize in stupid questions? Of course I don't. If I did. I'd be there.'

The faintest of raps at the door. Jonas was there in his winter coat and scarf. He looked forlorn.

'Are we done here?' Jarnvig asked the detective.

'Were you aware that Bilal hates Islamists?'

Jarnvig rolled his eyes.

'Oh for God's sake. He's done three tours fighting the Taliban. He knows what these people can do. What do you think?'

'I was asking you.'

'I think . . .' It was a good question, not that Jarnvig wanted to acknowledge that. 'I think he always seemed the perfect soldier. Conscientious.

Loyal. Obedient.' A pause. 'Obedient to a fault sometimes. He'd never get any higher than he was. He wasn't great at thinking for himself.'

Another cop came in from Bilal's quarters, said, 'Look at this. I broke open his locker. Interesting stuff.'

Clippings from the papers. All five victims, with photos, glued to card. Dozens of them.

'Perfect soldier,' the first cop said and laughed. He waved the clippings at Jarnvig. 'Make sure you let us know if you hear anything. The same goes for Raben. He's got plenty to answer for too.'

Jarnvig watched them go. When they'd left Jonas marched across the polished floor, hands swinging. Just like a soldier.

'You've got your jacket on,' Jarnvig said, bending down and doing up the top buttons. 'Have you been playing outside on your own?'

No answer. The usual blank look.

'Joakim and his parents are coming to take you to the cinema. That's good, isn't it?'

'Where's Mummy?'

Jarnvig smiled. It always seemed necessary when you lied to a child.

'I bet she'll be here by the time you get back.'

Another false grin and he realized for the first time it didn't work at all.

'That's what Daddy says,' Jonas told him in a low, hurt voice.

The boy leaned into Jarnvig's face, whispered in

302

his ear, glancing all the time at the two cops down the corridor.

'It's a secret, Granpa. He's waiting for you by the fence at the back. Where the tower is.'

Two young, accusing eyes.

'You won't tell, will you?'

Jarnvig tugged the boy's jacket.

'I won't tell, Jonas. That's a promise.'

Raben was waiting in some bushes by a fire exit close to a little-used guard tower. Jarnvig unlocked the gate, walked through, had Raben in his face straight away.

'Do the police have any idea where he took her?'

'They don't know a damned thing.'

He was in a grubby blue jacket that looked as if it might have been pulled out of a rubbish bin. He held one arm awkwardly.

'You shouldn't be here, Jens. You're sick.'

'I'm not helping in a hospital, am I? Where could he have gone?'

'We've checked all the army bases we can think of.' A pause. 'You're normally full of ideas. Where do you think he is?'

Raben shook his head.

Jarnvig put a hand on Raben's shoulder.

'People get hurt when you're around. I don't want that to happen to Louise. Stay clear of this.'

'We're equal now. We've got to help each other.'

'This is all your fault!' Then, more quietly,

'Louise kept trying to help you. Asking questions. Doing things she shouldn't.'

'I told you the truth all along. Why didn't you believe me?'

Jarnvig closed his eyes for a moment.

'Because I didn't want to. There. Are you happy now? Can we put this to one side and think about Louise?'

Raben looked happy with that admission.

'Bilal used to go camping on an old military site near Hillerød. We can start there . . .'

'You have to stay away.'

'And leave it to you and those idiots in the police?'

Jarnvig gave up, walked back to the gate and his green Mercedes G-Wagen. The phone rang. He answered so quickly he almost dropped the thing.

'Hello? Hello?'

A soft voice, faintly accented, distant and detached.

'We must stick together against the enemy.'

Jarnvig tried to picture the location. No traffic noise. Just the faintest sound of birdsong. Rural maybe.

'We're not the enemy!' Said Bilal said, his flat, monotonous voice rising. 'We never were . . .'

'Where are you?' Jarnvig demanded. 'I want an answer.'

'You're not my colonel any more. They took that away from you, didn't they?'

There was a strange mix of fear and fascination in his voice.

'Where are you?' Jarnvig asked again, aware Raben was next to him now, eyes shining, face full of curiosity.

'I did my duty. That was all. I did what I was told. Like a soldier should.'

'Where's Louise? She's nothing to do with this.'

The shortest of laughs.

'I won't take the blame. Never . . .'

The line went quiet.

'Bilal! Come back.'

'You turned against me. After all I did. All the work, all the loyalty. I still wasn't good enough. Just because of what I was—'

'No one turned against you! The police found evidence—'

'I didn't put it there. Someone's trying to frame me. Can't you see?'

A brisk wind was whipping up around this forgotten corner of Ryvangen. The sun was disappearing. Rain was on the way.

'You've got my daughter. Let her go. We can talk about this. I can make sure—'

'You can't do anything,' Bilal broke in. 'You're finished too. Tell General Arild. Say he's got to get me out of this. If it wasn't for—'

'What in God's name are you talking about?' Jarnvig cried.

A sudden movement. Raben's good hand snatched the phone from Jarnvig's hand.

'Let me speak to Louise,' he said in a low, calm, determined voice.

'I'm talking to Jarnvig. Not you!'

'Nothing happens until we hear from Louise, Bilal. Nothing . . .'

Said Bilal walked to his stolen Land Rover, opened the back door.

She was where he'd left her the previous night. Duct tape over her mouth. A military sock wrapped round her eyes as a blindfold.

Bilal ripped off the tape, didn't mind when she yelled at the pain.

The colonel's daughter. She looked down on him just as much as the rest of them.

He put the phone to her ear, underneath the blindfold.

'Louise?' Raben said.

Straight away, 'We drove for an hour and a half. A place underground—'

Bilal snatched away the phone, punched her hard in the mouth. Then again for sure.

He watched her hurting, listened to her screams. When they died down he put the phone back to his ear.

'Don't touch my wife,' Raben muttered in a low, hard tone.

'Too late.' Bilal looked around. This was a place he knew. They couldn't find it, not from what she'd said. 'I'll call again this evening. Get Arild. Talk to the police and I'll kill her.'

He opened the back of the phone. Took out the battery, threw it on the ground.

Louise Raben's nose had started bleeding. One red line down into her mouth.

She said in a cracked, pleading voice, 'Bilal. Let me go. What's wrong? I never hurt you.'

The young officer slammed the door on her, looked around, saw nothing but flat, bare grassland in all directions. Walked to the front of the vehicle, got in and started to drive.

Buch had been kept in an interview room in the Politigården all night, interviewed by a succession of surly PET officers who barely listened to a word he said. Around six in the morning they let him call home to Marie. That went almost as badly as the interrogations.

Now it was the middle of the day and a new shift, one young officer, one middle-aged, had turned up. They wore dark suits and blank, uncaring expressions. Neither of them sat down much. Buch had the impression they were biding their time. Wasting his. He wasn't a lawyer but he didn't believe for one moment he'd done anything that could lead to a prosecution.

'Tell us again,' the nearest PET man said.

Buch wiped his sweaty forehead with his right hand.

'This is a political issue, not a criminal one. Not yet. The Prime Minister was aware I had evidence of misdeeds on his part. The Defence Minister was ready to confirm this. Somehow Grue Eriksen knew. So the Prime Minister tried to shift the

307

blame to us.' Buch smiled at each of them in turn. 'Through you. How does it feel to be used?'

'The trouble is,' the younger PET man said, 'Rossing won't confirm your story. He's been released without charge.'

'That's because Grue Eriksen's got to him. Offered him a deal I suppose. It doesn't change the facts—'

'How could the Prime Minister know you were going to do this?' the second officer asked.

'Because someone warned him! Isn't it obvious? You've detained me all night for no reason.'

'National security's no reason?' the young one asked.

'I've done nothing to jeopardize national security. Quite the contrary. I've been defending it.'

There was a folder on a desk by the window. Both of them went to it, took out some papers.

'Let's see,' said the old cop. 'A confidential PET memo gets leaked from your office.'

'Not by me,' Buch insisted.

'You met with a suspended police officer, Sarah Lund. What for?'

'I was Minister of Justice. Lund was suspended only briefly. I believe she's back in service now. What's the problem?'

They didn't want to push that one.

'You visited your predecessor, Monberg, who took his own life.'

'Tell me how I acted illegally, please.'

'Your secretary accessed data without authority.'

'My secretary! Not me!'

'You obstructed PET's investigation. You defended Islamist organizations and their rights. You've been in contact with a journalist who provided you with confidential information she obtained while working for the Ministry of Defence . . .'

Buch felt like putting his head on his hands and going to sleep.

'Oh for pity's sake. Am I being subjected to an all-night interrogation because you and your new boss, whoever it is, doesn't like the cut of my jib?'

'We're at war!' the young one said and finally took a seat. 'There's a word for undermining our government and our democracy. It's called treason.' He waved his hand. 'Doesn't matter whether some Afghans got killed here or there. Treason. The betrayal of your own country.'

Buch groaned, closed his eyes, covered up a yawn with a tired, grubby hand.

'Are you going to persist with your accusations against the Prime Minister?'

'No.' A long, serious nod. 'Is that what you want to hear?'

'It's a start,' the young cop said, smiling at his colleague.

'Good,' Buch added. 'I intend to go even further. Grue Eriksen's the traitor. If you weren't the spineless, gutless creatures you are, you'd have him in here, shining a light in his eyes. Keeping him awake

309

all night. Hoping to break him. He's the traitor, and you nothing but his quislings . . .'

A knock on the door. Someone outside announced a lawyer had arrived. A tall, grey man came in and spoke quietly with both the PET officers out of Buch's earshot.

'Hello! What's going on here?' Another slam of his fists on the table. 'Am I invisible suddenly?'

The quisling crack was a touch too far, Buch thought. He might apologize for that one.

But then the older officer turned to him and said, 'There's someone outside for you.'

'Someone I'm allowed to see?'

'Sure. You can go.'

Karina and Carsten Plough were waiting in the circular vestibule by the Politigården stairs.

'I must say,' Plough declared archly as Buch came out, 'this is the first time I've ever had to spring a minister from jail.'

'First time for everything,' Buch declared. 'Besides, I'm not a minister any more.'

'Nor me a Permanent Secretary,' Plough added miserably.

'Well, you're free,' Karina said. 'That's something, isn't it?'

'Yes,' Buch agreed. 'But why?'

'Lund found something in Afghanistan.' She had a folder full of photographs. 'Take a look.'

A small skull with a bullet hole. A dog tag stained with smoke.

'That's what she was looking for when she went off limits,' Plough said. 'The police are chasing a Danish soldier now. He committed the recent murders to prevent the case being reopened.'

'And the officer who killed these people in Helmand?'

'The army say they're taking care of that,' Karina said with little enthusiasm. 'Though since they never found the bodies in the first place . . .' She looked at him. 'You can't win every battle, Thomas.'

This pair had stuck with him throughout. Damaged, perhaps ruined their own careers through nothing except an innate sense of justice.

'Thank you,' Buch said very earnestly. 'Is it too much to ask you to call a meeting of the parliamentary party? Without Grue Eriksen.'

'We can try,' Plough responded.

That note of caution never really left Carsten Plough's voice. It was a part of him.

'Say what you mean, will you?'

'You've got nothing on Grue Eriksen,' Plough insisted. 'I told you before. It's Rossing you should aim for. We know he was lying. We can prove it.'

Buch laughed.

'Ah. That old story . . .'

'It was the Prime Minister who got you out of here,' Plough added.

'Since he threw me in here in the first place that seems appropriate, don't you think? Can you arrange that meeting?'

Plough didn't move.

311

'I don't want you to snatch defeat from the jaws of victory, as they say. Think carefully . . .'

'I will,' Buch promised. 'Now can we get out of this grim hole, please?'

By the time Buch got to the Folketinget the word was out with the media. A full pack of reporters and TV crews blocked the entrance.

'Are you back in the government?'

'Do you support the Prime Minister?'

'Are you being charged?'

'Do you maintain your accusations?'

He knew now to do nothing but smile and push his way through. The experience had changed him. Perhaps made him a politician at last.

Kahn was waiting for him in his old office, still unoccupied ahead of the coming reshuffle.

'Where is everyone?' Buch asked.

'They asked me to come alone,' the Interior Minister said. 'Best not to make too much fuss.'

Buch realized he'd been so preoccupied he'd forgotten to brush his teeth. So he went to the desk, took out the brush he kept there and the little tube of toothpaste, poured himself a glass of water. Plough and Karina watched in silence from the bookcase near the door.

'I apologize for the mess,' he said, seating himself on his desk. 'I left in rather a hurry as you may know.'

Then he started brushing his teeth.

'We were hasty yesterday,' Kahn said. 'We

312

didn't know the full facts. We had to protect the party.'

'At all costs? At the expense of the truth?'

'Fine, fine. Bawl me out. You've got to admit. It was a pretty tall tale. We're all sorry. OK?'

'Accepted,' Buch said. 'Now we must act quickly. There are only two options.'

Kahn glanced at Plough and Karina.

'Either Grue Eriksen resigns,' Buch said. 'Or we force him to do so. Let's have a private conversation first and see if he'll do the decent thing and fall on his own sword.'

'There'd be a general election. One we'd lose,' Kahn said wearily.

'That's a reason for not doing the right thing?' Buch asked.

'Listen to me, Thomas,' Kahn pleaded. 'The Prime Minister wants to see you. He's appointing new ministers. You're looking at promotion.'

Buch turned to the window and the twisting dragons, walked to the door, pointed at it with his toothbrush and said, 'Get out.'

'You like being a minister!' Kahn cried.

'Out!'

Kahn walked through the door, sour-faced again.

'Krabbe and the Prime Minister are of one mind on this. Rossing won't help you. It's time to grow up.'

'Wait till I put Krabbe right on a few things. Thank you! Thank you! Goodbye! Chop, chop!'

Buch slammed the door behind him. Karina and Plough watched, wide-eyed and speechless.

'Well?' Buch asked. 'What else could I do? Krabbe!' He raised a fleshy finger. 'Let's find him.'

Carsten Plough put his hand to his eyes, shook his head, then wandered slowly outside.

Søgaard was still in the Politigården. Brix's personal decision. He didn't like the man and was in no rush to let him go.

The major now wore the blue suit of a prisoner and faced being charged as an accessory. Lund and Strange sat in the interview room watching him walk nervously up and down by the window. He was finally starting to look scared.

'Tell us about Bilal's contacts,' Lund began. 'Friends? Family?'

Søgaard dragged a seat to the table, sat down, glared at her.

'I was his commanding officer. Nothing more. Why in God's name am I still here?'

She tapped the pile of evidence in front of him.

'There's clear proof in the radio logs that some messages were deleted. You investigated.' Søgaard picked up the sheet and looked at it. 'Why didn't you find any of that?'

He didn't answer. Lund nodded.

'You didn't look into this yourself, did you? Too menial. So you delegated it. Let me guess—'

'Of course I asked Bilal to check them! He was the officer responsible for that area.'

Strange threw up his hands and laughed.

'So you asked him to investigate himself? Give me strength . . .'

She showed Søgaard the new photos from forensic. The skulls and bones she'd brought back from Helmand.

'We know for a fact these civilians were killed. No point in denying it now. An officer was there. Raben told the truth.'

'Raben was talking like a madman—'

'He told the truth! Bilal concealed those messages. Your men were witnesses to an atrocity. I don't believe for one minute you'd no idea something bad went on.'

'No.' He kept looking at the radio logs. 'I was assured nothing happened. I never knew about the messages. We never found anything at the house.'

'That's because you didn't look,' Lund threw at him. 'This isn't going to go down well with the next promotions board—'

A knock on the door. Strange went to deal with it.

'I can't answer for Bilal.' Søgaard leaned back, looked weary. 'Ask him.'

'You knew about the message five days before. The one that told you special forces were heading for the village. Who were they?'

A hand to his head.

'I never saw that message!'

She got up from the table, stood by the window,

hands on hips, staring at the rain running down the pane.

'You really weren't much in command at all, were you?' Lund asked, looking at the grimy glass.

'You don't know what it's like . . .'

'Listen to me, Søgaard. What future you've got in the army depends on the answers you give me now. The man who murdered these people used Per K. Møller's identity. Did Bilal know Møller?'

It took him a while to answer.

'No reason why he should.'

'Was Bilal there when the real Møller died?'

'I don't think so.'

'Was anyone from special forces . . . Jægerkorpset . . . any of these people around when that happened?'

'No. He was on his own when there was an explosion. He went straight to the nearest field hospital in Lashkar Gah.'

Lund turned and looked at him.

'Was he wearing his ID?'

'Why wouldn't he be?'

She picked up the photos, showed him the charred dog tag she'd picked up in Helmand. All in one piece.

'Explain that.'

'I'm not going to try.'

Lund didn't take her eyes off him.

'If you had a special forces officer come to you and say he needed a new ID for a covert mission—'

'Never happened, Lund! Don't go there.'

'*If.* You could just look through the recent deaths. Pick a name. Get a new dog tag made.' Her hand went to her head, ran through her long dark hair. 'Maybe Møller's did get lost. Or someone took it. If this is a covert mission they'll give him a new one anyway. Like a fake passport.'

Søgaard was rigid in the seat opposite her.

'But an order like that's above your pay grade, isn't it? Above Jarnvig's too I guess. It would need someone back here.'

'I never did anything like that in my life. I was never asked.'

'If you were?'

No answer. A knock on the door. Strange there.

'They've found Bilal's G-Wagen outside Hillerød. No sign of him or the woman. He must have stolen a new vehicle.'

She got up to leave.

'What about me?' Christian Søgaard shouted as she walked for the door.

'You can wait,' Lund said.

Outside the office was buzzing as Brix gathered a team. They'd placed a tap on Jarnvig's phone and captured the conversation with Bilal.

'What did he say?' Lund asked. 'This still doesn't—'

'He claims he's been set up. He wants Arild to get him out of this.'

Lund sat down next to an officer at a computer.

'Bilal's never been anything but a soldier. He's

317

going to want somewhere military to hide. The place he left the G-Wagen—'

'There's nowhere military in that area,' Brix said. 'We checked.'

'Nowhere now,' Strange said. 'During the Cold War we had lots of places up there. We thought the Russians were going to walk straight in, remember?'

Lund ran her finger over the screen, not minding how much this annoyed the woman detective perched in front of it.

'What kind of facilities?'

'All sorts,' Strange said. 'Underground barracks.' His mild face hardened. 'We were supposed to hide there and wait. Just sixteen Danish soldiers died when the Nazis invaded. The Russians weren't going to get off that lightly.'

'I imagine not,' Lund murmured, thinking. 'Have we checked for abandoned facilities?'

She got up, went to the wall, looked at the evidence photos. A blackened skull from Afghanistan now alongside the bloody photos of Anne Dragsholm and the four members of Ægir.

'I want someone to get hold of Frederik Holst,' she said to the nearest detective. 'He's an army surgeon in Lashkar Gah.'

There was a photo of the smoky piece of metal she'd dragged out of the oven the Afghan cop had uncovered at the back of that sad little house.

'Get through and ask him what happened to Per K. Møller's dog tag.'

318

A buzz of excitement ran round the office.

'Lund!' Strange yelled from the exit. 'We've got somewhere. Grab your coat. We're going.'

'Ask him if there were any special forces officers in the hospital at the time,' she added. 'Get me names. Is that clear?'

'Sure,' the young officer said. 'Will do.'

She got her donkey jacket from the locker. Looked at the gun in the locker, took it. Strange was right. She knew there'd been body armour sitting on the second shelf. It had been there ever since they took her back. No one mentioned it. No one ever told her how to use the thing. Not that she minded. She knew now.

The woods north of Hillerød were dense and dark. The green army G-Wagen moved slowly down the narrow lane. Jarnvig at the wheel. Angry.

'This is ridiculous. We can't keep looking.'

'Bilal used to come here,' Raben said. 'He told me about it. You could break in. Go underground. See all these places they used during the Cold War.'

He waved at the broken wire ahead. Flat green land beyond it, forest in the distance. No buildings. Not even a sign.

'We should call the police,' Jarnvig said again.

There was a shop along the road.

'Keep driving, will you?' Raben said.

'I'm taking orders from you now, am I? We

319

could get hold of Arild. Bilal worships him. If anyone could cut a deal . . .'

The roadside shop was for local campers. Fruit and vegetables. Gas. Clothing. General supplies.

'Let's ask someone,' Raben said.

He told Jarnvig to stop the jeep. The two of them walked into the ramshackle store. A short bearded man stood behind the counter.

'Can I help? We've got fresh potatoes—'

'We're from the army,' Jarnvig said. 'Looking for a deserter. Probably in fatigues. Acting a bit scared. He's—'

'He's sick,' Raben said.

'What kind of sick?' the man asked, reaching for something underneath the counter.

'A bad kind. He's young-looking. About twenty-eight. Dark hair. Dark skin. Immigrant. He'd probably want to buy food or . . .'

The bearded shopkeeper pulled out a double-barrelled shotgun, held it loose in his arms.

'Don't get many people this time of year. Those you do get . . . sometimes they act funny.' He looked at them. 'What kind of bad?'

'We can deal with it,' Raben said.

The man nodded at Jarnvig.

'You're the second squaddie who's walked in here with a gun on his belt. I'd get arrested if I went round like that.'

'Where did he go?' Raben asked.

He laughed.

'Come into a shop and you've got to buy something. It's only polite. Everyone knows that.'

Jarnvig muttered something, nodded at the cigarette stand and threw fifty kroner on the counter. 'Give me twenty Prince.'

'Prince cost a hundred out here, mister,' the shopkeeper said with a big grin. 'It's the transport, you see.'

Raben was getting furious. Jarnvig threw another note on the counter.

'Where . . .?' Raben started.

'Go left. A couple of hundred metres down he took an old track into the woods. Not seen that used in years. You ought to find him just from following the tyre tracks.'

'He had a woman with him?' Jarnvig asked.

'Not that I saw. You want to buy something else?'

But by then Raben was hurtling back towards the Mercedes.

Torsten Jarnvig sat in the passenger seat, shaken by Raben's crazed driving as they careered along the overgrown trail.

There was only one set of tyre marks ahead. He could have followed them. Would have done too. But Raben was a *jaeger*, just like Jan Arild all those years before in the Gulf, the Balkans and places they never talked about. Like dogs after a scent, they didn't pursue a quarry, they chased it down.

The woods were coniferous, thick and dark, even in winter. From the state of the ground it looked as if only one vehicle had been this way all season.

A crossroads. Raben didn't even stop before taking the Mercedes into a hard left swing, rounding the corner at such speed the vehicle almost toppled over. Jarnvig clung to the door handle, didn't say a thing. There was no point.

The track narrowed. There was open space ahead. At fifty kilometres an hour they burst into a clearing. An old black Land Rover was parked on a concrete pad. A rusty, low watchtower to the right. Raben stamped on the brakes, kept the wheels bursting in and out of lock, brought the vehicle to a halt in a dead straight line.

No one in the Land Rover. Behind it was an ancient fence topped with rolls of barbed wire. A yellow sign, rickety, now at forty-five degrees: *Military Area. Keep Out.*

Raben stretched out his hand. How long did Torsten Jarnvig think about this? As long as he did in the Iraqi desert, when he was alongside Jan Arild, wondering how to stay alive.

He took the army handgun from his belt and handed it over.

'Call the police,' Raben said.

'Do you want me as backup?'

That was a look Arild gave him from time to time too.

It said: *Are you kidding?*

'There's space enough for a couple of thousand

soldiers underground here,' Raben said. 'Their radios won't work. They won't know where I am.' A sour, hurt expression on his face. 'I'd rather not get shot again. Tell them that too.'

Then he worked his way through the wire.

It took a minute to find the entrance. Cold War. Built to shelter from a nuclear blast. They'd been mothballed by the time Raben came into the army. But the word was they were never totally out of commission. Some bright spark had realized the end of one conflict, even a half-century stand-off between the world's great powers, didn't spell peace on earth. The time might come again . . .

Raben remembered this as he edged through the open heavy iron door set into what looked like a derelict guardhouse surrounded by blackthorn and elder bushes. He had a torch but he didn't need it. The place was lit up like Strøget at Christmas. Two lines of bulbs in a whitewashed ceiling led down a stone staircase that seemed to go on for ever. The place had power. Was still breathing, alive.

Jarnvig's P210 pistol sat steady in his hand. He took the steps one by one, moving slowly down this steep artery into the earth. There was nowhere to hide in this freezing, dank refuge beneath the ground. Not for him. Or Said Bilal.

Buch found Erling Krabbe on the main staircase in the Folketinget.

323

'I left you some messages . . .'

The People's Party man looked even more evasive than usual.

'I was about to call you back. After my next meeting. Look . . .'

MPs and civil servants were wandering up and down, glancing at them. Krabbe walked down to the next landing, disappeared into the shadows of a corridor. Buch followed.

'Just tell me,' he begged. 'Will you join the Opposition in bringing down Grue Eriksen?'

Erling Krabbe bit his bloodless lower lip, said nothing.

'Dammit!' Buch barked. 'You know he's not fit to stay in office. The man's as guilty as hell. They found proof that family was murdered in Helmand.'

'You only have Rossing's word for that and he's chosen to take the blame . . .'

'Rossing's the scapegoat! And a happy one too. He won't get prosecuted. He'll be back in government in eighteen months. It was the truth. You know it too.'

Krabbe glanced at his watch so quickly Buch knew he hadn't even checked the time. Then he started to walk off.

Buch's hand came out and grabbed his arm.

'What the hell's going on here?' Thomas Buch demanded. 'I've got a right to know.'

Krabbe peeled Buch's fat fingers from his arm.

'I'm not going to get into bed with Birgitte Agger

324

without thinking it over. You don't honestly believe it's justice she's after.'

'This isn't about politics. It's about right and wrong . . .'

Erling Krabbe was staring at him, as if he'd seen something new.

'It really is that black and white for you, isn't it?' He laughed. 'I suppose it was for me once. But it isn't and it never will be.'

He went back to the staircase, started to walk down the steps.

'So it was you who spilled the beans, was it?' Buch bellowed, his voice echoing off the walls, making heads turn everywhere. 'When I told you Rossing had confessed. You went straight to Grue Eriksen like the lapdog you are?'

Krabbe came back, astonished. Hurt, Buch thought.

'What on earth are you talking about?'

'You're the only one I told!'

Erling Krabbe folded his skinny arms and waited.

'Apart from . . . my own people,' Buch said more quietly. 'People I trust, naturally.'

Krabbe laughed at him.

'Oh honestly. Did your week as a minister teach you nothing? There's no one you can trust in this place.'

A pat on the arm. A look that seemed almost kindly. He held out his hand.

'I'll call you when I've decided,' Krabbe said.

Buch shook his dry, cold fingers then watched him go.

Back through the endless corridors, into the Ministry of Justice, mind racing all the way.

Karina was at her desk alone.

'The Prime Minister's office called wanting a meeting,' she said when he marched in. 'I declined. I hope that was right.'

'I suppose.' Buch walked to his desk. 'Who prepared the documents yesterday? After Rossing came in here and I asked someone to make a note of what I told you afterwards?'

'Plough,' Karina said. 'I offered but he insisted.'

'Who typed it? Which secretary?'

She tugged on her blonde hair.

'Plough did it himself. He said they were busy with other things.'

'Could someone have seen his report and warned Grue Eriksen?'

'No! He printed it out and gave it to me. Then he went over to the Prime Minister's office . . .'

Buch looked at her.

'Oh for God's sake, Thomas! It was about that post in Skopje. You'd intervened on his behalf, hadn't you?'

'And the office called him in?'

'I don't remember. Ask him when he gets back.'

'Where is he?'

'I don't know. Now can we . . .?'

He went through more papers, scattering them everywhere.

'Who leaked that memo to Birgitte Agger? Did we ever find out?'

She folded her arms.

'Plough looked into it. He didn't get anywhere.'

Buch went to the nearest document mountain, started sifting anxiously through it.

'Where's the information on the military squad? Ægir?'

'Thomas!' Karina cried in a high, piercing voice. 'What's going on?'

Nothing in the papers. Buch picked them up, launched them at the sofa, watched them flutter round the room.

'Calm down,' she ordered. 'I won't talk to you if you're going to be like this. I'll walk right out of here . . .'

He kicked a pile of box files, stumbled to the desk. It was there all along. A list of the soldiers in Raben's unit. Mugshots, profiles.

She followed, trying to reason with him.

'Listen, Thomas. I know Plough was angry with Rossing. He's never liked the man. But he didn't want you to go for the Prime Minister because he thought you couldn't win.'

Buch flicked through the pages. Myg Poulsen. Raben. Lisbeth Thomsen. Photos, brief service records and a few personal details.

A head shot he'd never really looked at before. There'd been no reason.

'Does Plough have a son?'

She groaned.

'He did. He died last year. Plough took it very badly.'

'In a traffic accident, right?'

She nodded.

'Plough lives in Nørrebro? What street?'

'Baggesensgade. What's this about?'

'If I've still got a driver,' Buch said, heading for the door, 'tell him I'm on my way.'

'And if not?'

Buch ran his fingers through his pockets, checked the wallet there.

'Maybe you could lend me some money for a taxi?'

Karina Jørgensen handed over two hundred kroner then went to the desk and retrieved the file.

It was open at the squad member no one looked at.

Hans Christian P. Vedel. Killed in a car crash on the Øresund bridge. Suicide, the police said.

A picture of a serious, plain young man, gloomy eyes staring straight at the camera.

An address in Baggesensgade.

'Thomas . . .' she started, but Buch was gone.

Lund and Strange were in the first car to meet Jarnvig outside the underground facility.

The heavy iron door was open. A long staircase, lights all the way.

'They're in there. Raben went after him,' Jarnvig said.

'Is he armed?' Strange asked.

The colonel nodded.

Lund got out her gun, Strange did the same. More cars were arriving. Two cops from the first ran over.

'There are going to be more exits than this one,' Strange told them. 'See if you can pull up a plan or something. Make sure everyone's covered. Tell Brix nobody's to enter until we've checked it out.'

The first officer looked uncertain.

'If you wait a minute you can tell him yourself . . .'

'My daughter's in there!' Jarnvig yelled.

Lund set off down the long stairs, gun ahead of her, listening. The place smelled like a gigantic mouldering tomb, the air stale and fusty.

Strange was soon with her. They half-ran down the first flight of stairs, stopped at the bottom. The place changed here. The floor was cracked and damp in places. The walls looked as if they'd been hewn from the native rock. At regular intervals there were doors that must have led to subterranean offices, barracks, storerooms.

'How big's this place?' she asked as Strange went forward, looking left and right.

'God knows,' he murmured. 'How the hell—?'

A distant sound. Footsteps, loud and rapid, hard to pinpoint as they echoed off the walls.

Strange looked round, listened, pointed to the right and they began to run.

★　★　★

Raben was deep in the bowels of the underground camp, checking every door. The ones he met were open. And then he got to a closed one. Red paint and the number forty-four on the outside.

Put his good shoulder to it, felt the old iron creak then move under his weight.

Through, gun in one hand, low and ready.

There was another section here, rooms and corridors. All part of the hidden tide of fury waiting to loose itself on a Russian army that would never come.

A noise not far away.

Her voice. Crying with pain and fear.

Raben leaned against the damp wall, brick here, not rock. Then he edged slowly, quietly forward, got to the end, saw bright lights beyond in what looked like a wide room to the right.

One brief moment of reconnaissance. His head flew round the door, flew back.

In that fraction of a second he saw them. Louise on her knees, hands tethered. Bilal standing, a gun to her head. The place was a generator room. Vast antiquated machines down one side. Places to run for cover.

Not that it mattered. Bilal was a good soldier too. The moment Raben stuck his head round the door he knew he'd been spotted.

After a while Bilal yelled nervously, 'Step forward so I can see you!'

Raben stayed where he was.

'Get out of there or I'll blow her head off now.'

Raben walked straight out, hands down by his side, gun pointed at the floor.

Louise looked up at him with tired, terrified eyes. Her nose was bloody and bruised. Bilal's fingers wound into her hair, his pistol hard against her scalp.

Said Bilal didn't even seem frightened. Short dark hair, boyish face, regulation fatigues. Model soldier.

'Put down your weapon,' he ordered. 'Drop it!'

Straight away Raben crouched down, placed the black handgun on the tiles, then pushed it across the floor, hard enough so it came to rest in front of Louise's feet.

'Where's Arild?' Bilal asked. 'I told you not to come looking for me.'

'Sometimes things don't work out,' Raben said with a shrug. 'Let her go. You've got me now. Whatever it is you want. Take me. Not my wife . . .'

The gun came away from her head, pointed straight at his face.

'If only you'd kept your big mouth shut! None of this would have happened.'

'But it did.'

'They weren't civilians! They were Taliban informers. Bankrolling the bastards.'

'The kids weren't doing that—'

'Don't you lecture me about the kids! Don't . . .'

Raben's heart leapt. Bilal's gun hand was steady

as a rock. Then there were more footsteps and they were close.

Lund got there first. Walked to Raben's side, watched Bilal's gun turn to face her.

'Stop this,' she said as calmly as she could. 'Put down the gun. Let her go. You can't—'

His fingers wound more tightly into Louise's greasy black hair. The pistol went straight back to her head. She shrieked with terror and pain.

'No!' Lund yelled, took a step in front of Raben, gun out, two hands on the butt, aimed straight at the man in the army fatigues. 'Walk out of here. We can talk this over. I want to hear—'

'You're not army,' Bilal spat back at her.

'What's this to do with Louise?' Lund cried. 'Leave her out—'

'You're not army! I did my duty. What I was told.'

One more step towards him. Gun steady. She was a lousy shot. Maybe he could tell.

'I believe you, Bilal. I can help. But you have to let Louise go.'

Another step and Raben was edging towards him too.

Then the door on the far side burst open and Strange was walking through, weapon up, face taut and determined.

Bilal looked left, looked right, looked up for an instant, then at Lund. His fingers relaxed in Louise Raben's hair. His knee pushed her forward.

'Go,' he ordered.

Lund didn't watch as she half-stumbled to her feet then fell into the arms of her husband.

Something wasn't right here.

'Get her out, Raben,' she ordered. 'Get her upstairs and . . .'

Bilal was sweating. Weeping now. Strange had got in front, checking him over, gun steady all the time. Not taking his eyes away for a minute he edged round to stand next to Lund.

'I just did my duty,' the young officer repeated standing erect by the ancient generator.

'Which was what exactly?' she asked.

'You're not army,' he said again but more softly this time.

He held his gun loosely by his side. No real threat. Lund walked closer.

'They were just little things, Bilal. You deleted some radio recordings. Someone told you to. Who was the officer involved? What did the radio messages say?'

Without being asked he leaned down and let the gun fall to the floor. Then back to the stiff soldier pose again.

'Good . . .'

He wasn't listening any more. His eyes were ahead. Somewhere else altogether.

'Lund,' Strange said. 'I don't like this. Something's wrong.'

'Nothing's wrong,' she insisted, not that she believed it. 'Come on, Bilal. Let's get out of here.

We can go back to headquarters. You'll be safe. I'll get you a lawyer. We can talk . . .'

He was unzipping his jacket. She watched and felt her blood run cold.

A belt there. Wires and packets. Pink sticks of explosive like fireworks. The familiar pineapple shape of a grenade.

Strange didn't say any more. He raced away from the soldier, grabbed her by the jacket, almost picked her up as he pushed and shoved her back towards the exit.

A voice behind. Loud and certain. The words of an army man reciting a long-cherished refrain.

'For God, King and Country!' Said Bilal chanted.

The red door was getting closer. She could read the number forty-four. They were turning towards it.

The bellow of an explosion. The world turning the colour of fire. Something lifted her and Strange off their feet altogether, threw them into the corridor outside until gravity beckoned and the hard damp tiles bit at her body, her face and hands.

When she came to his arms were still over her, fingers holding down her head, shielding it, his body wrapped above hers like protecting armour.

Sparks flew around them. There was the smell of cordite and explosive. And behind that the fresh, sharp tang of blood.

Plough's house was as inconspicuous as the man himself. A plain detached bungalow down a long drive, almost invisible from the street. Thomas Buch realized he'd no expectations of what it would be like. No idea how Plough, a quiet, introverted solitary man, lived.

The lights were on downstairs. The front door was open. He knocked then walked in.

A kitchen with half-washed dishes and empty cartons of microwave food. Then a chaotic living room full of packing cases. A map of the world on the wall. Shelves of books.

Two boxes stood open on the desk. Medals inside. Military, from service in Afghanistan.

A set of photographs in frames. Mostly the same face, a young man growing from schoolboy to manhood. Smiling, not the surly, uncertain figure in the army mugshot.

There was a resemblance there, Buch thought, as he picked up the nearest photo. If Plough smiled easily he'd look like this. Perhaps he did once. Long before Frode Monberg, Flemming Rossing and – it had to be faced – Thomas Buch entered his life.

It was hard to let go of the picture. Buch thought of his daughters, wondered if either of them would want a career in the army. It was safe money these days and there wasn't much of that about. A way of paying off your debts to get through college. Security of a kind.

He heard familiar soft footsteps behind, turned and faced Carsten Plough.

'I'm sorry,' Buch said, putting the picture back

on the desk. 'I knocked but no one answered. The door was open.'

Plough was in a green and blue plaid shirt and jeans. He looked different.

'Hans Christian Plough Vedel. Vedel was my wife's name. In the army they always called him HC.'

The tall civil servant came over and looked at the photo.

'He was the only one in the squad who got out unharmed. It was a miracle, or so I thought.'

Plough's calm and gentle face creased with sorrow. He picked up some paperback books from the desk, tidied them into a neat pile.

'Hans told us there'd been some kind of incident in the village. There'd been an officer, and some civilians were killed. Then the judge advocate came along and called him a liar. A lunatic, like that Raben fellow.' A caustic smile, one Buch had never seen before. 'It wasn't possible, was it? A Danish soldier would never do such a thing.'

More books. Buch wondered if the man even knew what he was packing.

'He changed his statement when the army leaned on him. But I think that made it all worse. You see.' Plough tapped his head. 'In here he knew he wasn't mad. He was sure of what he saw. But the army said otherwise and the army didn't lie. So I believed the army too, and Hans became sicker and sicker.'

There was a grand piano by the window. He

picked some sheet music off the stand, tossed that into the box.

'Then, a year ago, he drove the wrong way down the motorway to the Øresund bridge. And that was that.'

He went through the pictures one by one, shook his head as if to say, 'Later.'

'It was the end of my marriage. Things hadn't been good since Hans came back.' The shortest, most bitter of smiles. 'I was a civil servant, you see. I was bound to side with authority. So afterwards I buried myself in work, even more than before. And then . . .' A bright, vicious note in his voice. 'One day Anne Dragsholm turns up asking for Monberg. My minister.' A possessive finger pointed at Buch. 'Mine. She knew Hans wasn't lying, any more than Raben. Because Dragsholm had done something all the clever people in Operational Command couldn't. She'd found the officer.'

More books. Then Plough carefully closed the lid.

'I won't forget that day. I sat outside on a bench eating my sandwich, drinking my bottle of water. Thinking I was the most loathsome, most despicable man on earth. Because my son had needed me and I'd thought him a lunatic and a liar. When all the time he was simply telling the truth.'

He lifted the box and placed it on the floor. Got another empty one. Fetched some more books from the cases.

'I'm a loyal, gullible man. So I believed Monberg when he said he'd look into it. But then Dragsholm was killed, and still he did nothing.' A cold laugh that seemed out of character. 'Instead, like a coward and a fool he tried to take his own pathetic life.'

'And then you get me, the new boy, dumb and innocent, waiting to be fed a line,' Buch said, alarmed by the venom in his own voice.

Plough looked offended.

'What else could I do? I'd tried Monberg and he let me down. I had to lead you to the case. So I leaked the PET memo. Yes! Me! Quiet as a mouse Carsten Plough, the most discreet and reliable civil servant in Slotsholmen. I made sure Karina found Monberg's private diary. I laid a trail of breadcrumbs for my fat sparrow and you followed them, Buch, every last one. More enthusiastically than I could ever have hoped.'

'For God's sake! You could have gone to the police!'

That bitter laugh again.

'Eight days a minister and still so much to learn. Of course I couldn't. Rossing had been pulling Erik König's strings for years. The two of them were in cahoots long before any of this happened. König answered more to the Defence Ministry than he ever did to us.'

'Then the Politigården . . .'

'Who would have turned the case over to PET in an instant. Give me credit. I know the system.

338

I invented half of it.' The books had been forgotten. 'But I had no proof. Not till yesterday. And then . . .' The broadest, happiest of smiles. 'I gave it to the Prime Minister.'

He smiled at Buch.

'There was no hesitation on Grue Eriksen's part. He didn't dither, like you.'

Buch closed his eyes and groaned.

'Of course not! He had his own skin to save.'

'No. Monberg as good as told me. He had a meeting with Rossing. As soon as he returned, the case was closed. There and then.'

Buch picked up a paperback on the desk. A cowboy story. It looked familiar.

'Thanks for giving me that,' Plough said. 'But it's not to my taste.'

'You should have told someone.'

'Who would have believed me?' Plough touched his arm, an odd and unexpected gesture in such a man. 'Not you. Not in the beginning anyway. Thomas . . . I'm genuinely sorry for the way things turned out. But you and Karina will do all right.'

Another book. A guide to Manhattan.

'When we talked the Prime Minister asked me whether I really wanted to go to Skopje. If there was anywhere else I'd prefer. So I said . . .'

Plough went through the photo frames, picked up one, showed it to Buch whose heart fell instantly.

'New York. Of course.'

A younger Carsten Plough. Dark hair. A pretty, happy wife by his side. A son with them, tall and smiling, no more than twelve or thirteen. They stood on the observation deck of the World Trade Center. Clothes from a different time. Everything from a different time.

'It was the most expensive holiday we ever had,' Plough admitted. 'I wanted it to be something we'd remember for ever.'

He gazed at the picture: lost faces, lost world. Lost family.

'There's nothing wrong with dreaming, is there? You'll be the crown prince now, Thomas. Karina can be your right hand—'

'All this time, Plough, all these years of service! And still you don't see how it works, do you? Monberg was screwing with you! What else are you hiding?'

A furtive look and that too was new.

Buch walked round the desk, tapped Plough on the plaid shirt.

'Tell me dammit or I'll take you down with them.'

'I'd like you to go now, please.'

The prim tone was back in his voice.

'Jesus.' Buch wanted to scream. 'You did just what they wanted all along. You helped the wrong man. You sucked up to the bastard who caused your own son's death—'

It came out of nowhere. A slap across the face. Like a challenge to a duel. Or a spat between children. Buch felt his cheek. It barely hurt. Not physically.

'The right people have been punished. I owed that to my son.' His arm stretched out to the door. 'You will leave now. I demand it.'

There were tears behind the staid horn-rimmed civil servant's glasses.

Thomas Buch picked up his old Western novel from the table, wondered why he'd given it to Plough in the first place. Even he wouldn't like these stories any more. Too many heroes and villains. Too much black and white and never a hint of grey.

'Goodnight,' he said then let himself out into the dark chill street.

Raben was back in a Politigården interview room, facing the same lawyer he'd seen the day before. He couldn't work out whether she was mad with him for fleeing the cops at the hospital or pleased he'd been proved right.

Either way it didn't matter. Louise now sat by his side. There was a deal on the table, a better one, though it still came with conditions.

'I don't think there's any doubt they'll accept your story this time,' the woman said. 'That doesn't change everything. You still need to drop your accusations against the police officer here.'

His arm was in a fresh sling. They'd cleaned up Louise's face. He didn't say a thing.

'It's clear your other allegations were correct.

That means you've served two years in custody for something that should never have happened. Whatever penalty you get for the crimes you've just committed I can argue the time you've served already covers that.'

'You mean I'm free?' he asked. 'I can go home? See my son?'

'You can see your son. But you'll have to be in custody until we can get in front of a judge. It'll take a week or two at the most.'

He glowered at her.

'You've waited a long time, Raben!' the woman cried. 'For God's sake be patient now. I've talked them into giving you a place at Horserød. It's an open prison. As pleasant as jail gets.' She glanced at Louise. 'You'll have family quarters there. The three of you can live together. Just a week, two or three at the most. Then I'll get you released. On bail at first. But they won't get away with opposing that. I can't believe they'd even try.'

'Jonas,' he whispered.

'And I advise you to sue for damages. You'll win. Big time.' She placed a piece of paper on the table. Raben looked at it. His original witness statement naming Strange as the officer in Helmand. 'But please . . . you need to sign a formal statement withdrawing that accusation against the policeman. As long as that's hanging over us . . .'

He looked at Louise.

'Can we have a moment to ourselves?'

'Of course,' the lawyer said then left the room.

He turned to the battered, tired woman next to him, didn't see the dirty clothes, the blood, the bruises.

'If we want . . .' he began.

Her head fell on his shoulder. Her hand found his. He brushed her dark and grubby hair with his lips.

'I'll do anything they ask,' he whispered. 'Whatever they—'

'So long as you come home I just don't care.'

His soldier's fingers found her cheek. They were too rough for her. Too coarse, too soiled by the work he'd done. But she never minded, and didn't now. She lifted her mouth, held it close to his, waited.

It was a brief and awkward kiss. The only kind he had. What was good between them came from her alone and she never even knew it. All he had to give was himself, his love, his dedication. And they'd failed somewhere along the way.

Not now though, he thought, as he held her, smelled the mud and mould of that underground hell they'd left behind.

Raben kissed his wife again then got up, moved his pained and aching frame to the table, and ripped the statement there to pieces, scattering the shreds across the floor.

Jarnvig was back in place in Ryvangen. Reinstated as colonel by Operational Command. Søgaard had been sent on leave ahead of an inquiry into his conduct towards those under his command. A new major, a genial man from the south, had taken his place.

They hadn't had much time to talk. Jarnvig had been on the phone constantly, to Camp Viking in Helmand, to contacts in Denmark demanding an immediate reopening of the investigation into the incident Raben had reported.

A distant voice in Afghanistan was listening to his orders.

'I want a military police team sent back to that place immediately. Look under every stone. Interview that Afghan officer Lund found. I can't believe she uncovered more in one day than we managed in three months.'

'I wasn't here then, sir,' the man said dryly.

'Well you are now, Major, and you've got a job to do. Get on with it and make sure I'm kept informed.'

He finished the call. The new man stood in front of his desk. Not stiff and severe like Søgaard. He looked more like a civilian who'd found a uniform somewhere.

'Any news about General Arild?' Jarnvig asked. 'I need to talk to him.'

'Not yet. We've got a new team arriving tonight. If it's OK I'd like to welcome them myself . . .'

'No, no,' Jarnvig said, not looking up from the pile of papers on his desk, most of them to do with the original report into Raben's claims. 'Thanks but I can manage.'

'I thought . . . Your daughter's back. She wants to see you. She looks . . .' He grimaced. 'She looks worn out. Really. If you need me . . .'

'Then I'll let you know. Show her in.'

The new man nodded at the window.

'She's in your house right now. Packing her things. I think she's called a cab to Horserød.'

Jarnvig took off his reading glasses.

'Horserød?'

Two soft bags full of clothes. Jonas trying hard to stuff his plastic sword into the second.

Ryvangen was a castle, a fortress of a kind. It protected her. It enclosed and trapped her too. Like family. A trade-off between security and freedom. She'd come close to making a bargain that carried too high a price. The bed beyond the door. Søgaard beneath her . . .

It was nothing to do with him. Nothing to do with Jens much. It was about being an army wife and mother. Another loyal servant inside the tribe. There was a time for that, and a time to break free, wrap your arms around the ones you loved, the people who truly mattered. And leave.

She'd stopped packing, was still staring at the unmade bed when her father walked in.

A smile for him. She knew what was coming.

'We've got to go now, Dad.'

'May I ask where?'

'Horserød. To visit Jens. They're giving us family quarters.' She picked up a scarf, put it in the bag with some of Jonas's shirts. 'It's easy enough to come and go. I can still be in the infirmary.'

She'd spent so long in the shower, washing off the filth and the memories of the place Bilal had taken her. The bruises were healing. There was a light ahead of them, dim and shapeless, but one she recognized. It had a name she hadn't heard in a long time. The future.

'We've got to get away from Ryvangen.'

'To live in a prison camp?'

'It won't be for long. The lawyer said Jens will be out in two or three weeks at the most.' She patted Jonas on the head. 'We can wait for that, can't we?'

He was more focused on his toys than their conversation, still trying to cram as many as possible into the bag. Plastic dragons, more swords.

She got up, went to her father, took the door keys out of her bag, handed them over.

He looked like a man betrayed. Deprived of something that belonged to him.

Soldiers, she thought. Good men. Decent men. Clinging to the things they loved for strength and confidence.

'Dad . . .' She put her arms round him, kissed his rough cheek. 'I'll see you tomorrow. The day after that. The week after that.' She touched his face, looked into his hurt eyes. 'We're not leaving you. Just Ryvangen.'

'Right,' he whispered.

Men were always lost for words when emotion raised its awkward head.

Jonas walked up and gave Jarnvig something. A warrior with a shield and a sword. Wrapped the colonel's wrinkled fingers round its body.

'The car will be here,' she said and kissed him again, very quickly. 'I'll call. Come on, Jonas.'

The two of them left, didn't look back. Jarnvig watched them go, clutching the toy soldier Jonas had given him.

Then he sat at the dining table trying to imagine what the house would be like without their presence. Bereft of Louise's energy and warmth. Of Jonas's childlike curiosity and games.

Dead, Jarnvig thought. One more brick box in the warren that was Ryvangen.

His phone rang. It was Søgaard's replacement.

'You wanted me to find General Arild,' he said.

'Yes . . .'

'Well he's here.'

Arild was in his office, smoking as he went through the papers on the desk. Jarnvig could only smile awkwardly as he walked in.

'Oh come on, Torsten,' Arild said. 'You're not going to play hurt with me are you? Like a little girl?'

Jarnvig took his chair. Arild grabbed the one opposite.

'I don't know what you mean.'

347

Arild gestured at the office.

'You're back here. Running Ryvangen again. The colonel. Louise came to no harm. Things aren't so bad. I could have put you in front of a court if I'd wanted.'

'Raben was right.'

Arild smirked.

'So what? He was a criminal on the run and you helped him escape PET. But what the hell? Water under the bridge.'

Jarnvig nodded, said nothing.

'What a business!' Arild added, still grinning as if it was all a game. 'Young Bilal running rings round us to make sure we never found out what really happened in Helmand.'

'You knew, didn't you?'

'Me?' Arild threw back his head and laughed. He looked like a young man sometimes. So fit he could go out on active service tomorrow if he wanted. Perhaps did. 'How could I? I'm a pencil-pusher in Operational Command. My life's even more boring than yours.'

Jarnvig watched him, becoming more convinced with every easy gesture, each casual denial.

'You do believe me, don't you?' Arild asked.

'No,' Jarnvig said with great certainty. 'I know how it goes with engagements like these. I worked them with you once . . .'

'That was a long time ago. These are different days.'

'Nothing on paper. No trails to entrap you. No footprints . . .'

'This is a fantasy,' Arild insisted.

'If you've got something to tell me, General, say it now. You can't cover it up any more. The police are involved. The Ministry. Tell me and I'll do everything I can to clear up this mess. I don't want to harm the army . . .'

'What a smug little cretin you've become,' Arild declared then blew smoke at the ceiling. 'Your horizons really don't stretch beyond these miserable barracks, do they? You've no idea how complicated the world's become.'

'A Danish officer massacres an innocent family. What's so complicated about that?'

'Lots,' Arild said. 'We have to protect our own.' His fist banged the desk. 'Our own! No one else will. The politicians play armchair generals in Slotsholmen. The media snipe from the side lines looking to belittle and blame us at every opportunity. And every year we send more men . . .' A shrug. '. . . and a few women to their deaths. For reasons we forgot ages ago, even if we ever knew them.'

'Either you lied to the police or you didn't.'

'Did I? Even if I did . . . so what?'

'I can't believe I'm hearing this . . .'

'Believe it, Torsten, or by God I will have you in front of that court. Yes, the police came to me. They had the name of a special forces officer. A man who served with courage and dedication.'

Jarnvig folded his arms and waited.

'They suspected him,' Arild continued. 'I told them I'd looked at the records and he'd been demobilized six months before.' His knuckles rapped on the desk. 'He wasn't even in Afghanistan at the time.' The short, muscular man flexed his shoulders, eyed Jarnvig. 'That wasn't strictly true. He was there. Not that you'll find that in the records.'

'That was our zone,' Jarnvig insisted. 'We should have been told.'

'It was none of your business. Why do you think I ordered Bilal to delete those radio messages? It was important there was no trace—'

'He killed this family!'

'You don't know what happened!' Arild yelled. 'He was a trained special forces commando. Not a hothead. Or a war criminal.'

Jarnvig grabbed a pen and a pad, began to write.

'Don't bother with that,' Arild ordered.

'There's going to be an investigation.'

'It won't go any further than the last one. The family who died weren't innocents. The father was funding the Taliban through drug shipments. He was an informer, a crook and a murderer.'

'There will be an investigation,' Jarnvig repeated.

Arild swore, shook his head, laughed more loudly than ever.

'You stupid little man,' he said, wiping his eyes. 'You never really understood, did you? You thought all there was to being a soldier was to listen and obey.'

'Get out,' Jarnvig said, staring at him.

'And you're right, for most of them,' Arild went on. 'But it's a shitty world out there. The Taliban don't play by the rules. If we do, then more fool us.'

'Get out!'

Arild didn't move.

'Do you know why I stopped going hunting with you?' he asked.

No answer.

'Because you didn't get that either. You used to wait for the prey to come to you. You thought it was enough to hide somewhere and hope it would come along.'

Arild stood up. Wiry man, active, general's uniform, handgun on his belt. He got his heavy winter coat from the stand.

'That's not what hunting's about,' he said. 'A *jæger* tracks his prey. Follows it. Identifies it. Gets to know it. Then . . .'

A hand as a gun, a finger as a barrel, aimed straight at Torsten Jarnvig's head.

'Boom!'

'Never show your face in here again. Never come near me or my men . . .'

Arild thrust his hands into his pockets and smiled.

'Do I make myself clear?' Jarnvig barked.

'You're overwrought. The strain I imagine. Take a week off. That's an order. When you come back I expect you to make the next team as strong and as ready as the last one. I'll be around to check—'

'No—'

'Torsten. Do I have to spell it out? Are you really so idiotic you can't take a hint?'

Arild patted his handgun, buttoned his coat, pulled on a pair of leather gloves, then looked at the man opposite him.

'Fuck with me and I will eviscerate you,' he said simply. 'Fuck with me and you'll wish you and your sorry little family were never born.'

A noise from the phone in his pocket. Arild looked at a message there then put it away.

'And now,' he said, 'you must excuse me. I have more interesting company to keep.'

She hated it when people started drinking at work. There were places for alcohol and the Politigården wasn't one of them.

Lund watched them gather as she sat at the desk she'd shared with Strange. He had a can of Coke, was moving from officer to officer, all genial smiles and relief. Brix was the leader, proven right in the end, a glass of whisky in his hand as if to show it. Ruth Hedeby hung on his every word, even though her elderly husband stood alone and bored at the other side of the room, silent next to one of the junior detectives who was too gauche and shy to mingle.

She followed Brix telling a joke, Hedeby giggling, gulping at her glass of wine, eyes glittering, never leaving his rugged face. There was something going on between those two. Lund just knew it.

Strange caught her eye, grinned, his ordinary face, so full of pain and uncertainty once, now happy, satisfied.

'Come on,' he mouthed, waving her in with his hand.

She smiled, said, 'In a minute.'

Then sipped at the bottle of beer Brix had forced on her and turned her back on them all.

The photos of the dead were still on the walls. Anne Dragsholm and Lisbeth Thomsen. Myg Poulsen, David Grüner and Gunnar Torpe.

No pictures yet of Said Bilal, blown to pieces in that underground warren outside Hillerød. No photos of an Afghan family murdered in their own home two years before. They would never get that dubious privilege. And soon the rest would be gone.

Case closed.

Madsen walked up.

'We need to take the files. Brix says best we get them in store before midnight.'

'Sure,' she said with a shrug. 'Why not?'

He nodded at a uniform man to come and start taking the boxes.

'Did anyone get through to Frederik Holst like I asked?'

Madsen looked guilty. A nice, quiet, decent unambitious man, she thought. The kind who always did as he was told.

353

'Someone gave him your number and asked him to call. Got a bit busy to chase. Sorry. Do you want me to . . .?'

'No.'

There was one other thing she'd asked for and that had turned up. Two sheets of paper from intelligence, records so old she didn't even recognize the design of the Politigården stamp. Lund read them as Madsen and the uniform man went to and fro with the boxes.

When they came back for the last one she stopped him.

'You were there when we searched the barracks a few days ago, weren't you?'

'Yeah,' Madsen laughed. 'What a place. Didn't they love us?'

'Why didn't you see anything in Søgaard's locker then?'

'Nothing to find. We looked. Bilal must have put that stuff there later, when he was getting desperate.'

The oldest intelligence file dated back to 1945. She couldn't imagine Copenhagen then. Or the Politigården making the difficult transition from being a part of the Nazi machine, struggling to be Danish, to be free once more.

'So we searched everything?'

'Dead right! Are you coming drinking with us or what?'

'I am, I am.' She watched him fill one of the few remaining boxes. Time running out. 'Did we ever work out how Dragsholm tracked down that officer? You know.' She tried not to sound sarcastic. 'The one the army are going after.'

'No.' Madsen frowned. 'I went through her case files. That was one angry woman. You could tell the way she wrote. We were all bastards. She had meetings with her soldiers. With other lawyers. With us supposedly.'

Lund stared at him.

'With us? Here?'

'No. Just one meeting,' he corrected himself. 'There was a diary note about talking to an officer in court.'

'That's how she contacted us?' she asked very carefully. 'Before she was killed? By going up to someone she met in court?'

He was getting bored with this.

'It's one line in her diary, Lund. I checked it out this end. There was nothing to confirm it. She never called here, that's for sure.'

'But she must have done. When she was looking into the case—'

'No,' he said firmly, 'she hired her own private investigators. Besides . . .' He shrugged, looked enviously at the crowd beyond the door. 'What could we have told her? We didn't even know something happened in Afghanistan until you came along.'

There was one last box file. She realized she had her hand on it.

'Can I take that one too? Then get you another beer?'

355

She held out the black box.

'Who was in charge of the first search at Ryvangen? Looking at the lockers and the rest?'

'Hell, I don't remember! We've all been working twenty-hour days. You've been to Afghanistan and back. Let's go . . .' He made a gesture. 'Glug, glug.'

'Was it Ulrik Strange?'

He had his free hand on the box.

'Right,' Madsen agreed. 'Strange. Why?'

Lund was thinking. He tugged at the box.

'Can I?'

'Take it,' she said and watched him go.

Holst's number in the hospital was still on her pad. Alone at the desk she dialled it, got through first time, said, 'This is Lund. When I ask you to call me I expect you to do it.'

'Sorry,' said the bitter drawl on the other end of the line. 'Things got in the way. Bombs. Bullets. Bodies. You know the kind of thing.'

'What happened to Møller's dog tag?'

Silence.

'This is important, Holst. What happened to his dog tag?'

'What do you think? I did what I always do. I cut it in half and put both pieces in the body bag. Is this important?'

'His parents never got a tag.'

'I put it in there, Lund!' he yelled from three thousand miles away. 'If it didn't turn up in Copenhagen someone took it.'

And made a new one, which was now in an evidence bag, stained with smoke from a baker's oven once full of human bones.

'Could they have taken it in Afghanistan?'

'What is this?'

'It's a question. Could they have taken it before the body bag went on the plane.'

'Not likely, Lund. We treat our dead with respect. More than they get alive sometimes. If someone got caught stealing a dead man's dog tag . . . I can't imagine.'

'Thanks,' she said.

The beer was empty. It was time to mingle.

It had to be Brix. No one else really listened to her. Not that he did all the time.

She wandered through the sea of bodies. Uniform men sweaty from the long day. Women from forensic. A few call handlers. It was turning into quite a party. Someone shoved another bottle of beer in her hand and she didn't even see who.

One side of the room finished. She was about to start on the other when a hand came out and stopped her.

Lund looked. Polished nails. Manicured fingers.

Ruth Hedeby was smiling for the first time Lund could recall in a while. It was a worrying sight.

'The people upstairs wanted me to tell you, Lund. Well done.'

She tried to walk on. Hedeby was having none of it.

'We got there in the end,' she said, keeping her hand on Lund's arm. 'No small thanks to—'

'You think?'

'I do!' The woman was loyal. Reliable. A drone. 'I must admit . . .' A flash of naughty regret as she fluttered her eyelashes. 'I had my doubts. When Lennart . . . when Brix sent for you. It seemed rash.'

The superior stare. She'd been hitting the wine.

'Seemed even more rash when I met you,' Hedeby added. 'First impressions matter. You should remember that.'

'What matters is looking until you get to the truth.'

Hedeby so wanted to be thanked. To share in the glory being distributed around this room.

'There's a good chance you won't be sent back to Gedser.'

'I like Gedser,' Lund lied. 'Lot of birds.'

'Birds?'

Lund's hands swept the ceiling. She made a tweeting noise.

'In the sky. Excuse me . . .'

Brix was talking to a burly man from upstairs. One of the suits who ran the place and never usually deigned to dirty their fingers with the troops.

'Can we talk?' Lund asked, carving straight into the conversation.

The suit went quiet, glared at her and walked off. Brix looked . . . disappointed. Again.

'What is it?'

'The day Strange went to the refugee centre in Helsingør. When I chased the man who killed Gunnar Torpe. Did someone check his alibi?'

'Yes,' he said with a pained look.

'He was with another officer?'

'No. They'd split up earlier. What is this?'

She looked round the busy room.

'Where's he gone?'

'Working,' Brix answered with a shrug. 'I don't know why. I could have found someone else.'

'To do what?'

'Escort Raben to Horserød. They're downstairs in the garage.'

Horserød. A picture in her head. The childlike drawing from the museum. Sad figures, starving, shuffling through the snow. Lund couldn't stop herself glancing round the room, wondering what this place was like back then.

'Have you been to the Frihedsmuseet?' Lund asked and watched Brix's interesting face crease with puzzlement. 'The Germans tortured people downstairs.' She shrugged. 'Some Danish cops did too. Then took them to Mindelunden and those stakes . . .'

'I do know that, thanks,' he said. 'Not now, Lund. Have a drink. Try to . . . I don't know. Wind down a little. If you can.'

A breezy voice over her shoulder.

'Lennart!' Hedeby all smiles. 'You must come and say hello to my husband.' She beamed at both of them. 'He's dying to meet you.'

359

'I bet he is,' Lund muttered then walked through the sea of bodies, out to the lockers beyond.

Downstairs. White police motorbikes, blue patrol cars. A warren of rooms and corridors leading off. She'd never thought about it much before but now it seemed obvious. This subterranean labyrinth was bigger than the sprawling Politigården itself, tunnelled underneath the street outside, the buildings beyond.

Seven decades before no one would have heard the screams. But they surely knew they were there.

Skinny, starving figures in Horserød. Ghostly voices in a dusty, stinking car park. The past didn't die. It lingered.

Lund walked on until she heard voices. Strange was there, next to his black Ford. A uniform man was helping Raben into the back. Couldn't help but push down his head along the way. Old habits . . .

'You can go now,' Strange said. 'I can take care of it. Have a beer for me.'

She watched from the shadows. The uniform man scratched his head.

'You're sure? There's supposed to be two of us.'

Strange laughed.

'He's got one arm in a sling and he'll be free as a bird in a week or two. I don't think we'll get any more trouble from this one.' Strange banged hard on the roof of the car, kept smiling at the cop. 'Will we?'

No answer from inside.

'Save a beer for me!' Strange cried, pointing at the uniform man. 'I'll be back in an hour or so.'

'No way,' the cop laughed. 'Every man for himself.'

Strange grinned at him. Watched him go. Looked surprised when she walked out from the darkness and said, 'I'm coming with you.'

A long pause.

'Why?'

'Because I am.' She held out her hand. 'We need to talk. Let me drive.'

'What is this, Lund? You're missing the party.'

'I'm not in the mood. Give me the keys.'

He grunted something, threw them over, climbed into the passenger seat. Lund got behind the wheel and looked in the mirror. Raben's bearded face was watching their every move. He had his seat belt on. The doors were reinforced and locked. He wasn't going anywhere.

'What is this?' Strange asked again.

'Horserød,' she said.

'It's inland not far from Helsingør.'

'I know where I'm going, thanks.'

She took them up the ramp, out into the busy night traffic, glad to get away.

Five minutes in and Strange was getting restless.

'That car's following us,' he said as they struggled to get out of the city centre.

'What car?'

361

'The one behind. That's following us.'

Raben hadn't said a word since they left.

'You're paranoid. It's traffic. Everyone's following somebody.'

'Yeah, well.' He looked at the dashboard. 'What about some music?'

He didn't wait for an answer. The radio was set to a classical station. Opera. Must have been his choice. It was his car. He wasn't an ordinary cop.

She listened for twenty seconds then turned the music off.

'So what do you want to talk about?' he asked.

'I'll get to that.'

They weren't far from Østerport Station.

'And why are we going the long way round?'

She glanced at him.

'I want to show you something.'

A little further down the road Lund turned off.

'Oh come on,' Strange cried. 'Horserød's straight ahead.'

'Won't take long.'

They were close to Ryvangen. Another piece of history came back from the museum. The Danish army had long used the barracks before the Nazis swept in and seized it as their base. The shooting range of Mindelunden was a practice area for soldiers, not a killing ground for the Germans. Only the railway track now separated the barracks from the memorial that Mindelunden had become. Soon they were on the park side, turning into a quiet dead end lane next to the long rows of graves, the statue of the mother with her fallen son, the three stakes in the ground.

'What the hell's going on?' Raben asked, worried from behind. 'My wife's waiting for me. My son—'

'You just stay where you are,' Lund ordered, then turned into the empty car park, killed the engine, got out and stood beneath the bare winter trees.

Clear night, half-full moon. Frost forming on the ground. The place was silent though beyond the memorial park she could see lights in the low wooden buildings of the adjoining schools.

Strange got out of the car. Lund used the remote and double locked it. He came and stood next to her.

'Something's wrong,' she said. 'It's Brix. He's covering up for somebody.'

He'd got a blue polyester vest beneath his light jacket. Probably felt cold. Not happy anyway.

'Brix?' Strange asked, shaking his head.

A train went past like noisy metallic lightning rumbling through the night.

'There's something you need to see,' she said when it was gone then walked over and forced open the wooden side door into Mindelunden.

'Bloody hell, Lund,' Strange complained. 'We're supposed to be taking a prisoner to Horserød. What is this?'

Past the long lines of names, past the graves and the frozen mother and son.

The moon was brighter than it should have been. Nothing here escaped its rays.

'Much as I'd love to be alone with you,' he went on, following her as she walked, 'this isn't very cosy. Can't we go for pizza and a beer or something? After we've dumped off chummy back there?'

'This is a memorial park for the Danish Resistance.'

The place it all began while she was chasing smuggled dope and immigrants in Gedser.

'I know that.'

The firm, hard sound of her footsteps rang up from the footpath.

'They were war heroes. Said Bilal saw himself as a patriot too. He would have worshipped them.'

He caught up, looked at her.

'Sadly we can't ask him now, can we?'

'Bilal would never have left Anne Dragsholm in a place like this. A graveyard for martyrs? She was a *stikke*, wasn't she? A turncoat. A traitor. Someone who wanted to drag the army . . . Denmark down into the gutter.'

He waved his arms in front of him.

'At the risk of repeating myself . . . we can't ask him now.'

She kept walking.

'Bilal erased those radio messages. Helped cover up what happened in Helmand. He didn't kill her. Or the others.'

He stopped, hands in pockets, a jaded look on his face.

'Then why did he take the Raben woman hostage?'

She shook her head.

'God you're slow sometimes. He wanted the army to come in and save him from being fitted up for something he never did. Fat chance . . .'

Lund turned and stared at the trees and the pale memorial stones.

'They were murdered by someone who felt differently about this place.'

'What's all this got to do with Brix?'

They were approaching the old shooting range, with the three sacred stakes.

Walking, walking, never looking at him.

'Brix is protecting the real killer.'

They looked like shrunken totem poles. Or relics from a lost Stonehenge. Part of a ritual, a ceremony most had forgotten, and those who remembered only dimly understood.

'Stand there,' she said, and got him to stop by the middle pole.

'What is—?'

'Dragsholm was terrified. She knew someone was going to come for her. Her house was full of alarms. She'd ordered sensors for her garden. She'd hired her own security guards.'

It was too dark down here beneath the branches of the overhanging trees. She needed the moonlight.

'Come,' Lund ordered and they walked up the steep bank behind the stakes, the buffer that once took the stray bullets that never hit their intended target.

Stopped at the top, a little breathless, looking around.

Then Lund stared at his plain face caught in the moonlight.

'But she never went to the police. She thought someone was going to kill her. And she never once called us.'

Strange shrugged.

'Maybe she wasn't sure.'

'She was sure.'

'Then—'

'She found him. She knew who the officer was. He'd been given Møller's identity deliberately by someone in Operational Command. They even forged a new dog tag.'

Strange hugged himself in the cold, kept quiet.

'Dragsholm knew he was working in the Politigården. She told Monberg. He did nothing. There's no other explanation.'

'Lund—'

'Nothing else fits. And then suddenly we find all that incriminating evidence at Ryvangen. Even though we'd searched the same place only a few days before. Don't you see?'

He stared at the frosty grass and shook his head. Lund came up to him, touched the front of his jacket.

'Someone planted that during the search.'

'I was in charge of the search. I didn't plant a thing.'

'Then . . .' She shrugged. 'It's got to be some-body on the team.'

His hand went to her arm. He peered into her eyes. She wondered about the expression there. It looked like sympathy. Pity even.

'This is what happened last time, isn't it? With Meyer. You won't let go, even when it's over.'

'That wasn't over. It still isn't.'

'Maybe not.' His arms gripped her firmly. 'But this is. Please let it die. For God's sake . . .'

Lund pulled herself away.

'Have you talked to Brix about this?' he asked.

'Not yet. Do you think I can trust him? He's going to send me back to Gedser.'

'We can stop that! Let's have a talk with him. Both of us. You're not going back to Gedser. But . . .'

His grizzled head lowered, his bright eyes bore into hers.

'You can't rock the boat for ever. We drop off Raben. We go back to the party. We have a few beers. Then tomorrow . . .' She remembered the time they'd almost kissed. He looked like this. Young and vulnerable. 'Tomorrow you decide. About everything.'

'Tomorrow,' she murmured.

'Can I have the keys? Can I drive?'

She looked back towards the graves and the memorial plaques with their endless lines of names.

'I couldn't find your grandfather on the wall.'

Strange blinked. Shuffled on his feet.

'I couldn't find his name in the memorial yard in the Politigården either,' Lund added. 'And that's odd. Every police officer who died under the Nazis is there. Even the ones who went abroad to the concentration camps.'

She looked up into his face.

'Why is that?'

No words. And his eyes were different. The way they looked in Helmand. Another Ulrik Strange was with her at that moment.

'I wasn't asking out of curiosity,' she added. 'I know the answer. I just want to hear it from you.'

Buch couldn't work out why he still had a ministerial car. But there it was waiting for him when he came out of Plough's house, Karina sitting in the back, arms tightly folded, face furious.

'Maybe we should get a taxi,' he said, sticking his head through the door.

'Why?'

She wasn't in a good mood. That was obvious.

Because this belongs to them, he thought. Like everything else. There could be a bug in the roof. Something that relayed everything he said straight back to the silver-haired man, the father of the nation, seated in the old king's office over the muddy riding ground where the horses went round and round. Just like him. Going nowhere.

'Just get in, will you?' she said.

He did and sat silent for ten minutes, thinking as they moved slowly through the night traffic. Then told her what Plough had said.

'That can't be true,' she cried, next to him in the back. 'You know Plough. He wouldn't leak a damned thing. It's not in his genes. Besides—'

'He did it, Karina.'

'I was with him every single day.'

'He did it! He told me!' The residential streets were long behind. This was the city now. Lights and noise and people. The grey island of Slotsholmen where Absalon once built his fortress and created a city called Copenhagen was getting closer. 'He was proud of it.'

'For God's sake why?'

There was a kind of logic there. Buch had to admit it.

'Because all he wanted was revenge. In his own head Rossing was to blame. Never Grue Eriksen. Not the grand old man.'

She howled with fury.

'He's not that stupid, Thomas! He must know something that implicates the Prime Minister. Something—'

'He doesn't.' Buch's gloomy stare silenced her. 'And even if he did he wouldn't say. Plough's part of the system. It brought him up. Made him what he was. It's hard enough to tear down one little part of it. To ask him to pull the rug from under everything . . .'

Buch put his hand on her arm, tried to make her see.

'We haven't been up against Rossing. Or Grue Eriksen. Certainly not Plough. We've been fighting . . .'

Slotsholmen. There it was beyond the windscreen. All the buildings, the ministries and the Folketinget, the little converted houses for the civil servants, the garden with its statue of Kierkegaard.

'We've been fighting that,' Buch said, waving his hand at the grey shapes ahead. 'Plough thinks he did the right thing. He was loyal. To the system to begin with. To his son in the end.' He glanced at her. 'And what were we?'

She was a smart, ambitious, dangerous young woman, Buch thought. He hadn't spoken easily with his wife Marie in days. A part of him, a part he hated, had looked at Karina, thought of Monberg, and wondered . . .

'Thomas,' she said very slowly. 'We know for a fact the Prime Minister was involved in a conspiracy that killed people. Killed them!'

'True,' he agreed as the long black car pulled into the Ministry entrance.

'We can't let him get away with that. How could you live with yourself?' Her hand fell on his, soft and gentle and warm. 'I know you well enough now . . .'

Buch took his fingers away, looked at the door he'd never walk through as a minister again.

He liked that job. He was good at it.

370

'I don't give a damn about my career,' she whispered, watching him, every expression on his jowly, bearded face.

The car stopped. The driver was waiting for instructions.

'I'm not giving up!' he said, too quickly. 'Believe it.'

'Good.' She patted his knee. 'So what do we do?'

Buch got out. The night was cold but there was no rain and the twisting dragons he'd learned to live with looked as if they were dancing in the clearest moonlight he'd seen in weeks.

He walked to the entrance, opened the door for her.

'What's Grue Eriksen up to now?' he asked.

'Talking to people about the reshuffle. He wants you there. To get your reward for keeping quiet.'

'How soon can you put a press conference together?'

'If I've got something good to dangle on the hook . . . thirty minutes.'

'Do it, please,' Buch said, then turned right to begin the long, interior march through the labyrinth of Slotsholmen, right and left, up and down until he found himself in the Christianborg Palace. There he asked a couple of questions. Found the room.

The Prime Minister was on his own. Slightly hunched, shoulders rounded, not that Buch had noticed before. Face so familiar most of Denmark seemed to have grown up with it. Benign. Dependable. Indulgent. A man to be relied upon.

Gert Grue Eriksen smiled when he walked in.

'Hi, Thomas.' He gestured at the seats round the table. 'Take one, will you? We've fences to mend, haven't we? I want this reshuffle fixed this evening.' Hand outstretched, Buch took it without thinking. 'I'm glad we've got the chance to talk first like this. That trouble with PET . . .'

The Prime Minister frowned.

'I'm afraid those officers became a little over-enthusiastic. They seemed to blame you for König's dismissal. Which is unfair and now they know it.'

For some reason Buch found himself staring at his hand after shaking Grue Eriksen's. Sweaty, ugly, fat fingers marked by the scars of his early farming days. The hand of a labourer, not a politician. Cautious, common men who didn't shake with anybody, not without looking them up and down first. As he had once.

'I owe you an explanation,' Grue Eriksen said as Buch sat down.

'Why can't you let things go?'

Strange stood in front of her, back to how he'd looked in Helmand now. A soldier. A man of duty. Forcing all emotion from himself. Getting ready to serve. To fight. To rage.

'I can let them go when they're finished.'

'Some things never finish, Sarah. It's best to walk away.'

'Your grandfather wasn't a hero. He was a *stikke*. He worked for the Nazis. He was the one torturing them in the basement of the Politigården. Bringing them here so they could be tied to these stakes and shot.'

Strange folded his arms and nodded.

'And then one day,' Lund went on, 'a group of Resistance fighters called the Holger Danske caught up with him outside Central Station. Gunned him down in the street.'

He didn't move, didn't speak.

'It's all there in the Politigården records,' she said. 'Not the Frihedsmuseet. I checked. So I guess . . .'

Thinking. Imagining. This was what she was good at.

'I guess one day a young police cadet comes in for work experience. He thinks his dead granddad was a hero. Because that's what his father told him. So he decides to look up the records for himself.' She moved closer to try to see into his eyes. 'And when he finds the truth he goes home and does what any kid would. He spills it.'

'You're not normal,' Strange murmured.

'This isn't about me. It's about you. Who you are.'

The eyes did flicker then, stared hard at her.

'It doesn't hurt any more. Sorry.'

'Did your father lie to himself too? Did he pretend . . .?' she asked.

373

'We all want heroes. We just don't like to think of the cost.'

'And then you run away to the army. God . . .' She shook her head. 'They must have loved you. All that inherited guilt. Talk about someone with a point to prove. An army man from an army family and what a secret to live with. When you brought Dragsholm here did it make it even? One *stikke* for another? How did it feel when they said that wasn't enough?'

Nothing.

Lund went back down the slope. He slunk after her.

'Come on, Strange. You said it yourself. You're a foot soldier. Not a leader. Someone put you up to this. Someone gave you the code to the munitions store in Ryvangen. Fixed that forged dog tag. Told you to kill those people and make it look so hellish we'd think some fake terrorist gang murdered them—'

'Cut it out.'

'You didn't enjoy that part, did you?' she went on. 'Torturing Anne Dragsholm. Cutting Myg Poulsen and the priest to ribbons. Locking a man in a wheelchair inside his own—'

'Give it a fucking rest for once!' he yelled at her, alive and jumpy.

Lund went quiet. Scared. At him in part. But more at her own growing fury.

Slowly, like a cat stalking its prey, he came over, walked round her once, returned to look in her face.

374

'You're not right in the head,' he said.

She didn't blink. Couldn't have done if she wanted.

'About this I am. Why did you go along with it?'

His hand came up, touched her cheek, ran across her dry lips, brushed the soft lines of her throat. Left her.

'Why?' Lund asked again.

'Because sometimes things come back to bite you.' He looked at the stakes, the little ramp above them. His voice had turned soft. He sounded younger. 'I was at a court hearing last summer. It was hot.' A shrug. 'I had a short-sleeve shirt. The Dragsholm woman came over wanting to talk about Helmand. Halfway through she saw the tattoo. All these questions. She must have looked in my face and . . .'

Strange nodded.

'She was like you. She wasn't going to give up. She knew. I knew. We all thought that nightmare had been buried. But . . .'

Lund got out her phone.

'You need to come in now. I'm calling Brix—'

He snatched the mobile from her fingers, flung it down on the grass below.

'You don't know what happened! Don't think for one moment you do.'

'I know five people got murdered. That's enough for now. I know you didn't do this on your own. Someone put you up to—'

'You don't understand a fucking thing!'

'Just tell the truth, Strange,' she said calmly. 'How hard's that?'

'I told my father the truth once. He didn't want to hear it either. Look where that got me . . .'

'Five people dead—'

'Every one of them a *stikke!*'

The noise, half shout, half scream, echoed around them in the little grove of Mindelunden. She couldn't think for a moment. Not even when she saw he had a gun to her chest.

'Don't you shoot me in the head?' Lund asked, looking him in the eye. 'Isn't that the way they teach you?'

No movement. No expression on his plain and ordinary face.

'You couldn't kill me before. You're not doing it now.'

She pulled away from him, turned her back. Aware he wasn't moving. Looked through the grass for the glint of an LCD screen. Found the phone, picked it up. Walked towards the three upright stakes.

No sound from behind. She put the phone to her ear.

Glanced to the end of this small open space in the Mindelunden trees.

Another figure there, where the riflemen would once have been. A body position she recognized. Legs apart, arms outstretched, a weapon held with both hands.

Lund was listening to the centre operator talk in her ear when it happened. Yellow flash of fire first, then the sound.

From behind a shriek of pain. She turned.

Ulrik Strange was on his knees. Hands to his chest. Mouth oozing blood.

Another explosion. He bucked back with a movement so violent it was like a puppet getting jerked on a piece of string.

The phone fell from her fingers.

Lund wheeled round.

One flash and when the shot hit her it was so powerful she staggered back, fell against something that could only be the first stake, stopped there, pinioned like a target under the bright silver moonlight.

Gasping for breath. Struggling to think.

Then another vicious burst of fire, an impact that threw her wheeling round clutching at her chest, leaving the stake for the thick cold grass, the darkness, the stink of grass and mud and death.

'No.' Buch shook his head angrily. 'I don't want to hear it. I've had enough of this. You can keep your ministerial offices. Your bribes.'

Grue Eriksen's eyes registered that news.

'I know Plough gave you the ammunition to blame everything on Rossing. One more puppet for you to manipulate, huh?'

The weakest, most political of smiles appeared on Grue Eriksen's face. He walked over to the door, closed it, made sure they were on their own.

'Do you think you can get away with anything?' Buch yelled. 'You can't bury this one. I'm calling a press conference. I'll tell them everything. Then I'll tell it to the Folketinget, the police, PET. Anyone who'll listen.'

'Thomas . . .'

Grue Eriksen thrust his hands into his trouser pockets, looked exasperated.

'I've got the documents,' Buch went on. 'I'll distribute them. Lock me up for breaching the Official Secrets Act if you want. The damage is coming . . .'

'Please—'

'You've been covering up for murder. People died because of you.'

'I'm the leader of this country. We're at war. The same war that killed your brother—'

'Jeppe died in Iraq!'

'Same war,' Grue Eriksen said quietly. 'It just goes on and on.'

Buch was thrown for a moment.

'Don't give me that shit,' he said. 'Don't . . . I know you were behind all this. I can prove it.'

He got up, went for the door.

'Do you really want to walk out of here without knowing why?' the Prime Minister called as he left. 'I find that hard to believe. You're such an inquisitive man. God knows we've all learned that . . .'

Buch stopped, fingers on the handle.

'I've been fed so much bullshit.'

'You have,' Grue Eriksen admitted. 'And much of it from me. It seemed right at the time. Perhaps I was mistaken. But . . .'

Buch started to leave.

'We weren't covering up the killing of civilians,' Grue Eriksen said in a loud, insistent voice. Enough to stop him, make him turn.

The Prime Minister frowned, folded his arms, leaned back to sit on the polished table behind him.

'Ordinary people die in war,' he said ruefully. 'Sometimes it happens by accident. Sometimes by mistaken design. But in the end . . . people forgive. They understand.'

'What then?' Buch demanded, marching back towards him.

'The problem was the officer. You see . . . he wasn't there.'

'Riddles, riddles . . .'

'That's just what they are,' Grue Eriksen agreed. 'Exactly. Do you think I sit at my desk in there and watch the whole world pass by in front of me? That I say yes or no to everything? Even with the domestic agenda I'm at best a distant captain, delegating to good men like you. As you delegate to others—'

'Don't flatter me, please.'

'I wasn't. The officer wasn't there. He was working on a secret mission. It hadn't been cleared with the Security Committee.'

Buch's finger rose.

'You have to do that. It's the law.'

'It's the law,' Grue Eriksen concurred. 'Tell that to the men and women we've got on the ground in Helmand. Let's say . . . they know a certain minor warlord is bankrolling the Taliban. Providing information, weapons, funds.' He looked at the ceiling, as if inventing all this. 'Let's imagine we get word that he's about to flee. He knows we're onto him, you see. So our forces have maybe a day, two at most to get in there. Interrogate him. Take him into custody. Well?'

'Well what?'

'When Operational Command comes to me what do I say? Do I tell them to wait until we've managed to check through all our diaries, ticked off our committee meetings, our lunch dates? Our evenings at the opera? In Monberg's case his assignations with his various mistresses? Do I say to these brave men and women fighting a hopeless war in a brutal distant land . . . wait a week or so, and maybe then I can get back to you with a yes or no?'

Buch said nothing.

'What would you do, Thomas? The moment a secret decision's committed to paper here it's a day away from the streets of Kabul. That I guarantee.'

'You knew who that officer was all along . . .'

'No, I didn't then and I don't now. Do you listen to what I say at all? I don't want to know. I wouldn't ask. All I understood was I had a decision to face. We were short of money. Short of troops.'

'You could have done something to stop it. When Anne Dragsholm was murdered—'

'This is the real world!' Grue Eriksen barked at him. 'Not the one we'd like. Denmark's at war and we're losing. The Taliban gain strength all the time. They exploit our every weakness. If we hand them a scandal on a plate . . . what do you think they'd do? Sit round the table and look for a solution? How do you think the mothers and fathers of soldiers coming home in a coffin would feel? Would they thank you for this? Or me?'

He pulled a chair from the table, sat down, briefly put his head in his hands. Gert Grue Eriksen looked old and tired for a moment, before the politician returned.

'When I first became a minister I was like you. Keen as mustard. Determined to do the right thing. To see justice done. But God . . .' His clenched fist hammered the polished wood. 'Nothing's as simple as that. It's a dangerous, fractured world we live in. Serve here long enough and you'll see it. One day someone will tell you there's something bad round the corner. So bad you don't want to hear.'

He opened his hands.

'And then what do you do? You ask for a report and options. And they say . . .' Grue Eriksen closed his eyes briefly. 'They say it's best you didn't hear. As you once said to me . . .'

Buch recalled uttering those very words. It seemed a lifetime ago.

'If we're not responsible,' he asked, 'who is?'

'Everybody,' Grue Eriksen answered in a soft, damaged voice. 'Nobody. You.' A brief, humourless laugh. 'Me, when it's late at night and I can't sleep. Conscience is a wonderful thing. Yours especially.' His hand clutched at Buch's arm. 'We need it here. To remind us when we go too far—'

'People died!'

'I know. And sometimes you have to tell that virtuous, nagging voice to shut up. To put democracy aside in order to fight for democracy.' The hand tightened on Buch's arm. 'I thought you of all people would understand that. If that brother of yours were here today—'

'Don't throw the dead at me,' Buch yelled. 'I've got enough of them in my head already.'

'Not as many as I have,' Grue Eriksen said in a voice close to a whisper. 'And they all know me by name.'

He looked round the grand room.

'We make a deal with the devil when we cross the bridge into Slotsholmen. You're learning that the hard way. I need you, Thomas. I need your intelligence, your innocence.' He laughed. 'Your infuriating naivety too.'

The Prime Minister got up, placed a firm and insistent hand on Buch's arm.

'If I make mistakes, you must tell me. Help me govern better. Make sure—'

'You must be out of your mind,' Buch said, removing himself from the man's grip. 'When I tell Krabbe and Birgitte Agger you're finished. You'll be gone by the morning.'

'Still not quite there, are we?' Grue Eriksen smiled. 'Still that childlike stubbornness holds you back—'

'I've had enough of this . . .'

'There's nothing to tell and no one to hear it. This secret's shared already. Come . . .'

Two large black double doors with star adornments stood at the side of the room. Grue Eriksen marched towards them like a little soldier himself.

'Meet those who've heard my tale already, Thomas. And agreed that the most important thing of all is to continue the good fight.'

'These games . . .'

'No game,' the Prime Minister said quickly. 'No sides either. When it comes to war we're as one. The way you always wanted it.'

The doors went back slowly. A gathering beyond. Buch came and stood to watch, breathless, sweating, knowing what he would see.

Erling Krabbe was there. Birgitte Agger too. The leaders of the minority parties. Every member of the cabinet. The political royalty of Slotsholmen, foes on paper, gathered together in unison.

Gert Grue Eriksen walked in, stood in their midst, turned, beckoned with a hand.

'Thomas!' shrieked a high-pitched voice from behind.

Buch didn't move.

'Thomas.' Karina Jørgensen marched in and stood by him. She was the one tugging at his arm now. 'The reporters are here. They need you. They're waiting.'

He shattered the passenger window on Strange's car with his Neuhausen pistol, freed the lock, dragged out the handcuffed man inside. Took him through the shattered wooden door into the memorial park, back to the firing range and the stakes.

Two still bodies on the ground. He'd need the keys to the handcuffs. Strange would have them.

He'd need a plan, a story too, and that was halfway there already.

Raben rolled on the grass, cursing and shrieking.

A boot in the gut, another under the chin. Then the Neuhausen in the face. That silenced him.

'Ungrateful piece of shit,' he said, and fetched him another kick, hard in the groin this time.

Wiped the weapon with a cloth from his pocket, crouched down over the wheezing man, squeezed the gun into his fingers, fired two rapid shots into the body a couple of metres away.

Watched Strange's corpse jump and twitch with the impact. The woman hadn't moved since he shot her. Too far for this trick. She could stay where she was for now.

A plan.

He'd brought two guns. Threw the one he'd just fired into the grass by the stakes. Took out the second Neuhausen, stood over the gasping, choking shape on the ground.

'You put him up to it,' Raben muttered then wiped his blue sleeve across his mouth, cleared away some grass and blood. 'They'll find you . . .'

He laughed.

'No they won't. Do you think shooting a worm like you counts for anything? Besides . . .' The man above Raben relaxed for an instant. 'You really don't remember, do you? I thought it was an act. But it's not . . .'

'Remember what?'

He crouched down, looked.

'You're the one who started all this. You shot that first kid. Strange was a good officer. Sound man. He'd kill anyone but not without a reason.' A shrug. 'You never put it in your statement. But Strange told us. So did your own men. Why do you think they were so scared of you?'

He rolled back his head. Laughed at the moon.

'All this time you spent chasing the monster, Raben. And you never knew. The monster's you.'

'Liar, liar . . .' Raben's voice was a low, frightened sound in his throat. 'You fucking liar . . .'

Two steps closer. The black barrel of the Neuhausen to his temple.

'Why would I lie? I'm about to shoot you. The way you shot her. The other kids. The mother.' A glance at the body behind. 'He got the father. But then the bastard was a friend of the Taliban so what the hell?'

'Shut up—'

'You started this. You and your fury. You murdered those kids because you just . . .' Free hand to head, finger whirling. '. . . lost it. And everyone was to blame except you. Come on . . .'

The barrel prodded at Raben's skull.

'Remember now? You were a snivelling wreck afterwards. All grief and regret. The good men we lost—'

'Arild—'

'Call me "General". For once in your sorry life act like a soldier.'

He went to Strange's body, rifled through the jacket, got a set of keys that looked good for the handcuffs. Came back and waved them at the figure on the ground. Raben was starting to weep, to choke and shake.

'Finally,' the man with the gun said. 'We've unlocked that memory, haven't we? A little late I guess . . .'

He took out his phone, called the Politigården, got through to what sounded like a party.

'Brix? Are you drinking?'

A caustic answer.

'Well, you can stop,' Arild said. 'I got a call from Raben asking me to meet him at Mindelunden. He said one of your cops was trying to kill him.'

Arild let that sink in.

'Raben's got a weapon from somewhere. He's shot them both. The lunatic's loose here.' A pause. 'I think he wants me next.'

'Stay where you are,' Brix ordered.

He snapped the phone shut, looked at the trembling man on the ground. Raised the gun.

There was a noise from somewhere.

A dog maybe. An urban fox.

A train went past, lights flashing. Arild raised the gun. Then something hit.

She hurt.

Hurt more when she crashed the police handgun hard into Jan Arild's head, sent him grunting to the floor, his weapon scuttling into the grass.

Lund coughed.

Looked at the still, sad, familiar shape lying there.

No movement. No breathing. That was clear in the bright moonlight.

It felt as if a horse had kicked her in the chest. Sick of the thing, she undid her jacket, stripped off the body armour she'd taken out of her locker for the first time that night, on the way to the car with Strange, fixing in her mind what she'd say.

It isn't magic.

She wondered when his gentle, inquisitive voice would leave her head.

Stopped when the man in the heavy military coat in front of her came to on the ground, began laughing, looking.

He had the face of a fox. Long sharp nose. Beady eyes. On her now.

'Raben,' she said quickly. 'Find the bastard's gun, will you? *Raben?*'

The figure in the blue prison suit was hunched up, a mess, drawn in on himself. Broken, maybe for ever.

Lund had heard every word of the exchange between these two, felt the fog clearing in her head as she did so. Strange was a special forces soldier. Capable of anything, provided duty and an officer above him called for it. But he didn't kill kids for fun. Only the enemy. And anyone who merited the name *stikke*, a curse that was too close to home.

Still no movement.

'Raben! There's a gun here somewhere. I'm on my own. I'm not . . .' What was the word? Her pained head hunted for it. 'I'm not good at this. You've got to help—'

'He can't, you stupid bitch,' Arild laughed back at her from the grass.

His fingers were probing the wound in his ginger hair. Blood, black in the moonlight. Not a lot.

'Thanks for that,' he said in his cruel, laughing voice. 'It all adds to the story.'

His head was off the ground. Arild was looking round. Right hand out, grasping.

Raben's moans were starting to get to her. The man was gone. Back in that room in Helmand, killing a kid because he felt like it, starting a blood-bath that would never leave him.

'You won't get away with this,' Lund said. She

held the gun in both hands. Kept it on him, not steady. That wasn't possible. 'Stay where you are.'

Arild grinned at her.

'This is nothing. I've buried better before. Better than you.' He wasn't afraid. Not for a moment. 'Who do you think you are? What? You're like him . . .' Arild nodded at Raben, rocking back and forth, eyes full of tears. 'One more pawn getting shoved round a chessboard you can't even see. I . . .'

He was on his knees, looking around him.

'I push you. Like I pushed Strange. And somewhere else . . . someone I can't see pushes me.'

A black shape glittered in the grass back towards the stakes. Within his reach. They both saw it. Arild watched her, head to one side.

'Your fingers are unsteady, Lund. Your arms are shaking. You don't even hold the gun right. You're a disaster, woman. You have been from the very start.'

'If you don't stay where you are I swear . . .'

But he was on his way already, quick as a wild animal on the hunt, rolling towards the black gun, the talisman he owned.

Now she saw it, felt it. The red roar rising in her head until there was nothing there except fury and hate, savage and raw.

The first bullet caught him in the shoulder. Arild bellowed with pain, skewed to one side, lay back on the grass, clutching the wound, staring at her, furious.

The second hit him in the chest and Lund didn't even know she'd pulled the trigger.

On the ground. Blood pumping from his gaping mouth.

She didn't count the rest. Lund fired and fired until the gun clicked on empty. Listened to Raben's howls then threw the hot, spent weapon into the damp thick grass.

Stood there, close to Strange's body and Arild's shattered, torn corpse. Sweat going cold beneath her jumper. Two bruises gathering where the bullets had smashed hard into Kevlar.

Sirens from somewhere. Blue lights on the distant road.

She walked towards them, eyes on the path. Out of Mindelunden not looking at the graves and the long lists of names. Or the mother with the dead son in her arms.

A shape ahead and she barely looked. Brix was there. Madsen too. Strange ought to be with them, face calm, eyes concerned, telling her to get in the car. To go home. To sleep. To forget.

To forget.

'Lund,' Brix said as she walked past, eyes on nothing but the night. '*Lund?*'

Torsten Jarnvig ignored Arild's final order and was welcoming troops for the next dispatch. Watching them stand to attention outside the Ryvangen barracks hall. Drilling into them the rules and rigours of the army.

In a warm and comfortable family apartment at Horserød open prison, Louise Raben sat on a sofa, Jonas half asleep on her lap, wondering when her husband would get there. Stroking the child's soft fair hair. Smiling at the thought of the future that lay ahead of them.

By the long line of marble slabs that listed the distant dead, Raben slumped in his grubby prison suit, mind gone, turned in on itself, capable only of tears, too afraid to go near the truth.

And on Absalon's island of Slotsholmen Thomas Buch stood in front of an open room, Gert Grue Eriksen beckoning to him. Birgitte Agger too. Krabbe, Kahn and all the others. The king and all his princes, friend and foe, half-smiling, arms open with only Karina's soft insistent fingers to hold him back.

He didn't look at her as he removed her hand from his jacket. Didn't look at her as Grue Eriksen closed the long black doors and led him into the crowd where glasses chinked, small talk ruled and no one spoke of a past that would soon be buried and forgotten.

There was nowhere else to go now and now he knew it.